EVOLUTIONARY

VERSA

VOLUME 1

EVOLUTIONARY

BRANDON NANO

Evolutionary

ISBN: 978-1-64318-019-9

1097 N. 400th Rd
 Baldwin City, KS, 66006
www.imperiumpublishing.com

A STORY INSPIRED BY KINETICA

PROLOGUE

OVER THE YEARS, MY RACE OF TERRANS, ONCE UPON A TIME CALLED "HUMANS" AS A WHOLE, HAVE ADAPTED, PROSPERED THROUGH THE HIGHS AND THE LOWS. We have united, divided in times of war and peace. Under the influence that we were not alone in a universe unable for exploration. Optimistic minds kept reaching for the stars, hoping to grasp their light while others maintained a pessimistic structure only clinging to what they knew instead of searching for the unknown. Whether we believed in religion for morality or science for immortality, we were not aware of the stranded continent that was Earth within a much bigger ocean of civilizations outside of our imagination. We all lived our lives and had our beliefs for centuries, for millennia, until one day, one solstice, when the universe showed Terrans that we were not alone. On June 21st, 2036, in Cape Town, South Africa, we were discovered by another species far more advanced and far more superior. At the time, that's what we thought. The alien came to us in its rayfish-like black and blue colored spacecraft, giving indication that our world was a whole lot bigger. The alien had an appearance Terrans could only describe as massive, muscular, and mechanical. We didn't know how to classify this unidentified creature, but then it said one word while pointing to itself reflected in the eyes of its initial audience, *Ragnarök.*

Days passed by as a newly formed committee called the Bureau of Extraterrestrial Affairs appointed language expertise to Cape Town for the translation of the Rokian's tongue. The process wasn't too long considering its native language was similar to English. The only barriers between our languages were the suffixes ending in "ix" or "ax." The lone Rokian explained to Earth that it had been searching for resources such as oil to prevent its planet from becoming obsolete. In exchange, it would provide us with technology. Earth agreed to the deal, commencing an era of innovation like never before. For the first time in our existence, every nation came together as a whole to approve of this pristine extraterrestrial alliance, leading to medical advances that would increase our longevity on top of decreasing fatality rates. No longer would a Terran die from an amputation, a heart attack, or a stroke due to the Rokian's artificial resource. A vital encounter that helped save a great portion of our race from the sudden eruption of supervolcanoes once called Yellowstone and Lake Toba. What should've been our race's breaking point quickly became our greatest thriving point. Our world became reformed in a manner both scientists and religious leaders could only dream and pray of; the Terrans were here to stay.

After renaming our planet UCE, the United Countries of Earth and labeling our epoch of survival as the Evolutionary Era in 2051, the alliance with the Ragnarök thickened. They saw the indissolubility within our race and felt the need to invite our leaders to the planet-like space station in the center of the universe called Unica. A luxurious complex station with native architectures from the Decalliance of Majoris planets: Ragnios, Gigalus, Crystia, Ghast, Arach, Legios, Arythro, Pasydanya, Graviathen, and Satania. At Unica, Earth was able to adapt, prosper by befriending seven more planets with an exchange system, allowing our existence to flourish even more within the Evolutionary Era.

The Ragnarök of Ragnios continued to provide their Technology while offering a few spacecraft for some more Oil.

The Gigallian Giants of Gigalus presented the toughest metal in the universe, Krone for our craft of Music and our art of Language.

The Crystallites of Crystia reformed our Currency from their land of crystals for the one crystal they lacked, Diamonds.

The Ghastallians of Ghast exchanged the premier Drugs in the universe for our definitions of Fear.

The Rachnidians of Arach offered the strongest silk in the universe, Wethro, in exchange for our Waste.

The Wardens of Legios recommended Weapons and Protection for our Prisoners.

The Ryths of Arythro rendered Architecture for a claim to the coldest place on UCE, Antarctica while the Pysceans of Pasydanya gave a new form of Beauty within their Shyre Attire for a claim to our Oceans.

Earth was able to please most of the Decalliance, profiting from their native advantages. All of the Majoris planets were behind Earth, except for two. Satania and Graviathen. The Satanians felt that our hunting skills were mediocre and weak, a scornful insult coming from a heritage infamous for following a religion involving the collection of bones from fallen foes. As for the Gravits, they had no interest in our resources and felt that the gravity of our planet was boring. An unordinary comment Earth understood better after learning more about the sleepless rogue planet with ever-changing magnetic fields that was Graviathen.

Once Earth stabilized an alliance with most of the Majoris planets, Unica declared our planet as "Innoris," a planet neither Majoris nor Minoris due to our superb resources combined with a lack of power and intimidation. Attempting to change our planet's status, we were introduced to the common ground between all planets, including the Hectolition of Minoris planets like Derry, Sylum, and Maradomum. A competitively high-powered sport called Versa racing where hundreds of racers compete against one another in armored exoskeleton suits where the wheels are magnetically attached to the appendages of the body. In Versa, racers rely on strength just as much as speed, shedding rivers of blood and fields of organs. A barbaric sport at best, and a sport Earth had to be involved in nonetheless.

Just like Earth did at Unica, we adapted, and we prospered, we competed, and we triumphed. Throughout our competition with the other species, we learned that there was one advantage Terrans had over the others, epinephrine, otherwise known as adrenaline. An internal chemical that could help us get stronger when attacking and become quicker when defending. This balancing attribute turned into our recipe for success. It kept us in the races through dire moments and had us evenly matched with unique creatures like the Rzurkins of Crystia, who had crystal javelins bulging out of their back with a rider at the helm, or the pyromantic Satanians, who could breathe three different types of flames: amber, azure, and noir. Every major species had their own abilities weaponized within the split-second dogfights of Versa.

Earth maintained a competitive edge against the other aliens in the universe's most popular attraction, Galactica. An Olympic-size contest consisting of a thousand racers from each qualifying Majoris and Minoris planet. It was a series that had been around for centuries, prior to their discovery of my planet. A series coined as unforgiving, agonizing, ecstatic, and immortal with a gargantuan prize translating its wealth to our quadrillion dollar bill. A temptation that caught the eye of every talented racer on Earth, including my father, Crank McGuire, otherwise known as The Heart of Earth. A racer who debuted in Galactica XLIV, claiming the first Galactic title for our planet in Galactica XLV, while adding onto the success with another in Galactica XLVII; because of Crank, the Decalliance expanded itself into a Hendecalliance for Earth. Undoubtedly the most iconic racer Earth has to offer, and arguably the best racer Galactica has ever seen. Now, at the age of 42, my dad is trying to become the first racer in Galactica history to acquire the hat trick, the Triple Crown, the trio of Galactic Titles. An accolade no other racer has seen since the birth of Versa. Officially one race, one win away from an immortal honor.

My name is Craven McGuire, the only son of Crank McGuire. It's July 26th, 2239, a day in which the McGuire's family saga changes forever.

ACT I
THEN & NOW

ACT I
CHAPTER 1

AN OLD LEGEND
VS A NEW LEGACY

"**L**ET'S GO EARTH!" THE CROWD KEPT CHANTING, RUMBLING THE HEAVENS FOR AN EPIC FINALE. The exclusively private booth I was in diminished some of the noise my young ears weren't ready to take. Above the Terran and extraterrestrial crowd, the booth had the perfect vantage point of the entire race track called The Twilight of Hera, a name originating from its tradition of racing at dusk. We Terrans clung onto the idea of riding into the sunset, which was why the final straightaway of this track headed into the great star's direction, a spot the booth had the best vantage point. Might have been the only thing the booth had a great view of because the rest of this humongous track was almost impossible to make out unless you had a binocular eyesight. Acting as a supplement to the blind spots, a cube-shaped hovertron floated in the twilight sky with live footage of the racers and their positions currently held in the historic conclusion of Galactica XLVIII. In the distance I could see the leading pack of racers boosting through the rail-less corkscrew loops over the great lake below the levitating stadium. Several racers lost their traction to the track at the loop's peak, falling into the war between the waves for a disqualification. The hovertron gave the fallen racers a pitiful lowlight along with the embarrassing tune of a high-pitched horn. It then eyed the man of the century, the green-and-blue racer representing my planet. The Heart of Earth, my father, Crank McGuire.

"There's our boy Craven," my animated mom, Lacey, pointed out. Her light brown eyes sparked the booth's dull walls from the sun's linear rays, bringing more life into her recently dyed hair. A look she'd never commit to if not for my father's doctorate in the arts of persuasion. Earth's colors, green and blue, weren't winning any elections as my mom's favorite pallet, and yet it somehow worked with her warm complexion. The shaven sides of her hair maintained the natural brown color while the branches of her long curls screamed blue with green tips. My father only wanted her to look a part suitable for his historic feat.

The universe would never forget my father's name when he achieved immortality. The Hendecalliance and Hectolition would engrave him on a pedestal out of a black hole's tug. History was the only thing my eyes were frozen on, taking in every detail of my father's suit glittering each shine on the hovertron's infinite resolution. The crowd reacted in a zeptosecond of his screen presence, injected by the final dose of his legendary tale. He'd been almost flawless in this race. There was just an early collision with some of the other racers. They were trying to take him out of this game early because of his experience, but he'd been in this position before holding a victorious resume against thousands of aliens across the galaxy. From the fish-like creatures of Pasydanya to the eight-legged freaks of Arach. Name a specimen, he had beaten them. He only craved one more ring, one more moment, one more reign of eminence, and I believed it was finally here, the final arc to his legendary career, the eudaimonia.

"Let's go Earth!" the people roared louder, all voices synchronized to wake an entire galaxy. Out of all the places to host the final race of the series, they picked Earth for the first time in Galactica history. No racer had ever won the final race at their home planet, but there was a first time for everything. Following the burst of energy within our cheers, the electrifying commentary team of Tokyn Hampshyre and Gradite Monroe was heard once more.

"Fifty racers and not enough winners! Too many races but one finish! We're here ladies and gentlemen! The last chapter of this extraordinary Tale of Galactica XLVIII! Whose heart will be broken? Whose soul will be collected? Who's got the one-way ticket to the immortal stage of Galactica?" Tokyn anxiously exclaimed to the audience. He was one of the most popular commentators and faces in the world. He was an iridescently sunny-orange Goldlyn from the planet of Pasydanya with a personality brighter than his skin along with their Terran partner, Gradite. There were times where I felt like he took his job a little too seriously, but who could blame him. These races had been unbelievable.

"I don't know Tokyn, something tells me that it could be The Heart of Earth Crank McGuire! He's edging closer to the front of the pack on those curves with fluent motion and a constant speed of 400km/h!" Gradite expressed as an answer to his partner's cluster of questions.

"You might be onto something Grad! Maybe it's your Terran instincts, eh?"

"Or maybe it's the one million standing strong beside the legend!" Gradite exploded, causing the crowd to increase its volume to the max. The chant eventually turned into the infamous "Seven Nation" chant, Earth's primary homeland anthem. The noise got even louder once the hovertron's image converted to the black and blue racer in the lead, it appeared to be the Rokian. An alien part of an aggressive species that was no longer a friend to Earth or any other planet. The representative of Ragnios wore a black mechanical suit with neon-blue tubes running through the legs and chest to the mask around its mouth, distributing xenon gas, Rokian's native air. The neon-blue theme matched the blurry-blue visor over its eyes and blue tips of its metal two-foot-long tentacles for hair. This Rokian named Thorax was a natural-born killer from a suffering planet on the brink of extinction. The Ragnarök were desperately in need of a win if they wished to heal any remnants of their planet from the recent wars endured against Crystia.

"You and everyone else can stand beside a legend! I'm going to stand behind the manifested alien from the black and blue, Thorax. It's only a matter of time before he ends this once and for all!" Tokyn surprisingly opposed, considering that he'd been a huge fan of my father throughout this series. I guessed the Rokian had made a believer out of the Goldlyn. Thorax had developed a lot of notoriety in this series as The Last Rokian. Just when we thought his planet and breed were down and out for extinction, a little spirit called hope appeared to continue the Rokian's violent but magical run for a globalized serenity. So far, he'd broken the record for the most kills in a single series. A record previously held by a racer named Skorge, a paled devilish-looking alien who had an unforgivable run in the past. My dad claimed Skorge was probably the toughest foe he had ever faced before the Satanian's death in Galactica XLVI. The record was 174, now it was 189, no 194. Thorax added five souls at the beginning of this race.

"It's An Old Legend vs. A New Legacy! The dream match-up that has not left us disappointed for one second!" Gradite exaggerated.

"Like I said earlier Grad, I'll keep my money on the new. Especially when the new has a 7.34 second split from Crank, who is still trailing in fifth… now fourth place!!!"

"Keep pushing Crank!" my mom shouted as if her husband could hear her through the "Seven Nation" chants.

"And here comes Crank, with one final push as he moves into third… now second place. He is right on Thorax's tail! I honestly can't believe what I am seeing! For the first time in this series, Thorax is playing defense! He is trying to take up as much space of the track as possible, but offensively Crank just won't quit! He will not take no for an answer!!!" Tokyn shouted with an overdose of vitality.

I could now see Thorax looking back on the screen. He was trying to shove his right-rear wheel into my dad's face so that he could scrape off parts of it, but my dad responded by grabbing Thorax's leg, fracturing it inward on the spot. Thorax tried to retaliate by swinging his right-front wheel at my dad but inconceivably missed. The nerves of failure within Thorax were beginning to show, and my father knew it. He took advantage of the flaw by drilling his left-front wheel into the gut of Thorax, scraping off all the armor and skin in that section. Thorax was now roaring for his life along with the galaxy of Ragnarök. Gears and wires were now sliding out of Thorax's gut along with a few ultra large intestines dangling along for the ride. The dark-purple extraterrestrial trail of blood now made its mark on the final stretch of this race. My dad was able to deliver a fatal blow that would end an entire species but instead showed mercy by placing his bloody left-front wheel back onto the track, officially passing Thorax for what might be the last time.

"And Crank takes first place! Never count out a legend!" Gradite yelled with excitement through the crowd that could now be heard from space.

My dad might have spared Thorax's life, but that didn't stop the alien from committing one last act of defiance by standing on his pair of rear-wheels, whipping his right-front wheel with torque at my dad's left leg. He was able to connect with the hit but my dad was still increasing in speed while Thorax was losing speed due to the lack of wheels.

"A 100-meter lead… A 200-meter lead… I can't believe what's happening! Crank has a 400-meter lead!" Tokyn informed the world while the hovertron began to show us an x-ray of my dad's left femur. The big bone had a crack stretching by the millisecond. Before the screen could show us the complete fracture, it quickly shifted to the wheel on his left leg losing magnetic attraction with the suit. "But that one wheel is starting to give out and it's becoming a little loose. Crank's got one more jump before the final straightaway of the race!" Tokyn explained while my dad traveled up the giant 100-meter ramp. He was getting ready to shoot himself off of the ramp for the final leap but before he could take it, the left-rear wheel detached itself from his suit. The technical error forced my idol to lose momentum throughout his leap.

My father couldn't control each flip he did in the air and eventually crash-landed onto his right shoulder. He didn't show us a sign of life after the fall. His suit was destroyed with each wheel scattered all over the track. Parts of the armor were crushed, especially around the section of his right shoulder. It was now dripping some type of liquid. It was not oil because it was not black. It was red. I thought it was blood. My dad eventually stirred to life as he struggled to eject himself out of the suit. He stood tall afterwards, revealing the gruesome injuries inflicted on his body. There was now a bone sticking out of his right arm, and his left leg was bending in a direction that it shouldn't. The graphic image silenced the crowd for the first time tonight, along with my mom, now covering her mouth with tremulous hands.

My dad was still wearing his helmet that now had a partially destroyed visor, a glass shield that typically protected the eyes. He slowly took the helmet off, showing us a disfigured face. I couldn't even recognize my idol anymore. Velvet streams coated his entire face with a few glass shards impaling the left eye and cheek. The image was unforgettable, but my dad didn't care as he hobbled down the straightaway to finish the race.

"I cannot believe what I am seeing ladies and gentlemen. The Heart of Earth trying his hardest to prevent a globalized cardiac arrest! What he is doing is legal! You can finish the race without a suit! Anything is legal in the Galactica!" Gradite preached with an amazed tone, bringing life back into the stunned crowd. The screen tried its best to capture my dad's perseverance before it transitioned to Thorax's right arm now transforming into a long blade. The Rokian was finally escalating the ramp.

"And here comes Thorax with one last statement!" Tokyn screeched. Thorax perfectly landed the jump in the puddle of blood splashing onto the abdomen of his suit, trying to catch my dad, who was only a few meters away from the finish line. This race was coming down to the wire.

The Rokian's bladed arm suddenly began to laterally rise for some odd reason before he could finally pass my dad at the last nanosecond. Thorax must've pushed my dad out of the way because Crank fell forward onto the ground afterwards. I couldn't tell if my dad won or not though, it was so close. We either took first or second, I wasn't too sure anymore. My exhilaration turned to confusion once I realized how silent the crowd was. My eyes quickly locked back onto my dad, who hadn't gotten up since the fall, a great puddle of blood forming all around his body like an ever-growing shadow. I glanced at my mom who had tears rapidly sliding down her cheeks. I still couldn't figure out what had happened. Hadn't we won? Weren't we getting first or second? Wasn't it one hell of a race? But when I focused back at my dad's body, I saw an image that I would never forget… the head of my hero severed from his body. Just like the rest of the crowd, my heart was shattered with the bittersweet symphony of black-and-blue fireworks exploding into the dark-orange sky.

"Thorax has made his statement…" Tokyn mumbled with shock and disbelief while Thorax ejected out of his suit, walking over to my father's anemic body. Other racers drove around the bloodbath to finish their race while the black-and-blue killer viciously stood over my dad's body, exhaling the light-blue gas from his mask. He then reached down to obtain the severed head, lifting it up as a trophy for the world to see. The lethargic eyes of my father resembled Medusa's, freezing anyone who stared, everyone except for me. The crescendo rhythms of my heart eradicated every ounce of my fear until anger had the home all to itself. "Ragnios is here to survive and the Ragnarök are here to stay."

Only One Winner…
No More Mistakes…
&
No More Tragedies…

ACT I
CHAPTER 2

ALMOST A
DOZEN SINCE

BEAUTY, THE MAGIC WORD OF THE HOUR FOR A DAY WHERE THE THERMOMETERS WERE ATTRACTED TO THE 70° THRESHOLD.** A perfect temperature for a life-changing day where beauty is anything but simplistic. No, beauty has layers, and adding to them was my fluent breeze through an important time trial within the 2250 Atlas and, man oh man, did she embody beauty. She may have started off as a work-in-progress, a theory, a fantasy, a trial-and-error process through a pedigree of Atlases, but she had turned into a Versa suit like no other. From the balance of weight to the manipulation of aerodynamics, she held beauty to a fault. Sure, her armor was a bit stiff. Yes, the right-front wheel's magnetic attraction had been wobbly at best, and of course it was damn-near impossible to avoid the subpar top speed of 420km/h when the market's median was 425km/h. But the love I'd placed into this suit could be seen outside of the Milky Way. Love had to be the most important ingredient because without it, perfection could never be obtained. I may have had my father's brain, but I also had his heart, and that is why his legacy would continue. That is why I had to excel in this time trial because tonight was the biggest night of my Versa career, and I did not plan on looking back, now entering the final obstacle, the 100-meter ramp.

"How much boost is left in the tank, MIKA?" I asked.

"Little over 10%," MIKA quickly replied.

"Let's empty it," I forcefully commanded while bursting onto the ramp faster than the speed of light. The only problem was that I could feel time slowing down once more. No. It was starting to happen again, wasn't it? My heartbeat was getting faster and stronger along with my muscles, which were now contracting tighter than a constricted snake. I closed my eyes so that I couldn't see it. Out of sight, out of mind, right? I still heard them chanting in my head over the drumming sounds of my heartbeat. The "Seven Nation" chants were now louder than ever. I could always eliminate one sense, but the others just seemed to overcome my resilience. I eventually give in by opening my eyes, instantly seeing him, the ghost in my head, the green-and-blue racer passing by. Of course, it was him. He was always here to come back for death. He never hit the brakes, nor did he change the mistake. Like usual, he only came back to reenact the dying minute. Now at the top of the ramp, he unintentionally mistimed the jump, losing his wheels along with control in the air. Again, to the tragedy's conclusion, he faded away in my head to restore my time back to normal. These events happened from time to time. Whenever time slowed down on this track, I could see his soul rise from the grave, like a ghost to take me on in this race.

"400… 410… 420!" MIKA informed me as I regained focus on the trial. When I got to the top of the ramp, I took the big leap. The sun instantly shone its rays onto my face while I was in the air. The light might've been bright, but it didn't prevent me from successfully landing safe and sound onto the last straightaway to finish the time trial stronger than ever.

The brakes were slowly triggered after crossing the finish line. I took a moment to stand up on my rear-wheels once I came to a complete stop. Quickly catching my attention were the appendiscs, a coin-size magnetic disc that kept the wheels attached to my arms and legs no matter where they were located. They were undoubtedly one of the most important intricacies to the suit. As a racer we had to make sure the discs were greasier than a triple-fried chicken because these bad boys were the reason why the wheels turned at top speeds. If lubed improperly, they could flare up to extreme temperatures and destabilize the magnetic attraction. A nonexistent issue by the pristine glares on each appendisc. I even dared myself to toad-lick one of them to see how hot they were and to my surprise they maintained an icicle degree.

Satisfied with the overall performance of this speed demon, my eyes ascended to the empty set of bleachers. They're empty, they're empty and yet I still heard them chanting, I always heard them chanting. I guess that's what I got for constantly coming back to the stadium floating over Lake Michinis. Coming back to my father's graveyard, I knew, was stupid; this track was the most accessible Naturis-rated track to practice on. They were the most extreme tracks, so if one could overcome them, one could overcome anything. Naturis ratings were only given to tracks requiring one to stay on due to the environmental dangers enclosing the race. For instance, any track that took place over water, fire, lava, clouds, sharp rocks, mountains, and so on were rated as Naturis, like The Twilight of Hera.

"What was the time?" I asked MIKA, stepping back into the more important reality.

"8:08, you've cut down twenty-seven seconds."

"Great, I can cut down twenty-seven more after I get my shipment of new parts," I replied as my wheels began to shrink down to cycle themselves into the wheel holsters of the suit. The holsters were located on the scapula and sacrum sections of the suit: my shoulders and lower back.

"Looking forward to it, Craven. Would you like me to shut off now?"

"How much battery life do you have?"

"72%."

"Yeah, get some rest. I'll see you again at Knightfall."

"See you then. MIKA signing off."

The 2250 Atlas commenced a shutting down phase as I ejected myself from the suit. The Atlas had been a suit I'd had my eye on for years, since a prototype was built for the *Tsarina* dealership. It was a concept that they chose to kill instead of pursuing, leaving an entrepreneur like myself to pick up the scraps for my own company, *The Blue Jay's Nest*. The suit catered to a mesomorph liking, granting musculature of armor around every major muscle like: The brachialis for the biceps, vastus for the quadricep, femoralis for the hamstring, dells for the deltoids, and latis for the dorsis. I already kept my physique up to the Versa conditions, constantly hitting the gym five times a week unless I was in-season, like now. Enhancing the muscles in my arms and legs had never been a problem in my life. As for my chest, heh, it was a goddamn mystery yet to be solved. For some odd reason, my muscles never develop there. It didn't matter how much of an attraction I added to the magnetic bench rack, they just never wanted to grow, which is why I'd added a layer of pectars for the pectorals. An illusion to the growth malfunction to help me resemble a hunk, and more importantly, present a suit attracted to an average Versa consumer. It took me three tries to get the intricacies to the current Atlas correct. I'd nicknamed the 2250 Atlas as Atlas III with Atlas Sr. and Jr. still back at the workshop. They always said that the third time was the charm, and after tonight, the Atlas would be just that, a charm in the Versa market.

As for MIKA, she was an Artificial Intelligent chip inside the back of the helmet. She could power the suit's controls when it came to triggering the boost or strategically mapping out where the wheels should be placed. The process was called axle adaptation. So, if I ever lost a wheel and was down to three, I'd have to move the wheels around to maintain a balance in speed. There were multiple transitioning positions to get into when there were only three wheels left like the tricycle formation, where I would hold onto one wheel with both of my arms together while both legs had their own separate wheel. A position inspired by the Martians, Earth's solaric rival. There was also the infamous motorcycle position whenever you had two wheels left which was a formation where both arms hold onto one wheel along with both legs. When it came to these game-changing situations, I needed to adapt quickly or else I'd fall behind in a race. This was why I had MIKA. She was very sudden with the transitions. She also informed me about the suit's condition. Basically, giving me intel on what was damaged and what was not. She was the A.I. of the 2200 Hermes, the legendary suit my father raced with during Galactica XLVIII. She served my dad well, a big reason why I snuck into the garage of my mom's house one night when she wasn't home to take MIKA from my dad's destroyed suit.

My mom would completely freak out if she knew that I'd been competing in natively sponsored Versa races for the past five years. I didn't understand why. I was a 22-year-old man for crying out loud. I'd been old enough to make my own decisions for the past few years and yet she still thought that I was like my dad and would suffer the same fate if I competed. But she was wrong, I was smarter than my dad and wouldn't let my merciful hand get me killed.

"It's mind-boggling! You race just like your father!" a voice shouted, followed by a lone series of claps over by the bleachers. It was my best friend, Trace Burretta, wearing a gray, long-sleeve sports polo with the Versa logo of an armored winged "V" at the chest. He loved that top as much as the sport it was associated with and liked to pair the look with some tan cargo shorts and running shoes. His shoes were heavily gripped at the bottom to offset Trace's obnoxious behaviors like leaping out of the bleachers to join me down on the hard asphalt pavement. Trace Burretta, where should I even begin about this guy? He had got short brown hair gently gelled back for a modest flow with hazel eyes. He always had a well-trimmed beard to cover both his rumpled cheekbones on top of the burn mark to his neck caused by an aggressively dangerous racer named Zane "The Raven" Maddox. A racer who maintained a dark cynical form of racing that was never a great sign for others. A polar opposite to Trace, someone I'd known since elementary. He helped me get over my dad's death almost a dozen years ago and convinced me to get involved with this blood sport. I was an only child, so I didn't know what it was like to have a brother, but I did know he was the closest person to a brother that I would probably ever have.

"You know I hate being compared to him," I reminded.

"It's just the truth though, and I know you know," he replied, grabbing my pile of clothes nearby. The notion made me eject out of the Atlas, revealing the light-gray Versa corium I had on. It was a bodysuit fabricated with the tight Dri-Fit technology to provide a comforting feel to the Terran body stuck within the suits, and it was very tight. Global warming had affected the "South Pole" since I first placed the corium on this morning. The uneased tension almost forced my restless body to rip the damn thing off instead of unzipping it for the better supplement of clothes now tossed to my feet by Trace. They were a dark-blue compression shirt, a pair of slim, dark-blue jeans, black high-top sneakers fused with neon-blue laces and canvas, and my favorite jacket in the whole world. *The Blue Jay's Nest* jacket specifically designed for the owner and could either be found around my body or in its vicinity. The jacket itself was mostly black with a double-layer of zippers I usually left half-way zipped because of its pair of high collars. The inner collar didn't reach higher than the Adam's apple, as for the outer collar, it reached out to my shoulders. The jacket was never too tight and was made of an eco-friendly material with a fairly tight cuff, but that's not what made it special, no, that came from the stitched-on neon-blue design of my company's logo of a blue jay spreading its wingspan along the jacket's back. Trace had stated countless number of times that it was the jacket I'd nosedive into my grave with. "Heh, he ain't wrong," I thought.

"So, this is the secret weapon that you promised to beat me in tonight?" he asked while I placed on my clothes, now examining Atlas III. When it came to Versa, Trace had a cocky mentality. Me being his other half hadn't suppressed the demeanor either, as I had bragged about the Atlas' groundbreaking birth into this world for the past couple of months. Honestly, it was safe to say that we both had a competitive ego, which came in handy for days like this. Tonight was the championship and I was positive he was going to fall to the back of the pack this time.

"I still stand by those words," I replied, causing him to chuckle while sending a sarcastic nod. "And besides, you've got a bigger problem to deal with in this race."

"What problem? Zane? What the hell is he gonna do? Not a damn thing. In fact, I'll pass his ass first, shift into reverse, bird the bird for good measure, shift back to normal and then pass your ass last. How does that sound?" Trace stated defensively, screening out his absurd vision with his pair of fingers boxed into a camera. Trace Burretta and Zane Maddox had been the main storyline to the Semi Leagues over the past few years. Their major rivalry had been around since my debut. So far, the two had broken each other's rib cages, collar bones, arms, legs, hips and hearts, leaving a countless number of scars in visible and non-visible locations. In my opinion, the most notable highlight in this rivalry had to be when Trace successfully frisbee'd his wheel into Zane's crotch while they were in the air during a race in Michinis. The doctors in the reports claimed that Zane was peeing pints of blood afterwards and had one of his testicles removed due to the infection. The two ferocious bulls have done a lot of cruel things to the other in a sport where much more can be done, which was why I prayed to all the gods in this universe that one of them wouldn't take their next moves too far.

"We'll see what happens. Were you heading to the nest?" I asked.

"Dunno, is a limped dick depressing?" he stated like a degreed student in the arts of smartassery.

"The plan was to go easy on you tonight. I take it that's not an option anymore," I responded to the wrinkle-stretched smile on his face. Arrogance wasn't my forte, and yet this asshole always yanked the dark side out. I'd known him for years and I still couldn't decide whether he was the best or worst part of me.

"I guess I can make a pit stop at the nest. I left a secret weapon of my own there to help you remember those poorly chosen words," he claimed backstepping to an exit off the track, maintaining a silent tone into the dark tunnel for dramatics. Heh, that sonuvabitch was definitely the best part of me.

Trace's trump card did leave me intrigued, but before I could follow him with my suit, I gave the setting sun one more hard look. The night was creeping closer and closer with my feet getting colder and colder. Knightfall was the biggest event in the Semi Leagues and would be all over the news. For the first time in my life, the Versa spotlight was going to shine brightly on the son of Crank McGuire, which officially made me a dead man walking. The big picture was that whether I won or lost tonight, my mother would find out, and when she did, there wouldn't be a god across the entire galaxy brave enough to save my soul.

NO RAYS, BLUE JAYS

THE CHICAGOLANDS, A CITY WITH FLYWAYS FASTER AND SMOOTHER THAN ANY OTHER. Like wind patterns, it added to the coined nickname of our home known as The Windy City by the majority. Never stuttering the hover truck's speed, Trace breezed through the secondary flyway, beating the emerging rhythm of traffic. It was not like the secondary flyway to be packed. That luxury was reserved for the primary flyway. It was typically the busiest filled with taxis, firefighters, anti-hackists, ambulances, and a hot pursuit once in a lunar eclipse. I remembered the epic chase that lasted several hours through the heart of The Windy City. The chase would've lasted an entire fortnight if not for the flock of birds intercepting the lawbreaker. Hell, Trace could've been that criminal based on how fast he was presently driving. It was almost as if he was sending a message on how smooth his skills were. To be honest, I didn't think much of it. If it got us to the nest, who was I to complain. His speed did make a lot of the holoboards seem like a smudge on a lens.

A half-finished descent of the sun lied on the horizon by the time we got to the tertiary flyway, now heading to the southwest corner of Lake Michinis near Calumet, a poverty-stricken area located on the lowest level of the city. Coined as an underworld by most living in the Chicagolands due to the lack of sunlight, but an absence of sun didn't necessarily resort to a creation of hell. The atmosphere down here was a lot more retro than most actually realized. Scattered across the walls were strips of neon lights shifting from a flaming-orange to a slow-strobing yellow producing an energetic virus roaming through Calumet's inhabitants. *An undying party*, is what Trace titled this place, and who could blame him. The inhabitants here knew how to produce something out of nothing, in other words, it was the perfect location for my workshop. A place hidden in the depths, ready for a culminating spark onto the Versa market. All of my best ideas had come from Calumet, and they were only going to get better Post-Knightfall.

"How packed do you think it'll be tonight?" I asked Trace out of curiosity.

"How packed…? You're kidding," Trace chuckled on a right turn. I glanced at him a couple times, waiting for an imminent analogy. "Let's just say that the stadium will be more packed than any Super Bowl."

"Did you ever get a layout of the track?"

"Before or after their reconstruction?" Trace questioned, leaving me a bit confused. No one ever told me about a goddamn reconstruction. "Yeah, Thardus told me that they've added a few things along with jammers to disrupt our A.I. from analyzing the additions. It shouldn't come as a surprise, though. We're both familiar with his nature, he's trying to boost the ratings with injuries." Of course, he was Thardus Leone, the president of the Semi Leagues. Ratings were all he ever cared about, desperately trying to compete with the A-list leagues in the world like the Pro and Galactic Leagues. It was easier to have a mindset like his when you were a spectator. An agent of chaos with a clean pair of hands—the man in a nutshell.

"Why does every finale gotta end with a bang?" I finished as we turned onto Nexus Ave, a street where the lights turned blue, and the underground Versa racers zoomed wild. The whiffles of burnt rubber and booms of turbos exhausting pulled us towards the nest. Anyone attracted to natural Versa senses would always end up here, where they belonged, at the workshop, at *The Blue Jay's Nest*, shining the fiercest blue light an iris could tolerate. A name brought to me by the people speaking volumes about a workshop once upon a time called *The Blueprint*. It was always my father's dream to create a workshop where every racer could start off fresh. Where big things could have small beginnings. Where gender, race, class, and even specimens could all be equal. A project that was merely a blueprint without a creator until a few years ago when I decided to make his dream a reality by using the jackpot of money obtained from his final race and even went as far as labeling it as *The Blueprint* in the bluest section of the Chicagolands. But that's the thing, I created it for him, not for myself nor others, and the irony to it all was that it was the people who made this place manifest. If not for them, this workshop would've been forced to relocate to the upper levels of the city, competing against the top dealerships on the planet like *The Golden Evolution*, a manufacturing company run by an entrepreneur named Luke Gold.

The Golden Evolution was basically the apex predator of the food chain across the entire galaxy of dealerships and didn't really have a manifestation of its own until Galactica XLVI. Luke's company was one of the reasons why my father had had a blueprint for his own shop. Claiming that my father despised Luke and his company would have been the understatement of the century to anyone following Versa. Luke was the lone Terran selling specialized suits exclusive to every Majoris planet, except the UCE. A risky move that easily could've resulted in Luke's excommunication from Earth instead deepened Earth's ties within the Hendecalliance, making Luke Gold the wealthiest man on the planet. In elementary, they told kids how Luke helped our planet by taking the greatest gamble imaginable, a tale any kid would buy unless their father was The Heart of Earth. To this day, I remember my father's words, his anecdote on hating Luke Gold.

"Imagine being with a band of Terrans, men and women you've fought, survived, and persevered with for years. The bond between you all is thicker than blood, but then a game-changer happens, the birth of *The Golden Evolution*. A company selling revitalized suits, gear, and weapons only for those who are not Terran, from a Terran. You and your band feel betrayed… no doubt a tough pill to swallow but you do feel like you've overcome rougher obstacles. You believe that this dilemma is tamable, until you witness your band, slowly becoming outmatched one by one against these new and improved suits. What was once a family now becomes a group of survivors. Only the surviving seven are left alive because of an upgrade that was given to every major specimen except your own, from your own." (Crank McGuire: February 14, 2197-July 26, 2239)

His words didn't just tell a story though, it was an actual event. I always saw my father as a top-notch racer instead of a survivor. To top it all off, Thorax wore one of the top-selling suits from *The Golden Evolution*. When it came to Thorax, I was driven by hate, when it came to Luke, I was driven by justice, thankful for Calumet. The nest was going to help me take down both one day, but until that day, the undying party would never stop.

"Home sweet home, eh?" Trace rhetorically inquired once the truck was parked in the lot of the nest. The crowd around the building wasted little time to greet us, revealing the glimmers upon the workshop's platinum exteriors. *The Blue Jay's Nest* stood two-stories tall, excluding the sign on the building's forehead of a blue jay spreading its wings while screaming to the heavens. The majority of the bird's head was black with its eyes and mouth contributing to the neon-blue atmosphere. A design I made to embody the spirit of a young boy soaring to the top with ferocity. I was 20 years old when I had the design first made, which was why the blue jay had twenty feathers, ten on each side. Undoubtedly the perfect fusion of what the workshop was and what it was going to be. The people always called this place the nest because of how I practically lived out of my office, continuously providing for the people, and because of the street name, Nexus. If we were being honest, the people never called it *The Blueprint* since the grand opening insinuating the name change. Trace suggested *No Rays, Blue Jays*, because it fused well with the environment while keeping my father's roots within the name, helping me think of a better name everyone would get behind. Hence, *The Blue Jay's Nest*.

"Y'all better be placing y'all bets on me," Trace reckoned to the swarming crowd. Guilty expressions could be seen by several, now squeezing their way to the back.

"If you place your bets on him…" I joined quickly, attracting every eye. "You'll be broke and lonelier than an anime fan on prom night."

"Don't listen to the false god," Trace stated, "I fucked the prom queen while binging Shaolin Heists."

"That's because you were the prom king!"

"I rest my case," Trace finished with his arms spread out like the blue jay, winning the debate before the crowd focused its attention on an exhibitional race now happening on

Nexus Ave. Taking our focus away from the race was one of my mechanics coming out of the workshop's garage on the building's posterior. It was the Russian expert, Vector Kuznetsov, an iron gem I snatched from the major Versa dealership ruling Eastern Europe/Western Russia, *Tsarina*. Arguably, one of *Tsarina's* top mechanics who never got the right amount of love and attention. Vulnerable to a departure, I took advantage of the opportunity by offering him the best contract a mechanic could drool over. Stuck in his head were still a lot of outlines for new suits along with connections still on the inside of *Tsarina* providing us with smuggled gear. The procuration of Vector had given me the much-needed royal straight flush, and my workshop hadn't looked back since. Neither had he, now coming closer for a crisper image of oil stains above his black beard and brown eyes covering up some of the wrinkles endured from *sarina*. They were also a major cause for the bald spot at the peak of his head. A subject more sensitive than most in Vector's eyes, which was why he had it covered with my workshop's snapback. I tried my best to avoid words or remarks revolving around patches, balding, alopecia, and so on. Trace on the other hand, proved how invested he was to the anime show, Shaolin Heist because he showed no mercy.

"What's up Baldylocks?" Trace stated to commence the war. Like I said, no mercy.

"You know one of days, boss and witnesses won't be around when you mock, pretty boy," Vector angrily replied the best he could with his broken English. The negative electricity between these two was so amplified, the neon lights began to flicker.

"I just wanted to know if Katia's here," Trace explained. Katia was one of the employees at my shop, and more importantly, Trace's fiancé.

"She's in the shop, Tracy," Vector replied with a concluding insult.

"You know what..." Trace began, unable to avoid my restraint. A blind eye could mistake me for an NHL referee due to the amount of times I'd been sandwiched between these two juggernauts. To fully restore the peace, I directed Trace to the shop's entrance. He claimed that they were just having a little fun on the way in before I could redirect my attention back to Vector outside.

"Vector, the Atlas is in the back of the truck. Is it possible if you can hook her up to the forge?" I asked. The forge was practically every racer's wet dream. It was a chamber specified for Versa suits where they could be analyzed, recoded, and/or redesigned by the possessor on a linked computer.

"Need battery too?"

"Possibly, but don't do anything else, I wanna give her some personal sparks."

"No problem boss."

"How did the deal go with your friend in *Tsarina*. Did he provide?" I asked for a steady nod.

"Plan worked to perfection," Vector added, explaining that the package his friend smuggled was already hooked to the forge. Heh, the hell would I do without Vector; this was why he got paid the big bucks.

The crowd on the sidewalks of Nexus Ave now began to amplify their cheers for a climactic finish. Curious about who they were cheering for, I rushed to the stairway of the workshop's western balcony overseeing the entire street. Coming down the northside of Nexus was a silver racer smothering his opponent with a cloud of steam, now crossing the red-lasered finish line. The racer wore a 2245 Zeus as they entered the parking lot. The smooshed inward craters of the Zeus' rotator cuffs proved that the race wasn't as pretty as the finish, helping me identify the racer before the helmet could be tossed into the crowd.

The avenue-sized smile of the 14-year-old racer lit up the entire lot as I came down the stairway to congratulate them. The silver-haired, young bear, freckled cheek, blue-eyed freak brushed off the crowd like a herd of zombies to hug me. Zero Jäger, a prodigy I'd been training since the workshop's beginnings. He was one of the many reasons why I loved this place. A native of Calumet, Zero had endured the struggles of poverty—the scars that helped someone cherish every meal, every outfit, and every breath of fresh air, constantly having dreams bigger than the small world they inhabit. Since the first time I'd laid eyes on this kid, he was innately driven with the one big goal of being the next Crank McGuire with help from a McGuire. How was that for fate?

"Oh, for the love of all the gods watching, please tell me you saw that race Craves?" Zero eagerly stated with the crackling voice every teenage boy gets through puberty. It was almost like the larynx didn't know what it wanted to sound like yet.

"I only caught the finish," I answered as he backed out of the hug, giving me a better look at his suit. It had neon-blue lightning strikes roaming all the way down to the calves along with a blue jay imprinted onto the suit's chest as homage to our home.

"Hell yeah, the ending is all I cared about," Zero expressed as the crowd caught up to share their love. "I honestly think I had a perfect race."

"Really? Perfect?" I questioned eyeing the dells peeling off with a few gunshot sparks for good measure.

"Ahh, that's just a scratch, they don't call Zeus, the God of Thunder for no reason," he smoothly brushed off. "Besides, this win is a foreshadow for the main event tonight."

"One would assume."

"The assumption's set-in stone because I'm gonna be watching."

"Since when could you afford Pay-Per-View?"

"Since now, Craves," he answered, fanning out the winning proceeds of his race. A disappointed look instantly engraved my face as the bitter taste of Zero's gambling sunk into my stomach.

"This isn't a good habit," I stated quickly, snatching the fan of money.

"It was for a good cause, though," Zero replied, reaching his hand out for the money. "I wanted to see you race."

"Fine, this better be the last time," I instructed, giving back the winnings. "You've got too little to lose."

"Well… I've made one more teeny weeny bet… but after today, my gambling days come to an end," he reluctantly explained.

"What the hell did you bet on now?"

"You winning Knightfall," Zero revealed. I honestly didn't know how to take the response. Yeah, it was a sweet act but come on, I refused to be the one responsible for his sinful addiction. It was bad enough that my mom would kill me after tonight, now I had to win so that momma and papa Jäger didn't do the same to him.

The guilty smile was the last thing I saw on Jäger's face, leaving him alone to temporarily enjoy his achievement. I entered the workshop to see how business was doing, and like usual, it was congested. The inside of the workshop had a more modern feel unlike the retro spirit outside. I found it important to keep the workshop's technology up to date but didn't want to make my customers uncomfortable from the platinum walls screaming wealth, which was why the lights had a dim touch with a popular choice of music symphonizing in the background. Adding on to the homey feel were couches, bars, and pool tables scattered throughout the workshop near each section separated by parts of an exosuit. One corner of the store focused more so on the helmets of the suit for those who needed replacement visors, A.I. chips, or just a brand-new helmet in general. I always tried to satisfy the demands for anyone in need at all cost. This sometimes required illegal exportation of products from a different country/planet or time spent on creating the product my-damn-self. If someone needed it, I'd have it, no matter what. We also ran the store on a grocery system online, a system that allowed someone to send us a list of all the things they needed or wanted so that we could package it, and have it sent to them via drone. Most dealerships were built on a similar system more legal than mine, but as a big offset were inexplicably priced too expensive for most living in an area like Calumet. Most top-tier racers had a large bank or a posse of sponsors aiding them financially for the right suit, and it shouldn't have been that way. The talents of a racer should outweigh their resources. It was why I love Zero so much. He was proof of my philosophy.

After reviewing the entire store, I noticed Trace talking to his fiancé, Katia Duran at the register. She was a short pretty girl with classy, faded gray-and-black hair. She had hazel eyes that seemed to shine a little more beneath her thick brown eyebrows. She came into the business near its beginning as a small-town girl migrating to the big city along with her three sisters, all searching for a name to themselves. One night, they ventured down to the so-called underworld with a group of friends to watch some of the exhibitional races that occasionally happened on Nexus. It'd be a false claim to describe the Duran sisters as unattractive, and yet Trace only had his eyes set on one. Head-over-heels the man was, overwhelming Katia with his charm. His rugged, half-broken, half-certain charm. He had good intentions; it was just that execution. Man, oh man his execution was hard to watch–like watching a bunch of legally blind drivers compete in a demolition derby. When I thought about it, that sounded like a fun event to watch, but anyways, the best thing my closest friend, my brother could muster from Katia's background was her need for a job. The vital intel had me hire her on the spot for my Trace's sake and he would grow on her over time because there was something Trace had always been great at and that was being persistent and primarily protective. Two key traits into Katia's heart, but at the moment, it must've been irrelevant because she was giving him an earful.

"What's going on?" I urgently asked as I approached them.

"She's getting a little scared about tonight," Trace answered.

"Well, I actually want to see all of my future husband while walking down the aisle, not parts of him that have been replaced with mechanical arms, legs, and organs," Katia aggressively stated.

"I'm not gonna get hurt, and I think you're over-exaggerating with the organs, love. If you think for one second that I'm gonna lose my perfect ass set of kidneys, then you got another thing coming."

"Another thing coming? Trace, every time you've raced Zane…" she stopped, glancing at his neck. The burn mark seemed more visible than ever. He could only look away knowing it was damn-near impossible to defend this case by himself.

"Katia, I'm gonna be right next to him throughout the whole race. If Zane attempts anything, I'll be ready," I explained to back my friend's case. It took Katia a moment, but she would concede.

"If he does get hurt, that blood is on your hands, Craven."

"And my hands alone," I replied.

"See, Craven's got my back. We'll just pop Zane's other testicle if he attempts anything," Trace said happily while patting my back.

"And we wonder why that lunatic hates you," Katia responded. Trace kissed her on the cheek which escalated to the mouth. I decided to temporarily give them some space by heading to the garage. The goal since that morning was to give my suit some updates and a paint job. As requested, the 2250 Atlas was hooked to the forge and a battery. Outside of the forge's chamber doors were the pedigree of Atlases. The 2248 Atlas was Atlas Sr., the 2249 model was Jr. Both were a tad grayer than Atlas III, but that was mainly due to the piles of dust coating their helmet and dells. Atlas Sr. was my first project which came out a lot bulkier than expected, damaging the handling. With an acceleration of a thousand stallions, Atlas Sr. quickly became a wrecking ball for every barricade on a turn. Just ask Zero, Atlas Sr. turned Nexus Ave into an asteroid belt of rubble through its homestretch. As for Jr., she was a lot smoother and smaller. The 2249's acceleration may not have been as strong as its predecessor's, but the speed, phew, there was nothing matching that. It could beat any fired bullet to their target. Jr., she had the caliber, but with armor more fragile than a toothpick's shaft, she just didn't have the protection. The bruises from the test run still marked my obliques and shoulders to this day, but what could I say, that's life. No pain, no gain, and it was the pain from Jr. and Sr. that helped me create Atlas III, the perfect median. Some might stay skeptical, but she was going to prove the haters wrong, especially with the new makeover I had stored for her in the forge, but she wasn't here alone. A second suit rested in a chamber next to her's. It was a Hermes that seemed more current than my father's 2200 model. It didn't look like it had the same power, but it did share the same intimidation factor. Especially because of how exclusive the Hermes was to Earth.

"Oh yeah, there's MY secret weapon. Bet you didn't see that coming," Trace confidently expressed while walking up beside me.

"So, how long have you had this beast incarnate, caged?" I asked. He stepped into the chamber to get a closer look at his suit, his eyes glimmering at the greatness his Hermes inspired.

"When your dad introduced the 2200 Hermes back in Galactica XLVIII, my father was determined to own one just like it. But because of how expensive and limited these models are, he decided one day to make one instead. The stubborn sonuvabitch actually allowed me to help him back in high school. It took us a few years to successfully complete her, but we did... and you should've seen the look on our faces, especially his. He was so proud of me. As a graduation gift, he gave me this reincarnated beast and told me to ride it down a path he never could," Trace explained. One could see the bonfire igniting in his eyes as he stared at his most prized possession. "What do you think? I honestly never wanted to show you this suit. I know what the Hermes means to you."

I began to analyze the suit for myself. It was mostly white with golden wing designs on the feet, hands, connecting their roots to the holsters on the back. Tiny gold wings were attached to the golden-visored helmet for presentational points, intentionally resembling the Greek God himself, Hermes, also known as the fastest God of them all. But there was one big folly about the suit, its armor was barren and lacked viscosity.

"What armor are you using?"

"It's a Hyper Velocitative Armour," Trace slowly replied. Hyper Velocitative Armour, the same thin armor I used for Atlas Jr. Thin and designed to absorb air and turn it into a boost. A racer ultimately went faster but was super vulnerable—the material more typically used in a long-distance race. I didn't think Trace to be so foolish. He was heaving a Hail Mary with that decision.

"That's why she's worried about Zane, isn't it?"

"Listen, I know the limits of what this suit can handle. Zane can only daydream about harming me tonight."

"Trace, you said it yourself! Thardus has reconstructed the track for ratings and injuries. Speed might not matter in the end."

"I'll be fine. I'm not..."

"You're not who... my father?" I questioned. There was a moment of silence between us. "Trace, you're a great racer but this is too damn risky."

"My nickname is The Ultimate Opportunist. I've gotta live up to that name," Trace proclaimed, glancing at the clock over the workbenches. "It's 8, we've got an hour to do whatever the hell we need to for tonight." I could tell that he really wanted to change the subject, but he was right. Knightfall's finale was only a couple of hours away, and too much time had been wasted.

ACT I

CHAPTER 4

POINT OF
INTEREST

METALS CLINGING, BLOW TORCHES SINGING HAD BEEN THE STEADY TONE OF THE LAST HALF HOUR. I couldn't say that I knew what Trace had been up to in his forge but in mine, the story had been about the addition of GripShift tires to the Atlas. Those tires had an inner layer of an adhesive substance that oozed out onto the outer by command. It's main purpose—keeping a racer stuck to the track, a precautionary move that would prepare me for any trick Thardus had up his slimy sleeve. The opportunity cost for the tires was speed, then again, I wasn't Trace who had taken a liken to the attribute. All about offense, Trace was. One of many reasons why they called him The Ultimate Opportunist, constantly attracted by small window solutions. The crazy bastard never ceased to execute the improbable. Personally, I believed it was luck. There was one race where he was practically married to last place until the final straightaway where every racer lined up diagonally parallel from one another. A look Trace saw as a pitch perfect opportunity to frisbee one of his wheels at the alignment, pinballing each racer off the track for an unlikely last second victory. To add insult to injury, the last racer the wheel impacted was me, and it was the penultimate race in this series. Lucky moments like that were why we all believe he had a horseshoe up his ass. Trace just refuses to get the x-ray. Heh, Katia once stated that Trace could crawl through a sewer of shit for seven seconds and sneak out with the holy grail.

Trace could sponge up all the luck in the galaxy. Me, on the other hand, I would rely on skill. The trait had gotten me where I was at so far, even Yama Tanaka, who just recently stepped into my chamber could vouch for me. He was a Ryukyuan mechanic I acquired from the Japanese manufacturer in Neotokyo, *Ion*. An overlooked company, in my opinion, which is why signing Yama wasn't as difficult as Vector. The amount of ideas I'd researched on *Ion* proved that their motto, *Only a Matter of Time*, was shaped more like an omen. They were planning on integrating a wingsuit mechanic to every exosuit, an innovative scheme that had not yet been perfected but if Yama's projection was correct, they should have a prototype by the end of the next year. *Ion's* under-the-radar appearance would be an afterthought with the wingsuit, which shouldn't have been the case. The only reason why Ion wasn't at *The Golden Evolution's* level was because of *Transcendence*, a company in Cape Town, South Africa. *Transcendence* had been the top native company on UCE for the past century due to the suits out there being combined with Rokian technology. This was based on a sacred bond the Ragnarök had had with the African culture. I could not say that *Transcendence* didn't deserve the recognition. The fact that the company, along with the Rokian land site, had helped turn Africa into a first-world continent on Earth was the underdog story of our existence. But a little love for *Ion* wouldn't have hurt.

At least *Ion* issued some love to *The Blue Jay's Nest* during the acquisition of Yama, who'd been checking the Atlas' progress over the past few minutes. He had long, black straight hair, presently in a ponytail, with a very tan complexion as a result of the potent heat of Arabia where I had him scout an expo of Versa suits. Without complaint, he went there with a beard and came back clean-shaven. I would have said that he was a changed man, but he was holding a container filled with unlabeled cylinder-shaped tanks. I had a hunch of what they were, but refused to jump to any conclusions. Maybe it was something he acquired from the expo.

"You've really placed a lot of work into this suit boss," he stated, examining the new features. It now had brand new gastrolocks which were magnets used for brakes on the calves of the suit. They helped increase magnetic attraction for rear-end stability. I'd also added a new primary layer of abdominises, a shield for the stomach. When it came to racing in these suits, racers had to hold a plank position on a four-point stance, requiring a strong core in the abs. It was something I'd been good with, but when it came to longer races, holding that position could be a grimacing feat. Sure, the better solution would be to not skip any Ab Labs on Tuesday nights, but in all honesty, Fuck Ab Labs. The shit they did made a prison camp look like a day at the spa. This was why I didn't plan on adding a fitness section to the workshop. I was content with my six-pack physique with no desire for an eight. To my rescue was the fresh layer of an abdominis preventing any first, second, and third-degree burns.

"I agree, the suit's maturing just in time. Check out the new platys-plates I got," I insisted to Yama. The platys-plates were the mechanisms of the suit connecting the horse collar to the helmet. The fresh plates I had installed were much more flexible than the previous, allowing me to pivot my neck a lot more comfortably.

"That should lower your visits with the masseuse. What about the product from *Tsarina*, did it come in?" Yama curiously asked.

"Oh yeah, I've got it equipped to the suit. It's a BrachiShield, a mechanism that can turn my right arm into a shield whenever I want."

"What the hell are you, a pacifist? Gear on arms are typically used for weapons."

"Everyone's a critic until they see it in action, then they're a customer."

"Oh yeah boss, how the hell are you gonna sell a product that hasn't even hit the shelves in Russia? I can already smell the lawsuit," Yama touched upon the potential problem while examining more portions of the suit. He kept eyeing the boost tank on the lumbar section of the suit's spina, proving my hunch correct. "What boost are you using?"

"No, no, hell no, not a chance in a Satanian hell, Yama. I'm not putting that Japanese shit into my suit," I angrily replied. Yama had been trying to have me use this boost he'd developed since his *Ion* days called the Komodo Fire. He claimed the durability of the turbo was out of this world and extremely fast. The major problem was that it ran dangerously hot. As a racer, I tried to avoid boost tanks with high levels of temperature to prevent the thin metallic tubes running down the suit's legs from melting. The tubes were like blood vessels. I chose to treat them with delicacy.

"Oh, come on boss."

"No, I've seen you use it once, and it turned your tires into aluminum foil."

"Well, that was just a prototype, this one is the final product. One must learn how to walk before they run, you know."

"I'm already using GripShift for safety. I don't need your Komodo Fire cooking my flesh well done."

"Alright. Alright," he mumbled as he left the chamber with the container. I didn't like coming off as an asshole, especially with Yama. I mean, he was from *Ion*, therefore it was *Only a Matter of Time* before he perfected the turbo. I just wasn't going to be the one cooked for an entrée when he did.

"Hey, what's this I hear about Komodo Fire?" Trace inquired from the other chamber.

"Oh, well you see. It's a masterpiece in the..."

"I'm not having you cook Trace's tires either," I yelled, ending Yama's proposition. I slowly noticed Trace staring at me from the outside of the chamber with his arms up.

"Really? Afraid that I'll smoke you with that tank," he stated while dropping his arms. Trace clearly suffered from short-term memory loss because it was his tires Yama fried last time. Then again, Trace's luck might allow it to come through.

"You'll be signing your death certificate with that boost," I replied.

"Come on, how many times have we cheated death?"

"Too many, and I'm starting to think that we're running out of spare lives," I expressed, remembering more reasons on why he was so damn lucky. The remark also made him chuckle while skimming through some of the memories that him and I had had over the years. There was this one time when we were at this abandoned hospital called Waverly Hills, declared by the majority as the most haunted place in the country. A modest title of a building that caught us in a paranormal war with one specific ghost, or at least we thought she was a ghost. I mean, we saw a transparent little girl whip a chair at us because Trace decided to steal the pink soccer ball the community warned us not to touch. Only kick, but never grab, they said, and what did this dumbass do, he brought to life a horror movie, almost resulting in us joining the poor little ghost girl in the afterlife. Trace sure knew how to spice things up, but that was one less spare life we could enjoy. Once Trace was done enjoying memory lane, I guided us both out of the forge to commence the final touch. It was a fresh design I'd created last week prepared for embedment.

"What's the plan for us after this race?" I asked trading the past for the future. "Do we finally go professional?"

"Well, Galactica isn't an option at the moment with the lockdown. It's funny how morality returns after Skorge's record is broken. I've been meaning to tell you this, but I actually got qualified for the Pro League series on Earth, Four Seasons," Trace responded after I plugged in the design I'd made for the Atlas into the computer to commence the painting session.

"What's Four Seasons?" I asked, closing the door to my forge.

"Let me show you," he replied while pulling out an iCube to set down on a table, a cubed device with a small square grid for social media interactions, health maintenance, and miscellaneous activities or in this case, television. The device was small, but for television, it summoned a grid for a virtual 50x50 inch screen. After his appeared, Trace started swiping through the channels until he reached the Unican Network, a channel that talked about Versa 24/7 on Unica. Right away, the Unican Network showed an interview with a man who looked to be the same age as us. He wore a black corium suit with golden lightning strikes branching out of his large pectorals. His hair had been buzzed, exposing the broad ears and nose along with the creased forehead. He also had fair skin, a five o'clock shadow, and heterochromia iridum eyes. The left iris, pomegranate red, the right, sky blue. A memorable distinction of an iconic individual I couldn't seem to name, for now.

"That's Midas, he's won the past three Four Seasons," Trace explained before the interview on Midas could begin.

"You've been on fire for the past six years. What's your mindset going into the next Four Seasons?" an interviewer asked cracking a minor smile on Midas' face. He continued to close-mouth chew the piece of gum he had, filling out the protruding cheek bones beneath the lightly shaded beard.

"Well, I just have to forget that I'm the champion. I've gotta be aware of the target on my back. You never know who'll come out of the shadows for a shot," he replied, initiating a shitload of follow-up questions. Eating up the elusive attention, he winked at the cameras for the trillion-dollar thumbnail. The narcissistic gestures triggered several sighs from Trace before he chose to mute the television grid, pulling up the social media application Way/Point on a separate grid with Midas' profile on display. Way/Point was the most popular social platform in the world allowing anyone to edit an avatar and club for the attraction of others. Being socially active for non-business affairs had never been my strong suit, unlike Trace who usually filled in the void of trends in the world. The headline to Midas' profile was labeled as "The Golden Scion," with an avatar of Midas rising out of a pool of liquid gold. In his club around him, were the eleven hundred avatars linked to him categorized as friends with 7.2 million avatars set up outside of the club as the followers. In a VIP section, closer to the golden pool, were a hundred avatars labeled as "close" with Trace's avatar among them. Heh, leave it to Trace to befriend an attraction.

"Four Seasons is becoming the biggest Pro League series on the planet. It happens every two years and this dude has achieved the hat trick."

"So, he's been doing this since he was an adolescent?"

"Yeah, but it's the streak that me and several others around the world are trying to beat. There's also a small portion of certain racers that have an issue with him due to some controversial issues, but it's the streak, man. He hasn't lost a series yet," Trace exclaimed in excitement, shifting to the basement of Midas' club revealing a silver-eyed cowboy patiently sitting in the shadows as one of the profile's enemies.

"Is it similar to Galactica?" I questioned, noticing the pair of loaded revolvers on the silver-eyed cowboy.

"No… well kinda… but honestly no. Every death that has happened in this series was an accident. Nothing's intentional, mainly because you'll get disqualified and punished by Pandora," Trace explained to keep me interested. I didn't know that Pandora overlooked this series. She was the Shepherd of the United Countries of Earth, the leader who represented our planet. Every planet had their own Shepherd in charge of the planet's stability—physically, mentally, socially, economically, and so on. Some planets organized their Shepherd terms into a lifetime sentence. As for Earth, we'd manipulated it into a 20-year-term, a native move established by the Absolution Act unanimously voted by the global population in 2054 to avoid tyranny or any politician holding a corrupted background that would endanger Earth's stabilization within the Hendealliance. A healthy system, Pandora Winfrey entered with ease as a Shepherd with her humble beginnings, illustrious acting career, and universal philanthropy across multiple solar systems of Minoris planets. If Earth had allowed other Majoris planets to vote for our Shepherd, she still would've been flawlessly invoked into the dreamland of power—a term she'd maintained since I was 7 years old, and to me, a proper overseer to an important series.

"Nothing's intentional, eh?" I remarked, still eyeing the cowboy. "Tell that to him."

"Every icon has an enemy, that's why you place them in the basement," Trace replied as the grid of Midas' interview showed him leaving with a pretty blue-eyed girl who could hook an iris.

"What about her? Who's she?" I impulsively asked, regretting my decision almost instantly. A smile the size of Jupiter ran across Trace's face as he backtracked to Midas' VIP section on Way/Point. He then pinned a spotlight on one specific avatar with the same striking qualities as the female in the interview. The avatar was a fair-skinned, rosy cheek and lipped belle with long, wavy brown hair holding a subtle balayage scheme to it. Trace then transitioned into her profile, revealing more of her in a black bikini standing in a body of water coming up to her belly button and back down to her hips. More striking than her was the onyx necklace with a golden dreamcatcher as the emblem dripping down to her big heart.

"That's his sister, Gabriella, otherwise known as Miss Earth," Trace beamed, providing a few nudges for good measure. She was beautiful, but Trace was taking the moment way too seriously. Just because she was Miss Earth, didn't mean I would go head-over-heels. Miss Earth was a title given to the prettiest girl on Earth after a series of modeling competitions. It also decided who would represent Earth during the Miss Universe beauty pageant which I believed had been crowned to a Syames of Pasydanya recently. Said a lot about my pop-culture knowledge.

"Maybe if you go into Four Seasons, you'll catch her attention," Trace continued.

"I'm not going into that race for a girl. But I wouldn't mind ending that three-time win streak," I answered, generating a series of slaps across my shoulder by the anxious Trace.

"That's what I'm talking about Craven," he followed up with intensity. Trace was so pumped for no damn reason. I still had to qualify for the Pro League series, but that was tomorrow's problem. Tonight was all about Knightfall. I couldn't let my mind get stuck in the fictional future. An intrinsic goal that instantly disintegrated into ashes as the television grid of Trace's iCube displayed an alien with metal two-foot-long tentacles for hair. The Rokian didn't excrete xenon gases, signaling their native environment. They sat in front of the camera without a mask, displaying the light-blue circuit of veins running across their mandible for a beard over their ocean-blue skin. Their eyes, those light-blue eyes. There will never be a concussion strong enough to dislodge an image of those Rokian eyes. I could feel every blood vessel in my body constricting uncomfortably, mistaking my body temperature for a fever. As of that moment, I was eye to eye with my father's black-and-blue killer, Thorax.

"Unmute it," I steadily demanded.

"You sure?" he asked. I instinctively nodded.

"So, with Galactica XLIX under lockdown. Are you worried that you won't ever get a chance to defend your title as champion?" an interviewer asked, stimulating a chuckle from the Rokian.

"F'nux, if I'm not able to defix my titax, it's because the gulactrix is afraid of what I'm capable of, and if I have to retirix because of it, then so be it. That's just one less gallox of xenix blux on my palmix," he replied with several native terms while looking into the camera as if I were in the audience. The grid suddenly vanished at the hands of Yama, killing the unpleasant vibe between a son and his father's executioner.

"I think that's enough for the day," Yama insisted.

"Yeah, and I think your paint job is done too," Trace added in agreement. I could tell that they really wanted me to take my mind off Thorax, but Trace was right. My paint job should have been done. The assumption convinced me to walk over to the forge's door, open it, and reveal my suit's makeover, giving Gabriella a run for her beauty title. The Atlas now had a charcoal abdomen of crumbled rocks for Abdomineses and Stonehenge boulders for pectars. Cracking each rock was a band of neon-blue chains, unbroken around the torso, and broken into shards around the appendages. Adding on to the neon touch were the blue spina processes to the Atlas, the section responsible for the automatic signals transmitting through the suit. In most exosuits, they had the spina process at the thoracic region with the cylinder-shaped boost tank in the lumbar region; only aliens inverted the anatomic schematic. I spent

F'nux=Fuck No
Defix=Defend
Titax=Title
Gulactrix=Galaxy
Retirix=Retire
Gallox=Gallon
Xenix=Alien
Blux=Blood
Palmix=Han

several days contemplating a barrage of ideas giving a potent homage to the Greek Titan, Atlas and, like any artist, knew when the masterpiece had implanted itself into my head. The only thing this baby was missing was a wing from a blue jay. I didn't know how it would correlate with the presentation, but I was sure I'd find a way to make it work.

"Damn. You really went all out on this design," Trace unexpectedly muttered.

"You're not the only one who can give an ironic Greek touch to their suit," I asserted. The Hermes personified Trace as the guardian angel who carried speed, but I was the unbreakable one, holding the world on my shoulders as The Heart of Earth's kin. Since we were kids, he and I had been always trying to one-up the other. When he sketched the idea of a Cerberus as his Versa gimmick in elementary, I topped it with a Chimera. In middle school, I qualified for a course in the Pyscean culture, he surpassed the achievement by attaining a course in the much bigger Gigallian realms, and in high school he excelled in mixed martial arts. I, sword-fighting. Now, here we were as a pair of Semi League competitors, one victory away from a career-boosting championship and he took up the image of a God to my Titan. It seemed only fitting that he and I would end up, at this point, now pleased with the major products of the intermediate chapters to our careers.

"Too bad the Atlas is missing," Yama began to say but stopped once he noticed the annoyed look on my face.

"Crap, it's almost 9. We gotta go," Trace urgently stated before rushing to the chamber, acquiring his suit.

"Go on without me. I'll see you there!" I yelled at him while he was heading out.

"Remember, they want us there by 9:30 and the race starts at 10:15," Trace explained before leaving the garage with the Hermes. I started unplugging the Atlas from the battery, slowly pulling her out of the chamber for a travel-ready status.

"Yama, can you take this suit to the company truck?" I desperately asked for a confirmation. With the suit taken care of and my jacket over my shoulders, I hustled to my office at the back of the shop for a charm and ergogenic. Once I entered it, I could see the mess of papers and Versa parts scattered all over the floor, along with the half-empty glass of water left on the desk from yesterday morning. The junkyard reminded how awake my body really was. It hadn't slept in over a day. I guessed time flew by when you spent all of it at a race track experimenting on one of your suits. The half-glass-full outlook of it all was that my body was restless. As for the half-glass-empty view, I was a slob who needed an intervention and was now forced to tiptoe their way through the piles. Once I got to my desk, I saw and grabbed the backpack of goodies resting next to the chair. Inside it were caffeine pills, creatine, smelling salts and the painkillers I instantly ingested with the glass of water. I then placed the backpack on the desk while I accessed the safe behind everything so I could retrieve the good luck charm resting inside. It was one of the many championship rings my dad had. He always kept it in a safe place, claiming he'd lend me one of the rings on the day he felt his boy became a man. The special day could've been my 18th birthday, my debut race, or the day I finally grew a beard. I would never know when that day was, which was why I went on a scavenger hunt back at home for it. I was still a boy at heart who believed in the supernatural forces and believed that his father could only protect those who wore the ring. It may have been a stupid belief, but it was a belief that incorporated my father's spirit into my work. What more could a young and dumb boy ask for? The ring was on, and the goodies were packed. The painkillers were kicking in, and the positive mind was intact. I, unfortunately, couldn't say the same for Katia who was standing by my door with a worrisome face.

"Hey, I just wanted to tell you to be careful against Zane."

"I told you, I'll be ready for anything, and I'll keep him away from Trace," I reassured her.

"But can you keep Trace away from him?"

"Trace isn't going anywhere near Zane."

"But if you're in trouble, Trace will stop at nothing to protect you," she explained. I eventually went up to her to give a much-needed hug to calm any tension. I then gripped her shoulders, reminding her of what I'd already confirmed.

"I'll bring him back in one piece, I promise…"

ACT I
CHAPTER 5

RITUALS WITHIN THE KOLOSSEUM

THE NOCTURNAL TWIN OF THE WINDY CITY NOW ILLUMINATED THE SKYLINE. As rayless as the depths, the flyways kept an uncongested current, providing me a direct way to The Kodiak's Kolosseum, Knightfall's starting line. On the way there, sections of the reconstructed track could be seen gliding through the tight quarters of the floating skyscrapers like a snake slithering through air. A relatable sense, considering how my body felt like an extension of the hover truck, soaring its way through the Chicagolands. It was better that the painkillers kicked in now than later. I had races where the effects took their time sinking, giving me an intimate sensation of Zane abrading the side of my hip with his patented wire-brush rims. The surviving nerves typically burned whenever I thought about that altercation. The acetaminophens coursing through my bloodstream proved that the joke was on The Raven this time around… God help me.

Bear-clawed exit signs eventually appeared, cueing my departure from the primary flyways, instantly throwing me onto New Lake Shore Drive, the city's main street currently sponsored by *The Golden Evolution*, running along the great lake of Michinis and more importantly, straight to the Kolosseum. As much as I hated Luke's logo of a naked man growing wings of golden crystals, the group vandalizing the sponsor were worse. The Re-Versables, a faction of activists who stood against the sport due to the acre of casualties. It felt like humanity had backtracked, embracing the spilt pints of blood in the water. To them, every racer tainted the future of their kin, morphing into a more animalistic path, an insanely subjective perspective. I got that my opinion was no different, but at least it had honor behind it. I thought I could speak for a lot of racers when I stated that I'd chosen my path, not the other way around. I could've bathed in a pond of sorrowful tears after my father's death, which would've made me weak, isolated, and lost. Instead, I transformed those same tears into sweat and blood, now able to walk the path destined for me much stronger, more surrounded, and very well discovered.

The Kolosseum's height grew to the heavens the closer I got. Mirroring the original in Rome, with its limestone exterior of pillars and radial walls. The major difference between the two was that the Chicagoland's version restructured it into a tower-like behemoth with the use of hovering systems separating the poly-layered landmark. The Kolosseum, if I had remembered correctly, had five layers with the top marked as Alpha and the bottom as Epsilon. With the parking garages in the Epsilon level, the Kolosseum itself was designed as an ascension to heaven, an area where the best seats were on the Alpha-level looking down at the Beta-level where the main stage was set. Through the early fall and winter seasons, the stage was owned by The Windy City's ruthless football team, the Chicagoland's Kodiaks. Prior to the Evolutionary Era, that was all this place was ever used for. Back then, it didn't look like a Kolosseum. It was, instead, just a regular stadium. The crave for an architectural makeover didn't occur until the Terran race took a trip to the largest planet in the galaxy, Gigalus. Near the planet's capital was the Wrathican, a place the Hendecalliance referred to as "The Greatest Kolosseum in the Galaxy." The Terrans who witnessed the galactic landmark firsthand claimed that the remarks were understatements at best. They even went as far as saying that the Wrathican could fit the entire country of Iceland, a claim my father had supported since his first of many visits to the Gigallian structure for competition purposes. One day, I'd hoped to see the inconceivable attraction for myself. Until then, the next best thing was the one towering over my hover truck.

The entrance to The Kodiak's Kolosseum was guarded by a checkpoint sandwiched in between two bronze kodiak statues pointing out to the Great Lake of Michinis. At checkpoints, guards typically asked for tickets and then instructively guided a pathway towards a suitable parking garage. For my sake, the guidance should have been more direct and a lot less clogged. The racer's way of getting onto the track was always a fluent skip through a summer blooming meadow from every experience I'd had thus far.

"Where the fuck have you been McGuire," the headguard named Dick instantly greeted. The authoritative spirit instantly caught me off guard causing me to accidentally leave the car in drive, slowly strolling past the evil eyes of Dick before I could fully stop. A couple of stomps forward placed him right by the truck's window. "Do you know what time it is, son?"

"Yeah, it's…" I started to say, glancing at the truck's time reading 9:04. No, wait. There was something I was supposed to do to the company trucks that I never got to because of how busy I'd been. Shit, I was supposed to readjust every clock because of daylight savings the previous weekend. We'd lost an hour. "Trust me when I say that I can get to the track in ten minutes or less."

"For your sake and mine, you bettuh. I've got a hundred-thousand bones on your ass tonight," Dick revealed, escorting me down into a cleared-out parking garage with an elevator leading straight to the locker rooms and onto the red carpet each racer, apparently, would be showcasing their suits on. After labeling my tardiness as a minor inconvenience, things quickly turned around because the parking lot had been exclusively cleared. The only things here were the racer trailers of the competitors. The most notable one was The Raven's. It had the designs of a black raven soaring through purple-lit skies. A tease for an amazing presentation I was sure Zane currently showcased. I'd always enjoyed seeing the artist within him morph from a blue jay to a raven; it was a damn shame he was psychotic.

An elevator within the parking lot was in my sights by the time I parked the company truck, forcing me to commence my pre-race rituals. Instead of taking the time to put on the corium, I had to make do with my jacket and jeans for protection and insulation, gently sinking in back first into the Atlas' opening. The tight inner-layered cushion compressed my body before I was fully inside. It was too early to initiate MIKA and the suit, but with a helmetless head, it wasn't too early to intake a few creatine patches along with a whiff of smelling salts. The purpose of using these goodies was to stimulate all the adrenal glands in my body to help it move faster for the big race. It was the one unique thing Terrans had against the rest of the galaxy, so I would use it to my advantage like my fellow competitors. The smelling salts usually burned the nostrils after the big inhale, but the painkillers protected me from that too.

Even though the ritual was rushed, it was done. The only thing I had to do was grab the Atlas' helmet and head to the elevator. Almost aware of the situation, the elevator doors opened fairly quick, getting me directly to the lockers leading straight to the tunnel with a red carpet, six suited racers, and a shooting range of flashing lights from photographers on the perimeter. Like a re-enactment of Miss Earth at a bar of single men, the necks violently turned to me, the last racer attending the main event. As someone who already felt they were floating, being blinded by the flashes didn't help the situation. Somehow avoiding a mass collision with the photographers, my proprioception kept me on a straight line. By the time my vision returned, I saw a racer in front of me with his arms laterally raised in the Hermes.

"This is crazy, eh!" Trace exclaimed, attracting more flashes by standing close to aid me through the tunnel of lights. I followed him up a ramp into the fray of the Kolosseum where the skyline of skyscrapers could be seen lacerating the fleet of stars above the tens of thousands in the Alpha-leveled stands roaring our names. As tempting as it was to absorb the Kolosseum's energy, observing the other racers became the priority. My father once said, *you base your suit and strategy only off of your opponents, never yourself.* I could tattoo those words onto my bones because if one based their strengths off of everyone else's weaknesses… checkmate.

Like the trailer in the parking lot, the first racer I noticed was Zane Maddox, the sadistic Welsh capable of quelling his cold-hearted nature. Always holding onto a sunbathed vacation tan to enhance the dark, orbital lair of purple irises. To add more cynicism, he concealed the small layer of baby fat with a short black, thick scruffy beard. One could argue that his curly purple-and-black mohawk daunted the track. I'd argue it was his black-painted teeth. Katia even made a claim to Zane's black plague doctor mask of a helmet with a raven's beak as an addition to his profusive presentation. Another reason why he'd been nicknamed The Raven. A nickname enforced notoriety in the sport. Whether it would be good or bad, a racer must live up to theirs, and Zane was no exception. It was one of his redeeming qualities—another is his intellect, especially when it came to crafting an original suit. The 2245 Nevermore handmade by The Raven himself for others to envy. Whenever a racer had a creator's mindset, they pursued it because it enabled them to provide exclusive qualities that couldn't be found on any other exosuit in the market. The quirk Zane dispensed onto the torque-heavy Nevermore was the six adrenia-injecting pistons upon the latis to supplement the holsters he clearly didn't need if the wheels had black wire-brush rims that could make a gentle heart gulp. It was very rare to have pistons, let alone adrenia injectors, and yet this madman fused them together. Adrenia was a man-made element mixed with Ghastallion drugs and epinephrine. Like an epipen, adrenia stimulated the adrenal glands, but it never exceeded a threshold unsafe for the heart. The fairly young adrenia officially titled Zane Maddox as the pioneer of the unlikely combination. Again, this guy was a genius! How could a racer not admire the Nevermore? From the purple scissor cuts around the black skin to the black robotic raven connected to his tree branch of a right arm, the exosuit shed an unholy amount of envy. I just wished that the Welsh boy from Tregaron had invested in some sanity because he hadn't taken his eyes off of Trace since we had stepped onto the track.

"Do you ever have that feeling like someone's watching you?" I asked Trace.

"Yeah, it's not my fault I'm too damn gorgeous."

"And we wonder why he hates you," I stated, causing Trace to chuckle into his lane. Walking towards us, in another lane, was a racer wearing an opal-white 2195 Icarus. If the Hermes was regarded by most as the best exosuit on the market, then silver undoubtedly went to the Icarus. The classic was an angelic sight for sore eyes with its most notorious feature being the white three-dimensional wings fluttering out of the holsters. Unlike the Hermes, the manufacturer came from *Tsarina* as their logo of a fringe tiara was embedded on the helmet's crown. The Eastern Europe dealership was not a bad one by any means, they were just a hit or miss, and the Icarus clearly hit the bullseye. The exosuit may have been a beauty, but she was a rare breed. There was only one person in the United Countries of Earth who raced in an Icarus at the moment, and his name is Roy Fathom, The Prestige Angel.

"Craven, it's about time you showed up," Roy stated, staring at a make-believe watch around his wrist. He had super short black hair that seemed to gray on the edges. His appearance showcased experience, but it also expresses his eldered age. His gray eyes matched the opal pearls of the pectar, but contrasted the bright spectrum of tan skin not nearly as modest as Zane's, considering that Roy couldn't tan. He can only become apple red. Regarding his notable background, he was one of "the surviving seven" in my father's story about *The Golden Evolution*. Like Trace and I, the two legends shared a brotherly bond blood couldn't match. I was surprised to see him in the Semi Leagues when I began my career. He claimed he'd gotten too old for the Pro and Galactic Leagues, and yet could still kick my ass in a race from time to time.

"I got held up," I finally responded.

"The important thing is that you're here now. I haven't announced it to the public, but this race is my eudaimonia. After Knightfall, I'm retiring."

"Why?"

"Aye, I might not look 52, but my body, on the other hand, does and can't handle the races like it used to. Plus, my first race took place within this Kolosseum, so it only feels right for it to end here too."

"No matter what happens tonight, it was an honor."

"Likewise, and may the better racer win," Roy stated while we shook each other's hand as a sign of respect and sportsmanship. Roy had really filled the void of not having a father figure over the years and had helped me grasp the tricks to Versa that I'd been relaying to Zero. He was someone who felt responsible, especially because he competed in the same race my father died in. I didn't blame him for my father's tragic end. I blamed him for claiming, without warning, that this was his final race. I was sure that he had a few more great years left, but when a racer made the eudaimonia statement, it was damn-near impossible to convince them otherwise. Eudaimonia was the finish line every racer wished to cross. The pinnacle achievement of serenity; the, so to speak, *last ride* into the sunset, or in this case, moonrise.

After ending the brief discussion with Roy, I glanced over at the hounds, Meta and Beta Breckenridge who were trying to flirt with Kira Brink, the only female racer to qualify for Knightfall. She had short and wavy, dark-pink hair with a fluffy bang to soften the bare forehead and crisply blue eyes. Her skin was pale, so it made her pink hair glow all the more. She might have been pretty, but I never let it fool me. Out of all the racers I'd competed against, she had to be the most strategic—someone who didn't like resorting to offense right away. She tended to keep her pair of aces hidden unless she absolutely needed to reveal their presence. Nicknamed The Cerebral Assassin because of how she outsmarted every competitor that stood in her way. She competed in a dark-pink 2240 Venus with a barbed wire heart in between her pectars. Like Zane, her suit was homemade, but contrasting Zane's unbranded label was her family's company, *Brink Industries*, engraved as a handwritten signature across the platys-plates. The Indie-Swiss company owned by her parents, Levin and Mila Brink, didn't capture the same notoriety as many other workshops across the globe, but their statement of a Venus was turning a lot of heads. Kira's success couldn't have been obtained without her exosuit's determining speed. Too bad the speed hadn't helped her escape the hounds just yet.

Meta and Beta were the annoyingly charismatic identical twin brothers who had been nicknamed The Yin and Yang Hounds, a nickname originating from their appearance. Meta was the six-foot-tall hound with white medium-length hair and black eyes. He always competed in the anteriorly convex 2250 Yang, a suit that had been redesigned into a white hound with black wheels on the palms of the suit and black teeth and eyes on the helmet. Beta was the antithesis of Meta with black hair and white eyes, and his suit the posteriorly concave 2250 Yin—all-black with white wheels, teeth, and eyes. Their designs were unique, especially with the dog fur running along the spina of their suits. The presentation captured their Norse-influenced logo of a Yin and Yang symbol represented by two hound heads. One black head with a white eye and one white head with a black eye, both sticking their tongues out. The 2250 Yin and Yang was one of *Ion's* critically acclaimed suits because as standalone suits, they were mediocre, but when combined, they become faster and stronger. It was possible to finish a race in a tie and the hounds had done it numerous times. They were a deadly duo when racing together. Competing in compatible suits was very tough and only worked with a strong chemistry. Something that Meta and Beta easily possessed. A strong bond was needed for a pair of suits manually operated without a chip. Once combined, both twins were basically synced together on the controls. This process was rarely pulled off successfully. I guessed one would need a twin for it to work.

The theatrics and modification of my competitor's exosuits were as expected. Heading towards my lane, I had a sensation of confidence, now glancing at the ticking countdown on the hovertron above the Alpha-level.

100 seconds

"Craven!" Trace randomly shouted while pointing at me, slowly guiding the finger to his derrière. "I hope my ass looks good because that's all you're gonna be seeing till the finish line."

I could only shake my head to the comments, contemplating whether or not I should hand Zane a seam route straight to Burretta. He continued to relay kind words to others as I entered the third lane, a lane reserved for me due to the standings. I'd scored the third highest amount of points throughout this series, and at the starting line, the lanes were lined up diagonally from left to right based on the standings. If a competitor had accumulated the most points, then they started in the first lane. If a competitor had scored the least, then they started in the last lane. All racers wanted to be in the first lane for the 10-meter head start from the second lane. The second lane had a 10-meter head start from the third lane and so on. Trace had acquired the first lane by luck and was only augmenting the target on his back with his words. He was calling Kira, a knock-off barbie brat, Meta and Beta, horny mutts, Roy, an arthritic who didn't make the cut for Luke Gold's logo, and Zane an autistic peep. In all honesty, Trace had had better days for insults.

75 seconds

"I want all racers standing up!" the Initiator in the black-and-white striped top shouted, causing all of us to stand up in our lanes. "If you haven't already, place on your helmet and turn on your suits." Not wasting any time, I swiftly placed on the Atlas' helmet with ease so that it could connect itself with the collar bone section of the suit. I had to commence the activation protocol.

"Turn on, MIKA," I commanded after the helmet was fully attached to the platysplate. This command woke MIKA from her comatose state so that she could take full control of the suit. The wheels attached to the sacrum and scapula sections of the suit began to inflate while magnetically moving to my elbow and knees.

"Hello Craven, I see that you've made a few changes to the suit," MIKA affirmed during the protocol.

"Yeah, let's pray that they were good ones."

"A BrachiShield? Hmm, this should be an interesting race."

"What, don't you like it?"

"It's an odd call, but I can respect it. Gear on arms are typically used for weapons, you know."

"Everyone's a critic," I finished before the Initiator could go over the rules. It was always fun having these pre-race conversations with MIKA. She might have been an Artificial Intelligence system, but she spoke like an actual person. We had conversations about anything and everything. The relationship between us started off tenuous because of the strong bond she originally had with my father. It could be a challenge for an A.I. when it came to changing racers, especially if the previous had been killed. A scenario like that actually generated guilt within them. They had feelings and emotions like any other living organism. That was a misconception the ignorant didn't realize about A.I chips. They were more than a chip, they were an actual soul.

50 seconds

"Now let's go over the rules one last time. Amputations are legal. Decapitations are illegal. Low blows are legal. Heart attacks are illegal. Is that clear?" the Initiator announced, asking for confirmation on our knowledge of the rules as the overseer of stipulations to a racer. Quality assurance to avoid controversy. In a Merce-based series like this one, they reminded us not to kill. The title was named after Logan Merce, the first Terran to win a race without killing. People like the Re-Versables always said morality was non-existent in Versa racing, but they couldn't overlook the Initiator's purpose, even in a Wreath-based series where killing was legal. In those series, the Initiator was more of a death row pastor than a rules expert.

"Remember this is just the starting line. The finish line is all the way at the top of the Sirius Tower. The track will lead you there and we will not allow any improvised short cuts that take you off of the track, are we clear?" he continued with more expected confirmations.

25 seconds

"Good, now if you would kindly get down on all four and await the siren," he concluded while making his way off to the side of the track. The crowd went silent as each of us went down on all fours to wait for the explosive tune. The starting position had the wheels already arranged on the extremities of the body. Every racer had to hold a mountain-climbing plank position where the stronger leg was flexed up to the stomach with the other extended back. The position helped us get a boost from pushing off the strong foot, a technique inspired by Track & Field's block starts.

We had to stay on the track the whole time, and the finish line was all the way at the top of the tallest building in the city. The analysis of the entire track caused everything around me to slow down, even with the heavy amount of ergogenics in my body. The only thing I could hear were the pounding battle cries of my heart getting stronger and louder by the pound.

"50… 400… 1,000,000… 7.34…" I could finally hear Tokyn and Gradite talking in my head, the darkest hour of my life, the first four numbers they consistently preached at the start of every race like a blessing at a feast. "Fifth… Fourth… Third… Second… First… 100-meter… 200-meter… 400-meter…"

My father suddenly appeared in front of me, standing tall on the rear-wheels of his damaged 2200 Hermes. He always appeared in this portion of the monologue with Tokyn simultaneously restating his words side by side with "one" in my head Followed by the "Seven Nation" chants.

"One… One more jump… Final straightaway… Only one winner…" I stated to myself once the monologue was over.

"No more mistakes," MIKA softly added like always, convincing my father's ghost to fade away.

"And no more tragedies," I concluded before the siren could officially scream its melody.

DARK KNIGHTS

AS SOON AS WE HEARD THE SIREN, WE ALL BURST INTO A STATE OF ACCELERATION. The low dubstep-based siren momentarily shook the entire stadium from its shockwave. Couldn't speak for the other racers, but the siren's quake threw me into a calm state coming off of the starting position. I usually had a poor reaction time, but this one felt perfect. It kept me in front of the fourth-place racer, Kira. The first-place racer, Trace was able to maintain his position in front of the second-place racer, Roy throughout this 10-second process. While holding third. I kept my eyes on the nearest racer, Roy. In the past, my best performances had come while I was the chaser instead of the chased. I think it had something to do with my ego. Whenever I was comfortable in first, my head tended to inflate with an arrogant persona, typically resulting in my downfall. That was why Roy was my target as a chaser. This was my strategy for success, each racer had got one, the trillion-dollar question was who could execute it in Versa's version of chess.

The track quickly led us out of The Kodiak's Kolosseum through the radial walls and had us loop around the perimeter a few times. The curves were pretty bumpy and purposefully had cracks planted all around. I was thankful to have GripShift tires equipped, but a tire could only take so many sharp cracks before deflating. For the first time, it felt rough within the suit's inner cushion, I was actually developing a headache from all the bumps. It also affected my plank position. Maintaining it through all of the cracks while lapping around the stadium like an ancient NASCAR racer was tough as hell.

"How much longer is the lapping?" I quickly asked MIKA as each lap around the stadium hovered us higher and higher above ground level.

"We're approaching the last pair of turns. I've also detected a ramp that'll shoot us over the lake," MIKA replied before I could complete the last turn. Each of us held our starting placed position as we approached the 300-meter ramp, but I could feel

Kira drafting behind me, an aerodynamic technique used to conserve energy within higher speed levels. She was using me for now. On the protracted ramp, Roy began to make a move against the leading Trace by slowly passing him to claim first.

"MIKA, should I use the boost for this ramp?"

She didn't respond right away like I wanted her to, so I triggered a little bit of the boost myself to slowly pass Trace. The boost also took Kira off my ass from the reddish-orange flames gusting out of the Atlas' exhaust tubes like a Satanian's pyromantic breath. If Kira was a clumsy racer, she'd be roasted on an open fire.

"Kill the boost! I can't see anything past the ramp, there's nothing but water!" MIKA roared, shutting off the boost herself.

"What do you mean?" I instantly asked while slowing down. My change of speed allowed Trace to pass me, along with his beaked-rival, Zane, who was using his boost early to get on Trace's tail. Roy was now at the peak of the ramp, taking the leap of faith, followed by Trace and Zane. I finally took the leap to suddenly see the swarm of drones circled above the lake, flashing bright-white colors. The drones were cameras for exclusive fans so that they could have an up-close point of view of the race. The combination of colors they flashed always represented the colors of the leading racer which was Roy at this point. After noticing the swarm of drones while I was in the air, I tried to search for a part of the track to land on, but there was nothing but water from the lake. What type of fucked up reconstruction was this? How the hell were we supposed to continue this race?

After questioning the layout of this track, a sinkhole suddenly began to appear in the lake. We all had no choice but to fall through it. When we got inside of the pitch-black sinkhole, lights started to appear all around the hole along with a few white flashes from the drones that decided to follow us inside. Holy shit! This was a vertical tunnel. The realization made me shift the momentum of my body toward the nearest concrete wall of the tunnel in order to stick my wheels onto it.

"The wheels officially have a grip. Your boost is ready whenever you are," MIKA informed.

All of the other racers were still free falling along the walls of the tunnel. They were trying to develop some type of traction on the walls. Each of them were failing and actually destroying parts of their suits due to the lack of traction. The leading racer, Roy made attempts at connecting his right-front wheel, but instead lost chunks of rubber, causing the tire's remnants to fly off, cracking Trace's visor during impact, and stripping the control of momentum Trace had on his free fall. Now diagonally cartwheeling down this tunnel, Trace collided shoulder first into the wall multiple times on multiple occasions, losing parts of his thin dell armor around his right shoulder. That was what his opportunistic ass got for using Hyper Velocitative Armour, maybe he'd learn his goddamn lesson this time. His beaked-rival, Zane was surprisingly in a better position, carrying out a better plan. The purple-and-black racer had his wheels shift to his injecting pistons, so that he could hold a falling torpedo pose, a position where the racers fell downward head first with their arms tucked into their sides. Zane gradually gained speed the longer he held the pose. Once an appropriate speed was obtained, he slowly reached out his right arm while a wheel shifted to his palmix in a twirling motion, easily creating traction on the wall. He was in a perfect position for first, but there was no way in hell I was going to let that happen.

"How about we take first early," I proposed to MIKA, triggering the boost to snatch the lead away from the adaptable raven. Lights from the drones and tunnels began to express neon-blue and gray. *Thank you Thardus, can't believe that I ever questioned your ways.*

After expanding on the insurable lead from the others, I decided to turn the boost off for conservation, I might need it later. I was enjoying the lead as an offender, but quickly had to transition into a defender because the tunnel was starting to curve upward into a 180° straightaway. The walls of the tunnel were now transparent, showing the abyss of Lake Michinis. It's a good thing I used neon-blue and gray to represent myself because it matched so well with the environment of the race thus far. What was I saying, of course it matched with me. I was the best goddamn racer in this series.

"How are you liking first place, MIKA?"

"Definitely familiar territory, but let's not get too cocky, Craven."

"Oh, come on, we've got a good lea..." I began to say before a Hermes zoomed right by to reclaim first place. The swifty action changed the lights to white and gold.

"And that's why you don't get cocky," MIKA pitched once more, deflating my head. A robotic raven then flew over my right dell, landing on Trace's right-rear wheel. The bird stuck its sharp beak into Trace's now smoky wheel. Oblivious to attack, Trace kept racing with false control over first.

"How much boost do we have? I've gotta help him out."

"I don't think this is the best time, look at the glass walls," MIKA instructed, pushing my eyes to the expanding cracks all around the underwater tunnel. *More ratings and injuries*; I should've known the tunnel was too good to be true. Water was now starting to squirt from each crack above and beside us.

Before I could trigger my boost, I felt a racer's presence eerily growing on my right side. Instinctively, I transformed my outer bicep into the BrachiShield, simultaneously beating a blade's drive into my bone marrow during the transformation. The shield may have originated from my bicep, but it completely covered the anterior side of my arm, successfully defending me from the impaling attack. The black and purple from the attacker's helmet revealed their identity, The Raven himself was attempting to make a crucial move against me in this finale. Once the blade was pulled out of my shield, I immediately slowed down, sweeping his pair of rear wire-brush wheels from underneath with my shield. The action caused Zane's legs to dangle along the track, creating a lot of sparks with the screeching screams of metal. Zane was now trying to adapt by transitioning one of his front-wheels to his scraping legs in order to hold the motorcycle position. The axle adaptation eventually forced him to fall behind. This inconvenience then signaled the robotic raven on Trace's wheel to retreat back to its master, but before it could, I used the sharp edges of my BrachiShield to slice off one of its wings, causing it to crash-land into the glass walls of the tunnel. The collision shattered the tunnel's glass, welcoming in Lake Michinis.

"Still criticizing my shield?" I shot at MIKA who was actually speechless. "Yeah, that's what I thought."

"It was a good move," MIKA finally replied after clearing her throat. "Who says that a shield can't be used as a weapon?"

As the tunnel slowly crumbled apart, Roy quickly passed Trace and I to take the lead once more in this race. Trace retaliated by triggering his boost to fight for first-place contention. The two were consistently shoving each other for the undisputed lead, but neither racer ever gained a concrete upper hand. The dogfight between the two racers kept changing the lights back and forth, flashing the trifecta of opal, white, and gold. It honestly felt like I was back in the photographer-filled tunnel. It was getting harder to race in this tunnel because of the escalating water levels, but before the levels could get any higher, the tunnel shifted upward. It felt like another ramp, no, it was another ramp.

"This ramp is leading to a straightaway hovering on the outside. Boost is ready when you are," MIKA informed, convincing me to activate the boost, snatching first from the hands of Roy and Trace. Once I took a huge leap from the peak of the ramp, I instantly saw the swarm of neon-blue-and-gray flashing drones waiting for us along with the skyline of bright lights coming from each skyscraper; they were neon-blue and gray too. The acknowledgement of my colors sent chills down my spine while bringing my heartrate to a lifetime high. I really wished that this moment in the air could last a bit longer, but in the words of Isaac Newton, *what goes up must come down.*

During the descent, I noticed the hovering straightaway that MIKA pointed out prior to the leap. I successfully landed on the strip that was about 30m wide, so it didn't take long for Trace and Roy to pass me once again. The lights to the city's skyline now shone white and gold, glimmering their colors off each window. The track then started to make several turns in between all of the buildings, turning this race into a close-quartered one. We could see all of the people cheering for us behind the windows and balconies to each building. After slowing down for a sharp right turn, the dark-pink Kira passed by to claim third, challenging Roy for second with a few shoves of her own. She actually had him at the edge of the track but wasn't quite strong enough to push him off.

The infused black-and-white fur-shedding twins briskly passed by to capitalize on a developing opportunity. They saw the exact same thing as me on this modest straightaway, a pair of top-tier racers stuck on the edge of our world. The double-stacked twins instinctively emptied the last of their boost to try and ram both racers off of the track, but before they could, Kira intuitively activated her emergency brakes while the 52-year-old vet somehow leapfrogged himself over her longest hair strand. The counters from the two defending racers caused the twins to soar off the track and into one of the buildings. Hope they didn't land on any spectators.

At the moment, I had second place and was directly behind Trace who was leading us into a pair of vertical loops. I couldn't catch him on the first loop but got close enough to draft with him on the second. The track transitioned the vertical loops into corkscrews. Maintaining a constant speed through each loop made my stomach feel a little nauseous due to how never-ending they felt. The spinning white-and-gold lights from the buildings weren't helping the cause, either. The brainwaves within my head were intersecting at 100km/h, briefly damaging my motor functions. The effect relaxed my abs onto the track, scraping off parts of the abdominis.

"Focus Craven!" MIKA shouted to wake me up in this race. "Your right-front wheel is losing traction, so focus!"

It must've been damaged when I used my shield to destroy the robotic raven back in the tunnel. I guess I didn't think my actions through clearly. A poor mistake from someone who likes to stay three moves ahead of everyone's gameplan.

"Then I'll have to go easy..." I tried to say now noticing the sparks sprinkling over my dell. I glanced back to see that it was The Raven himself trying to get even with me. He maintained stability by having the lone front-wheel planted onto the track with his left arm while the other arm freed itself to form a brachial blade.

"If only you had a FemoriShield," my snarky MIKA implied.

"Oh, shut it!" I responded stressfully, trying to avoid the swings from Zane's blade. He was trying to amputate my legs, but Trace suddenly appeared out of nowhere, ramming his rear-wheels into Zane's cranium, rupturing both the beak and glass to Zane's black visor. As collateral damage, Trace's hit unintentionally rattled my head within the helmet, briefly altering my sense of sound. The only thing I could hear was a steady high-pitched noise echoing off of my eardrum. Trace's collision into Zane gave me the lead, turning the city neon-blue and gray while the track shifted into a sideways straightaway, positioning the neon-blue-and-gray lights above and below us.

Trace started to rub one of his rear tires into Zane's beak, severing the helmet in half, but Trace didn't stop there. No, he kept his rear-wheel in Zane's face, shredding through the thick beard until the blood gushed out. The cheek then began to rip open horizontally, showing the broken shards of black teeth inside Zane's mouth. Abrasions masked the left side of The Raven's face with blood leaking out like oil. Zane eventually retaliated with his blade by cutting off the rear-wheel that Trace was offensively using. The wheel fell off of the track and onto the street. I instantly triggered my brakes to help Trace in his dogfight with Zane. Swinging my shield into the injured side of Zane's face was my first move. The strong hit didn't even phase Zane as he quickly retaliated by shoving his only front-wheel into my visor, producing a crack that diagonally ran across the entire visor, affecting parts of my vision. The only things I could see were the black-and-purple shines from above and below this sideways track.

"I can't see much of anything MIKA. Detach the visor."

"Are you sure Craven? Your eyes will be vulnerable."

"I don't give a shit, detach the visor!" I aggressively roared, forcing the visor to fly off of my helmet. The bursting rhythm of winds now impacted the vulnerable parts of my face. The sharp winds naturally forced me to squint and tear up. It was something that I would have to adapt to, at least my vision was kind of normal, right? Damn, detaching the visor sounded better in my head.

The sideways track was now entering another series of corkscrewed loops with The Raven somehow maintaining a questionable lead over Trace, who was now beginning to give a few good swings with his right-front wheel. The fury of swings unfortunately came to an end once Zane sliced off Trace's right-front wheel, but that didn't stop Trace from jabbing Zane's injured cheek with the free right hand. Zane eventually impaled his blade into Trace's right bicep, amputating the arm. Blood geysered out of the open wound while the loops of the track came to an end.

We were back on a normal straightaway, but the bad news was that Trace was still losing a lot of blood. He looked fatigued with his abdomen rubbing itself on the track. Trace was super vulnerable, and Zane knew it. He instantly rammed himself into Trace's suit, forcing Trace's lethargic body to fall off the track and onto one of the streets below us.

With all of the aggression I still had left in my veins, I gave a thunderous roar. The outcry made Zane glance over his left dell. I briskly caught up to him, ramming my shield into the injured side of his face, disorienting his cognition. I then stood up on my rear-wheels, vertically hammering my front-wheels into Zane's occipital lobe, which caused his forehead to ricochet off of the track. In an unconscious state, Zane's Nevermore began to free ride off of the track to join Trace, who I hoped was still alive.

"Trace will be alright, Craven. We just have to finish the race." The statement from MIKA helped me notice the Atlas-colored spirit of the city. I was currently leading the race with Roy on my tail. I had a good lead on his Icarus as the track began to transition upward. We were now driving up the side of the Sirius Tower with the finish line in our sights about 200m away.

"You still have 25% boost in the tank," MIKA prompted as 25% slowly dwindled to 0% to maintain the lead I had on The Prestige Angel. I glanced over my dell to see that his Icarus had supplemented a last-minute miracle with a highly raised middle finger. Roy's final act of defiance for his defeat and my first championship as I crossed the finish line to see the stacked-up bleachers of fans waiting for us on the roof of the tallest tower in the Chicagolands. They all were chanting my name through the showers of confetti. This win should have brought a huge smile to my face, but it didn't. I just couldn't enjoy the moment. I had made a promise to Katia, and I couldn't keep it. If it wasn't for Trace, I wouldn't even have been in this position. So many negative things were racing through my head as the fireworks and chants got louder and louder. It might not have been the prettiest of victories, but I had to accept the fact that I was the Champion of Knightfall.

A KING WITH NO THRONE

STUCK BETWEEN THE PAST AND PRESENT, I STOOD IN FRONT OF THE GIANT DARK-OAKED DESK STATIONED IN MY FATHER'S OFFICE. Behind the desk was The Heart of Earth himself wearing a minty-white long-sleeved collar shirt. The lumberjack beard hid most of the wrinkles on his cheek, except for the giant ones that stretched across the maxilla to the hawk nose. The scrunched lines between the brows indicated how focused he was roaming through the highlights of his competitor. As usual, I'd watch the footage with him, sometimes attempting to mimic the hand brush he occasionally did through his short, wavy thick hair as a stress reliever. Each racer he focused on usually had a championship on their resumes, displayed for both of us to see. In his head, he was thinking about their weaknesses. As for mine, I was wondering how the hell these racers handled success. It seemed like something a racer could lose themselves in. Aware of how focused my father was towards his work, I asked him how he did it. How did he handle the success? At first, he smiled, then he took a long look at me with his light brown eyes and decided to shut down all of his homework.

"From what I've seen, there are two different ways of handling success," he told me. As a child, I remember getting into a cross-legged position on the floor, ready for another chapter of my father's wise storytelling. "One way is to let the success settle in your head, the other is to have it sink into your soul. The big problem is that both ways lead to heartache. If you let the success settle in your head, you become aware of what you've done. You've ended the stories of one or possibly many competitors. That's the thing they don't teach you in Versa. To obtain success, there's a great chance you have to end another's, and the price is heavy. It's never easy, ending another's story, and once a racer realizes that, it takes a toll on the head and can eventually destroy it.

"After hearing that outcome, you'd think the answer would then be to have the success sink into your soul, right? But that's the thing, even the soul has a catch when it's engaged to success. If you let it sink into your soul, you're going to feel immortal and question whether or not you're actually a god. Imagine that, being one of the best racers in the world. Imagine it for too long, and it'll corrupt you. It'll make you condone the very characteristics you've often condemned. Whether or not your body has survived the day, week, year, you won't realize that your new soul is rotten to its core."

"Which way have you practiced?" I hesitantly asked.

"Neither," he quickly responded, throwing the image of himself onto the screen surrounded by those he loved on a finish line. "I've pioneered a new way, which is placing success outside of you. Never letting it touch your head or soul. You instead keep it far away, living each moment, day by day, hour by hour, second by second. Every racer has to realize that there will always be a moment that tops the previous, which is why you have to live in it, never letting it corrupt who you are on the inside… you never know when it could be your last…"

Those final words tossed me back into the present where the confettis were blowing and the cheers were growing. The rooftop to the Sirius Tower quaked the tectonic plates of an entire city. Atlas-colored fireworks filled the sky, echoed in the drone-swarm of lights and in the glimmering eyes of each fan. This was it, the success my father taught and warned me about. The choice was simple, and yet I couldn't make it. The success almost felt non-existent at the moment with my focus on my fallen brother, Trace. He was the reason why I won this race. In my scrambled train of thought, I eventually took my helmet off, now eyeing the helmetless Roy walking up to me.

"Really? You had to flip the bird?" I asked him. He just shrugged with a modest smile on his face.

"What can I say, it's my last race. I can do whatever the hell I want now," he finally replied. We both noticed Kira crossing the finish line to claim third place.

"You think he's watching?" I asked.

"Of course, he is, and he's prouder than ever," Roy stated while patting my back. Heh, Roy never lied, and it was obvious how joyful my father was, wherever he might be. It was the reason why I shared his memories, wore his rings, and honored his blue tints. The healthy thought altered my mindset in a more positive manner as Kira came over to share the moment.

"Oh my god Craven, congratulations!" she shouted in her teenage boy tone of a voice while hugging me. She was someone who had supported me along with a few tough love lessons since my debut race a couple years ago. She was the smartest girl I knew, and being friends with her and *Brink Industries* has only made me smarter. "You've been working your ass off since day one, and now look at where you are."

"I know, but I owe it all to Trace," I responded. He'd helped me throughout all of my childhood, and yet I couldn't do the same in this race. The thought made my head slowly tilt downward toward the floor. The action forced Kira to pull my head back up with her hand on my chin.

"Craven, he landed softly, I saw it all. It's Zane who took the hard fall. He crash-landed into a car below and rightfully so," she explained, cheering me up. It was a good thing too, because we could now see all of the reporters rushing from the stands. They were all shoving each other out of the way like it was some type of mosh pit.

"Well, here comes the media. Take it all in Craven. Better you than me," Roy concluded with a smirk. He then began to steadily make his way off of the rooftop.

"We'll be in the skydeck one floor down. The post-race party is being held there," Kira informed me prior to joining Roy. They immediately left the roof to avoid all of the reporters. It really made me feel like an amateur, but then again, I was the champion. I had to accept the spotlight sooner or later. The reporters were confronting me, each of them shouting my name as they pointed their microphones at my face. I couldn't hear myself think with the unsettling amount of questions shooting my way like bullets. Seeing them continue to forcefully shove each other out the way made me feel even more uncomfortable.

"Jesus Christ! One question at a time!" I blasted out loud.

"How does it feel to carry on your father's legacy?" The female reporter asked with a video camera suddenly masking my face. I really should've followed Roy and Kira downstairs because the reporters didn't care about personal space. Arms-length away was the standard, right?

"I don't know; but I know he's always watching," I replied to the first question.

"What's next Craven McGuire? Are you hoping that Galactica XLIX comes out of lockdown so that you can avenge him?" a different female reporter asked.

"No comment."

"Are you afraid of Thorax?" the male reporter in front of me quickly followed up.

"Next question."

"Craven, you came into this race wearing blue and gray. These are colors similar to Ragnios' black and blue. Is there any relation or hidden messages within these tones?" the same reporter asked with a puzzled look on his face. The other reporters repeated the question for a much-needed response. I was trying my hardest to keep the success on the outside, never letting it touch my head or soul which only damaged my head some more.

"50...400...1,000,000," I could hear Thorax' deep voice echo in my head through all of the pressure and the thousands of words whipped at me like dodgeballs.

"Listen up everybody!!!" I exploded, silencing them all. "I don't care about Galactica... and I sure as hell don't care about Thorax! The only damn thing I care about is going downstairs to celebrate a night that you all are beginning to ruin, thank you."

I pulled myself from the horde of reporters after the mic-dropping outburst. Guards rapidly came to my aid, restraining the reporters from prying more answers. I made my way down a set of stairs to enter the skydeck of the Sirius Tower. The post-race party instantly gave a sense of relief. It was filled with a hundred fans who paid for VIP Passes to the party that were more expensive than Zero and Dick's winnings combined. All of them went silent once I appeared so that they could begin the series of applause, starting off with one brave soul followed by a few others, then the entire crowd. It was something that sent chills down my spine for the second time tonight; a major upgrade from the reporters.

There were tables all around the whole floor filled with expensive extraterrestrial entrées and desserts like salar, raptr, lachli, and a Grace of Gluttony. Salars were

Pyscean's version of the salmon fish. Unanimously declared by every chef as the toughest fish to cook because of the salar's thin layer of adipose which provided a saccharine taste. Raptr, on the other hand, was more of a steaky meal from Gigalus. Similar to the velociraptor that roamed Earth in the Jurassic Age, this creature had an easy-to-pull-apart muscle structure with special enzymes great for a Terran heart. There was a limit to how much a Terran should eat in a single month as it could damage the cardiac muscles from the collective pack of enzymes strong enough to survive our digestive system. It was still worth dying for, though.

Held in the center of the dessert table was the mountain-shaped Grace of Gluttony—a gateau that was arguably the greatest dessert in the galaxy due to its seraphic flour from Arythro. Its sweet taste upon the first bite was great but nothing compared to the angelic after taste triggering every nerve within the body. It was typically used as a lustful method into a woman's heart or their... it didn't matter. It was an amazing gift from the Ryths for their claims to both poles on the planet. Next to the dessert table sat the food I was searching for, lachli, a cherishable herb from Ghast that had been crafted into a Terran's favorite salad. A necessity for every Versa racer due to its healing effects on the body, something I could presently use as the painkillers faded away.

Quickly digging into the lachli, I noticed a lot of people hanging out by the windows holding an amazing view of the race track and, quite frankly, the city itself. They were noble enough to give me space while I ate, waiting in line for pictures and autographs once I was finished. I felt really comfortable around all of them. Most of them were outgoing, some a little more than others. Like any crowd, there were some shy ones who held back. I tried to help them open up. I knew what it felt like to be shy. It was a stage I went through after my dad's death. Hell, there was a plausible chance that I would still have been shy if not for Trace. In an exclusive setting like this, no one should have been an outsider. After meeting a good portion of fans, I ventured my way over to the dessert table with Roy and Kira standing nearby in their coriums, conversing about the race.

"I thought two heads were supposed to be better than one, and yet they fell for our bait," Roy joked to Kira. His wobbly stance revealed how buzzed the vet really was.

"You should've seen how far they flew off," Kira joyfully said, raising the pink complexion in his cheeks.

"Please don't tell me that they flew into that insurance building, because I heard glass shatter in the background," Roy struggled to ask, laughing while Kira slowly nodded her head. Roy eventually pulled me into their discussion once he regained a little focus.

"How was the fifteen seconds of fame?" he asked, taking a slice from the Grace of Gluttony cake.

"I think you already know the answer," I responded.

"Don't worry. It gets much better. Just think about all of the sponsorships that you'll be getting from this experience. It'll help your workshop out a lot," Kira explained.

"Oh, there's someone that wants to say hello, Craven," Roy suddenly added while trying to quickly finish off the slice of cake he had. "I'll be right back."

He finally placed the plate down to search for the mentioned individual. Kira and I talked about what we might be doing next. Her family had been promoting the Pro League spectacle that was Four Seasons. Apparently, it was more popular than I thought. A lot of people were chatting about it and the golden poster boy, Midas. I still wasn't too sure about competing in it though. Trace's health was the main concern.

Roy came back with a woman dressed in white, with long blonde hair, brown eyes, and skin that was slightly tanned. It took me a second to recognize her due to the substantial amount of weight she'd lost, now bonier than ever. She represented Earth in Galacticas XLIV-XLVIII. Her name was Kriss Fathom, Roy's wife. Another one of "the surviving seven," last of the ones still alive. Catelyn Brannigan, Fiona Welsh, Adonis Angelos, and J.C. Ripa as the other four had been dead longer than my father. Catelyn's lover, Fiona was killed in Galactica XLVII by a Minorist, who Catelyn would later get vengeance upon in Galactica XLVIII, but the price paid for it was her own life. Adonis, someone my father claimed had lost his mental faculties after seeing the majority of their Terran team wiped away, died in Galactica XLVIII by Thorax's hands. J.C. Ripa had been the only one out of the seven who had passed away from the wounds accumulated from Galactica XLVII. Roy and his wife, Kriss were the only ones who had witnessed eudaimonia, but not without a fault. During a race on Ghast, Kriss ingested an unforgivable toxin that would damage her reproductive system. It was an injury she never recovered from and left her husband childless because of it. That was one of the reasons why Roy took me under his wing at the start of the career. I guess one could say that I became the son he never had.

"It's been so long Craven," she said with a few tears coming down her cheek. She used to be good friends with my dad, so she was always a bit emotional because of how I resembled him. They were known as The Terran Triforce, the greatest trio of all time, and I did not speak subjectively. This was a fact.

"It's been almost a decade since you've last seen him," Roy stated.

"Yeah, I guess it's been a long time since we last met," I affirmed after realizing the timeframe. She used to be one of the racers I looked up to because of her chemistry with Roy and my father, almost as if they could predict each other's next move whenever they ganged up on their foes. If anyone was ever at a disadvantage against The Terran Triforce, they would pretty much guarantee an upcoming obituary. Not even the other four of "the surviving seven" could stand a chance in their primes. I would back that argument to my grave.

"It's been way too long, and I see that you've been running into success. It's a natural trait that runs in the McGuire family. Has the same fortune been with Lacey?" she asked.

"She's had better days. She just found out that her son's a Versa racer," I replied, noticing the priceless look on Kira's face, slowly shaking her head. Clearly, she hadn't dealt with the same dilemma with her Versa-embraced family. A daughter of *Brink Industries*, lucky you.

"Well, some secrets are kept for the best," Kriss responded.

"Yeah, but a light ends up shining on them sooner or later," I concluded. Before the discussion could continue, Thardus Leone and two beautiful models suddenly appeared, heading our way with a sword, a crown, and a briefcase filled with money.

"Here they come," I silently muttered to myself.

The sword was made from the toughest metal in the galaxy, krone. It had a bright-white grip with a miniature chrome-tinted knight's helmet on the pommel. At the center of the sword's guard was a metal emblem of the Greek Titan, Atlas holding onto a chrome Earth. Enclosing the emblem were two black crosses on the edges of the cross guard for an ironic but fitting representation of Knightfall's Champion. The crown had an inner layer of a black cotton blend, an outer layer of a silver metal caged around it with onyx pearls scattered all around the cage, and a metal cross in the temple of the cage with the same black pearl in its origin. In my honor, Thardus was coincidentally rocking out a neon-blue and gray suit. He had that typical mobster look of a flabby belly, a bulbous nose inhaling the whiffs of his fresh cigar and slit back gray hair.

"There's my money maker," Thardus complimented with his crunchy voice. "What did you think about the new race track? Impressed with the recently acquired features?"

"Words can't describe how I feel about it," I told him as a clever lie. It was a dangerous track that almost killed us. I would have called him sardonic, if not for the victory.

"I take it that it'll have a special place in your heart because I most honorably present to you the King's Crown and Sword of Knightfall. Plus, the winning grand prize of ten million big ones!" he announced for everyone to hear as they started to cheer. The pair of models slowly walked over to my side, slowly placing the crown on my head while seductively handing me the sword. A few fans delivered some arousing whistles. "May more accolades come your way, but for now... Long live the king," Thardus finished after handing the briefcase of money. The skydeck began to quake the city once more from all of the cheers and pictures. I tried to enjoy it, but Kira caught my attention instead by pulling my arm.

"One of the fans just told me that Trace is in the medical center on the 6th floor," she urgently reported impelling me to hand off the prizes so I could check on my brother's condition.

ACT I
CHAPTER 8

BROTHERLY LOVE

THE ELEVATOR RIDE TO THE MEDICAL CENTER COULD NOT HAVE BEEN LONGER. I expected the ride to be quicker, considering it was within a building holding onto more than two-hundred floors. The annoying 20th Century jazz music didn't help, either. My heart was racing a storm, worried about my best friend's condition. My brain was battling a black hole, trying to avert depression. My rage escalated by the second, stuck inside this snail-paced elevator ride. The silver lining to this whole situation was the plate of lachli I took for Trace and Kira's willingness to take the crown and sword before my departure; I would've looked like a fool wearing that bejeweled shit.

Once the elevator doors finally made the wise decision to open, I urgently rushed into the spacious dimly gray-lit waiting room. There wasn't a nurse or an attendant behind the main check-in counter, but there was a pair of gentlemen, sitting down in a pair of chairs against the far-right corner of the room. It was the hounds, Meta and Beta Breckenridge, arguing with one another while continuously banging the back of their heads into the wall. My main goal was to check on Trace, but I couldn't ignore how loud, vulgar, and obnoxious the twins could get in defeat. Somewhat sounded like an individual arguing with themselves because of how identical their voices were. If it wasn't for the distinction in hair color, telling them apart would be impossible.

"It was your dumbass idea to combine," Beta stated, ending his rhythmic thuds against the wall.

"Yeah, but it was your smartass idea to shove them off of the track," Meta redirected, continuing his series of thuds.

"Well, it would've been a badass idea if you hadn't triggered the boost."

"Did not!"

"Did too!!!"

"Now why would I trigger the boost?" Meta asked, shooting his twin a scrunched up facial expression.

"Because you were jealous that Kira picked me over you. That's why you wanted to shove her ass off the track," Beta explained.

"Oh, here we go again with the jealousy card."

"Hey, are you guys alright? Didn't know hounds could fly," I said to dampen the argument. Let's just say this wasn't the first, second, or tenth time they'd butted heads during the Semi's due to the other's folly. Believe it or not, the arguments were much worse when they were winning. At times they would argue about who the best racer was in Versa history, who should be in the running for the next Shepherd of the United Countries, or where they should go out to eat. Meta had major cravings for Ol'McDonald's burgers, while Beta, on the other hand, preferred Burger Kingdom. One would think that twins would share the same cravings, but that was not the worst thing about them. No, that came from their beliefs about The Terran Triforce, an overrated trio due to my father's success. People didn't understand the war I was willing to wage on that topic. The hounds and I would argue during pre-races about who was better, and it damn-near drove me to an asylum on the moon.

"Oh, that's just part of the bullshit," Meta exclaimed on the flying hound topic.

"We actually crashed into a shitty cubicle of an office, flat-bedding a fucking custodian," Beta informed, cracking up the hounds.

"We sure scared the fucking shit out of him," Beta comically issued through his adolescent laughter.

"Why are you two idiots laughing? The custodian is probably gonna sue your asses, and to add insult to injury, you didn't even win the money to cover it all," I reminded them, silencing the howls of the hounds for the first time.

"B, remember the look on the custodian's face?" Meta reminded, triggering a series of laughs once again. He fell to the floor in front of his brother's feet. Water began to flow down their cheeks, creating a river of humorous tears. Personally, I thought these two knuckleheads should have been diagnosed with concussions.

I left the hounds to themselves, making my way through a doorway that led to the patients. A long hallway led to rooms filled with patients on each side, and a tall male doctor in a long white coat standing outside of the third room to the left. He was filling out an evaluation report on a holographic tablet.

"Excuse me doctor, can you point me in the direction of Trace Burretta?"

"Craven, you son of a bitch!" I heard a voice shout from the room that the doctor was standing near.

"He's in the last room on the right at the end of the hall," the doctor eventually answered after the unsettling verbal explosion. He looked annoyed, clearly used to temper tantrums.

"One more question. The custodian who suffered from accidental injuries, is there any updates on their status?" I asked as the doctor used the side of his right hand to wipe off the amount of sweat forming on his forehead.

"Bruised sternum, fractured ribs, damaged liver, along with a few more unidentified contusions," the doctor explained. "He'll be alright."

The news definitely lightens the dark vibe typical of the medical center. I didn't know why, but just had to know the condition of the injured custodian. Maybe it was the fatherless little boy within me, the one who had empathically linked with those who had lost loved ones to the collateral damages of this sport. It was a good thing that little boy disappeared during the competition, or I might have been the next casualty.

In Trace's room, I found the identity of the patient stressing the doctor's nerves. It was The Raven, Zane Maddox strapped to a bed with half of his face covered in sanitatium bandages, an extraterrestrial metallic substance from the planet, Ghast. It basically looked like a shiny sheet of aluminum foil that perfectly masked itself onto another's face. Sanitatium was primarily used for skin cell regeneration; it could restore a lot of skin cells when applied immediately, but Zane's face was catastrophically abraded with a sliced open left cheek, leaving rocks in the middle of his bumpy healing process. I guessed this made Zane and Trace even when it came to facial scars.

Hesitantly stepping into Trace's room, afraid to find out what a broken promise looked like, I discovered him relaxing in bed, watching the Unican Network on his iCube like he was on vacation. Stuck in a patient's gown, stripped from his corium, wearing a calm demeanor, Trace had bandages wrapped around what was left of his bloody right arm.

"There's the man of the knight," he joked. This was supposed to be a serious moment but Trace was pretending like nothing ever happened. It was not the first time that he'd reacted like this. He was the same way after receiving the burn mark on his neck. The scar made him happy, made him look tougher. *It builds character*, was the dumb statement he expressed to the Versa universe with a strip of sanitatium still glued to his neck.

"Are you alright?" I asked.

"Alright? Nah, I'm all-left," Trace chuckled, making an attempt at the terrible joke without laughing but failed miserably towards the end.

"Is everyone on drugs here?" I muttered to myself because Trace was never this punny.

"Dude, check it out. You're on TV. Unican is talking about Knightfall and everything," he indicated while pointing to the screen showing highlights of the race. The main footage they kept playing was the malicious hit I inflicted on Zane with the headline reading, "The Dark Knight of Earth?"

I walked over to the television grid, shutting it off before the nonsense of theories exploded.

"What the hell was that for?"

"You just lost your arm in a race, and you're treating it like it never happened."

"It builds character, and besides, I'm southpaw."

"I know that but..."

"But you're the better racer, and most likely always will be. I'm not the one who had something to lose in this race, you were. You're the one with the bright future. You're also the one who's gonna take down Midas at Four Seasons," Trace explained.

"I'm not doing Four Seasons, not after this, not after tonight."

"Like hell you are! I saved your ass from Zane, so now I believe that you owe me one."

"Damn it Trace. Don't force me into that series."

"I'm not forcing anything onto you. Versa's your second nature, and it's what you were born to do, Craven. You just need a little push, hell, we always need a push."

"How the hell am I supposed to qualify then?"

"I've already qualified, but as you can see. I'm not gonna be medically cleared. But I can substitute myself with someone who is, and that's where you come in. They allow you to make a move like that in the Pro's. Especially for a Semi League Champ with your stature and legacy. For you, the future is written in stone. All you have to do is experience it," he explained.

"I'm sorry, but my answer is still, no."

"Fine Craven, you win. I won't push you anymore because I've recently found the confidence to race on three limbs instead of four. If the Martians can do it, so can I."

"Why? You'll just make things worse!"

"Doesn't matter cuz I've already thought of a new nickname. Call me Trace, The Southpaw Trident. It's got a catchy ring to it. Might have to buy a 2250 Neptune or Poseidon to add on to the presenta…"

"Fine, I'll fucking do it," I quickly interrupted, finally convinced of Trace's determination. He'd definitely find a way to compete if I refused.

"Come on Craven. I don't want you to feel like you're held against your will, even though you are. I just want you to have some type of motivation. Think about Miss Earth, do it for her. I know you like her. I saw the way she caught your attention."

"She didn't catch anything; she was just on TV," I replied while leaning against the doorway.

"Eh, she was, but you had a relieved look when I told you she was Midas' sister," he added with a smirk on his face. "Oh yeah, Trace knows. Trace understands, and Trace will help your lonely ass out. The ladies love it when you smoke their brothers in a series, especially if it involves an undefeated streak."

"Good to know that you're alright. Let Katia know I'm using the winnings to pay for your replacement arm, maybe it'll postpone her assassination attempt on me."

Replacement limbs were easy to acquire if you had money nowadays. The best product on the market from *Transcendence* was a hybrix, a mechanical arm with artificial skin and Rokian technology picking up on one's daily motions through their DNA and muscle memory. The full calibration could take a few weeks, possibly months, but it was better than being armless. Plus, I'd heard good reviews on it. *Transcendence* knew how to perfect a brand new limb and organ, the company's only flaw was not having anything for the spine. Creating nerves that adapted to the body was one thing, creating an entirely new central nervous system was another. It was better to lose limb instead of fracturing the spine. As of right now, there was no coming back from paralysis.

"Shit, how the hell do you think she's gonna react?" Trace questioned, obviously stressed.

"Why are you freaking out, you're not the one who gave her a promise before and after you left the nest."

"Yeah, but you're not the one who has to sleep with her every night."

"Heh, you're right."

"How do we cheat death this time around, bro?"

"Trace, something tells me we'll find a way," I said, turning his television grid back on and making my way to the door after leaving the plate of lachli on his lap.

"Where are you going?"

"My mom's house."

"Forget about my bittersweet heart. You're as good as dead if you head there. That's uncharted territory, bro."

"I know, that's why I gotta face my demons," I said as I left the room. Trace was right about me possibly digging my own grave, but it was the least that I could do for my mother. She and I didn't see eye to eye on Versa-related topics anymore. That was why this confrontation was so important. I had to find a way to heal that bridge, the prestigious bridge my father built for the McGuire tree so long ago.

MANOR'S MANIA

THE FULL MOON WAS AT ITS HIGHEST POINT, SHINING OVER WINCHESTER ESTATES, A NEIGHBORHOOD NOTORIOUS FOR SOME OF THE MOST ICONIC SPORTS FIGURES. Only the best of the best live there due to the pricing of each mansion. Names like Aiden Moore, one of the best quarterbacks of all-time, or like Corbin Prowler, a four-time MVP as a centre in the NHL. In the sports industry, my father was highly ranked as one of the top-tier athletes based on health and performance, only making it fitting for him to live in a top-tier community like Winchester.

A couple years back, this place used to be my home, the only place that I could call home, never on the move. The advantage of a wealthy lifestyle. I didn't see that until I met my best friend, Trace one sunny day at a park closer to the city. We were both wearing the same Versa shirt of my father. Like gems on a ring, we were fused together, convincing my father that I should apply to the same public schools Trace went to. Trace's lifestyle was much different than mine. Working-class family, which wasn't much compared to the higher classes. Witnessing some of his family's economic struggles helped me appreciate certain things I could've easily taken for granted. At one point, I actually hated being wealthy from all of Trace's remarks. He was the only person on the planet who would make fun of someone being rich. I guess you can say that I'd taught him how to appreciate another's social class too because I didn't hear him complaining about the nest, my new home. It had been that way ever since I left the Winchester Estates. If only my mom would understand.

I couldn't believe what I was doing, finally crossing the damaged bridge. My mood sunk down even further once I was in the parking lot to the McGuire Manor, a tanned triple-floored mansion with a stony exterior structure and a five-car garage my father traditionally used as a mini-workshop of his own. I always loved seeing The Heart of Earth work on his projects in the garage as a kid. Just like Trace's father, mine allowed me to aid him with certain Versa suits. It was the main inspiration for *The Blue Jay's Nest*. Man, those father and son moments felt invaluable. I eventually stepped onto the front porch of the house to ring the doorbell, but all I heard was silence. I kept ringing the doorbell, replacing the song of silence with the symphony of annoyance, knowing that my mother was home from all of the lights lit up inside.

"Mom, I know you're in there!" I yelled so loud that the neighbors five houses down could hear me. "There's something we need to talk about!"

"Go away or you'll regret it!" I heard her shout from the inside of the house.

"Like hell I will," I impatiently said to myself, pulling out my iCube to auto-connect with the manor's security system. I secretly linked the facial, voice, and x-ray recognition to my iCube before I moved out and resorted to it whenever I wanted to sneak back into the house without my mom ever knowing. It didn't take long to pass the security for the brown double-door, granting me access to the unwelcomed manor. My mom's German Shepherd, Max, instantly came to greet me. Barking up a storm instead of licking my face from the last time I saw him and my mom at Christmas. The 7-year-old black-and-orange behemoth even attracted the matriarch herself.

"Really?" my mom cried, now stomping down the left set of arched-staircases. The steps were vanilla-white with black railings matching the textures to the entire manor. She was in her pajamas, and still looked the same from the last time I came to visit. Her hair was naturally brown again, but she had a few more wrinkles around her light-brown eyes. A common symptom for a mother stressed at their son. "You might have your dad's skill and looks, but you also carry his stupidity."

"So, the secret's out?" I inquired, already knowing the obvious answer before she could march up to me with a ferocious slap across my face.

"No shit!" she screamed while grabbing my arm, yanking me into the living room. I could see myself on a recently cracked 80" TV screen that was paused in the center of the room. The sight made my heart rate increase to a brand-new lifetime high because I was officially dealing with a She-Hulk. "Really, after all we've been through. How the hell can you find any love for this crap?"

"Well… Trace…" I tried to explain, clearing my throat a couple times.

"I'm gonna stop you right there. So, you're telling me that Trace, the same Trace who just got his fucking arm cut off by a lunatic, convinced you?" she asked with a crescendo of ferocity. The debate was beginning to look one-sided as I slowly nodded. It felt worse listening to the argumentative question than it had been experiencing it.

"Wow, this night just keeps getting better and better," she continued while stepping into the kitchen to place dishes away. The kitchen itself was still clean, enormous, and illuminated by a few dozen soft-white flood lights scattered around the ceiling. Taking up some of the space was an island counter with a black marble top, black appliances, and a pair of dinner tables that could cater a party of twenty. There were also pathways to the garage and a straight flight staircase to the second and third floor.

"You can't blame Trace for this, if we're being honest. My involvement with Versa was inevitable," I stated, provoking her to slam the dishes into the sink, followed with a devilish stare.

"Inevitable? You call a kid witnessing their dad's death and getting involved with the sport he died in inevitable? I call it betrayal."

"How is it betrayal? I'm a fucking McGuire. This was something that he would've wanted to see."

"Why? Why can't he see it Craven? He came an inch away from the finish line to his career. Perfection was the imperfection that got him killed, and it's the same delusion that'll get you killed, too," she cried, staring at the broken dishes. Tears were falling into the sink.

"Why do you keep crying like I'm already dead? I'm still here and there's not one scratch on my body."

"I'm crying because I can already see how your road ends, and I refuse to be a part of it. Now please, get the hell out of my sight," she forcefully demanded with her eyes still locked on the dishes. I wanted to challenge her, but decided not to and left the kitchen. I had to give her as much time as possible to help her cope with my lifestyle. I could see Max sitting at the end of the hall to the garage with his paws around the ears.

"Sorry," I whispered like he could understand what I was saying before I went upstairs to the second floor. Along the walls of the stairs were framed family pictures. The first one was the wedding picture of my parents in Newcastle, Australia, the gorgeous city where they first met. The story went that my father took a little time out after experiencing a near-death altercation during his Galactic race in Sydney. He had heard great things about the beaches of Newcastle and decided to never leave his suit after the race and drove north to the destination. A breath of fresh air was all he wanted as he sat on the beach next to his suit until a curious female lifeguard approached him, asking if he was alright. "No," he replied because he was blinded by the lifeguard's beauty. My father had a charm that would cast a spell on any girl, but instead was caught in one. For some miraculous reason, he felt like he could leave the suit behind on the beach for this girl, mainly because, for once, somebody didn't know who Crank McGuire was, and that was somebody he wanted to spend the rest of his life with—a textbook happily ever after.

Next to the wedding picture was an old photo of my mother's parents, a pair of family members I never got to meet due to their early passing. They were strangers to me. The only thing I knew about them was their names Ward and Lauren, and that they were buried somewhere in Salt Ash, Australia. The strange thing was that my mother's family tree ended there. She had no sister, brother, aunt or uncle. Ward and Lauren were all my mother had which was why this picture of them was so important. It also connected both my mother and father because his family tree had the same issue, making me the last line for both sides. I'd been curious about the family tree, but never got around to asking my parents. I always felt like I'd be wounding their hearts if I asked.

Leaning towards a lighter memory was the last picture of my parents and I at Dessnia, Florida, otherwise known as the happiest place on Earth. It seemed like everything went perfectly on that hot summer day, it was the 21st of June—a sudden trip my dad planned out behind the scenes. He knew everyone's schedule would be open on that weekend for a proper family memory. We actually got to hit up every rollercoaster there while having enough time to watch the evening fireworks show near the Castle of Dessnia. It's how we got this special family picture with green, blue, purple, and red fireworks exploding in the background. At the time, I was a 10-year-old, thinking to myself that the moment was a small sum of many more moments that I would cherish going forward. If only I had known that this would be the last photo of us taken as a family. Unica broke the news to the universe that Galactica XLVIII was coming out of its temporary lockdown the following day. It was a Galactica the Hendecalliance had to think about, knowing Ragnios was on the brink of extinction. My father was hooked to the spectacle's resurrection, knowing he could achieve one big thing, the hat trick.

"Perfection really was your imperfection," I mumbled, ignoring the other pictures as I stepped onto the second floor catwalk. It had great views of the game room on one side and a vantage point of the kitchen on the other, still of my mother's presence throwing away the broken glassware. At the end of the catwalk was a right turn to another set of stairs that curved itself along the wall to the third floor, a left turn to the pair of arched-staircases that my mother descended earlier near the entrance, and a straight pathway to a Y-shaped intersection of hallways. Down the hallway were guest bedrooms, theater/game rooms, bathrooms, and a universal library where my father spent a lot of time studying the history of all the other planets and specimens. The library was the main reason why I came upstairs, so I quickly made my way to it at the end of the left hall.

One of the reasons why my father called this room the universal library was because of the ceiling's holographic design of the galaxy. He wanted the library to be an environment he could be comfortable with, an environment that personified his work, and what better choice than a scenic view of the Milky Way. Adding to the library's comfort were comfortable couches and chairs near every coffee table. Possibly too comfortable with a cushion rate equivalent to a cloud in heaven. If we weren't reading in this library, we were sleeping. I'm honestly not too sure how my dad got any studying done in here from all the times I caught him napping. Whenever I woke him, he would smoothly play it off by saying he was resting his eyes. He actually fooled me one time with a holographic recording of open eyes covering his closed eyelids.

On the shelves were expensive books a Versa racer would die for if they ever went up against another specimen. My father had each shelf categorized for the sets of books. There were categories like: Anatomical books dealing with the strengths and weaknesses to each extraterrestrial body. Astrogeological books showing maps and climates of every Majoris and Minoris planet. Paroikological books explaining the historical growth as a culture for each specimen. Theological books expressing each extraterrestrial belief and ritual system, and Kinesiological books demonstrating the mechanics of alien movements. It was also the category my dad spent a lot of time analyzing during the creation of his Hermes. I, on the other hand, spent a lot of time reading Astrogeology. The maps and layouts of all the discovered planets was a child's imagination brought to life. Every single dream world a kid could fantasize about was basically the terrain of another planet. A child who loved a Jurassic world with giants would love to travel to Gigalus, or a different child who loved to create junkyards more messier than my office, they'd probably keep a close eye on Arach. A planet known for turning shit into an angelically silken environment, then again, if the kid was like Trace and hated spiders, scorpions, beetles and every other specimen with eight legs, well, I would advise them to avoid Arach. There's a world for everyone, including the sick and twisted. Those were the books my father kept concealed. Out of all the books here, my favorites were the Pyscean stories about Pasydanya because of all the creatures. The amount of different ethnicities were extraordinary, and the fact that all of them would unite together as one to fend off the beasts merging from the depths was astonishing. That wasn't the craziest part of it all, no, that instead came from the immersion I had in the readings. I got that a reader could lose touch with reality from a captivating story, but the immersion I had felt was stronger than that. It was almost as if the Pyscean oceans themselves were coursing through my veins. Then again, that could've just been a hats-off tip to the writer.

As of right now, my eyes were set on one anatomical book about the Gravits of Graviathen. At a red light on the way here, I noticed blood dripping off my right arm from the minor cut delivered by Zane's blade during my shield's transformation. The shield was a prototype, so having a flaw in its defense was expected. This is why I'd flushed out an idea to act as a plausible solution with the integration of Gravit blood cells. It just required some research. Next to the Graviathen book was a strange book I'd never seen. Sealed under an unidentifiable white metal, the book was titled, *Ampyre's Fall*. The book's natural fabric glowed like a sun with a lonesome image of a black halo as its cover. I've never seen anything like this, but at the end of the day it was irrelevant to the situation, so I placed it back to collect more dust.

Once I had what I needed from the library, I made my way down the hall, stopping at the sight of a cracked open door to my father's office. I wanted to convince myself to leave it be, but a few deep breaths stimulated my curiosity. It had been almost a dozen years, and for almost a dozen years, that door had been sealed shut with neither my mother nor I daring one another to open it.

I gently pushed the door open, softly hearing the creaking noises of the slightly rusted door hinges until the sight of my father's office was full and clear. The first thing I could see was my father's giant oak desk on the far-left side of the room with his black leather chair behind it. Straight ahead from the door were four black metal filing cabinets side by side against the gray walls. The sight made me think of a memory that somehow felt present. It was a vivid memory of my dad opening up some of the cabinets, searching for a certain file. Vibrant chills ran through my bones from seeing the ghost of my father coming to life from my memory, still searching for a specific file. He had that sleepless look on his face with the eye bags piled underneath his light-brown eyes like a mountain of dirty clothes. I honestly never really knew what was in the cabinet. As a child, I figured if it made him stressed and sleepless, it would do the same to me, and I wasn't trying to look like a zombie. I guess I had to find out sooner or later.

The walk to the cabinets helped me get a whiff of my dad's natural cinnamon-like scent. Definitely a somewhat haunting feeling. He was dead and yet his presence still floated around, airborne and very much alive. I had to wash away the thought before it could haunt me more by pulling open the top drawer of the far-right cabinet. It was filled with holomarks, a transparent square file that resembled a sturdy piece of paper. The only way to see the file was with a hologramer, and that was when it hit me. My dad specifically had a unique hologramer implanted on the wall across from his desk, which coincidentally had the remote. I took out one of the files before heading over to the desk. With the remote in hand, I pressed down on the power icon, initiating the hologramer until the wall's screen turned completely white with the *Holo* trademark appearing in the center. I launched the hologramer and planted myself into my father's leather chair, staring at the holomark in my hands. Anything could be on this file, there was no telling what hologram was going to appear in this room. The proper way of using one was to hold it up at the hologramer, which would cause the holomark to shoot a bright flash at the hologramer, revealing the holomark's file.

Once the hologramer was ready for a flash, I held the holomark up, only to see a mysterious three-horned monster miraculously appear in the center of the room, frozen still, holding up a humongous hammer with one arm, staring at me with its hauntingly black eyes. I slowly rose up from the chair, dropping the holomark to take a closer look at the horned-figure. The body was pale and covered in bones from what seemed to be from other aliens. The mysterious hologram was about 7-feet-tall and had a long bull-like head which resembled a skull from how far inward its eyes were. I would make the assumption that this was a Satanian but felt a little thrown off from its skin color. Satanians typically had dark obsidian skin, but this thing was different. After I was done observing the horned-beast, I noticed writings on the hologramer's wall. They were formatted into a traditional racer's bio. The screaming black-tongued creature didn't look like a racer, but that thought quickly changed once I read the name. It was Skorge, the racer who previously held the record for most kills in a single Galactica series. The rest of his bio read:

Name: Skorge Z'IV
Sobriquet: "Zata's Fourth" & "The Apex"
Weight: 329 lbs (149.2 kg)
Height: 7'5½" (2.27 m)
Native: Crescienna, Moon of Zata

Appearance: An Albino Cresciennic Bullasian w/three horns, one protruding out of his occipital lobe, and two out of the parietal lobes with a hornspan of 4½ feet. The two front-horns are bright white with black tips in an arched upward formation. The lone rear-horn, on the other hand, arches forward over the top of his head, resembling a bonehawk with small 3" black spikes aligned symmetrical on the horn. Skorge's species has a head that's similar to the skull of a bull from the United Countries of Earth, hence the Bullasian classification. The dark eyes within the eye lobes add on to the already morbid look to his species. Covered with albino skin, Skorge's rare epidermis makes him invulnerable to any type of pyromantic attacks, except for the even rarer Satanian noir-blaze.

Bio: Due to the unique pyro-resistant skin, the Bullasian has been declared by Satanians as the fourth spawn of Zata, Goddess of Satanian Gods. Hailing from the moons of Satania, Skorge has manifested his "spawn" title into the apex predator of Satania, a status even more prestigious than a Shepherd. The Apex's violent nature helped him form a faction called R'lanqa (Relinquisher), a group known for hunting down all of the Satanians, osculated or unkindled, with the intent of endangering the race. Instead of conducting a civil war, the Shepherd of Satania saw an opportunity of eliminating Skorge by placing him in the unforgiving series, Galactica against all specimens, but the intention backfired with Skorge's milestone record of most kills in a single series, building upon The Apex's resume.

Highlight: Galactica XLV - Setting the record for most kills in a single series with the kill count of 174 out of 1000 racers. The most notorious kill out of the 174 was the beheading of Onitus, the largest Gigallian in Galactica history, sitting at 22'6" (6.86 m), carrying the weight of 2300 lbs (1043.3 kg). Classified as a David vs Goliath match-up, except, it was Onitus, playing the role of David. A one-sided affair that left Skorge unsullied and flawless, howling their title as The Apex across the entire universe. Skorge would go on to carry a part of Onitus, as his own by detaching the right femoral bone of the giant and forging it into his own colossus-size hammer with skulls implanted onto both sides of the hammer's guard, naming it Sularis Snatchera (Soul Snatcher).

Galactica XLVI - Becoming the first racer in Galactica history to have more than three-hundred kills in their career with fifty coming from the planet he represented, inevitably resulting in a grudgeful death by a Satanian osculated with Zata's noir-blaze, who now keeps the remnants of Skorge alive to this day, wearing The Apex's Bullasian skull as a helmet while being the new keeper of Sularis Snatchera.

Status: Deceased

Jesus, the Bullasian might've been dead, but that didn't prevent his resume from unsettling my stomach. I'd only heard short stories about my dad encountering this foe, but never dove deep into his bio. My father once claimed that Skorge's death was the worst thing they could've done for the afterlife. Made me wonder about who the new apex would be if Galactica ever came out of its lockdown.

Having the beginner's luck of picking one of the most intimidating racers in Galactica history diminished the curiosity I had toward my dad's files. On that note, my business in his office was finished. I turned off the hologramer on the way out, and decided to head back downstairs to the garage instead of traveling to the third floor where my old bedroom was. I didn't need a reason to stay the night if my mother and I were at odds.

When I got to the garage downstairs, the motion-sensing service lights quickly illuminated the garage filled with my dad's relics scattered all around. There had to have been about a dozen Versa suits, each one owning a story of its own, told best by my dad as a child. One of my favorite stories came from the suit placed against the right-side wall, the 2185 Perseus, my dad's go-to suit before the birth of the Hermes. It had dark blue skin with green vines wrapped around the limbs, similar to the Atlas' design of broken chains. *To this day, the best race I ever had was in this suit. Percy was with me from the beginning, helping me claim a name, followed by my first and second Galactica titles*, my father had explained about this suit. Percy was the nickname he gave for the elder suit, holding onto scars that aged even more from the rust and scratches of past races. Not too sure if this Ole Yeller had another race within him.

Another story that stood out was the exosuit in the far-right corner of the garage. It was the silver 2220 Legacy, a brute with heavy armor and artillery. He used it to defend himself in a desperate race labeled as a "Kill or Be Killed" race against a family from Earth's solaric rival Mars, also known as Red Minor. The story started off with my father falling into an elimination race against the Korn family consisting of Armrak Korn, the father and his quadruplings, Boomer, Lockett, Pryst, and Qale Korn. The battle resulted in my father winning with fractured ribs, and a dislocated hip, but that was nothing compared to the scars left on the Korn family. The two brothers Boomer and Lockett were killed by my father causing Armrak to retaliate with vengeance, resulting in him ending up with a lone eye, arm, and leg. A grudge I bet the Martian family still held to this day. It was a good thing they never had a chance for redemption.

Next to the Legacy was my dad's last suit, a partially reassembled 2200 Hermes. She was just sitting there next to the rest of her broken parts, collecting dust, developing rust. I would always remember that unforgettable moment when he debuted the suit at the opening race in Galactica XLVIII. It was on the planet Pasydanya. The other racers didn't know what was coming, including Kriss and Roy, who were also competing. *A Flawless Victory* was the headline on the Unican Network after that race. "Not a scratch," Tokyn had said, following my father's astonishing performance. There was also the time my dad got cornered by this four-horned Satanian with a huge hammer. Holy crap, I can't remember the Satanian's name, but I do know that he was Sularis Snatchera's new keeper, pushing the Hermes to a breaking point with the weapon. MIKA pulled off some magic by guiding my dad out of that predicament. As a kid, it felt surreal seeing him perform magic in the Hermes. Prior to the Hermes, I had only heard stories about his greatness, but witnessing it was a whole different story.

I could only stand by the Hermes, frozen from nostalgia. I eventually wiped the dust off of the helmet, allowing the blue and green to shine once more. The combination of colors that represented the UCE in the past still had its glimmer. I had to pick it up for a closer look. I even took the liberty of blowing off the thin coat of dust on the visor. My mother stood in its reflection.

"You can have it," my mom softly offered while calmly walking up beside me.

"Is that forgiveness I hear in your voice?" I gently asked, noticing the first smile of the night on my mother's face.

"Don't push it kiddo," she warned, slowly grabbing the helmet, taking in its memories too. "Do you think that Martian family still hates us?"

"Nope, I honestly think they've got a batch of cookies waiting for us in the near future."

"You've been hanging with Trace for too long, his smartassery is beginning to rub off on you."

"What do you expect, he's the closest thing to a brother that I'll ever have," I stated, receiving another understanding smile.

"The both of you were so in love with the sport when Crank was competing," she reminded, allowing tears as she thought about him.

"We were. Why do you think we wanted to be like him? We wanna make him proud. Trace as a fan, me as a son," I responded.

"He is proud, but you have to promise me something," my mother stated with her hand on my shoulder. "Every race you compete in will always be on Earth, nowhere else."

The hard-hitting promise was one I couldn't deny, and she quickly took away the option of second-guessing it with a comforting hug. My mother wasn't stupid, she knew how much I loved my father. I was the only other person in this world who gave her a run for that loving title. That was why she had to make sure I wouldn't pursue anything hateful. Like any strong mother, her loving hands gripped tight around me. She didn't want the hate towards my father's killer to consume me, but that was the thing. I'd been living with this hate for almost a dozen years and was the only one in this world who could carry out the justice destined for the Rokian. I'd already broken one promise today, so breaking another wasn't going to drop any more pellets of sweat. I wanted blood and would be counting down the days until I could get it because that was my eudaimonia.

ACT II
FOUR SEASONS

THE BRUTE, THE DIVINE, THE AVENGER, & THE NIGHTMARE ON ELM

A COUPLE OF MONTHS HAD PASSED BY AND THINGS WERE STARTING TO LOOK GOOD. The relationship between my mother and I had pretty much healed. The paparazzi was slowing down, and Trace was finally getting the hang of his new right arm. He and I also had to survive the wrath from his fiancé, an altercation that lasted for nearly three weeks. Man, Katia placed the fight between my mom and I on a peewee status from all of her screams and threats. She actually contemplated leaving the shop, but eventually calmed back down to a reasonable state of mind. Those three weeks were more life-threatening than any race I'd been a part of. That was another spare life that Trace and I could subtract from our set. Note to self, never make a promise you can't keep with Katia.

Thankful for a peaceful period, Four Seasons was less than a week away. Enjoying the timeout I had before entering the fray on the horizon, I was experimenting with a month-long project involving my shield's upgrade. The prototype of it was finished and had passed several tests flawlessly. With a few re-evaluations at *The Blue Jay's Nest*, I had to make sure its progression of success wasn't a fluke.

Stationed in the workshop near the forge, the disconnected right arm of Atlas III was separately connected to a computer for testing operations. I'd spent most of the day here, ignoring how the shop itself was doing on supplies and demands. Building a better name for myself at Four Seasons was the goal, that was why this new and improved shield had to be perfect. I reached my right arm into the socket while manually commencing its shield transformation on the computer. The new addition to the shield covering my entire arm was more visible than ever. It was an outer layer of black spherical hæmalytes from Graviathen. With the aid of Vector's friend smuggling in more BrachiShields, I was able to brainstorm the hæmalytes' configuration to the shields by using Atlas Sr. as my test dummy. In luck, the elder survived the failures, but that was only because the hæmalytes kept rolling off of the shield's improper attraction. The follies convinced me to reformat the equations for a hot streak of successful tests. The only problem was whether or not I could recreate the success for Atlas III.

Briefly distracting me from the experiment were the crying voices coming from the television grid of my iCube I left on for background noise. The footer read, *Damnation to Xenners*, and had footage showing a pair of Xenners being dragged out of their houses with the muzzle of a double-barrel pushed into their craniums. The pair of Xenners had disfigurations of oval eyes, cleft noses, spiked shoulders, gray rubbled skin and superiorly arched spines. Xenners were also known as Xenobred, an immoral act most often justified by impulsive individuals like the ones in the footage. The feedback then transitioned back to a reporter explaining that this act was happening in Greymouth, New Zealand, an area highly prone to Xeno-breeding due to how close the country was to Pyscean Reserves. The act of Xeno-breeding was frowned upon because of the results. In most cases, the births resulted in something out of our ideal Hell. If it hadn't been for the Satanian religion elaborating their beliefs towards Skorge's existence, one would believe he was a Xenner. *We fear what we don't understand*, summed up the perception of Xenners, but if it was possible to come out like Skorge, could anyone blame the communities for taking action? Only nightmares could give someone an empathetic sense of what it was like to be a Xenner, something I was thankful not to be, even though there had been a very small margin of cases where the Xenner came out looking normal.

"Guess what Craven!" Trace anxiously shouted. His entry startled me away from the news in Greymouth.

"Jesus, man," I briefly replied, catching my breath and noticing the huge smile on Trace's face. "Are you trying to give me a heart attack?"

"Quit whining, you've been through worse, guess what?" Trace asked again, rushing the question. He took a seat on the computer's workstation.

"What?" I finally replied, annoyed, tending back to the Atlas' shield.

"Katia and I, we've got a date," he exclaimed.

"A date… you and her… Whoa!" I sarcastically asserted. "Get the fuck outta here."

"No, it's for the wedding," he clarified to my surprise.

"Wait, seriously?"

"It's on May 21st, 2251 at the Windy Lakeside, and I need you to be there as my best man," Trace revealed, his smile contagious. The Windy Lakeside was a critically acclaimed venue near the pier, traditionally used for weddings. I accepted the offer, simultaneously pulling my arm out of the Atlas' socket and congratulating Trace with a hug. "What the hell have you been working on? This better be a new secret weapon."

"Sorta, it's the BrachiShield with an extraterrestrial enhancement," I replied, guiding my arm back into the socket. Trace leaned over for a better look.

"Are those balls on the shield?"

"They're not just balls, they're oxidized hæmalytes!" I said. Trace was unable to comprehend the foreign language I spoke. He even glanced at my chest for subtitles.

"The fuck is an oxi-diced him-a-light?"

"Oxi-dized hæmalytes are from Gravits. It's their blood. I remembered my dad racing against them on Earth and how their blood turned into balls when it oxidized, pioneering a theory in my head. Gravits are magnetic and can control said magnetic attraction through their blood, so I figured, if I could get a hold of some of their blood, and oxidize it, I can maybe just maybe, use its spherical form as a booby trap."

"Soooooooo, it's basically armor. Why do you do this Craven? You always play shit out safely."

"And that's exactly what I want you to think. It's more than a shield, let me show you," I explained, searching for my Knightfall sword. "Try to look around for the sword, I want you to swing it at my shield."

Trace began to examine the entire workshop while I stood up with some of the computer cords still attached to the inner parts of the Atlas' right arm. Trace, after some time, concluded his scavenger hunt and used his new mechanical arm to hold the sword.

"You see Craven, you should be using this sword, instead of that shitty prototype around your arm," Trace said with disapproval, getting into character as a knight by holding the krone-edged sword straight up with two hands around the handle and the blade aligned with his nose.

"You're about to eat those words, swing away," I commanded, quickly bracing for impact by holding the shield up in Trace's direction. Under an advantage with his new hibrix arm, the force from his swing was stronger than expected, but that was why I needed his help for the test. The swing caused my right arm to slightly whiplash backwards, but overall the force was absorbed. I couldn't see much with my head behind the shield. I could only hear Trace blurt the words, *The hell is this?* I then pulled the shield down to glance over its arc, seeing all of the hæmalytes swallowing the krone blade like a leech. Taking advantage of Trace's stupor, I instantly yanked my shielded arm away, unarming the sword in his hands.

"Checkmate," I finally stated with a smirk. Everyone was always a critic before they were a customer. "Don't worry, you can take your time with the apology."

"I'll admit, I'm impressed and… I'm sorry," Trace apologized. "Maybe a defensive game plan is the way to go."

"Why should I attack first when I can attack last," I proposed, setting the Atlas' arm back on the workbench. The shield naturally increased its magnetic attraction, rearranging the hæmalytes back to their original positions.

"I seeya Craven, turning into a little Versa Einstein," Trace complimented as I took my arm out of the Atlas' socket. "So, what are you calling it, the GraviShield?"

"You know, I actually thought about that, but it's not original."

"How bout Aegis? It'll match the Greek Titan feel you've got going on with your suit."

"What the hell was it?"

"An ancient shield used by Zeus. Trust me when I say it'll match the presentation. The shield was magical, powerful, and unbreakable," Trace described, finalizing the name.

"Aegis it is then," I answered, receiving a pat on the shoulder from his hibrix. "How has the arm been?"

"I don't know…" Trace began, examining his arm. By choice, it was still uncoated, showing its natural baby-blue pigmentation, one of the reasons why Katia was mad for so long. Bundles of tiny mechanical strands designed like tendons and ligaments were attached to rollable sections of Rokian metal resembling the actual muscle. The schematic design made it seem like the mechanical arm could flex whenever the bundles pulled the rollable sections. Displaying the design was probably one of the reasons why Trace refused the coat of skin in the first place. *It builds character.* "Strange's the word I'm looking for, like I know it's fake, but it feels so similar to the real thing."

"It's not strange, it's better," I affirmed, softly patting his shoulder in return. It didn't take long for Trace to play around with the sword once it was detached from the hæmalyte's grip. It pulled our conversation down memory lane, taking a pit stop at our high school years. We talked about the two-week long competition we had in gym class called Gladiator. It determined who the best agile student was, an evaluation through a series of events like archery, sword fighting, lifting, running, et cetera. My shining skill was in sword fighting, hence why Trace was bringing it up. He severely sucked at it, so I had to brag, stating that if it were the real deal, I would've been racking up on the kill count. He insisted on adding the sword to my arsenal as The Unchained Knight, a recently acquired nickname. Always loved having talks about the past with Trace, he and I had come a long way and still had a long way to go, but it didn't mean we couldn't reminisce.

With the Aegis diagnosed as ready-for-action, Trace and I made our way to the office. On the way, there were a lot of Calumet residents getting hyped for the Pro Leagues. The chants of *Craven, Craven, Craven* echoed the depths whenever a blue-lit spot shone on my face, and the hype didn't stop there. Vector and Yama produced holomarks all around Calumet of the Atlas torching Midas' suit with the Komodo Fire equipped for practical effects. The suit Midas had on resembled a Cronus, the only Terran suit manufactured by *The Golden Evolution*, but it was hard to tell from the Komodo properly being used for the correct reason. Almost like a shrine, the holomarks in Calumet always produced a horde around it with a few drunks tossing their beers into the flames like molotovs. Calumet spoke volumes for the Chicagolands to hear, and Four Seasons hadn't even begun. I couldn't comprehend the imminent parades on Nexus Ave if I were to win the Pro League series. All I knew was that Zero would be at the helm of that bonanza since his gambling days had only gotten worse. Trace and I had to give a few ass-kickings because of it. In his defense, he'd been undefeated with the bets, never dropping himself into a ditch he could never escape. He just needed to stop betting on me. It was too much pressure, and I got that I chose the Atlas because of how I always felt the pressure of the world and my father's legacy on my shoulders, but come on. I didn't need the financial future of my prodigal son resting on my shoulders too. Then again, that was a possible story for every fan-base, especially one so potent.

Trace was speechless once we got to my office. Oh yeah, for the first time in the nest's history, my office was spotlessly clean. He was used to my sloppy demeanor at home, but only because I felt most organized when I was unorganized. If I was sitting at the desk, working on some expenditures and I suddenly felt dehydrated, I could be organized and try to remember where I last placed my water bottle, or I could be unorganized and see one randomly rolling across the floor like a tumbleweed. Between the two, I usually chose the latter, but I was getting tired of both Trace and Katia calling me "Sloppy Joe," a relation to my middle name Joseph. It was really annoying when they called me that, like come on, no one ate that 20st Century junk. The new "cleansed" me made Trace inspect the office for any signs of grime as I laid on the chair for some rest, the first time for it since Knightfall.

"Is everything in order Inspector Burretta?" I asked as he slid a pair of fingertips across the desk. He then brought the fingertips to his eyes for examination, hoping to see the speck of dust.

"I don't know, there's some bull-shittery here," he responded taking a seat across from me. "That or someone's disguised as my best friend."

"Hey Sloppy…" Katia staggered upon entry, noticing the same thing Trace had about my office.

"That's right, I'm no longer sloppy, so you can just call me, Joe," I stated, kicking my feet onto the desk.

"I guess you were right, babe," Katia said, stepping next to Trace. She held a package at her waist. "A woman can truly change a man."

"Wait, what?" I quickly asked while she dropped the package on the desk. I knew that her comments were linked to my alleged crush on Miss Earth. A hot Calumet rumor flourishing by the second because of these two.

"I knew there was some bull-shittery," Trace added.

"Cute, this little connection between you two is cute. I was gonna congratulate you lovebirds on the wedding, but I'm instead gonna leave it buried with Sloppy Joe," I responded, taking a look at the package labeled as "Four Seasons."

"He's a beauty when he's mad, isn't he?" Trace asked. Katia agreed before she gave him a kiss on the way out.

Inside of the package was a rulebook, a deck of 4x8 cards with information on each racer, an exclusive passport granting me access to reserved jets and hotel rooms sponsored by Four Seasons, and a QR coded vid-drive that could be scanned and downloaded onto any iCube. Trace swiftly pulled his out, which created a holographic image of a man in a green and blue suit with long blue slit back hair, trimmed blue beard, and green eyes. It was the famous Versa commentator, Gradite without his Goldlyn partner, Tokyn.

"Hello competitors, if my appreciable appearance of Earth hasn't given it away already, my name is Gradite Monroe, here to give you the ground rules for… Four Seasons. This year, we've got competitors around the globe returning for the second, third, and fourth time with others debuting for the first. Among these competitors: a golden streak, an unchained legacy, a Celtic brute, an Aboriginal avenger, and A Nightmare on Elm, go figure. The rules should be clear for both parties when I state that this is a Non… Killing… Merce… based… series. This won't be the first or last time you hear those words either, so try to keep them somewhere safe.

"Just like every other Pro League series on Earth, there's a point system to help separate the fifty-two racers. Points will be decided over the first three outta four weeks of competition. After the trio of weeks, thirty-six competitors will be eliminated with the top-sixteen moving on to the Semi-finals. Similarities might be found in the pointing system from all parties, but don't you dare feel that there's an unfair advantage of being a returner, because for the first time in Four Seasons history, the amount of Naturis tracks are being increased from eight to… get ready for it… are you ready yet… a whopping sixteen tracks, scattered all over the series with the exception of the first week.

"The returners are familiar with the series' structure, but I'll elaborate for the newcomers. The first week is what we like to call the 'Fall' week, a week filled with amusement park themed races, you know, areas like: Arabia, Neotokyo, Dessnia, and so on. Typically, the favored week that gets you into the rhythm of things. The second week is known as the 'Winter' week and every track in this timeline will be Naturis. Held in dangerous locations like: Antarctica, Greenland, Nunavut, and parts of Asia. This won't be a kind week for the cold-blooded, no, that kindness isn't given until the third, otherwise known as the 'Spring' week. This'll be a warm week that all racers will enjoy, weather-wise at least. A lot of it takes place in the Amazon, but if you're lucky, you'll be competing in either Australia or the Islands of Samoa. The fourth and final week will only be for the top-sixteen, labeled as the 'Summer' week, a week where the four elements play their roles for the four groups of four among the four by four. Heh, try saying that ten times faster.

"The four randomly assigned quadrants will be called Water, Wind, Earth, and Fire. Water will compete in an aquatic region with Wind in a windy region, Earth in a rocky region, and Fire in a volcanic region. If you haven't guessed it yet, each of these will be raced on Naturis tracks. The winner of each region will proceed to compete in the final race held at The Twilight of Hera…"

"50…400…" the numbers ranged in my head, forcing me to lose focus on Gradite's monologue. Out of all the race tracks to use for the final race, they picked the one my father died at. Yes, I had done time trials there, but a time trial was much different than an actual competition. It didn't take long for Trace to understand what was ramming through my head as I sunk further in my seat.

"It's happening again, isn't it?" Trace touched upon the sensitive subject, shutting the television grid off. I gave him a slow nod. He was aware of my mental fallouts, it was clearly not the first time I'd had it with the most recent fallout occurring several times at Knightfall. Like at my father's wake, Trace always knew when to tone his demeanor down. Instead of reminding me that my father's death wasn't my fault, like everyone else, Trace suggested that my father only wanted a head start to the Versa Leagues in the afterlife. He even claimed that my father was smoking Christ's ass in a championship race. It was kind of funny. Trace sold the afterlife league to a point where he could've made the sanest individual commit suicide just to join my father in the promise land. But like he said, that was a place neither him nor I planned on going for a long time. In the meantime, I had to fight these traumatic moments. I swore to all the Galactic Gods and Goddesses that they were getting worse the older I got, and Trace could definitely see it. "Was it The Twilight of Hera?"

"Yeah, it was just a minor trigger, but I'm fine. I think I've got the layout down. I'm curious who the other fifty competitors are. There's me, Midas, and…"

"Well, there's you, Midas, and… oh boy…" he commented with an unpleasant reaction after grabbing the deck of racers. His mix of facial expressions transitioned from disturbed to joyful, and back to terrified. He went on to finish the deck with a surprised look. "Okay… there's a lot of big names in this deck. There's Midas, Kira, Meta, Beta, and believe it or not Zane, the crazy son of a bitch. He's tough, I'll give the beaked-freak that."

"Yeah, I already know their styles and have beaten each of them, except for Midas."

"True, but then there's other big names like Warlock, Creed, Law, Krueger and… shit… The Carnivore Family."

"I'll handle them."

"You don't get it, these guys are Galactica worthy when it comes to ruthlessness and finesse. They're gonna give you and Midas a run for your money," Trace claimed going into further details about some of the information on each card.

———————————————

Name: Warlock Neit
Sobriquet: "The Devil's Shamrock"
Weight: 317 lbs (143.8 kg)
Height: 6'8½" (2.04 m)
Native: Dublin, Ireland

Appearance: A tall bodybuilding-caliber Irishman with a long red braided beard, carrying a spiked-up mohawk. His skin is pale, bringing more glimmer to his hazel eyes, but don't let his eye color fool you, it's typically covered in red.

Bio: A fearless Irish-born fighter from Dublin who doesn't mind losing a few limbs on the way to the Finals. Has mastered the art of war in races with a reputation of giving others hell on and off the track.

Highlight: Four Seasons 2248 - Qualified in the Water Quadrant of the Semi-finals, only to lose to Nicholas Hauschka in a heartbreaking fashion during the last meter of the race. Not taking the results kindly, Warlock remarkably ripped off Hauschka's arm, continuously batting him in the head with it until Hauschka was unconscious. To this day, Nicholas Hauschka has been unable to compete in another race, suffering from traumatic brain damage.

Trace's Comments: "His last name, Neit, is actually the name for the Celtic God of War, so it's probably best that you don't get on his bad side."

———————————————

Name: Credo "Creed" Velasquez
Sobriquet: "The Paled Crucifier"
Weight: 197 lbs (89.4 kg)
Height: 6'2" (1.88 m)
Native: Las Heras, Argentina

Appearance: An albino priest with short brown hair. Has shining blue eyes and a barbed wire tattoo that runs diagonally, vertically, and horizontally across parts of his face.

Bio: A racer that is pretty handy with the set of hatchets he carries in every race. One of the best racers when it comes to close-contact fighting and has had some success in Broken Velocity, a series where killing isn't prohibited.

Highlight: Broken Velocity 2246 - The Argentinian had an unforgettably gory debut performance. In a Wreath-based series, he purposefully had his eyes set on the defending champ, Hunter Lansley. During the race's climax, Creed sliced open Lansley's stomach, pulling out parts of his large intestines. The wound did not kill Lansley, instead, it left him vulnerable for an even worse fatality involving Creed wrapping Lansley's intestines around his neck, dethroning the champ by choking Hunter to death.

Trace's Comments: "To sum things up, he's a walking contradiction."

Name: Lawson "Law" Pierce
Sobriquet: "The Corona's Bandit" & "The Reapa's Revolva"
Weight: 203 lbs (92.1 kg)
Height: 6'4" (1.93 m)
Native: Aputula, Australia

Appearance: Always has a mask with grayly fractured skull designs on it along with a cowboy hat to cover his silver eyes. Aside from the presentational appearance, not too many have seen the outlaw without a mask lately.

Bio: An Aboriginal bandit from the outback who has been known for bringing guns and spiked lassos to each race. A calculative racer that never misses a shot whether that's with a molten magnesium-filled bullet or a photo-finish; he's always in the right place at the right time. Unfortunately, he's recently been on the wrong side of tragedy regarding the death of his older brother, Orin. A death in the previous Four Seasons series that has built controversy over the offseason and has created a movement called The Full Metal Jacket, a group filled with outraged fans seeking justice for the Pierce family.

Highlight: Oceanic Typhoon 2248 - In the most popular Wreath-based series in the Pro Leagues, Law entered an FMJ-filled stadium and left a bloody highlight reel for The Golden Scion, in a competitive 10-man finale, becoming champion as the last man standing covered in everyone's blood except his own in what has always been labeled as The Ironman's Series. Trent Green was probably the only racer who stood a chance against Law's onslaught but ended up getting hung by Law's lasso on the final loop of the race. The words, "Four Seasons" were carved onto his stomach by Law's knife for the world to see.

Trace's Comments: "Law's a bloodthirsty racer searching for vengeance. Due to the anarchy that happened in the Semi-finals a couple years ago, he blames Midas for his brother's death and is looking to even the score. It's an inevitable clash that I reckon you avoid."

Name: Krueger
Sobriquet: "The Clawed Cardiac"
Weight: N/A
Height: 6'0" (1.83 m)
Native: Unknown
Appearance: Unknown

Bio: An unknown racer who has recently made a name for themselves in the offseason. Has been smoking competitors in races while disappearing off the track after. Notorious for the unorthodox pair of thickly sharp krone claws used to slice open a countless number of faces. A racer that has been titled as Krueger due to the resemblance of the horror icon, Freddy Krueger.

Highlight: Bermuda's Locker 2249 - Walked into the Wreath-based series as an unknown, coming out as the grim reaper's love interest, responsible for the deaths of most of their competitors.

Persian Gulf 2250 - In the conclusion of the Merce-based series, Krueger spent the entire race toying with The Prince of Arabia, resulting in a finish with Krueger implanting their claws into the spina of the prince's suit, somehow shutting it down inches prior to the finish line. Krueger's unfamiliar weapon increased his career record to an undefeated 20-0.

Trace's Comments: "Krueger has to be the hottest racer coming into this series with an undefeated record, or at least we think he's undefeated. We only have clips of him dominating racers in the Persian Gulf. A lot of people have money on this racer, so they're undoubtedly a racer we need to keep our eyes on."

Trace didn't give much info on the Carnivores. He just told me that they are a mobile freak show with a few aliens in their family. Off the track, they were involved in a circus located in Dessnia and tended to bring some of their idiosyncratic talents to the races. He also told me that they'd won the numbers game with ten qualifying for the series.

"This is all of the competitors. The forty-seven qualifiers, the three wild cards, the one supplement, and the three-time defending champ," Trace concluded.

'Who are the wild card racers?"

"It's some young Italian chick, an advocate from your favorite company, *Ion*, and the prince who squared up against Krueger. They're being brought back by Earth's Pro League Committee after failing to qualify the first time around," Trace explained, giving me the gist of each racer. I could tell that this was a series he really wanted to be a part of from all of the research. I just hoped I didn't let him and myself down going forward. "Once you're done with all of your final touches here, pack up because you and I are heading to the airport. The opening race is held in Dessnia, Florida."

"Wait what? Why? It's Wednesday, and the series doesn't start until Monday," I pleaded, rising out of my chair from the sudden change of events.

"Why? Correct me if I'm wrong but weren't you late to Knightfall?"

"Man, you gotta let that tardiness shit go," I replied, falling back into my chair.

"11:00 P.M., be at the airport at 11:00 P.M.," Trace ordered while snatching the tickets from the racer's package, taking away my freedom of choice before leaving. Admittedly, I was nervous for this series, my first Pro League competition, and I was dealing with a lot of racers who had trained day and night for it in unfamiliar territories.

When the afternoon came to a close and my Atlas' touches were finalized and ready for departure, I handed off my responsibilities of the nest to Katia. She wished me good luck and, surprisingly, told me to keep Trace out of trouble. I agreed to it, but didn't promise anything, thankfully. Giving her the power was a bit weird, though. I mean, this was going to be the first time I'd ever been this far away from the nest for a lengthy time-period. The feeling really sank in after talking to the pair of mechanics. They were more than willing to deliver care-packages of ergogenics, replacement parts for the Atlas, or new products in general. They gave me a bag of flare grenades as a distress for the packages, something I didn't expect and couldn't help but hug them for. They'd been the primary advocates for this workshop and myself for a while now, so it was time to make them proud. The last person I gave my farewell to was the prodigal son himself waiting at the entrance surrounded by his posse. We shook each other's hand, slowly bringing them in for a respectful hug. I told him that I was going to kick his ass again if he placed any bets on me. He responded by saying, "Good because I'm gonna return the favor in a couple years when I compete in Four Seasons!" I could only smirk at the promise, knowing he was currently close for competition. He was growing up, but when he was in the big-boy leagues, I would be ready. At the moment, his support was all I needed, and it was something I couldn't take for granted. I had to live in every single moment, surrounded by those I loved because I'd never know when it would be my last.

ACT II
CHAPTER 2

DESTINED
TO DIE

THE FLIGHT TO DESSNIA WASN'T TOO BAD; IT WAS POSTPONED BY A DAY BECAUSE OF THE TROPICAL STORM PASSING THROUGH, BUT OVERALL IT WAS GOOD. It was my first time in a private jet. As for Trace, well, let's just say that he knew exactly where to find the stash of whiskey on the plane. He didn't drink too much though. It was very easy for him to turn one drink into a dozen. While he enjoyed his minor shot of whiskey, I ventured onto the Way/Point grid of my iCube. My profile was recently updated by Trace and Katia, Post-Knightfall, changing my avatar into a charcoal knight, screaming, breaking out of its chains. The avatar's "club" was the nest's parking lot. The knight's hoisted arms aligned with the wingspan of the blue jay, providing a neon-blue outline around the avatar. The fresh additions increased the number of followers from 672k to 2.6 million over the month. An impressive feat from someone not too great with social platforms, and despite the vast amount of cyberpunks who roamed through the platforms. Some of them had tried to infiltrate my profile under a Thorax-driven alias, an issue Trace demolished with the help of a few goons in the Calumet area capable of searching and destroying the cyberpunks. Because of Trace, the basement, or in this case the sewers, to my profile were empty compared to Midas' who still had a silver-eyed bandit in the shadows. If enemies could come into our lives with ease, then why was it so difficult to befriend the world? All my life, even with the McGuire name, it had been a struggle. The 95 friends were laughable compared to the 1.1k in Midas' profile or the 2.1k in his sister's profile. Was it because of looks, personality, power, luck? I know for a fact that it wasn't because of money, otherwise I wouldn't have had the lethargic problem.

Times like this were when I hated how socially inept I was on grids like Way/Point. For crying out loud, I was on a jet ride to the biggest racing series on the planet, and all I could do was stare at the ocean-blue eyes of Miss Earth's avatar, crisper than the great barrier reef. If a newsfeed was to claim that she was extraterrestrial, the world wouldn't gasp. It was the only logical answer for how gorgeous she was—nearly impossible for a

Terran to resemble a goddess. A friend request appeared above her avatar. Way/Point's advice for me to send her anything if not a simple wave. I swiped the guidance and profile completely away as if I was on the dating grid, senZation. I remembered this one time when Kira accidentally matched on the senZation grid with Zane. On the senZation grid, people provided their profiles with the best four-dimensional holograms of themselves with a plausible summary in the bio tab usually underneath the image. Kira herself was equally as beautiful as she was intelligent, so someone matching with her was second-nature. Now as for Zane, he was, of course, a bit different. Apparently prior to his Versa days, this dude had some modeling gigs, and believe it or not was actually hot. A jaw-dropping eight-pack was hidden underneath the corium with pecks arching out to the width of a football and shoulders inflating into a bowling ball. The hunkish image of The Raven quickly attracted Kira before she read the name, damn-near sinking her into a coma. Oh man, Trace and I to this day held it against her. We could be brain dead and still somehow find a way to remember the frozen look on her face after realizing that she had matched Zane Maddox. It made Trace and I pass a kidney stone from how hard we were crying on the ground. For what it's worth, she found happiness in love after all. Since Knightfall, her and Beta had had lustful momentum. Beta's charm was something Trace and I couldn't trifle with anymore because he got the yes from The Cerebral Assassin and hadn't looked back since. As her new training partner, Beta had improved her skills, boosting her stats to an unimaginable level. She'd been on an exhibitional hot streak, winning seven straight races to acquire an entry into Four Seasons along with Beta and his twin. It was because of Beta that Kira was smarter than she'd ever been. Who would've thunk it.

Resting on the thought of love pushing a racer to incomprehensible levels, I took a closer look at the deck of racer's qualified for the Pro League series. The holographic cards had the pictures of each competitor in their suits on one side with their information on the other.

The first in the deck of racers was Midas.

Name: Midas Gold
Sobriquet: "The Golden Scion"
Weight: 186 lbs (84.4 kg)
Height: 6'2½" (1.89 m)
Native: Nuuk, Greenland

Appearance: A Greenlandic buzz-cut racer with a faded beard, fairly light skin, and special heterochromia iridum eyes that carry red and blue within the iris.

Bio: As a three-time Four Seasons Champion, Midas stands on top of the mountain as Earth's best racer, still defending his title. Some of that success has come from the innovative gear received from his father, Luke Gold. Undoubtedly one of the most dominant racers in Four Seasons history with one issue that developed towards the climax of the previous series regarding the deaths of several racers at Blackstone Park.

Highlight: Four Seasons 2244 - Not taken seriously as a top-tier racer at the age of 16, Midas was able to catch everyone's eye in the Semi-finals and Finals, dethroning the champion at the time, Orin Pierce, creating one of the most exciting rivalries in Four Seasons history.

Four Seasons 2246 - Defending his title at the age of 18, luck was not on his side. With all the focus on the Gold vs Pierce rivalry, it was easy to forget the return of the Gora sisters, an Egyptian kinfolk notorious for their homicidal tendencies. Clear on teaching the young champion a lesson, Midas showed his special agility, surviving attacks from machetes, chainsaws, and bullets eventually defeating the sisters in their own game, resulting in their banishment from the Pro League series due to their life-threatening offense against many racers throughout the series. The elimination of the Gora sisters opened the door for the Gold vs Pierce rivalry in the Finals, leading to a repeat on Midas' behalf.

Four Seasons 2248 - In a series with the lack of threat, Midas easily became the first racer in Four Seasons history to three-peat, obtaining the very rare hat trick of titles after being the lone survivor of an unfortunate technical error within the series in the Fire Quadrant, controversially claiming the lives of three racers, including the talented, Orin Pierce.

No wonder why Midas seemed so familiar.

"When were you going to tell me that Midas is Luke's son?" I immediately questioned Trace after he was done with the whiskey.

"Didn't want the drama," he replied while placing the drink away.

"You know that this is going to be one of the top stories of the series. Son vs Son, Legacy vs Legacy. They'll make the most out of what they can."

"Well, who won the match-up when it was Father vs Father?" Trace inquired while trying to frame the hovering headline in his head.

"I'd like to say that my dad won, but he didn't. He died by the hand of a Rokian wearing Gold's product."

"The match-up this time is different, though. History won't repeat itself."

"We'll see," I stated before he could take a seat across from me. As stressed as I was, I would have been in denial if I thought that Midas' presentation wasn't cool. He had a golden Guy Fawkes-masked helmet sharing the same black mustache smile. The rest of his suit continued the golden look in *The Golden Evolution's* 2250 Cronus with black three-dimensional lightning strikes orbiting down the left arm like a cape.

I continued my examination of the other racers by going through the deck some more. The next racer in the deck was Warlock Neit. He had on *Tsarina's* dark-green 2250 Celtic with a clawed red paint design on the helmet. There were also a lot of more violent designs to the suit like the sliced open stomach design on his abdominises, as if it had returned from war. His representing colors were basically shamrock-green and bloody-red based off of this presentation.

The next racer in the deck was one that I didn't recognize. The racer had on a black, crimson, and gold 2230 Corallinus, an aerobic suit with a lot of artillery. The exosuit had an insane amount of gold bullets and shells wrapped around it that auto-fed themselves into the equipped guns on both arms. The right arm had a golden 0-gauge plasma-filled shotgun while the other arm had a golden 10-barrel rotary machine gun. I wasn't sure who gave off the better war-like presentation, this racer or Warlock. I turned the card around to see who this racer was, most likely another threat.

Name: Jackal "Jack" Amaryllis
Sobriquet: "The Blackjack"
Weight: 233 lbs (105.7 kg)
Height: 7'2" (2.18 m)
Native: Dessnia, Florida

Appearance: A man that has been named the most attractive Carnivore. With long blonde hair, hazel eyes, and a black trimmed beard, resembling the figure of a Norse God.

Bio: The weapons specialist who brings some of his tricks from the carnival of Dessnia onto the race track. One of ten members from the Carnivore family competing in this series. Arguably the best Terran member of the family when it comes to racing, holding a Red Sea Classic championship in his background of accolades.

Highlight: Red Sea Classic 2248 - Survived a devastating sandstorm of the Sahara Desert in the Finals of the Merce-based series as the last man standing, supposedly having no connection to the disappearance of all the other seven contenders in the finale.

"No connections to the disappearance of all the other racers, so basically we can assume he killed them. Why the hell am I competing in this damn series? It's filled with alleged and unalleged killers!" I angrily stated, slamming the deck of cards onto the table. I also didn't know if unalleged was an actual word, but for the sake of my point, it would do.

"Ah, I see that you're aware of Mr. Amaryllis," Trace chuckled while organizing the cards scattered all over the table.

"This isn't a joke, Trace. Someone's destined to die in this series. If I wanted that person to be me, I'd be competing in Galactica instead."

"Technically, you can't compete in Galactica…"

"Cut it with the smartass comments."

"Chill out, Craven, we were gonna cross this bridge sooner or later. You're a great racer who doesn't have to worry about getting killed. To be honest, you might not even see him in a race because of the scoring system, so again, chill out. You're in control of your own destiny," Trace preached to calm my nerves. I gave a few nods of approval to show that I was back to normal. He continued to clean up all of the scattered cards which caused me to see the one of an alien.

"A fucking Rokian's competing?" I quickly uttered, picking up the card to take a closer look at the alien named Primax. I could only wonder how I'd mentally walk away from racing a Rokian, if I could walk at all afterwards.

"I told you that the Carnivores had a few aliens in their family," Trace reminded me as I flicked the card at him for forcing me into this series. To add to the bad luck, we were now landing at the airport of Dessnia. There were loads of people inside the hangar for our jet. It was the media. The sun had just risen, and they were already here to annoy me. Media—a disease that plagued every racer. Fortunately for us, there was a lot of security present in the hangar, pushing them out of the way. The guards opened up a pathway leading to a black hovering limousine with tinted windows.

"Wow, a limo. I've never been in one of those before. Looks like this series is really turning around after all," I sarcastically uttered to Trace who gave a displeased look, quickly reaching for a glass of champagne. The guards placed all of our stuff in the trunk when we got into the limo. They also told me that my suit would be transported to a private locker room near the starting line, a spot that I could have all to myself in case I needed to do any pre-race rituals. Once I was seated in the limo, I tried to tell the driver to take us to the Marriott, but Trace instantly suggested a different location, the Lotus.

"What's so damn special about the Lotus?" I asked. It was one of the many hotels sponsored by Four Seasons, but it was not like Trace to gravitate towards high-class things.

"Umm...it's a classier hotel, and they serve a mean raptr there," he replied while rubbing parts of his belly. "Trace hungry as hell right now."

God, I hated it when he spoke in third person. Obviously up to something, I curiously laid back to see how his plan was going to play out. Riding through the main streets of Dessnia helped me remember the beauty in this spectacle of the sunny city. A sleepless land with an amusement park on every block and hologramers of Dessnia's hottest stars floating over every palm tree like a drone, welcoming visitors to the happiest place on Earth. Embracing the upcoming series, some of the trees actually had holograms of racers instead. The message of Four Seasons didn't truly sink in until I saw the hologramer of myself in the Atlas, contracting its body out of the broken chains. The feeling of pride was quickly tainted by a holoboard sign, recently hacked by Re-Versables. The sign had a political cartoon of their president, Jess Prey as the Statue of Liberty, but instead of holding a torch, she was holding up a bloody sword, pointed at the first Rokian ship to land on Earth and a beheaded Rokian in her other hand. This is another reason why I kept my workshop hidden in Calumet. The activists were just as extreme as the picture and would do whatever it took to destroy the sport of Versa.

On a brighter note, we were instantly greeted with care upon our arrival at the Lotus, the kind gestures continued with some of the employees coming out to take care of our belongings. Now that my hands were free from that task, I ventured to the front desk, claiming one of the reserved rooms. I was given some interesting intel about where we were staying. Informed that our room was directly below Midas' penthouse, Trace had awakened my internal demon. I was not even going to give him props for his pitiful attempt at a surprised look.

"Well, if it isn't The Unchained Knight and The Ultimate Opportunist. What a pleasure," a casually dressed woman expressed while walking up to us from the courtyard of the hotel. She had long bright-blonde hair with brown hair layered underneath, and icy-blue eyes with black eyeliner that made them shine a little more.

"Wow…umm…who are you?" Trace asked, flustered by the lady's attractiveness.

"Azzrelia Perris, but most of my clients call me Dr. Perris. I specialize in Psychiatrics," she explained. She was very pretty, but her looks could not counter the fact that she was a doctor. Over the years, I'd learned that there were two types of doctors; ones who promoted the Re-Versable movement because of the incurable injuries like paralysis, and others who wished to capitalize on the fortune of curing said injury.

"If you're here because you hate the races, fuck off," I insisted while leading Trace and I away.

"No, I'm actually all for the races. I'm here for a different type of reason," she said, stopping Trace and I. "A lot of doctor's complain about the expenses when it comes to helping all of the racers, but I feel like there should be attention placed on the racers who don't get injured. Kind of like you two, with the recent exception of Mr. Burretta. I feel like we need to place our focus on the condition of each racer's head. The Terran brain can't withstand the amount of punishment some racers endure. That's why I'm here, offering my expertise of work for those of you interested."

"So… you're thinking that we might be slowly deteriorating, mentally?" Trace questioned, trying to understand the proposal.

"Sort of, it's more of an examination of the racer's head. Overtime, I've recorded multiple racers on multiple occasions, slowly documenting permanent mental malfunctions due to the races. I'm trying my best to prevent that so racers like you two can have extensive careers," Azzrelia claimed while handing us her business card.

"A mental illness would explain a lot about Trace," I joked while taking her card. She told us about the offered therapy sessions, too. It was something to think about, but when it came to the races, I thought he and I were mentally sane for now. The encounter with Azzrelia did cheer me up a bit considering I was still a little pissed at Trace. The media was going to be all around the Lotus due to the fact that our room was below Midas'. The bit of anger I had swiftly faded away once we stepped into the massive suite Four Seasons had reserved for the racers under a first come, first serve basis. The whole suite had a platinum theme to it. Platinum walls, platinum tables, platinum floors, and they even had a platinum toilet.

"You see, Craven, this is why I chose the Lotus," Trace preached as the employees transported our stuff into the room.

"Oh, cut the shit, Trace."

"Brotherly love, Craven, that's what brotherly love is. Honestly, you know what will cheer you up? A medium-rare raptr with hash browns on the side," Trace insisted while glancing at one of the employees.

"I'll have that done right away sir," the employee said as they left the room. I decided to ignore Trace by stepping onto the suite's balcony. It had a good view of Dessnia, a view

I remembered so intimately. The castle's appearance was no different than the one framed at home. My father planned out the family trip so beautifully. My mother had always been a fan of Mickey Mouse, from her days stuck in Australia, hoping to claim a stuffed animal of the icon. An animatron toy version of the mouse could be found anywhere, but the classically stuffed version on the other hand was a bit more challenging. That week, there was only one throughout the whole park stationed at the courtyard of the castle floating as high as fifty feet. My father's undying love towards my mother soared higher than the castle's tallest tower scraping through the clouds as my father competed in a quiz-based game against a few other contestants with the game-winning prize none other than the stuffed animal. I remembered my mother relaying answers to my father who didn't know jack-shit about anything Dessnia related. The host allowed the relay of answers out of pity. My father was a headless chicken stuck in no-man's land that day, but he did win the stuffed animal, so what more could a loving husband ask for? Hell, what more could I ask for? The opening race was at the happiest place on Earth, holding the happiest memory of my father. That had to mean something, considering where the final race was at, if I even got that far.

"Guess what?" Trace asked, joining me on the balcony. He had an envelope in his hands.

"What? Are they out of hash browns?" I sarcastically replied.

"No, thank goodness," he answered in relief. "You were invited to the party that Midas is hosting tomorrow night."

I applauded Trace's D-leveled acting, but his pre-season plan was executed to perfection.

"You're a clever man, Trace. A clever man who doesn't give a damn if I'm late to this series, just one that cares about my attendance to this golden party."

"Well, I heard Gabriella's gonna be there. So, excuse me for being Cupid," he stated. "And besides, some of the other racers are gonna be there too."

I couldn't believe it. For once, the man actually had a point and an answer for my rant earlier on the jet ride. I needed to head into this series with allies, and this party issued a buffet of them. The thought of Miss Earth being at the party didn't offset the amount of reporters pitting Midas and I against each other like the Montagues and Capulets, but the realistic thing was to put to rest this Cinderella story of me catching the prettiest girl on the planet. Entertaining the idea would only make the failures that much harder to bear.

"I'll go, but it's only because I desire friends."

I heard Trace mutter "And a date" to himself after I was done talking. We spent the rest of the day relaxing because we knew that there was a great chance of a never-ending night tomorrow.

ACT II
CHAPTER 3

ICONS

WHAT STARTED OFF AS A PEER-PRESSURED TRIP TO FLORIDA, EVENTUALLY TURNED INTO AN IN-HOME STUDY SESSION ABOUT THE TALENTS OF ALL THE COMPETITORS USING THE VERSARCHIVE, A CLOUD DATABASE FOR ANY RACER TO LOOK AT LIKE THE DECK OF CARDS. It provided descriptive backgrounds on the racer's weapons, gadgets, and exosuit attributes such as top speeds, velocities, and so on. After dissecting the highlights, I was able to pick up on some of the tactics each racer carried into their races. One habit I found interesting came from Creed whenever, and I mean whenever, a nearby racer leapt into the air. They were met with a hatchet thrown into their torso for target practice. I mean, Creed never missed once. Another tactic I discovered came from Zane during one of his recent exhibitional races. It involved him utilizing the robotic raven as an ally in competition by having the bird fly around the racers in front of him with a blade coming out of the bird's mouth. The robotic raven sometimes faked the bladed kamikaze forcing a racer to avoid short-cuts, and other times it was ready for impact—a ballistic approach that wasn't nearly as soul-punching as an FMJ-filled crowd at every race Law entered. Like a cult, each of them wore an eye-covering cowboy hat and a mouth-hiding bandana, standing tall next to one another waiting for their maniac of a messiah to step out of the shadows and into their light. Every track Law raced on felt like his home as the FMJs took over the atmosphere, usually scaring off the other fan-bases from the brutal assaults even the security guards had not found an answer for—another gallon of gasoline for the Re-Versables.

There was something unique about each racer, but one specific talent had my full attention. It was Krueger. There was so much to study when it came to The Clawed Cardiac. For starters, he shared Zane's craftsmanship of a homemade exosuit nowhere to be found on the market. I gave The Raven credit for his integration of adrenia, but the talent receiving the gold medal at this year's science fair had to be Krueger. Their unnamed and unsullied suit was primarily black and had a secondary pallet of red manipulated in a way I'd never seen before. The secondary color was used as an x-ray of their entire body. Something I thought would be a disadvantage because, if a bone like the ribcage breaks, then a racer had to try their best to conceal the injury, but how Krueger used it was so diabolically impressive.

He would have the x-ray show a broken arm or leg, attracting other racers to attack its false fracture. The illusion would always confuse the attackers, leaving vital sections of their exosuit vulnerable for Krueger to slice open. That was just one tactic, the next was psychological warfare. Perks to having a man-made suit was the incorporation of native technology like the hologramer embedded in Krueger's black helmet, transitioning into any image he desired. Krueger's preferred look was a red Jack-o-lantern, but it would sometimes change into a horrifying image of their opponent's loved one.

Don't get me wrong, Krueger was freaky as hell, but I couldn't help but take notes on someone as intriguing as him. It actually made me lose track of time. The sky had already gone through a full cycle of light-blue, light-orange, light-pink, flaming-orange, and black with white pimples of stars. Trace actually had to be the one to break my trance on the racer named, Krueger, helping me bring my focus back onto the real agenda of the evening, increasing my friend's list. To be honest, my heart pounded harder than a load of bass drums during a Blue Man Group performance because there was a chance that Krueger would attend the party. I'd give the man my goddamn workshop if it meant being friends in this series.

Thankfully the party didn't require a specific dress code because I hated dressing up. It was just something I never felt comfortable doing, plus the first time I ever wore a suit was to my dad's funeral. That played a factor. Never deprive me of my blue jay jacket, was how I saw it. Doing that was a quick reservation to my Way/Point sewer.

Welcome to all racers and fans as you are, the invitation said. With the amount of Re-Versables and FMJs in the area, I reckoned it was too welcoming. Trace and I expected a long night, hoping it would be in a good way. But not too good, as I'd probably lose my shit if I saw Krueger there. The thought made me anxious of the venue, forcing Trace to calm me down, an unusual sight as it typically went the other way around. He didn't want us to appear desperately early. His plan was for us to wait for several minutes after the music started playing to finally head upstairs. A boring ass plan that made birdwatching look like a climatic event.

Once we arrived, the doors to the penthouse were already open, and we were greeted by some of the guards at a golden entrance. The theme grew into gold this, gold that, not to mention, Midas' last name was Gold. But it didn't stop there, oh no, I wish. The walls were painted gold, and the lights were slightly dimmed, which made the golden colors razzle and dazzle. There were also art pieces of the Greek King Midas painted onto the ceiling. As a racer, we were supposed to give off a creative presentation, but this was taking things to a whole new level. A great example of a racer who provided the right amount of presentation was Zane, but this surpassed The Raven's threshold.

The setup to this event was similar to the after party back at Knightfall. There were tables all around filled with the same extraterrestrial entrées and desserts. The only difference was that there was a dance floor occupied by most of the guests. But at the center of the room was Midas in a black-and-gold tuxedo, primarily black. He stood beneath a chandelier, so the spotlight was literally on him. The man was practically a goddamn Great Gatsby. It didn't take long for the wealthy and proud icon to notice Trace and I.

"Well, well, well. If it isn't The Unchained Knight himself, Craven McGuire, son of Crank McGuire. It is an honor to finally meet you," Midas greeted while reaching his hand out to shake mine. "And of course, The Ultimate Opportunist himself Trace Burretta. I am truly sorry about your accident. I was really looking forward to racing the both of you."

"Likewise," Trace replied.

"So, what do you think of the party?" Midas asked for first impressions.

"Dunno yet, I'm still trying to figure out the theme."

"Good one, the party might be an extension of my name, but the main idea was to get every racer here so that they could have a good time before things got serious again," he explained as he glanced around at the party. "I was actually hoping that Krueger would show up."

"Me too," I blurted.

"You're friends with Krueger?" Trace asked Midas.

"No, far from it apparently. Krueger has a problem with me. He claims that I'm fake and that I've cheated on my way to the top. He sends me messages, claiming that my luck is running out. The man is treating me like some type of Versa tyrant. To counterattack the ignorant propaganda, I had some of my security send messages all around Dessnia to every hotel Krueger could possibly be staying at. I welcome the anonymous figure with open arms because it's about time he faced me like a man," Midas explained concluding with a slightly angered tone.

"Well, you know what the people are saying these days, they believe he can be another threat to your title!" Trace exclaimed.

"The Gora sisters were a threat, not this wannabe. Racers like this talk the talk but never walk the walk. He'll fade away, and I honestly can't wait to see the look on his face when I pry open his false identity of a mask, finally showing him and the world who I really am once again, The Golden Fucking Scion," Midas promised, showing a less humbled side.

"Pride comes before the fall," Trace responded at the promise.

"Maybe, but with all the tension set aside, I'm primarily looking forward to racing you Craven. I'm pretty sure it'll be me against you in the Finals. Mano a Mano, Champion vs Champion, The New Legacy vs The Legendary Legacy," Midas exclaimed with Trace agreeing. He was already excited for this series, so Midas' words acted more like adrenia. Now catching our eyes were the trio of racers entering the party. It was Kira, who was with the twins.

"Well, make yourselves comfortable. I'm gonna greet the new arrivals," Midas said, heading to the entrance but quickly stopping to issue one more thing. He and Trace must've been talking lately on Way/Point because they were now discussing an important poker game that was supposed to be going on tonight.

Once Midas was gone, Trace and I drifted apart. He was here to have a good time. As for me, I was here to make some new allies. He left me with a statement about choosing my allies wisely because I might regret it later. It was a good point, but I was confident that I could take care of any problems that might occur. When it came to meeting new people, I was comfortable. I was secure that I could befriend the first soul I met.

The first place I checked was the bar, I knew there had to be a few racers there. The bartender was serving a silent man in a thin white jacket. He had pale skin, blue eyes and a barbed wire tattoo that went across parts of his face. I couldn't see much more of his face covered with a hoodie. What I could see was the diamonded rosary wrapped around their left hand with a drink in the other. Creed, *the walking contradiction.*

"If you're so one with God, then why do you contradict everything he stands for?" I asked him, requesting the same drink he was having, whiskey. A sardonic smile stretched across Creed's face distorting some of the barbed wire tattoos. His cheekbones didn't have any baby fat either, so the retracting linings were similar to a walrus' neckline.

"I love my God, but the world has changed, and there are too many beliefs in this universe to actually decide which one of them are true. I honestly chose Christianity because their God was the most forgiving. I may not believe it in the same way as most, but I respect it more than a lot of corrupted shit in this universe," he preached to me in a voice that was soft and low.

"I guess that kind of makes sense... a little," I replied remembering he was a priest too. Jesus, I wondered what church he homed in Argentina.

"We all have our opinions," he said, taking another sip of whiskey. Just in time for the bartender to grant me the same beverage.

"Why the tattoos?" I asked because every single time I looked at this guy, my mind tangled from all of the strange combinations going on.

"The Terran body is merely a cocoon. I tattooed it to visually narrate a story the world could understand. It's something people will be able see when I'm in the afterlife, but that won't be for a long time," he explained with a brief chuckle. I swear to every God across the Milky Way that I didn't know why I was laughing. I'd double down on a conversation with Zane any day over this guy.

After ingesting a gulp of whiskey, a Hercules-chiseled brute appeared next to us asking the bartender for some Guinness. I quickly recognized the man once I saw his red braided beard. It was The Devil's Shamrock. Warlock.

"It doesn't take a genius to know what beer you would've asked for," Creed shot at the Celtic.

"Hey sunshine, your snowflake skin is brighter tan my lily-white ass, so tere's no need for us to use words as weapons," Warlock replied, provoking Creed to down the rest of their drink.

"You're right, we've got other options," Creed proposed, pulling out a hatchet from his sleeve. Warlock clearly had been looking for a fight all day because the brute had already braced for Creed's attack with fist-clinching krone knuckles. I quickly got up to intervene and told them that they would have plenty of time to tear each other a new one during the races, and that they shouldn't be getting disqualified over some dumb party. Creed heeded my words by walking away, but Warlock launched a cheap shot by calling Creed, Father Casper.

"I take it you're Warlock?" I asked as we both took a seat at the bar.

"What gave it away, was it tee accent tis time?" he asked in his scrunchy deep voice.

"No, it was your rugged charm," I replied, making him spit out the beer in his mouth with laughter.

"Wow, you're a funny man, I'll have to add tat trait to my resume."

"So, what's your story? How does a clichéd Irish-born, brawny lover of fighting end up in a sport built upon speed?"

"Shit, you've done your homework, MaGuire," he said, taking another drink of beer. His potent accent seemed to make him pronounce my last name differently. "I don't know. I've always loved tee fast-paced action of the sport. It uses strength as a weapon instead of an insult, and brawn doesn't affect your speed if you know how to use it. I guess tat's why I love tee sport."

Finally, a violent racer I could understand. Warlock's brief background made a lot more sense than Creed's.

"So, how about you? What's your story? Is it a tale of vengeance against tee Rokian, or redemption for tee Heart of Earth?"

"I guess I'm not the only one who's done their homework," I responded as he began to raise his drink in agreement. "I guess it's just a story about inevitability, where that might be."

"You know what? You're alright MaGuire," Warlock claimed, and started to compare me to someone he knew back in Ireland named Darragh Bel, who was a bare-knuckle brawler responsible for Warlock's design and presentation. Typically, someone Warlock consulted with jokester qualities always told the brute himself to lighten up from time to time with a few drinks.

I told him that I had a friend like that as I eyed the hibrix-armed man partying on the dance floor with a drink at hand. The joyful look on Trace's face disappeared as screams interrupted the party. Trace joined a huge crowd of people surrounding the problem.

"Finally, some action!" Warlock exclaimed, bulldozing his way through the crowd like a man-size bowling ball knocking down the pin-size people for a strike. I decided to follow him. When we got to the center of the crowd, we could see a man aiming a revolver at a defenseless Midas. The man with a goatee wore a cowboy hat that cast a shadow over the red in his eyes.

"This is payback for Orin," the man yelled at Midas, who didn't really seem to be scared. Was this Law? Fully unmasked?

"Is this really how you want to win?" Midas said, walking up to the gunman so that the nose of the revolver would be planted onto his forehead. "Like some cheap low-life thug who killed the champ before becoming one himself. If so, then stop wasting my fucking time, and pull the goddamn trigger," Midas continued provoking the gunman, but when the man in the cowboy hat pulled the trigger, the revolver only made a clicking sound.

"He's not afraid to end it that way, don't ever forget it. He's gonna make sure you pay. You're gonna burn in hell, and he's gonna be the one who personally sends you there with a one-way ticket," the triggerman announced trying to head towards the exit but was instead tackled and unarmed by the guards.

"It's not Law, just one of his idiotic followers," the guard explained with the FMJ member still pinned into the ground.

"Good, I'd be a bit disappointed if it wasn't," Midas stated with relief as the crowd began to surround him like moths to a flame. The guys fist-bumped him while the ladies caressed his body, sliding their hands south. Heh, they must've had some Grace of Gluttony.

"Wow, right when tis party was getting good, it goes back to shit. I'm gonna need another drink," Warlock uttered, shoving his way back to the bar.

I decided to leave Warlock alone and started heading to the balcony of the Penthouse. It was quiet. The balcony was similar to the one in my room. It had a great view of Dessnia, which was more exuberant at night. The image took me back to the night of my last family vacation. It was a memory of my father and I standing on the balcony of the hotel we were staying at. Staring at the stars above the iconic castle, I told him I was going to be a star one day. Heh, he responded by saying, *If you are, it's because I'm the supernova who created you.* The unforgettable statement brought a lonesome tear down my cheek just like it did then. My grip on the balcony rail tightened.

"Sounds like a party out here," a girl said from behind just in time for the lone tear to dry up. I turned around to see a fair-skinned woman with curly long balayage hair wearing an unzipped leather jacket, tight black jeans, and high-heeled ankle boots, bringing her to match our heights. The golden lights from the Penthouse revealed the unforgettable face of Miss Earth, except that her eyes weren't piercing-blue like her avatar on Way/Point. They were, instead, pomegranate-red and sky-blue like her brother Midas, and she had a small pack of freckles scattered underneath and across her snubbed-nose.

"Well, I was getting tired of all the drama in there," I replied, a little shocked by her presence. My Aphrodite, was she beautiful, flawless. She wasn't even wearing makeup, and her smile damn-near knocked me off of the balcony.

"Same, some fresh air here and there really does the trick, eh?" she asked, stepping next to me. She had a husky voice to fit the badass outfit, not at all what I was expecting. I thought she'd be walking around in a golden dress with a golden tiara and an ego igniting every corner. All I could do was stare at her as she leaned over the balcony to admire the view. When my eyes finally escaped her trance, the first person I saw was Trace through one of the windows smiling at me with two thumbs up. Screw it, I was already in the right position, might as well admire the view, too.

"So, how many enemies does your brother have?"

"It seems like a lot these days, but that's the price you pay when you get your hands dirty," she replied with a sigh.

"What do you mean?"

"That's just how things go in this series for those who have power. Don't get me wrong, he's skilled enough to get into the Semi's, but beyond that, our name pays the way," Gabriella began, explaining how her brother paid off all the officials so that he could be placed in the volcanic race, a track that had a blind spot within the volcano of the race. His acclimated suit had an electromagnetic pulse, a weapon that primarily affected automatically operated suits, which was the majority of suits, including Orin's. There were very few manually operated suits out there, making me think of Krueger, someone who had a man-made suit. "If investigated properly, Midy would be stripped of his titles, but when you've got money and power, well, you can get away with anything."

"And that must be the reason why Krueger's after him too," I added, a bit annoyed at what her brother actually was—a lie. I had to give her some props, she knew a lot about the sport. She actually grinned once Krueger's name was mentioned as if she was his biggest fan.

"How much do you know about Krueger?" she eventually asked leaning a little closer.

"Well, from what I've seen, he's an intriguing racer. I honestly think that he might be a genius. The highlights show an innovatively self-made suit, but that's just the suit. The attachments are a whole 'nother story," I began to babble but restrained myself before getting out of hand.

"How do you know about all of that? The suit? The features?" she asked.

"I own a Versa workshop, so I know every single part of a suit that exists in this world. Everything that's on Krueger's suit is unheard of. I've never seen anything like it. It's ambitious, it's innovative. It's…it's…" I said, now losing restraint, officially nerding out. I started explaining the capabilities of Krueger. There were sleeping giants in Versa, but Krueger was the nightmare that would wake up those giants. I eventually realized that Gabriella was smirking. "What's so funny?"

"It just sounds like you've got a crush on Krueger."

"Ha-ha cute. I just know a Versa Einstein when I see one," I replied to Gabriella as an unintentional reference to Trace's quote a couple days back. The conversation paused as she took a long look at me with her heterochromia eyes. I swear those eyes could cause paralysis in anyone, especially when she was not smiling. She looked like an angel when she was smiling, but when she was not, it was like staring into the eyes of Skorge. There was a devil in there I couldn't seem to comprehend, and it frightened me a bit.

"That's who you are. What's Mr. Knightfall doing at a crappy party like this?" she asked, relieving the tension by making us both laugh.

"I actually came here to find some allies."

"Smart, and how has that been going?"

"I started off well, talking to Creed…" I revealed, giving her the opportunity to fill in the blank, which produced a laugh.

"Let's ditch this party then. I know where you can find some allies," she said, making her way back into the Penthouse. I could continue to watch her walk away in those heels, seeing each hamstring contract in those tight jeans, or I could blindly follow her. As usual, I chose the latter, finding my way out and into the lobby of elevators.

"Where are we going?" I asked her once we were in the elevator.

"To the most famous carnival in Dessnia," she answered as the elevator doors shut. I had an idea of what she was referring to. "Have you ever heard of the Carnivore Family…?"

FIVE OF
A KIND

MY TRUST WAS NOW IN GABRIELLA. I FELT SOMEWHAT INDIFFERENT ABOUT HOW SUDDEN ALL OF IT WAS. I knew how odd that sounded as a racer who dealt with fast-paced situations all the time. But when it came to my life outside of the track, I liked having control, and as of that moment, it was in the hands of another. We weren't even traveling in a limousine. Parked in a lot near the Lotus was her own hover, a 2220 Lamborghini Legalus. This car expressed power due to how rare they were, it was the Hermes of a hovercrafts. I would admit, the lady had class, and good taste.

Our destination took us to the outskirts of Dessnia where hundreds of anorexic trees covered most of the terrain, and skylines of theme parks now resembling the glow of a UFO crash site. The damp Earth exhaled their chilly breath in the quiet evening. The Lamborghini's radio listed its archive of classics. It left me wondering what Gabriella's favorite genre could be. Did she share the same favorites as Kira who always leaned towards Pop, Trace who inherently bonded with Rock, or Zane who matched their ferocity with the hard screams of Metal? For all I knew, she could've been attached to a genre much worse than all of the above combined, Country. *Oh Yahweh, Osiris, Zeus, Juno, Odin, Zata, and any other powerful god above the rest, please, and I mean please don't let her pallet be linked to Country.* I would have nosedived out of this speeding car if she had favored Country. Her hand reached for the radio's control systems. Breaking the silence, I heard the broadcast channel for the Unican Network. On it, a discussion about how the wagers had been conducted. The betting odds of Midas four-peating came out to a whopping 6-1, with an 8-1 ratio for racers like Law and Krueger. I never knew how these geniuses came up with the odds, always thought it was a ridiculous wet dream for the gambling industry.

"What made you get into Versa?" Gabriella asked to finally break the silence between us. "I know your dad was a racer. I just figured it'd shy you away after… Sorry, I'm an idiot for asking."

"No, no, you're fine," I told her, knowing how awkward the feeling may have been. It popped up at least once in most conversations involving my father. People often felt like they were triggering a wire for detonation, fearing the spontaneous combustion of a response. I guess that was how most felt when talking about a deceased loved one. "I just loved the sport too damn much before… and always felt like it was in my blood, as clichéd as that might sound."

"Must be an extraordinary feeling, having the Versa instincts."

"Only when I'm winning," I joked for another glimpse of her smile. "Were you a fan of my father?

"Of course!"

"What was your favorite performance from him?" I questioned to test her knowledge. The typical fan would say *the race that got him the galactic title for Earth, duh*, but he'd had more memorable moments. An answer from her didn't come as quickly as I thought.

"I think it has to be the race against Dante Cage in the Finals of the Barbaric Grit," she finally responded, shining light on a part of his career that not many cared too much about.

"That was an underground series, how the hell did you know about it?"

"Like I said, I was a fan. I believe he debuted the 2185 Perseus against Dante's 2190 Dionysus. I loved everything about that race, Dante brought out the best of Crank, along with Crank bringing out the best of Dante. Both, so smooth with their glides along the track. It was a Wreath-based series, and yet they didn't have to kill anyone for the title. They just let their skill inside the suit speak for itself," she explained, reminding me of an early bright moment in my dad's career. Something not too many people had done. I usually had to look at an old model my father drove for remembrance. The only person who'd ever really told good Versa stories about my father was either Roy or my father himself.

"Percy is actually at my mother's house," I said, noting as Gabriella lost focus of the road, nearly crashing into oncoming traffic.

"No way!"

I responded by pushing the steering wheel downward to avoid an accident.

"Sorry, I just… I just almost had…"

"A nerd attack," I muttered once she drove down an exit. She responded by punching me in the shoulder with a friendly force. I silently stared at her for the reaction, like if you were a nerd towards the sport, accept it. There weren't any Re-Versables nearby.

"Fine, I'm a Versalyte, but don't tell anyone. People tend to treat me like Miss Earth more than a Terran who might be an actual fan of the sport. It just gets a bit annoying sometimes," she vented as a carnival suddenly leapt out of the forest with the array of bright-orange strobes. A giant mouth of a clown's face lay at the carnivals entrance and was the most noticeable landmark at the parking lots entry.

"Well, some people can be ignorant shits. You love Versa racing, own it. Doesn't matter if you're Miss Earth, it's a dumbass title anyways."

"Hey! Actually, it is a pretty dumb title," she accepted once the hovercraft was parked. "Thanks though, hopefully we can find you some allies."

I agreed once we were out of the Lambo, ready to enter the carnival. It was an enormous spectacle, formerly an abandoned theme park previously owned by Dessnia. The owner of the carnival, Joseph Kershaw who refurbished the park, consistently changed the theme of the park for those who were looking for something different. Joseph was actually a mastermind when it came to making something out of nothing; he also had a very kind heart. He was the same guy who notoriously created the theme park called "Limitless" on the north side of Dessnia for those who were handicapped and couldn't afford to properly treat their disabilities with overpriced medical supplies. The name "Limitless" was meant to open an idea of possibilities for those who didn't feel they existed. The thought of his inspiring work inspired good feelings for what might come from this park. A feeling that increased after we walked up to the carnival's front entrance with a bright red and white diagonally-striped sign with its peculiar font, *Step Right Up, Cirque De L'abime. Circus of the Abyss*, Gabriella translated. The proper home of the Carnivore family—a family Joseph Kershaw had co-ownership of, which made me believe that I was actually going to end this night with a new batch of allies added to my Way/Point profile.

Entering the Carnival, I could see Illusional Coasters, Floating Ferris, Four-Dimensional Gaming Stages, Concessions, and every little scratch that builds up an identity of a carnival. Gabriella kept following each Cirque sign, leading us to the back of the park and a humongous black tent with a blue trident at the top. It was connected to an even bigger amphitheater behind it. Spotlights were all around the tent shining into the night sky waving back and forth, attracting an audience of all interests.

From all of the attention, it was a surprise that our identities were kept incognito to the Carnivore's tent. At the entrance, people gathered all around to see one of the performances going on nearby. The performance was taking place at a shooting range on the outskirts of the tent. Hard to see was a tall blonde-haired man holding a .50 Caliber Sniper rifle and asking for volunteers through a hovering mic. There were a few out of the many who were chosen to step up, taking their designated positions along the shooting range. The staff members around the park were setting empty bottles upon each head and shoulder of the chosen, as for the man with the rifle, he had a piece of cloth tied over his eyes.

"That's Jackal. On paper, they say he's one of the best shooters. In reality," Gabriella paused. The staff members commanded the audience to stay silent as a blindfolded Jackal raised the behemoth of a rifle at the chosen on the range. After a brief series of inhales and exhales, he took several shots, exploding each bottle with zero casualties. The exhilarated crowd rapidly cheered as the adrenalized Jackal dropped the rifle down to take off his blindfold.

"Thank you, thank you!" Jackal shouted through all of the joy from the crowd. His voice fluctuated in a garbling manner. "I only ask for you NOT to try that at home, enjoy the rest of the show folks." Jackal embraced the cheers with a supernova smile that could turn a black hole back into a star, but it seemed to vanish once he spotted Gabriella and me in the back of the crowd.

"He is the best; let's head into the tent," Gabriella instructed, leading us into the belly of a freak show beast. An anaconda-like line at the entrance gave me a better look at the towering size of the trident-topped tent. Arguably the same size as The Kodiak's Kolosseum, the tent's four protruding corners around its center cone encapsulated the trident emblem with ones of their own. Amongst the four emblems: a red moon's crescent, a pair of black horns, a giant gray quaver, and a tiny light-blue rayfish-like spaceship. Each emblem must've represented the aliens associated with this family as mentioned by Trace. The sight turned my gut. I'd never been up against an alien before and for once was hoping that the spectators were right about my performances being similar to my father's. He had always made the best racers from the other planets seem like trainees coming to work for the first time. Maybe, I would be able to do the same thing. If only I was paying attention to Gabriella a bit more instead of the giant tent because she was now handing me her leather jacket, revealing the sleeveless black and gold, hollowed-out dress top designed as a V-neck underneath. She tapped on some black mascara beneath her eyelids and added an onyx necklace with a golden dreamcatcher as the emblem, which dropped down to the revealing cleavage.

"Before we go inside, I have to explain one more thing to you," she finally said, coming to the end of her transformation. "I've made some agreements with this family. We're not all friends, but we do have common interests."

"And what interest is that?"

"Making sure my brother loses."

"Okay, so what's the problem?"

"The problem is that the Carnivores have trust issues with the outside world. They're a group of rejects who perform for the accepted. It took them some time to trust someone like Joseph Kershaw, so you can only imagine how long it took them to trust me. A lot of things can go wrong inside."

"Then why are we here?"

"We're here because you need allies, but in return, I'm gonna need your help with something," she stated as she slipped a diamond ring onto her left ring finger. "The leaders of the family are fond of me and strongly believe in the bonds of love. It's what got them through tough times, so that's why I need you to pretend we're engaged. It'll help them trust you." A lot of emotions rattled around my head. A part of me almost screamed, "Say yes you damn moron!" As for the other part, well that roared, "This girl is too suspicious!" Stuck in between, I couldn't squeeze out an answer.

"Do you want allies or not?" she said, giving me the second ultimatum of the night. I was running out of time, now inches away from the tent's interior, forcing me to make the choice.

"Of course, sweetheart," I answered, grabbing hold of her left hand as we entered the congested tent. The interior was a lot bigger than I thought it would be, definitely more complex than most circus tents. Right away, I could see three pathways with a pair of knife throwers down the left path, and a giant boulder down the right. Both paths had attractions for all the guests, but the one that caught our attention was the man waiting for us down the center. He had white shiny skin that complemented his gray eyes and slit back black hair. Dull shadows beneath the long cheekbones extended down to the widely arched chin. The face was a recognizable one, considering this man's name had been mentioned multiple times in the past hour. He was the co-owner of the circus himself, Joseph Kershaw, and he knew how to dress for the occasion. He wore a dark-blue vest over a white collared shirt with a blue tie. Over the vest, a dark-purple suit with a pink rose pinned an inch above his white handkerchief. Dripping around his neck was an unwrapped light-purple scarf that reached all the way down to the purple cane his hands and body seemed to heavily rely on for balance.

The smile on Joseph's face grew large once Gabriella and I were toe to toe with the big man. The crowd of people gave us some room by detouring around to enjoy the spectacle Joseph was hosting.

"Lovely night, wouldn't you say," he greeted with his low-bass English accent—fitting for a man reaching out to Gabriella's left hand so he could rest a kiss on her slender fingers. The kind gesture instantly brought her diamond ring to his full attention. "Oh, how interesting you are my darling."

"What can I say, I fell in love," Gabriella said. The notion intrigued Kershaw while she retrieved her hand.

"Did you now?" Joseph questioned, gazing at her pseudo-lover. "Well, I think introductions are in order, wouldn't you say, Mr. Knightfall?"

Gabriella introduced me as the one responsible for the rock on her finger, helping me befriend the man who seemed five steps ahead. I let Gabriella do most of the talking because I didn't think there was anything I could say that he would buy, especially after she referred to him as the brains of the Carnivore operation. His nickname was a combination of the first couple of letters from both names fused into one. JoKer. Such an appropriate name for the man in purple who never seemed to stop smiling.

He had everything to smile about as he voluntarily went into detail about the family he'd invested in and how he met Kingsley "The King" Amaryllis at a showcase in Neotokyo. Kingsley and his longtime wife, Gwenylin "The Queen" Amaryllis performed illusionary acts involving swallowed fireworks that supposedly blew them to smithereens, only to suddenly teleport elsewhere safe and sound. Impressed by the extraordinary act, Joseph provided them with a deal that allowed them to settle in one location versus constantly traveling. Of course, they accepted it with an addition of Kingsley's much younger brother, Jackal "Jack" Amaryllis, a remarkable sharpshooter Joseph kindly insisted we check out as Jackal typically stole the show in Dessnia. Gabriella counter-proposed a meeting with Kingsley and Gwenylin instead. Before Joseph could answer, a storm of cheers erupted from the crowd down the left pathway. All of them stood around a booth called The Blades of Quinn, which Kershaw explained were his newest additions to the family.

The two fresh assets were named Harley and Harlene Quinn, a pair of knife-throwing siblings. Joseph silenced himself so they could explain their skills for themselves. It was a knife-throwing competition where Harlene would attach herself to a standing wheel that spun clockwise at what seemed like a hundred kilometers per hour. Harley began to dance around before randomly slinging a blade at the spinning wheel. The death-defying actions made the crowd squeal as the blade came a centimeter away from making Harley an only child. I wondered about the amount of trust that went into this performance. Harlene was lucky her brother wasn't Trace. His tragic eye-hand coordination would've produced a lawsuit at Joseph's venue. The following wave of blades did not disappoint either. Harlene eventually maneuvered herself into a contorted position and held it until Harley was out of knives. The final image of the performance was a chalk outline of blades around a living and untouched Harlene Quinn.

"Such an amazing talent, wouldn't you say, Craven?" Joseph insisted, gently nudging his body into mine a couple times. The irritated Gold quickly turned the conversation back to Kingsley and Gwenylin. Joseph agreed to introduce us, and we followed him down the right pathway from the tent's entrance. I stopped to watch two aliens standing in the spotlight of a massive stage down the center pathway. One of the two aliens had black obsidian skin with an exterior set of ribs covering the torso and chest of his body and two minotaur-like horns with gray tips bulging out of the sides of his cranium. The horns looked more menacing paired with his black eyes.

"Hold on, my darling. Craven seems rather curious. Perhaps we should let him see a Satanian in action, yeah?"

A Satanian, in the Carnivore family. Trace hadn't informed me about that. These creatures were known for hunting their victims and collecting their bones for clothes as honor. Joseph instantly confirmed the custom by explaining how their hunts were a sacrament to their red moon Gods and Goddesses. If there was one thing a Satanian feared, it was a spawn like Skorge from their Gods as an act of damnation to their sacrilege. I never read the books in my father's library, so I wouldn't know, but what I did know was the Satanian's ability to breathe fire. An ability that Joseph claimed was extra special in his Satanian, named Lucretia "Lucifer" Xiagra. Lucifer was one of the rare Satanians who was unkindled—they couldn't breathe fire. This is something most Satanians quickly condemned, but for Lucifer's sake, his mother got him a safe passage off of the planet and into a different universe. An act that cost her life so her son could find a new one, a life Kershaw chose to redefine.

"For centuries, your species has been trying to discover the limits of the Terran body," the Satanian said with a strong Romanian-like accent. He grasped a hold of the blades attached to his back. "Like a clock, you continuously wondered what makes the body tick."

Before Lucifer continued, he revealed the handles to his blades— blackened humorous-shaped bones with a ball at the end. JoKer informed us that those bones came from the last existing pieces of the Satanian's deceased mother. It was crazy. I didn't know Lucifer but thought I already understood some of his heartbreaking truth. Gabriella knew I could relate. Her warm hands gently wrapped mine. We briefly glanced at each other before Lucifer pointed his blade at the mummified companion standing next to him.

"Did I mention that Lucifer was a two for one deal?" JoKer abruptly said while the crowd held their breath.

"Here to help us, answer the big question, a spawn of the great Satanian Goddess, Vanta. Originally discovered as an unclassified Terranoid from the Cresciennic realms of hell for reasons like this," Lucifer said with a strong horizontal strike to the mummy's stomach, opening up the abdomen like a stick of butter. A ruby-toned waterfall eased out of the mummy's wound while the audience squealed for the umpteenth time tonight. The creature then fell onto its knees, giving JoKer an opportunity to explain why this act existed. The creature's name was Bayne, and even though there was a religious origin to the creature's story, the Satanians didn't really know how to classify Bayne other than the fact that the thing was a teardrop of their Goddess of Mystery, Vanta. They didn't even know Bayne's gender, classifying the spawn as Innara Tarrysys, abbreviated to their term of "IT." Unsure and afraid of what to do with IT, JoKer ran into the Satanian dilemma during Lucifer's adoption process. He figured that if the Satanians didn't want IT, why shouldn't he, an acquisition that proved to be astonishing as the rivers of blood began to rewind back into Bayne's stomach. The incision then stitched itself back together, finishing the stunning regeneration process for an applauding audience. "Do not let the Terranoid term fool you. Bayne may resemble a Terran, but I can assure you, they're anything but." The spawn slowly smiled as Lucifer, the Satanian, sheathed his blade and gave his friend a hand.

"Bayne's one of the racers," Gabriella whispered into my ear.

Her words broke the spell. "How the hell do you beat IT?"

"You don't, you befriend IT," Gabriella responded as JoKer finally led the way once again, through the right pathway, a little less congested after the conclusion of the Satanian act.

"Is that the first time you've seen a Satanian in action, Craven?" JoKer asked as we walked up to the boulder.

"We're wasting time, JoKer," Gabriella stated.

"I'm sorry, my darling, I just thought your love should know what he's going up against next week… That is the point to this little ruse, yeah?" JoKer asked, not at all fooled by our act. He shifted our attention to a storied tall giant with a triple-neck guitar easing its way to the giant boulder. "Take a look at the Gigallian named reliQ Qalmantine, otherwise known to most as 'Titan,' an attraction one must see for themselves."

Gabriella became uneasy. Like myself, she couldn't tell whether or not we should trust the man. Was a proper preview of the Carnivore family genuinely a kind gesture, or was it a taste of the hell to come in the Pro League series? Whatever it was, I had no choice but to play as the pawn to his game.

The giant took a moment before he was ready to toss up his sylonzer, a ball-shaped device from Ragnios that temporarily created a transparent bubble of lasers which canceled the noise from anything outside of it. Once the sylonzer was fully operational, the giant took a seat on the boulder. He appeared straight out of medieval times with all of the gray scaled armor he wore. Fragile skin and organs were one of the few things that prevented the Gigallians from being the apex specimen of the universe. Organs and music, we couldn't forget about their love for music. Similar to the weird sensations I had with Pyscean scriptures, music matched with the Gigallian nervous system like snowflakes resting on a glacier. It also explained why the giant nicknamed "Titan" had a gray triple-neck guitar natively crafted from the Gigallian metal, krone with some not-so-native wethro guitar strings from the Rachnidians. The foreign quilled webbing wasn't the only unique part of the guitar though. The eye catcher was the sharp edge of the guitar with an ivory lubricant.

"What's the substance leaking from the guitar?" I whispered to Gabriella while Titan tuned his instrument.

"Irizan, it's a Ghastallian chemical from the Great Lake of Hall. A liquified nerve agent that instantly attacks the iris of its victims. Helps them hallucinate things that can end up killing them," she explained, flexing her knowledge on an alien she seemed more familiar with. She told me that the giant was a nomadic one. He lacked the ability to speak, which had apparently ostracized him from Gigalus into a nomadic journey signified by several sections of his instrument.

"Let me guess, he races with that guitar."

"Of course; he sometimes uses it as a tomahawk. The guitar itself is capable of splitting into three parts, but you shouldn't worry, everything's gonna work out. I hope."

A comforting statement followed by the giant's acoustic cover of a rare 20th Century classic by a notable ancient Terran named Johnny Cash. I couldn't say that I was a fan of the artist, but I could confirm reliQ's talents as a guitarist, performing a breathtaking solo that echoed its high melodies off the sylonzer's perimeter. The song was powerful, but so was he. I hoped Gabriella was right or that destined-to-die rant I'd preached earlier was going to act as an omen.

reliQ continued to play a variety of songs to stretch the length of his concert. Gabriella, on the other hand, pulled me out of the sylonzer and into the climax of another performance not too far from Titan's. It was taking place within a giant tank of water that was now turning red. Before I could make an assumption, a hammerhead Pyscean leapt out of the water with a lifeless great white shark in each hand. The audience cheered in amazement.

"What a way to represent Earth," I commented sarcastically upon what was left of the great whites from my planet.

"Do you see what he's wearing?" Gabriella pointed out, convincing me to carefully observe the Pyscean's body. Coated around his skin was an adaptive suit matching his light-blue skin. There were a bunch of small tubes running across the appendages of his body. Tubes filled with water. "He's another racer who'll be competing next week and can't survive on dry lands without that suit. I figured it'd be a relief to know that somebody here has a weakness."

"Ahh yes, the Pyscean," JoKer indicated, catching up to us. Like all of his other acquisitions, he discussed the strengths of the Pyscean, unlike Gabriella who was trying to provide frailties. The Pyscean's name was Krakyn, but more specifically, he was a Hamer Chondryck. A group of Pysceans classified as half-man, half-shark, innately resembling a hammerhead. The Pyscean within JoKer's circus was the most ambitious alien in his Quintet. Independent as the only alien who came to the United Countries merely for fame and performing arts, which was why a trident representing Pasydanya sat at the center of the tent's rooftop. The declaration of Krakyn's importance made Gabriella cackle at the conclusion of JoKer's tale of the hammerhead's tape of a 7'3" (2.21 m) height, 303 lb (137.5 kg) weight, and 3,500 psi bite force. JoKer only focused on what I should be afraid of, and Gabriella knew it. She shed light on Krakyn's deficiencies until I understood that he was the weakest card in JoKer's five of a kind. Apparently the Pyscean was the most desperate Carnivore here and was willing to do whatever it took to be the most important.

"You seem to know a lot about the resources here, my darling, even for a Miss Earth," JoKer finally said following her barrage of counter-statements on the Pyscean.

"I'm just a Gold who wants to protect what they love, is that so hard to believe?"

"None whatsoever," JoKer replied, conceding to the credits of his performance by pointing outward towards the quadruple set of doors. They were designed as the four suits of cards for the tent's amphitheater below the white lettered holographic sign reading: An *Amaryllis Exosphere*.

"What's in there?" I asked JoKer.

"Your love's wish of The King and Queen," he responded, lowering his arm back down to his cane's handle. His stability was beginning to weaken by the looks of his rattling arms. "They'll be beyond those doors, hosting the main event. In there, I trust that Gabriella will give you that something you seek ever so desperately."

"You're not coming with?" I questioned, causing Gabriella's eyebrows to press together. The wide-eyed reaction made Joseph chuckle, granting Gabriella more wishes from his genie lamp.

"Unfortunately, this is where my journey ends, I can't rely on this cane forever," he affirmed. He said farewell, giving us the opportunity to enter the amphitheater. Time would only tell what was in store for us beyond those doors. At the top of this theater were five emblems: a pair of black horns for Lucifer, a red moon's crest for Bayne, a giant gray quaver for Titan, a centered trident for Krakyn, and a rayfish spaceship for an alien I assumed was a Rokian. I wasn't sure who this Rokian was, but if one was beyond these doors, I could only guess how traumatic the turn of my day would be this time around.

ACT II

CHAPTER 5

THE KNIGHT
OF OUR DREAMS

THE SPIRITS OF A FRECKLED SKY GRACED THE AMPHITHEATER'S OPEN ROOF, PRODUCING A SETTING LIKE NO OTHER. The seating was arranged for half of the amphitheater's circumference. The other half had a large crack that ran through the walls behind the main stage with a great view of the lit-up Castle of Dessnia in the distance. The stage itself was a rectangular platform with walkways leading to a pair of tunnels on each side. Tunnels I assumed were filled with restless performers while the Florida chill settled its way into the vast room. The breeze brought a strong sweet scent of funnel cakes. Not something my body wanted, no, it was something my body needed. Gabriella, on the other hand, seemed more so saddened about the night so far.

"I'm sorry for being such a pain in the butt," she said.

"It's no biggie. Trace has increased my tolerance over the years," I said putting another smile on her face. "And besides, being here with you beats being with him at the poker table."

"I take it you two are close?"

"He's my brother. It may not be by blood, but he's the closest thing I have to a sibling," I stated, adding a few stories about how The Ultimate Opportunist pushed me into this series, on how he gave me a journal specified for trash-talking one-liners and how it was because of him that I was sitting next to her at all. He was the one who got me to Florida and Four Seasons. Without Trace, I was not much more than a man who shared the name of a legend. "What about you and Midas? Are you close?"

"Yeah, I guess you can say he's my Trace. I can't live without him," she explained, exposing a part of her that felt more real than the rest. "He might be the older sibling, but it always seems like I'm the one protecting him… that's why… that's why tonight has to work."

"Is everything alright?" I asked.

"Only if you trust me," she replied, gently lying her hand over mine on the arm rest. We locked our eyes for a moment. Before I could give her a proper answer, the lighting of the amphitheater drew us to the glowing stage and a man wearing white dress pants, white blue vest top with blue buttons over a blue tucked tie, and white alligator skin shoes. He had long blonde hair and a beard which covered the collar strap of a long blue cape with cotton edges—a royal garment. Atop his head he wore a sapphire jeweled crown. I would have bet the lease to the nest that this was the one they call, The King.

"Good evening, Dessnia," Kingsley announced through a mini-mic arched around his right cheek. His hoarse voice attempted to talk over the sensational crowd. "If there's one thing Dessnia is known for, it's story-telling, and this show will be no exception. Awaiting you in this theater is an epic like no other..."

"...A masterpiece, yet to be discovered," a woman in a long white dress suddenly followed, stepping out of the tunnels for the spotlight. She wore a similar sapphire jeweled crown but instead had a silver cape covering her shoulders to match the long gray hair draped on the cotton edge. Clearly not as tall as her royal partner, but that didn't stop her from matching heights with silver heels capable of sending her to space. If I'd already gambled my workshop on Kingsley's identity, then I'd have to bet my mother's mansion that this woman was his counterpart, The Queen. "A tale of four souls, attempting to slay the darkness bestowed against them."

"Such a folly," Kingsley added, offsetting Gwenylin's much more soothing voice. "This story will teach us about despair…"

"...Passion..."

"...Sacrifice..."

"...Perseverance..."

"...Unbecoming..."

"...And at last, new beginnings," Gwenylin finished, now side by side with Kingsley. "Like all great sagas, they are not without length."

"Have no worries, though, as we know that with great length, comes great responsibility," Kingsley stated, causing some of the immature members of the audience to chuckle. "Which is why there will be an intermission to the show."

"An intermission where you can chat with us and get a better look at what it's like…" Gwenylin explained as the lights to the theater began to dim.

"...To enter… *An Amaryllis Exosphere*," Kingsley finished as a foggy coating of air filled the theater's crack to obstruct the view of the castle in the distance. Out of nowhere, a spacecraft uncloaked itself within the cracks, revealing the head of a Rokian ship stuck in the wall from a "crash-landing." The ship was a shrunken prototypical version of a Fellix, the spacecraft used by the Ragnarök. Fun-size had to be their only option for the showcase as most Fellixes were ten, maybe twenty-times larger, and were only held at spaceports like the one in Florida called The Aldrin Spaceport.

Facing the crowd was the hockey-shaped visor of the Fellix illuminating the room with its light-blue shade, causing the amphitheater to mirror the Milky Way. The stars of the cosmos tie-dyed themselves around the Fellix before a Rokian slowly ascended out of the ship's rooftop. My heart skipped a beat when my eyes locked on the alien native of Ragnios. Fortunately for me, the colors of the Rokian's armor were violet instead of blue which could've… It could've… It wasn't blue. That was all that mattered.

"I am Primax, your destroyer of worlds, here to carve our name into every history book," the Rokian announced in his rotund voice, leaving the crowd more afraid than silent. A glare from the xenon gas carved into a scythe, wrapping itself around an aorta. Like a Gold, his eyes were bicolored. One biologically purple, the other artificially red. Around the artificial eye were red protruding sites of soldered material to hide the obvious battle scars inflicted on them. There was no question why Primax was cast as the villain. His image has been the personification of villains for centuries, maybe even millennia, and his speech about galactic domination was the cream cheese on the platter. Holographic visuals of other planets crept closer to his ship, now preparing to fire its weapons on the landmarks. Four distinct supernovas suddenly appeared to corner the Fellix. Two of the supernovas were red, one was black.

"These are the children," Gabriella whispered.

"Of who?"

"The King and Queen," she answered as the explosions of the supernovas began to compress and solidify into four Terranoid figures. "They'll be competing too."

An Amaryllis Exosphere, it wasn't just a trademark, or a play on words, it was an objective statement. There were four more branches on the ever-growing family tree, each appearing within the blink of an eye to save the day. Volunteering her narration, Miss Earth provided me backgrounds on each youthful Amaryllis. They appeared in order of their ages with Spade the first to show his true identity as the eldest child and son. Next, the second oldest and eldest daughter, Heart. Like the three petals of the flower, Club appeared as the third child and younger son. As the fourth, Diamond took the title as the youngest daughter and child of them all.

Spade Amaryllis was the head of the quartet serpent and was the one Gabriella claimed should be the most worrisome opponent. Undoubtedly the most gifted of the four and always called the shots as the eldest. If not for him, the other three would disintegrate into ashes as they tended to rely on the strengths of one another. Diamond was The Greatest Contortionist, specializing in submissive holds where the wheels could penetrate weak points. Heart was The Greatest Aerialist, an adrenaline junkie who only found comfort through the soaring skies, never crashing or burning off of high-altitude environments. Club was The Greatest Acrobatic, an agile racer relying on the manipulation of another's momentum and using it against them. On top of being the eldest, Spade was The Greatest Showman, as he excelled in all three categories mastered by his siblings. A balanced racer who fused the elements while adding his own enhanced ability of proprioception, something he relied on all the time. Gabriella claimed that he did it for the thrill, but actually believed it was to impress his parents who seemed to focus their attention on the youngest, Diamond—a daughter they'd wanted for a long time and had procured several abortions after Club just to cap the four suits properly. How about that for presentation?

The show continued with the four main stars dressed in their angelic outfits, floating across the skies and finally into Primax. Now coming out of the Fellix were fully robotic Ragnarök, clearly created by Primax as his henchman for the performance. Henchmen that would divide and conquer the quartet of Amaryllis children, sending the three youngest to a rainy Pasydanya, while Spade took on Primax at a freezing Arythro. The vast holographic design let us observe all the clashes happening simultaneously, which was when the "Despair" section of the story kicked in as the three youngest were eventually defeated and killed, leaving Spade one-on-one with Primax who would then take the vision of the eldest child with his bare hands.

The Greatest Showman then fell to the icy surface of the Ryth glacier for Primax to stand over, glaring back at the ghastly crowd; more specifically… me, and that's when things… that's when my head… it took over the show as the lone surviving Rokian deprived me of Spade's redemption arc by morphing himself and the environment into Thorax standing tall over my father's corpse on the dark race track. I couldn't tell what was real anymore, now trapped in a child's body stuck in the private booth next to my mother. And just as I did that day, I got up and walked out to the stairway leading to a dark hallway. Did I travel through time, or was I going insane? Whatever the answer, I stopped in my tracks and dropped down to one knee, now feeling my heart attempting to claw its way out of my rib cage.

"Craven," a woman said. In the background I heard Tokyn's closing statement regarding the Ragnarök being here to stay. The woman I assumed to be my mother grasped my shoulder before kneeling down to check on my condition. Her eyes weren't light-brown, though. They were, instead, red and blue. "Are you okay?"

"Yeah," I muttered, checking to see if the woman truly was Gabriella Gold, analyzing every detail, from the freckles roaming across her nose to the lips like Goldilocks. The polished skin to the unnecessary layer of mascara. The iridium eyes to the draping dreamcatcher. "Yeah, I... I'll be alright."

"Is it because of Primax?" she asked.

"Yeah, he sort of turned into… him."

"I can see that, but you shouldn't be afraid of Prim. He's all looks and lacks direction and efficiency," she explained, going into further detail about the violet Rokian. A shell of their former selves, the Rokian had been recruited by JoKer for visual presentation to the liking of the Amaryllis' storytelling. Primax, along with his insane brother, was apparently exiled by Ragnios for his questionable decisions as a high-ranking general. They were the ones notoriously known for starting a war with Crystia, Ragnios' galactic rival. An issue that led to Ragnios' debt-status entering Galactica XLVIII. No one knew where his brother disappeared to, but I knew that Primax was here, and he was a Carnivore, ready for next week's competition, nonetheless.

Gabriella didn't need to be right here, right now by my side, but I was thankful that she was. Her presence lowered my heart rate back to normal, and I even cracked a smile when she insulted the Rokian's cheesy outfit. She promised to slap some sense back into me the next time I feared, in her words, *Barney the Dinosaur*. We got back to our feet just in time to catch The King and Queen wandering around the circus to check on the other acts. It didn't take long for the royal couple to recognize Miss Earth.

"How nice of you to stop by Gabby and with…the MehGuire boy?" Kingsley began to scrunch his face into a betrayed look.

"Don't worry, I just wanted to answer the rumors going around the family on who

I've been seeing behind the scenes. It was something I, I mean, we wanted to keep from the world until the time was right, and an engagement I think is the right time," Gabriella explained while raising her left hand to show the ring. Sparkles struck the irises of the royal couple while they grasped Gabriella's bejeweled hand.

"Oh! How amazing, and here I was thinking the worst. Would you please forgive me and my misconception of what you were trying to display?" Kingsley revived with joy.

"Course not sweetie, our little jewel knows how we feel about the others, she's our family," Queen said, wrapping her hands around Gabriella.

"She's a very special type of jewel these days. It takes a mighty STRONG man to maintain someone like her, Sir MehGuire. Be a good lad and always take good care of her," Kingsley demanded.

"He will, and I don't want anything to happen to him during the races. I care about him too damn much," Gabriella said with a serious tone. The damn girl should've been a part of the Amaryllis showcase based on her performance. It really convinced me of her love, something that brought wings to my heart. Her words were about to grant me an alliance with a family who had positioned themselves as the biggest threat to this series thus far. "I… I don't think… I can handle… losing…"

"My dear, my dear, have no worries. I'll inform the rest and make sure that they look out after him, but you need to go talk to Claire Voyant. The outcome that was promised has changed. Your golden shite of a brother is supposed to fall with my own blood, Jackal rising in their place, but the only one who's manifesting is the infestation called Cougar. You've made the claim of placing us on the top of this series, and I still trust in those words, but if Cougar ends up as champ instead of Jackal, I'll have Prim and Loosh tear your brother inside out 'til the tracks are saturated in velvet gold," Kingsley said with much ferocity.

Gabriella looked on in disbelief. I too was in disbelief, but for a different reason. There was no way this dumbbell called Krueger, Cougar.

"That's where I come in, your grace? I can take down... Krueger?" I offered to repay Gabriella, pulling her out of this dilemma. It made me sound like a fucking idiot, too. The cape and crown actually sold the royalty for me. I didn't know who was more shocked by my "your grace" statement, me or Gabriella. It was times like this when I was thankful Trace was absent. He would've ruptured a spleen if he'd heard me just now. "I know how Krueger thinks based on his suit. I've got access to top of the line shit that'll send him to the sidelines. If there's a weakness, I'll find it and expose it."

"I like this MehGuire boy; he's got an astounding amount of integrity and initiative," Kingsley rejoiced.

"That's… that's why I love him," she responded, caressing my waist to sell the relationship more than their royalty. The gesture made Kingsley's smile broaden just before the siren to the show's intermission could go off.

"Head over to Claire. Maybe she'll have some good news now that the MehGuire boy is aboard," Gwenylin firmly instructed prior to the herd of people coming out of the doors to surround the royal couple. Heeding Gwenylin's words, Gabriella led us to the far west side of the tent to a room called A Date with Destiny. The closed doorway had a sign stating, *when the doors are sutured, do not harm another's future*. The rhyme left me confused, honestly. I thought it was a classy way of saying wait your damn turn, which was exactly what we did outside of the purple doorway with steam creeping out of the cracks.

"Soooo… this is what it feels like to have allies," I said while waiting.

"I'm sorry I didn't tell you the full story."

"The man threatened your brother, I think the story speaks for itself," I stated, causing her to shake her head.

"There's more to it though," she gently spoke as a massive cloud of smoke imploded the purple doorway. A customer came out of it wearing a soon-to-be trillionaire smile followed by a very tanned woman in a bright-purple robe with bright-purple eyes, lips, and short hair. The only non-purple thing about her was the glowing eye of providence tattooed on her forehead, the all-seeing eye usually associated with an undying myth known as the illuminati.

"Claire, I can explain everything," Gabriella instantly stated once the trio of eyes had been locked on her.

"You fucking doughnut, why did you bring him into this?" Claire Voyant demanded. "On second thought, step into my room, both of you, now!"

We entered the quiet misty room with more eyes of providence scattered on the six glowing white walls. Candles on the floor formed into a hexagram star. Each end of the star pointed to one of the walls, and at the center, a hovering spirit ball for show and tell. One could only hope that she was going to usher out some great news as with the previous customer, but from how stressed out the two grumbling ladies were, that was as mythical as everything else in this damn tent.

"I can't keep covering for you Gabby. I'm being forced to think of lies and bendable truths that could aid us, but that's been a pain in my ass due to the proud drama queen, JoKer, notching closer and closer to our plan. He's catching onto my false trails. I had no choice but to bring up the name Krueger," Claire revealed as if Krueger was a friend. Was he a part of this?

"I know. I think everything is under control now. I've got insurance," Gabriella replied, flourishing her hands at me like a magician capping off their trick with a voila.

"How is everything under control? You brought him here, our last line of defense. Do you know why it's called the last line, because it's the last damn line. Not the 'I'm gonna use ya halfway through the fight' line. You can't prevent Midas' fate by bringing Craven into the situation. Midas is going to die no matter what… unless… you do what I've been telling you to do for the past few weeks, unmask yourself! Only then will the future change."

"But if I unmask myself, I'll die."

"When you prevent one death, someone else must take their place. So, whether fate chooses you or not, someone's gotta take the bullet," Claire explained.

Out of frustration, Gabriella began to punt the candles into the walls. This was the rest of her story, the thing she'd been hiding, the reason why she wanted me to trust her. The reason why she wanted me here at all. She was trying to save her brother's life, but the only way was by unmasking herself. What the hell did that even mean? Was she trying to open up to me, or somebody? I could not say I was against the idea by any means, I just wished I had a better understanding.

"What if bringing Craven here changed something?" Gabriella questioned out of desperation.

"It didn't," Claire quickly said.

"Can you at least check, look into his eyes, maybe there's something we missed, please?" Gabriella pleaded. Claire attempted to deny all of the possible actions. After tiring from the stubborn Gold by my side, Claire eventually glanced over at me.

"Are you okay with this Craven?" she finally asked. I took a brief second to think about the question and instantly remembered the same Gabriella who had helped me escape an overrated party, who had pulled me out of a traumatic nightmare, and had granted me an alliance with the toughest family in the series. Declining Claire Voyant's offer would've been disrespectful if not futile. What did I have to lose? She'd helped me, so now it was my time to fully repay the debt. I eventually nodded. At Claire's request, Gabriella left the room. Claire prepared for the prophesying ritual by planting her cold fingertips on the sides of my forehead. Her eyes then closed, and a clockwise flurry of mist hovered for effect. Out of nowhere, she began her poetic chant, stating: *Where fire is felt, lives can melt, so bestow the cold, and save a gold.* An unclear future, but it did seem to have a happy ending, I thought.

"Does that mean he lives?" I hesitantly asked once her eyes were opened.

"I don't know; we'll have to find out," she said. "Changing history won't make things better because history always has a way of evening out, even if it's in the future. So, try your best to heed the words instead of hunting them."

I would store Claire's advice in my head, as it could come in handy for later. She felt pleased by the prophecy, but at the same time, it seemed like she had gone through hell and back. I gave her the much-needed rest by stepping out to the eager Gold awaiting me. At this point, there was no way I could look at the glass half-empty, now ready to tell her the first thing on my mind.

"Your brother lives," I confidently stated, receiving a genuine hug that could've lasted forever.

"I knew bringing you here was a good idea."

"How about we leave this freak show and actually enjoy the rest of the night?" I proposed, leading us out of the tent and to a nearby booth that sold a very special craving I'd been wanting to hunt down since our entry into the amphitheater. It was a booth selling funnel cakes, a proper treat that helped the two of us sit down and actually open up like normal people.

I asked her about her eye color and why they were different in her pictures as Miss Earth. She said that it was to attract more people. She felt like the world found a blue-eyed girl more attractive than a bicolored one. A notion given to her by her mother who was once upon a time, Miss Galaxy. Her mother, Catherine, thought that giving her blue contact lenses would get the votes, and there wasn't a sane person in this world who could argue with the conclusion. Maybe that was why I was alright with being insane for the rest of my life. Gabriella with the two eye colors was much prettier than the tourist attraction of a poster stuck to every boy's bedroom wall, and I had no problem saying it. I told her that it was what made her, well, her. She countered the statement with the expectations constructed by her family, a relatable topic causing me to bring up a similar situation with my own mother. I told Gabriella about what my mother had to go through after my father's death. The grieving process was hell, which produced a lot of guilt as a racer who had been married at birth to the sport. Sure, it wasn't in the exact same realm of expectation, but I felt it was close to the ballpark.

The conversation then shifted to an inevitable question about my jacket and why I always wore it. She apparently found it funny, seeing a racer leap out of their suit in a jacket at Knightfall. She had me dead to rights. I explained that I was rushed into my suit that night, hence why I wore the jacket. It more importantly opened up an opportunity to explain to her about my workshop in Calumet and how she should stop by when this fuss with her brother was over. The proposal was a few moves ahead of the curve, but it was something that brought her and I a bit closer, just in the nick of time, too, because the circus had now issued their closing announcement to the park.

"Not a bad date, eh?" I asked, thankfully getting one more smile while the herd began to leave the tent.

"I've had worse," she responded, finishing off the cake. "Who knows, maybe you're the knight of my dreams."

"If I had a nickel for every knight pun I've heard in my day."

"Aye, I actually thought it amazing."

"It was," I finally said to end our tenure at the carnival. It had been a long day with mixed emotions, but we were able to cap it off on a high note now making our way back to the Lotus. The food coma gnawing away at our energy levels didn't hit its mark until we reached the elevator, forcing us to lean against each other. When the elevator reached my stop, we gave each other one final hug that seemed to last longer than the day itself. We just held on to the other without saying a word because the silence spoke louder than Dessnia's nocturnal heartbeat.

ACT II
CHAPTER 6

FALL

FOUR SEASONS WAS HERE AND ALMOST A WEEK HAD PASSED. In that time, I'd experienced an opening ceremony, a long-awaited debut, a reality check of a loss, and a real date with Miss Earth. To start the unforgettable Fall week, the opening ceremony required all fifty-two racers to attend, even though eight out of the fifty-two were ready in their exosuits for the opening race that took place directly after. Only one non-competing racer was absent from the event, and that was Krueger. Apparently, it was an excused off-the-record absence. It only left me more and more intrigued about the mysterious racer.

The ceremony itself was similar to Galactica's opening: lots of fireworks, spotlights, and fan-bases going nuts during the televised event. I felt relieved in the Versa spotlight not having to wonder whether or not my mother was watching. She and everyone at the nest kept messaging pictures of me on TV, claiming that I seemed a little stressed. I didn't realize the internal emotions were visible on my face at the time. They would have been stressed too if they had known that my agenda wasn't to win the series but to protect Midas, someone who was part of the opening race. An opening race I wasn't even competing in. The worst thing to it was watching, not knowing if something tragic was going to happen to him early on, but luckily for my stress levels, there was no Law, no Krueger, or Carnivores competing as one of the eight. Realistically, the other seven were nobody's. They were mediocre at best, getting their asses handed to them by the supposed best, leading to the greatest thing about that race, which was who I watched it with.

At my side was Midas' sister, Gabriella, a true fan of the sport calling out schemes her brother should've been attempting. Diagnosed with an earworm, I could listen to her commentary all day. An apathetic feeling drowned my emotions when I should've been excited. Her brother had won the opening race without a scratch on his 2250 Cronus. Living the moment like it was my last, I asked her out because it would've been too damn painful to spend another day without her. When agony reached a climax for me, I treated it, and the yes I received was just the prescription I needed. Even though her and I were still in a pseudo-engagement for the Carnivores' sake.

The opening night of Four Seasons gave me the momentum for my debut race the next day. Unlike Midas, I didn't have Gabriella watching, but I did have my brother Trace, who provided a high-octane pep talk revolving around Miss Earth. His awe-inspiring speech had lines like: *She doesn't accept punkbitch losers, Craven!, She's with The Unchained Knight, not The Unchained Shite!*, or my favorite line, *You're Craven McFire!* As absurd as the speech was, it helped me place first against a similar batch of mediocres which helped me understand the scoring system with the ten points I acquired. The series ran on a 10,8,6,5,4,3,2,1 format.

The victorious debut did boost my ego as a racer leading me to a match-up against Midas in our second race. Just like our openers, there were no threats competing with us, leaving it as a lone test for our skills against one another. The 2250 Cronus was a lot faster than I thought. I spent most of the race drafting with him, trying to strategically use my boost with the help of MIKA. Midas had some skills but had the same bad habit as Zero, which were poor turns. The Golden Scion always rushed the straightaways, never giving himself enough time to pull back on multiple sharp turns. He actually used one of the barricades as an obstacle to ricochet off from a bad turn. He was lucky I wasn't a Carnivore. If someone like Krakyn had been on his ass during that turn, they would've had an opportunity to fracture a pair of ribs with a compressive collision. Even though the turns were poor, Midas' suit was fast enough to outperform mine for now, claiming first place while I took second for my first Pro League loss. It had a bitter taste to it, but I felt relieved that it wasn't in front of his sister. She had to miss the race for some modeling errand. Eighteen points was nothing to be ashamed of, I just needed to stay at the top of the standings. Midas had ended the three-race Fall week with thirty points, staying undefeated in the series, moving on to the premier bracket of the Winter week, a bracket that I had to be a part of for Midas' protection or else I'd be sent to a different location.

Winter Week Standings

Premier Bracket: 21 points or more = Greenland (Tumblers & Zane qualified)
Axial Bracket: 20-11 points = Antarctica
Danger Bracket: 10 points or less = Nunavut

Three points was all I needed for advancement into the premier bracket and the next race would be my toughest yet. Taking place at the Kingdom Come race track with contenders such as an analytic assassin, a pair of hounds, a kin-bladed devil, a desperado hammerhead, a muted giant, and an undefeated Krueger. It was a challenge I would be ready for but prior to it, I only had one thing on my mind—Gabriella Gold. We were on a late afternoon date on the balcony of my room. The sunset in the background set the tone for our entrées of medium-rare raptrs. Trace would have tossed us into a black hole if he'd known we were eating raptrs without him. It was a good thing he wasn't here.

"What in the holy hell is that smell?" I suddenly heard from inside the suite.

"Is that Trace? Thought you said he was busy?" Gabriella questioned as I took a brief look inside to see that it was indeed my best friend.

"He was," I exclaimed, now conceding to the date's plausible demise.

"Well, I'll be damned," Traced exclaimed on his unpredictable arrival. Gabriella and I tried to treat him like a tyrannosaurus rex by being still and pretending he wasn't there. Maybe he would go away, right? Then again, this was Trace. "That's cute, I like how you two are ignoring me."

"This was actually supposed to be a private date. Just throwing that out there," I said, knowing that he would try and make us feel bad. We didn't.

"Oh, I'm sorry, I didn't know that this was private, my bad," Trace apologized, finally going back inside.

"Thought he'd never leave," Gabriella said, sighing.

"Don't worry, he's like a fly, you just have to swat him…" I tried to explain but was cut off by the screeching metallic sounds coming from inside. Trace drug a chair out onto the balcony, setting it at our table to join us once again.

"More like a cockroach," Gabriella affirmed. I think she was beginning to understand that Trace was part of the package when it came to her and I.

"Words don't really hurt me darling. You see, I'm the reason why Craven is here, competing in this series. I was the one who gave him the motivational speech before his debut," Trace started explaining, taking a cut out of my steak. "Go ahead and tell her what happened in that race, don't be shy." He nudged my shoulder for the response. The man could be impulsive at times and was definitely killing the mood on purpose. I had to take a deep breath before answering his question.

"A win," I quietly whispered.

"Pardon?"

"A win," I replied in an annoyed tone for the second time.

"A WIN! I'm 1-0 as Craven's coach, beautiful, so let me provide my client with another great talk. He's got a tough bout tonight."

"Don't you mean 1-1? He lost against my brother," Gabriella quickly stated. "I highly doubt he needs your motivational lectures if they're only 50% accurate, and besides, he's got me."

"Ha, I remember the last girl who said that. I believe it was Craven's ex. The hell was her name? Cherry. Chelsea. Chas… Chastity, that's what her name was. I created that jingle for the both of you, Craven and Chastity sitting in a tree, S-E-X-T-I-N-G."

"Don't you have somewhere to be?"

"Don't you?"

"The race isn't until 8."

"It's 6:42," he bickered. He always sought to embarrass my love interests. Even if it was in front of the prettiest girl in the United Countries; that may have given him more of a reason to do so.

"How about you trust me when I say that Craven's going to be just fine. He's very aware of the stakes tonight," Gabriella reassured, ending the fuss between Trace and I. She read the puzzled look on Trace's face. Like the rest of the world, he didn't expect her to know much about Versa. "I know that he's going up against a pair of hounds under the influence of a cerebral manipulator. I know that there are a trio of extraterrestrial Carnivores, each bringing an element of desperation, deception, and descent. And there's also an unmatchable nightmare who happens to be a combination of all of the above."

"Damn, didn't take you as a Versalyte. I guess you're more than just a pretty face Ms. Gold," Trace stated.

"Tell me about it," I muttered. Trace then challenged Gabriella's Versa IQ with a few trivia questions. Who was the first Terran to get a kill in Galactica (Adam "The Cardinal" Wreath), or who was known as The Lone Shark? (Catelyn Brannigan). Gabriella was flawless, quickly providing an answer before Trace could finish each question. The girl could've won a trillion dollars if she was on an actual game show, unlike my father who barely won a stuffed animal. Her knowledge impressed him enough to leave me in her hands for the night's race. He apparently had plans with Midas and a few others in Greenland. Trace expected me to be there next and had strong faith in my capabilities.

Once he was gone, Gabriella decided to honor my best friend's request by getting me to the track on time. Making sure to avoid the late afternoon airway traffic, she left to get her sports car. I was to meet her separately in front of the hotel, so the media didn't find out about our relationship. Heh, I'd say that we had been pretty good with our discretion.

On the way to the lobby, I noticed a lot more Re-Versable posters along the walls of the hotel. Security and Staff were urgently ripping them down in the defense of their Versa guests. Hell, there were probably enough posters to keep them busy after the race. The activists' numbers were growing by the second, and they had a lot of balls pulling off a stunt like this. If anything, they caught Dessnia's attention by the looks of people walking past the posters now leering at me. The Re-Versables may have turned some heads in the Lotus, but that wasn't going to stop me from competing. Seeing the posters honestly gave me more of a reason to fight tonight. Four Seasons was the biggest series on Earth, and it was Merce-based. If Midas were to die, this would only give the activists more fuel for their fire. The thought killed all of the nerves, instantly gifting a game-ready mindset. The internal advantage didn't last long, unfortunately, due to what awaited outside. A barrage of flashes from cameras blinded me, and I was peppered with a symphony of questions.

"What's this relationship between you and Gabriella Gold?"

"Are the Golds and McGuires allies?"

"Would you say that you've got an edge on Midas by bringing his sister into the equation?"

"What's your endgame Craven? Will Thorax ever come into the picture?"

I might've been temporarily blinded, but I could see the oval eyes of Thorax through some of the flashes. Those light-blue eyes that could paralyze a soul. Why did they always bring him up? The Rokian was always on their minds. Yes, I wanted him dead, but I didn't need life reminding me every damn day.

Suddenly, herds of people leapt onto the grass and concrete as if their lives depended on it. A black hovering Camaro suddenly appeared rumbling its muscular engine, shouting a battle cry. The windows of the black car were tinted, so I couldn't see the driver, but that didn't stop me from diving into the vehicle's opened passenger side door. The momentum from the car's acceleration planted my back firmly into the seat's cushion, slamming the door shut. The image on the windshield blurred before the ascension into a flyway. After declaring my escape successful, I glanced over at the driver. Gabriella gave me the biggest pink smile I'd ever seen.

"You were going to run them over, weren't you?" I said once I properly buckled into the seat. Rightfully so, she had to have been going 160km/h over the speed limit.

"I honked," she cackled in her raspy voice. "They're a pack of wolves who sometimes need to be taught an aggressive lesson."

"Well, that was unethical."

"Craven, you're a Versa racer, I'm pretty sure ethical standards have been tossed out of your window a long time ago."

Ethical standards. I had a group of activists on one shoulder and a group of fans like Gabriella on the other. It made me think of the obvious; the reason our alliance turned into a relationship. I'd been letting things progress out of curiosity since the carnival, but that had to change. I couldn't keep playing dumb for much longer. It was time for another big answer.

"So, how does Midas die?" I asked, creating goosebumps on her arm.

"Truthfully, I don't know," she revealed, leaving me a bit agitated. How the hell were we supposed to prevent his death if we didn't even know how it was supposed to happen? "When I first met Claire, she told me a reaper had a bullet with Midy's name on it, inferring Law. We made a plan that involved me creating an alliance with the Carnivores. Ten racers would prevent a specific outlaw from killing a champion, an easy plan leaving my brother unharmed. There was one catch from Kingsley—making sure his younger brother Jackal would be crowned champion afterwards. I didn't have a problem with the deal, but the same couldn't be said for the tumblers."

"So, the tumblers are who we should be on the lookout for?"

"They're not exactly assassins though. If they were to kill Midy, it'd be direct, resulting in Pandora's wrath. No rewards come from that risk which is why I begged Claire for more information. A fallen general was the best she could provide, inferring Primax."

"So, it's Primax? Or did things change again?" I asked. Gabriella raised her eyebrows. Lucifer had to be thrown into the picture due to Kingsley's promise of slicing Midas, and she mentioned multiple times that Krakyn was desperate for attention. "Basically, the alliance backfired."

"Not for you, they'll help you. We can use it to our advantage," she stated without hesitation. I didn't know how I felt about that, especially because of how uncertain I was towards the aliens' compliance.

"What about the unmasking bullshit, and your connection with Krueger?" I questioned, testing more of her secrets. I recognized how Gabriella and Claire used Krueger's name in a friendly manner. Gabriella gave me a few side-eyed stares, and we carried on the silence. For a moment, it felt like we were in a dark room with Gabriella trapped in the corner with all the answers to how we got into the room in the first place. "Look, I get that you've got some barriers up, and I respect that. There are just certain things I gotta know. It's not like I'm racing the guy tonight, oh wait, I am."

"I know who Krueger is if that's what you're asking, and yes, we're friends. Is there anything else you wanna ask?" she replied, agitated by my sarcasm. "How about this, we each meet up at the penthouse tonight? No more secrets, just the three of us laying our cards on the table."

Still questioning the situation, I gave a nod. By right, I deserved answers. I'd come this far to help her brother. I just couldn't be in the dark for much longer—no more stones unturned so that we could find a way to bestow the cold in order to save a Gold. I still didn't know what that meant, but I had to heed it.

Ahead of us on the flyway was the tip of the tallest tower of the floating castle, piercing through the pink clouds, trying to create a gateway to heaven. Once we were off the flyway, Gabriella's speed decreased in light traffic. The street's image was no longer a blur, showing us a blossomed garden reflecting the clouds of the happiest place on Earth, Dessnia Kingdom, Florida's central park. Scattered around were pillars topped with Dessnia's most popular animated figures in exosuits. I don't know what was funnier, seeing the infamous Mickey Mouse dressed in a golden 2250 Cronus or his companion Goofy in a combined 2250 Yin and Yang. Would've been better if they had Goofy in Zane's Nevermore. Mr. Maddox must've wisely kept the copyrights to himself.

The traffic picked up the closer we got to the floating castle. It took 10-15 minutes to reach the crowded gates of the kingdom, and it was a kingdom. It had its stables, its Victorian-styled buildings sandwiched in between one another with actors dressed up as princes and princesses all around. The gate itself was massive—two stories tall with security maintaining authority over fans impatiently waiting to obtain their seats. This was where Gabriella and I had to part ways. She had to park the Camaro, and I had to get inside. She wished me luck with one long hug, letting me know that she'd be watching at an exclusive location.

Once we were separated, I squeezed my way through the tight crowd, gaining instant access through the gate after one of the guards came out to check on me. Dick had a shiny addition to his outfit—a hylec that could only be purchased through the galactic market as the material came from the opulent crystals of Crystia. It may not have been as thick and sturdy as the popular onyhylec catered to the Crystallite Knights, but it was still an amazing material to have. He had his hylec fashioned into an arm sleeve with the diamond patterns of the crystal shining their foggy salmon textures in the air. I took it that his Knightfall winnings were paramount as the Crystallite currency was worth a dozen souls compared to our dollar bill.

"You sly sonuvabitch," he stated, heaving me out of the crowd with a firmly grasped hug. "Please tell me you're here to make me rich again."

"Has anyone ever told you that you've got gambling issues?" I asked him as he led me through the gate. He made a quick glance at the starting line, which was also the finish line. The long opening and final straightaway ahead had bleachers and booths along the sides, eventually curving right around the floating castle. The route back could be seen through the clouds covering the edge of a large ramp scaling itself over the tip of the castle's tallest tower. I muttered words more colorful than the rainbowed sky after scanning how high the ramp was. "The landing's gonna hurt."

"As long as it doesn't hurt my bank account, I'm sure you'll be fine." Dick added, leading me through a tunnel under the left set of bleachers with the racer's locker at the end of it—a facility used for any type of pre-race rituals for its competitors. There was one at every race track across the galaxy no matter how high of a Naturis rating the track had, something that would be a factor next week.

Like some of the previous lockers, this was structured like a multi-storied house only with guest rooms. This one had eight rooms, with four on the first floor and four on the second, each designed specifically to the racer's presentation, with their nickname engraved onto the outside of each closed door. For once, my room was on the top floor. Dick led me past the rooms labeled: "The Harmonic Titan," "The Rammyng Trydent," "The Unkindled Demon," and "The Clawed Cardiac." The thought of being less than a hundred yards away from Krueger drew curiosity. It was perfectly legal for racers to make physical contact with one another. It was just illegal to kill.

After heading up a stairway to the second floor, I had to pass three rooms marked as "The Cerebral Assassin," "The Yang Hound," and "The Yin Hound" to get to mine labeled "The Unchained Knight." The architecture within the room was created from actual neon-blue chains and gray knight armor. On the main wall in front of the centered bench was Atlas III. The Pro League Committee had been good when it came to the safe transportation of my exosuit and restocking of ergogenics in my goodie bag. They always kept the Atlas refurbished and perfectly ready for each race, then again, the suit hadn't been physically tested for what was to come in the future. That was why having a few flare grenades in my back pocket was an advantage for the upcoming dire dilemmas.

The clock in the room read 7:27, giving me more than enough time to get ready. This was why I was never early. There was never anything to do in here, not like other racers who spend hours properly getting their shit together. Putting on my father's championship ring and ingesting goodies was as much of a ritual as I needed. Simple, and it got me into the right mindset nine times out of ten. Lately, I'd been keeping the ring attached to the Atlas' index finger during intermissions. In the spare time that was left, I sat down on a bench to watch the highlights of earlier races I'd missed from my tenure with Gabriella. There were new competitors joining Midas in the premier bracket.

Warlock was one of the few, finishing his race in Sandusky, Ohio by cutting in front of a heated Rokian to claim first place on the final turn. The two brutes brawled it out afterwards with Primax actually receiving the bitter end of Warlock's signature weapon, a pair of electric gloves with krone knuckles, knocking the scarred Rokian out to Antarctica instead.

In the airborne city of Volador Vegas, Law and Creed made a temporary alliance against IT, someone who had to defend their lead using a scythe, which created problems for the young alliance. It took a vise grip around the shaft of the scythe from Law's lasso to grant Creed an opportunity to sever Bayne's right arm. It took away the scythe Bayne had been using for defense. Law then flattened Bayne's tires with a hail of gunshots, giving the deadly alliance a tiebreaker for first. That sent them to Greenland with Bayne heading to Antarctica to join his friend Jackal, who made a comeback finish in Neotokyo.

By the time the Unican Network replayed its highlights for the third straight time, the Way/Point grid popped up. The iCube was notifying me that someone had sent a request as a VIP candidate. I directed my attention to the social platform and an icon of a closed envelope above my avatar's head. The only one's close to my avatar in the VIP section of the nest's parking lot were Trace, Kira, Meta, Beta, Roy, Zero, and Katia, but they would soon be joined by the avatar of Miss Earth when she opened the envelope. Her avatar walked up to mine and grabbed ahold of one of the chains to disperse the lustfully pink smoke—a Way/Point signal of a relationship, which instantly doubled my number of followers. I had no choice but to swipe the grid away, as it could've distracted me for the rest of the night. This was the first time I had a notable social status. I wished I could've cherished it, but tonight's race was more important. I could lose everything I'd gained up until now if I didn't obtain three points. *No pressure, Craven.* I'd picked the Atlas as my symbolic suit for these types of moments.

With still more time to kill, I began to wonder around the locker. I learned that Beta was absent from his room of black furry walls with a full white moon on the ceiling. It was such an amazing design that one could only smile at. The Yin Hound instead chose to spend his pre-race ritual with Miss Brink in her room. A morbid but appropriate room with hearts constricted in barbed wire on the wall. I assumed the hound had been accepted by the Brink family as I'd heard from Kira that her parents could be over-protective. Like me, she was an only child, so her parents tended to spoil her. Heh, imagine if they spoiled Beta. *Brink Industries* wasn't a heavyweight, but if they ever catered to the twin's trademark of a combo'd suit, heads would surely turn. Better yet, imagine if the company paired with *The Blue Jay's Nest.* We could be like one of those superteams in the NBA. A bird could only dream.

My fantasy paused once I confronted Meta outside of his blinding room filled with the shining-white fur that could be seen from Pluto. Thankfully the moon in his room was undergoing a lunar eclipse. The lone hound for once wasn't annoying, maybe it was because he was alone. He seemed more focused than usual, preparing himself for whatever the Carnivores had in store. He told me that up to five racers from this race could enter Greenland depending on the outcome. I didn't really think much of the calculations. The only point-scenario I'd been paying attention to lately was mine and Midas'. Meta was getting ready to explain everything but was interrupted by the music coming from downstairs. I went to investigate it myself due to Meta's contemplation of meeting a Carnivore.

The music became more recognizable down the stairway. It sounded like Mozart's "Requiem" played on an ancient record player. I glanced into reliQ's room to see if the music originated from there, but only saw the seated giant lubricating his triple-necked guitar with the Ghastallion nerve agent Gabriella noted. I almost felt bad for Titan, like how the hell did he even fit into the locker. His room might've been bigger than the rest, but the grandé treatment would end there as the tunnel to the track echoed its Terran-size structures. I pondered upon the thought until someone yanked me by the collar away from reliQ's room, tossing me onto the hard pavement of a room with obsidian walls and red moons on the ceiling. Mozart was playing louder than ever, and an image of a dripping wet hammerhead stood tall over my grounded body. It seemed like I was taking a shower from all of the water dripping off of Krakyn's adaptive suit.

"Look ova here Loosh, izza doozie!" the shark enthusiastically said. His voice was very vibrant, almost as if they were talking underwater. There were streams of liquid gushing out the small-teeth spiked mouth. The 18th Century music lost its volume. "Whazzo special bout you?"

"For starters, I'm a friend," I replied to the shark as he bent over for a greater look. Krakyn was a lot larger in person with his head doubling the size of mine in height and width.

"And a lova of the Gold gal, you spect may to believe that? You chew are the Romeo and Juliet of Verza."

"Well, I didn't take you for a lover of Shakespeare."

"You callin may incompatent?"

"Well, I'm not calling you a bonehead," I said sarcastically. The shark's eyes dilated as he wrapped his wet giant hands around my neck with a huge grumble. A sharp end of a blade then pressed itself into the center of Krakyn's forehead, contracting the shark's eye back to normal. He loosened his grip.

"We were told not to harm the boy," another voice stated in a soft, calm tone. I leaned my head upward to see the Satanian standing in front of Krakyn.

"Hear may, Loosh!"

"I do hear you, now hear me. We do not harm the boy," Lucifer stated once again, scramming the shark away. They slammed their fist into the wall on the way out. Crumbs of obsidian fell onto the floor. I thanked the Satanian as I got back onto my feet, readjusting my drenched jacket. It was good to have a peaceful understanding with the one alien that spoke fluent English. "Krakyn is right, we know that this… ugh… engagement is a farce."

"What makes you say that, don't believe in true love?" I told him, getting a good view at his smooth light-gray face with white unpyrolytic veins running up the side of his cheeks to his black eyes where the white veins were most noticeable. Similar to the eye's color, his lips were black and had the tiny black bones of his jawline protrude out of the skin in a Satanian beard.

"A month ago, she was pulling the strings of Jack. Then, all of a sudden, she's pulling yours?" Lucifer pointed out, seeing right through the lie. Gabriella had failed to mention her acquaintance with Jackal—another of her secrets.

"Why the protection if you know it's a lie?"

"Because it's the best move, for now," Lucifer stated as a horn went off in the background, alerting the racers of a ten-minute countdown. Lucifer placed his katanas down to turn on his Satanian exosuit from *The Golden Evolution*. An all-black 666 Hades Z-Model with Terran bones as armor around the torso of the suit. Tubes also ran along the arms, connected to some type of machinery on the back where the turbo tank should be. I couldn't quite tell what it was though. "You ought to be getting ready boy; won't be able to protect you on the field."

I made the wise choice of heeding the Satanian's advice, leaving him be in his room, taking a long glance at the closed door labeled, "The Clawed Cardiac." If there was any room I should've entered, it was that one, but it didn't matter anymore because time was of the essence. In less than ten minutes, we were finally going to welcome the nightmare named Krueger.

LAYERS OF INSANITY

CLOSED MY EYES TO THE RUMBLING HOLLERS OF PEOPLE ERUPTING IN THE STRAIGHTAWAY OF BLEACHERS OUTSIDE, PROFFERING THEIR LOVE TO THE COMPETITORS AWAITING THE SIREN. FIREWORKS SOARED INTO THESE HEAVENS, AWAKING THE GODS FOR OUR MAIN EVENT. Expanding metal ran across the hair strands on my body, compressing my suit's interior cushion into each relaxed muscle of my body; acclimating itself to the over-exaggerating inhales of my lungs, fluently pushing the streams of blood to every needed cell, and cooling the temperature.

"Feels good to be online," MIKA said, as I opened my eyes to the inner screen of the helmet's visor. Scrolling paragraphs of coding appeared on the top left corner, booting the layout to the race track called Kingdom Come with puzzling sections, each completely different from the other. The Milky Way section on the east side of the park was a dome with an unknown interior. Next was the Living Forest around the park's perimeter. The following section was the Haunted Caverns on the west side of the park. My visor's outline of the track showed the caverns as a labyrinth—every racer's worst nightmare. The last section took the track to the center of the park around the floating castle where there were a lot of ramps including the final one.

"Have you uploaded the logs of each racer?" I asked MIKA through the Atlas' booting stage.

"Should I?" MIKA questioned, implying it would be irrelevant due to the superb performances of the past two races. I was not the only one who could get cocky during a hot streak.

"For the safety of our lifespans, you should probably upload the log."

"If you say so, the other racers shouldn't be a huge problem…" she said, trailing off. "Since when did Earth allow Non-Terran competitors in their Pro Leagues?"

"Story for a different day. Is it possible for you to access past recordings of races with my father squaring up against Satanians, Chondrycks, and Gigallians? Any type of info regarding weaknesses would help out a lot." I urgently requested, really wishing I had grabbed a couple books from my dad's library on the way to Florida.

MIKA was going to need some time to skim through her archives, so I had no choice but to venture downstairs. Every locker door stood open to an empty room, every room except for one, Krueger's. His door was still closed, provoking me to ram the Atlas' dell through the doorway. The image of Krueger's room sparked another set of questions with zero answers. The sight momentarily made me pull off my helmet. An empty gray room, pristine and untouched, lacking any trace of a racer's presence. No spot for an exosuit, no bench, nothing! Who the hell is Krueger, a goddamn ghost?

"We're gonna need you on the track McGuire," the guard named Dick ordered from the locker's tunnel. I glanced over my shoulder to ask him if he knew anything about The Clawed Cardiac. He shrugged, just as clueless as I. "Damnit Dick, you had one job."

"Yeah, making money off yo sorry ass," Dick replied as the time for questions had reached an end. There was only one place in this world right now that could give me answers, and it was calling my name, now more powerful than ever.

"CRAAAVENNN!

CRAAAVENNN!

CRAAAVENNN!

CRAAAVENNN!

CRAAAVENNN!"

I could hear the crowd chanting in sync from outside. The chant interfered with the neurological signals from my sense of touch creating a ghost-like sensation of levitation, more so than any painkiller. I couldn't feel the pounding of my heart, the expansion of my lungs, the grip of my helmet, or the soles of my feet. Ghost status.

Like a moth drawn to the light, my soul was linked to the chants, instinctively guiding me through the tunnel, hoping to give the crowd what they were pleading for. I was met with a standing ovation with hands and holosigns beaming into the air reading: *The G.O.A.T.'s Heir, Our Knight & Shining Armor, A Shield's Mightier Than A Sword.* This was an unfamiliar feeling, something I had not experienced from previous races.

There wasn't enough time for me to absorb the fan-base's energy. I couldn't even find Gabriella, didn't know what she meant by an exclusive spot. There weren't any booths above the stands, only a swarm of drones hovering over the entire straightaway. There had to have been at least a thousand drones, all beaming the colors of my suit, neon-blue and gray. Below them was the real incarnation of the race, each competitor standing in their lane, 10m diagonally in front of one another. The closest racer from the tunnel in the eighth lane was Meta, rambling at his fellow competitors in lanes six and seven. The pair in those lanes were Kira and Beta, both of them wearing the same suits from Knightfall.

"Hey, I hope your boyfriend doesn't try to shove you off of the track this time," I warned Kira, quickly tapping her shoulder as a friendly gesture.

"Aye, that was Meta!" Beta shouted defensively.

"No, it wasn't," Meta revealed. "I was the one who turned on the boost. You were the one who tried to shove them off."

"So you did trigger the boost!" Beta exclaimed. This started an argument between the hounds as Kira's hands covered her face. She'd gone almost an entire week without hearing the two argue, but then I happened. If only I felt bad for them.

I placed my helmet back on after realizing who was in the fifth lane. In the navy-blue 2240 Glaucus HC-Model, a specified suit made for Hamer Chondrycks from *The Golden Evolution*, was Krakyn. The suit came with a unique helmet that wrapped around the ends of the hammerhead for armor with a glass visor that covered the entire face. At the moment, his helmet was off as his saliva spattered onto my visor during his growls. I should have invested in wiper blades for the Atlas' helmet.

In the fourth lane was the Satanian in his gray bone-covered Hades with two double-edged katanas in its sheath along the sides of a revealing turbo tank on the suit's latis. Tanks weren't meant to be that large. The larger the tank, the bigger the combustible target, even for a Satanian. Our helmets eventually locked visors, sending a nerve-wrecking chill down my spine. His helmet had a horse's skull with black retracted visors in the eye sockets. The jaw to the skull was replaced with black tubes leading to a showerhead-shaped mouth. A similar pair of black tubes ran around the arms and legs of the exosuit with open ends near the hands and feet. The clever sonuvabitch was using the turbo tank to kindle the flames he was unable to do himself. Great. If his katanas weren't deadly enough, toss in a flamethrower.

The bowl of mixed feelings continued to stir as I reached the triple-sized third lane occupied by the giant in a gray 2250 Colossus, a specified Gigallian suit with eight wheels instead of four. Best known as the semi-truck, a truck that stood skyscraper tall. For the first time in my life, I felt like a dwarf standing next to Titan. The distal portions of his arms and legs were covered in krone armor with a more flexible layer of metal armor around his torso to prevent suffocation. The flexible layer was more importantly breakable—a weakness I expect him to defend heavily with the triple-neck guitar strapped to his latis. In the second lane was the Initiator waving his hands inward, signaling me to come closer, letting me know the lane was mine. In other words, a giant was going to be on my ass at the start of the race. Great. This left me with one racer to play catch-up with on the straightaway, and they were nowhere in sight.

"Kruuuuuueeeger

    Kruuuuuueeeger

        Kruuuuuueeeger

            Kruuuuuueeeger

                Kruuuuuueeeger!"

The chants grew louder and louder, forcing me to search all around like a paranoid politician. First at the tunnel, then the gate, followed by the bleachers. He was still nowhere, but that's when all of the drones came together to form a wall in front of the starting line, beaming all of their lights bright-white. Some of the drones near the bottom of the wall began to turn their lights red with several more near the top doing the same until the image created a smiling red face of a Jack-o-lantern. The presentation made the entire crowd go nuts, causing all of the drones to scatter back to the night sky revealing the racer waiting behind the wall. It was him, it was Krueger, finally in my sights. The unfamiliar black suit that Krueger wore had its wheels still holstered, showing how sharp and shiny the claws were. Just like parts of reliQ's armor, the claws were krone. An expensive metal for Terrans to acquire and yet Krueger had it on all twenty anatomical digits.

Knowing what their score was, Krueger claimed the first lane without any words or actions, standing still, calm, and collected. He was going to have to maintain the given lead from all of us if Krueger wanted to keep his momentum. Out of all of the racers, he had the biggest target on his back. There was no telling what the Carnivores were going to do when they caught him. Gabriella shouldn't have been worried about me harming the guy. I was the least of his worries.

All of the hovering drones kept their red-and-white lights on to represent the leading racer even though the race hadn't even begun. That must've been less than a minute away because the Initiator was telling us all to have our wheels out and ready, ordering us to get down in the starting position. I instantly felt the inflation of the wheels, smoothly transitioning themselves down my limbs, stationing themselves in each palmix.

"So, I was able to find some encounters where Crank prevailed in battle," MIKA began to inform me once I was on my knees getting a few torso stretches in, contorting the muscles into a proper stance. "Chondrycks rely on their water supply like any Pyscean, take it away and you have something weaker than a Terran. Gigallians as we know have brittle skin, but they also have sensitive nerves in the limbs. They typically coat the area with small trims of krone. As for Satanians, Crank only went against the osculated, where weaknesses revolved around their pyrolytic veins. Without the flames, Satanians are as equal as Terrans, lucky you."

"Yeeeeaaaah, about that," I said as the flamethrower ignited in the background, blowing its fire in the air like an ancient dragon.

"You're kidding," MIKA muttered in a stressful tone.

"Don't worry, we'll find a weakness, thanks for everything," I told MIKA, trying to bring my breathing patterns into a zen-like state. Each inhale longer than the previous until the drones in the air aligned their Krueger's colors into a 10...9...8.

"50...400..." Tokyn's commentary began in my head like a broken record. The curse in my head that would never die, somehow slowing down time once the drones showed "7." It wasn't just the timer, it was everyone. The fans in the bleachers were now moving in a frame-by-frame manner, some of them landing their jump with others still in the air screaming. The Initiator, walking backwards with his right arm held high, waiting for the drones to show "0," and Krueger, who was slowly looking up at someone standing in front of him. It was another racer in a blue-and-green suit with a shattered visor on the helmet. The dangling parts of metal streamed blood onto the ground, adding onto the layers of insanity. I knew who the standing figure was. Of course I knew. The unforgettable image of my father, always haunting me in the races. Always reminding me that I was not normal.

Krueger looked over his dell at me until our visors locked. I could only see the reflection of my own helmet in his black visor. The ghost of my father began to ooze more gallons of blood from his carotid artery. Krueger's helmet then displayed the red smile we were all used to seeing. Leaving me frozen as a siren went off in my head. Krueger launched himself down the straightaway along with all six of the racers behind me. I fell to last place in a matter of milliseconds from the shaken state. I couldn't hear anything, feel, smell or taste anything. I could only see the sight of every single racer getting smaller in the distance. I closed my eyes only to open them to a swarm of drones now spelling 4...3...2...1. I was jolted back to reality and the ghost of my dad was nowhere in sight. Streams of sweat ran down my cheeks, fogging some of the inner parts of my visor. I launched myself to the side of Krueger's leg once the drones showed "0."

My timed reaction may have eliminated Krueger's lead, but the incredible jolt of acceleration from his suit helped him control first place. I thought for sure that the lights were going to shine my identity, instead the heavens only displayed red-and-white clouds. Another set of fireworks crackled and boomed their colors over the castle, the only thing on this straightaway that wasn't a blur from our top speeds. The first turn curved us right and wasn't tight enough to alter our speeds. It was a turn good enough to increase Krueger's lead. The outer end of the curve forced me to cover more distance. He developed a suits-length lead at the end of the turn. The track started straightening itself out into the first corkscrew loop of the race. MIKA placed the suit's boost on an activated status for the corkscrew's highest point. It put me right beside Krueger with an inch of a lead, an inch that turned the sky neon-blue. Krueger frowned during our stare down, then smiled after he reclaimed first. A master view of the dome could be seen at the end of the loop, guiding us to the entrance.

"...HIND YOU!" MIKA rushed in the nick of time, shuffling my suit to the left, avoiding the quaking slam of wheels with a loud ding of sparks coming from the separated neck of reliQ's guitar. Remembering how fatal a blow from the guitar could be, I triggered a bit of my boost to maintain second.

Krueger led the way into the darkness-filled dome. Speckle-size lights were all around the dome's interior like the stars of the galaxy. At first glance, a striking image, but it wasn't good enough for a clear vision of the track. MIKA turned on the visor's night vision, revealing the corkscrew of loops that could ravage the strongest colon. Some of the loops introduced multiple pathways, separating us all. None of us had any idea which way we should choose. Each path was another loop that tangled our minds even more in this mind-boggling galaxy. Racers chose to leap onto other pathways instead of speeding through each one like I did. An agonizing choice that became more and more unbearable from all of the loops. My vision blurred from what seemed like the umpteenth loop, unsettling my stomach. I was headed for a nauseating climax before an exit suddenly appeared at the end of the final loop.

A red and white covered sky turned neon-blue once I was outside, now heading into the Living Forest. The asphalt track turned into dirt. My suit, shining in the sky, kept me moving forward before the trees began to crash down onto the tight paths in front, decreasing my speed to zero. The track's layout on my visor didn't show how big the damn forest was, it instead marked my location at the center point of the woodlands. It was official, I was lost and fucked because the lights of the sky were strobing multiple identities, every identity except mine. I moved the rear-wheels up to my patallises to explore the forest.

MIKA encouraged me to observe the environment once I was at the apparent center. To the east, a parade of dancing flames crackling the leaves, killing the forest. To the west, a dark-pink racer climbing up to the top of the tallest tree, searching for an exit that seemed to be north, but the sounds of branches snapping grew louder and closer from the south. A roar developed from the same direction forcing me to leap out of the anarchist's pathway. A blurry silhouette zoomed by, stopping with a sideways brake.

"Friend or Foe?" MIKA questioned as I stared at the racer hidden in the darkness. We both stood up, almost synchronized, looking at the shadow of one another. The fresh flash of red and white unveiled the hammer-shaped head.

"FOE!" I shouted, running north of the burning forest, not wanting to be Krakyn's target. There was a hate-at-first-spite bond between us. The rams of metal dwindled in the background, giving me a chance to reset. The sudden chase prevented me from resetting my wheels, a fault that wouldn't hurt me as I noticed a long blade lodged into the stem of an unburnt tree. The handle to the blade was made out of bone, raising a smile on my face. I raced over to pull it out, causing my right arm to transform into Aegis once the blade was at hand. Several drones caught the true image of a knight as a highlight that would probably headline the Unican Network and my Way/Point avatar for the next week.

My location was discovered once again by the Pyscean, thrashing through a tree. I was ready for the clash and could see him gazing at the burnt trees nearby. Fire had never been his friend, helping me realize that he was nothing without the supplies of water to his suit. It gave him an advantage over me, especially via strength, something more obvious than ever as he deadlifted a destroyed tree over his head to toss at me. I dove out of the way, making my body a landing strip for the Pyscean. I surged into a lunged position, bracing my shield for the hammerhead attempting to batter my arm in half. The impact made the hæmalytes lock themselves around the attacking end of the head. Now in a peculiar position, Krakyn squirmed rapidly out of panic. Snatching the upper-hand, I severed the water tubes around his torso, setting the streams free. The roaring screams turned into suffering groans as the water drained out, slowing his movements ten-fold. I then used the katana to slice off the hammer's end locked into my shield. The Pyscean catapulted me through multiple trees once it was detached. Several sections of the latis felt like a bed of fists, making it harder to breathe. I lost my grip around the katana during the launch but found I didn't need it because Krakyn was busy trying to place pressure on the opened tubes, eventually driving away.

"Why attack first when you can attack last," I uttered once the coast was clear, resting my eyes on the image of a Krueger-colored sky beyond the leaves.

"Your dad isn't the only McGuire who can best a Pyscean," MIKA added as I placed my focus back on the race but froze in place, now eyeing the ghost of my father standing atop of the leveled trees. The leaves around us rattled with the rumbles of the ground. My father raised his arm, pointing in the direction behind me, past the burnt portion of the forest, revealing what seemed like a torpedo booming through the woodland. If anything, it was creating a pathway; possibly a way out. I quickly ordered MIKA to scan the area for Lucifer's katana, knowing I was going to need it later. I got down on all four once we found it to tail the wrecking ball out. The debris of shattered wood chips and leaves kept sticking to my visor until the surface turned asphalt. A smooth familiarity that relaxed the muscles I didn't realize were contracted. A short-lived feeling once I spied Krueger unorthodoxically riding a Gigallian like an ancient mammoth.

The drones didn't know whether to shine red and white or gray and ivory, so I provided them with a definitive answer by boosting past the competitors to take the lead. Just like the start of the race, Krueger and I locked visors. Three out of the four clawed limbs were implanted in reliQ's back with the one free arm used for balance. It didn't take long for Krueger to wave at me with that arm.

"Craven, I don't know how, but Krueger's controlling the Gigallian's suit," MIKA stated as the rider and I stayed side by side during a trio of turns. The grip I had around Lucifer's katana could've been classified as ossificated. I was ready for Krueger to shove me off of the track, but the action never came as we entered the underground section of the race, the Haunted Caverns. This should have been the third and final puzzle, eliminating our sight of the drones. Left in the unknown, Krueger and I were separated. The night vision of my helmet acted as an attribute inside this cave, almost lost in the darkness. The multiple pathways ensured moments of deja vu. It might not have been as disorienting as The Milky Way, but it was surely stressful. A thunderous vibration suddenly quaked the cavern like the impact of an asteroid. Rubble fell onto the track combined with dust covering my sight. Blinded, I collided with the cave's rock-solid wall, placing more pressure points of protruding metal into my body. Breathing in the suit became more difficult so I had to stay calm through the misery. MIKA was able to save the day by highlighting a pathway out of the cave before we were stuck in there for good.

The drones in the sky shone my colors as the lone racer on this track, now circling around the floating castle to the big ramp. I felt comfortable enough to cruise the rest of the way, but the lights quickly turned back to Krueger's colors. I couldn't see the racer anywhere on the track, but I sped up anyways, reclaiming the lead. The drones continued to play a game of ping pong with our colors until I took the big leap off the ramp's peak, revealing the racer who was driving upside down underneath the track like a spider the whole time. The smile on his face seemed bigger and redder than ever. We both landed on the final straightaway at the same time, prepared for the concluding blows from each other that never came. Krueger was actually slowing down, surprisingly handing me first place.

The fans and reporters stormed the track to admire my performance, preventing me from catching the racer who was undefeated once upon a time. Like the other races in this series, the people were patient, unlike the Semi Leagues where they were shoving, grabbing, and shooting random questions about my father's legacy. All of them scattered around the track preventing me from confronting Krueger who was making his way to the locker. The reporters kept their questions short and sweet with fans requesting selfies, a comforting feeling I could adapt to if we stayed on the topic of today and not tomorrow. There was a sudden pause as another racer crossed the finish line. An ignited Satanian made his claim for third place, extinguishing the flames with a tight grip around the lone katana. The herd of people opened up a pathway for Lucifer and I to meet halfway for the handoff. I thanked him for losing the katana that ended up saving my life. I could see the small grin on his face once our helmets were off. I honestly didn't know what he was going to do, I've never read about thankful interactions with a Satanian. The moment was interrupted by the racer claiming fourth place, Kira Brink, followed by the hounds combined as one for fifth. Meta, who was on top of his brother had steam escaping from multiple portions of his suit during the detachment process.

"That sonuvabitch right there!" Meta shouted once his helmet was off, pointing at the Satanian beside me. I quickly noticed the cut marks near the steamy entries of his suit, putting two and two together.

"No pain, no gain, right?" Lucifer replied, aggravating the hound into a contracted motion choking out an invisible figure. His brother eventually came over to calm Meta down while paramedics checked to see if the cuts were fatal.

"Did you win like usual?" Kira asked, slightly nudging my arm.

"Of course," I replied, remembering Kira's standing with the five points obtained from this race, letting her know where we were going next, Greenland. It would be the first time since the start of the series where she would be without hounds as they missed the premier threshold, only acquiring twenty points each. After the small talk, Lucifer and I made our way into the locker, leaving Kira with the hounds and the herd. Our first stop was Krueger's room, which was empty once again. Lucifer was hoping for the confrontation. Apparently Krueger caused reliQ to crash back in the caverns—the source of the quake. Revenge for his step-brother would have to wait. I gave him some space, also remembering the piece of Krakyn still stuck in my shield, hoping the Satanian wouldn't notice.

Luckily for me, I was able to leave the locker in one piece, avoiding any form of conflict. I did leave the piece of Krakyn's head in his room, knowing that forgiveness was a shot in the dark. I wasn't sure if I was supposed to wait for Gabriella, so I ordered a ride back to the Lotus on my own. The Re-Versable flyers were all gone once I returned, saving some of the hotel's reputation towards Versa racing. The bruises on my back lessoned, pain-wise, by the time I reached the elevator. I went to my room first for ice, instantly smelling the seasoned, sizzling raptr on the dinner table. There was a note on it from Trace reading,

"One streak down, One to go brother.

Yo Boy, Trace"

His support temporarily relieved the pain. I heard the loud thud of a slamming door from the room above. It had to have been Gabriella or Krueger, either way, the time for secrets had to come to an end. I left the prepared entrée in my room for later to discover whatever truth awaited me. For the first time, there were no security guards in front of the Gold's penthouse. With my hand firmly on the door knob, and my heart pounding in my chest, I was finally going to meet The Clawed Cardiac.

The black carbon fiber helmet to his custom suit rested on a golden table in front of a couch. Gabriella stood on the balcony. She had a glass of wine in her hand, wearing her go-to leather outfit while staring at the fireworks bursting near the castle. I slammed the door loud enough for her to know that I was here, instantly seeing the big smile on her face.

"Soooooo, where is he? Where's Krueger?" I asked.

Gabriella put down the glass of wine. "Well…he…is actually a she… I'm Krueger."

ACT II
CHAPTER 8

GOLDEN WRATH

GABRIELLA WAS KRUEGER? I HADN'T SEEN EVEN A HINT OF IT. She was the last person I expected Krueger to be; the suit itself was designed for a man. Female suits typically had a wider hip threxis and protruding pectars. I understood that a custom-made suit could create an illusion, something Krueger had been notorious for, but I was just mad that I couldn't catch it. My father's ghost even hinted at it during the race, and I never caught on.

"Well…" Gabriella said with opened arms. It may have broken the silence, but it didn't kill the tension. How the hell could I respond to my girlfriend disguised as the baddest racer in the baddest sport with one of the biggest targets on their backs? Roy vented about his wife, Kriss, competing countless number of times, making irrational statements about how distracting and stressful it could be. Catelyn Brannigan, one of "the surviving seven," saw her girlfriend get torn into pieces during a race. "Claire told me to unmask myself, so here I am, unafraid."

"It's not me you should be afraid of," I finally said, killing the smile on Gabriella's face. I took a seat on the couch trying to unscramble the thoughts in my head. My tired image reflected clear as water in the helmet's visor.

"I thought you'd understand," she said, testing my temper to the situation.

"Understand? How could I possibly understand? First, you tell me that we have to stop your brother from winning because his life is on the line. Then I'm told about the branch of enemies on his ass, and now to cap it all off, you're actually one of them," I yelled for all of Dessnia to hear. I was out of breath from the exertion. There was only so much one could put their body through in one night, let alone an entire day. The depletion of energy caused my hands to tremble. Gabriella could see it too and came over to hold them, calming me down a bit.

"I'm sorry, I just wanted us to trust one another," she softly answered. The words seemed genuine from the look in her eyes. For once, it actually felt like Gabriella had let her mask down.

"The Carnivores are gonna kill you when they find out."

"My life isn't as important as my brother's."

"If it ever comes down to you or him, you've gotta believe that I'm choosing you each time." The statement provoked her to let go of my hands. She must have known she was becoming too important in my eyes.

"You can't ever do that in this series. There's a lot of crap my brother's death triggers."

"What happens?"

"Claire… she told me… his death… it resurrects Galactica… leading to Earth's extinction," she revealed. I didn't know how to feel about that. It had to be fake. How could one man's life decide the fate of billions? "The death creates a storm of wrath that my father will oversee. He's an impulsively selfish man who only cares about the Gold's name and will create anarchy in order to protect it. Power, Catherine, and Midy are pretty much the only three things he cares about in this world even though he equally abuses all of them. He'd snap if he ever lost one of the three, especially Midy. My father will unleash hell on everyone involved in the Pro League, including the aliens. He'll break galactic law. Earth's controversy won't sit well with the Hendecalliance, resurrecting Galactica to avoid a war. It'll also kill the exchange system Earth has with the Hendecalliance, including my father's company. He owns most of the planet's wealth and his arrogance will gamble it all on the team that he'll create, and you can basically figure out what happens next."

"We lose," I responded to Gabriella's revelation. "It'd be Ragnios all over again." I got up to head over to the balcony for some fresh air. It didn't take long for Gabriella to come up to my side. She wanted me to promise that I'd always pick Midas over her in this series. That just wasn't a promise I could make. I told her Claire's revelation, *bestow the cold to save a gold*. It might now refer to Gabriella. And I didn't care whether her brother lived or not.

"Why was I considered the last line of defense?" I touched upon for some clarification. She told me that her father's animosity towards my name kept him from letting me aid with Earth's defense in Galactica. I, instead, would be equivalent to Thorax in the following Galactica series, hoping to reclaim the riches that were once lost as Earth's last line of defense. Claire's insight on how I would fare was apparently blurry. Gabriella figured why not use me now instead of later, which was why she stepped away from Jackal—someone who was temporarily her ally until he became one of the possible candidates in her brother's demise. Based on Lucifer's statement, I knew that there was something between her and Jackal, but it didn't matter anymore. The entire Terran race was on the line, and we couldn't let stupid shit get in the way.

More fireworks began to burst into the night sky. There must have been more races going on, but none as important as the one to come. There had to be a strategy for how Gabriella and I could prevent a tragedy.

"So, If Midas wins?" I proposed.

"The Carnivores kill him," Gabriella responded. "If we get carelessly sent to a bracket Midy isn't in, and he ends up racing against Law, then he's dead."

"So, we basically have to babysit him throughout the entire series, no matter what happens."

"No matter what," she quickly replied, resting her head on my shoulder. "Craven, as long as we have each other, nothing's going to happen to him."

"That's easy for you to say, I'm still trying to figure out how to bestow the cold."

"The Winter week is our next challenge. I reckon there'll be a lot of cold factors," she inferred, reminding the obvious. What was once an unbearable moment of truth somehow switched to an unimaginable moment of peace. I finally felt glad that she was Krueger. I mean, I'd been constantly stating how amazing this racer was, basically nerding out in front of Gabriella on multiple occasions, unaware of who she really was. I wanted to know more about her story, on how she came up with the character, the design, the abilities, everything really. She was the blooming rose in a pile of shit that we were stuck in, luckily for Earth, we were stuck in it together.

The tension of the long night came to a close at the conclusion of the fireworks. We made the most out of our final night at the Lotus by spending it together, knowing that we were going to have to create a clever scheme that could keep Midas alive through the Winter week, or better yet, bestow the cold that saves the Gold.

ACT II

CHAPTER 9

FORT KNOX'S PLATEAU

ABLINDING SKY BLURRED MY VISION. It kept drifting in and out, in and out, in and then out to a cracked image. My eyes slowly focused on more cracks stretching further across the white sky, a sky that began to cry frozen white tears that fell without ever reaching my face. There was some transparent shield around my face, protecting me. It wasn't the sky that had a crack, it was the shield around my face. I gently twisted my head to the side to see more of the landscape. Whiteness, more and more of it, stretched beyond a curly-haired woman in a black tank top sitting next to me. It didn't take long for her image to fade away. I then noticed my arm covered in some type of metal armor with a bone sticking out of it. No, this couldn't be a race, I thought I was… wasn't I just with the… the tank-topped woman… the one with a long curly ponytail… Gabriella?

"The legendary Crank McGuire has accomplished so…" a man's voice uttered in the background. I felt like I recognized it. The tone of the voice was so similar to the one's I heard in my head all the time. Whoever it was, maybe they could help. I didn't know how I got in this position, but I had to do something before I was buried in the sky's tears. I twisted my head in the other direction and saw a man staring down at me. He had the same light-brown eyes and hair as me, except there were shards of glass penetrating his left cheek. The brutal injury didn't stop the man from offering his hand to me. I knew that my right arm was broken, so I decided to reach up with my left. I heard the crunching getting louder. I opened my eyes. I was still in bed, watching the bright-white clouds drift by a window. My heart was racing faster than normal, but slowed down after realizing I was only dreaming, but the crunching sounds continued. I looked over at Gabriella, staring back at me. She was eating French toast and had a lot of crumbs on her shirt.

"Burrfast?" she tried to say while eating, offering me the piece in her hand.

"McGuire has accomplished so much, therefore his son's got the seed for greatness," a man's voice uttered, once again making me sit up to see who it was. Across one wall of the room, an image of a blue-haired man with a blue beard was talking to another person behind a table. The words, "Unican Network" marked the bottom corner of the man's image.

"Grad's been talking about you all morning. When is he gonna talk about me?" Gabriella asked, talking like I was wide awake. I was still trying to get myself together. I recognized the show she had on, though. It was called Vice Versa—a show where Gradite and his co-analyst Lenny Jackson, an older African American man with a bald head, a goatee, and a lone mole isolated on his lower right cheek acted as opposers. Like a match made in a Satanian hell, these two would bicker for an eternity if it brought validation of their opinions, and we, as the audience, would always tune in. Their personalities were the main attraction.

"I believe that we are in the midst of something great. There's a unique sense of excitement that rushes through my veins whenever I watch this boy perform," Gradite said, gesturing his hands all around like a helicopter ready to fly out of his seat. The image on the TV then transitioned to me in the Atlas, gripping Lucifer's katana in front of the burning trees. "I dare ya to tell me that you don't see greatness, I dare ya."

"That was a badass image," Gabriella tried to add while eating. A line of words ran across the screen reading, *A True Knight's Tale*. Gradite began to argue my potential against Lenny who was counter-arguing and singing the accolades of racers like Midas, Jackal, and Law. Highlights of them in their races appeared until Layla Rose, the Moderator of the show mentioned Krueger. Gabriella finally cheered. Gradite had some derogatory points about Krueger, comments that brought out a more vulgar side of Gabriella, considering she hardly swore. The group of analysts then shifted their discussion to the opening race of the Winter week in a couple days. A 13-man race taking place on a brand-new track called Peak, a Naturis track running along the edges of Greenland's center mountain. A race that included the likes of me, Gabriella, Midas, Law, Warlock, Creed, Kira, Lucifer, Zane and the tumbling Amaryllis children. This was the premier bracket, a list of talented individuals in the analysts' eyes, but not in ours. Gabriella and I only saw threats. Five Carnivores, one gunslinger, one raven, and a pair of brutal forces that we'd forgotten all about. The challenge killed the serene start to the day and pushed us to think of a game plan. Footage of the young track showed a lack of railings, making Midas' survival damn-near impossible. Gabriella pushed out of the bed to get dressed. She explained that she had a hidden workshop in Greenland near her family's manor and that we would have to regroup there pronto.

We chowed down the rest of the breakfast before going our separate ways, leaving our Way/Point grids open for conversing. I caught the scent of a leftover steak. There on the dining room table lay an uneaten raptr Trace would never forgive. It was a good thing he wasn't here. I threw away the evidence before dipping into the shower. Red, purple, and jaundice marks pigmented my body, making the pounding impacts of water in the shower almost unendurable. These were the tolls of being a Versa racer. I was beginning to understand why Roy called it quits. The Semi Leagues were nothing compared to the Pro's, and I didn't even wanna know how to reference my state to Galactica. Roy always talked about the distinct satisfaction of Galactica, always calling it the sui generis nature of Versa. An adrenaline rush like no other. Even a pacifist could get addicted. He knew about the agony and the ecstasy of the galactic competitions. From the universal respect of talents to the gambled life-spans our technology couldn't even extend. Roy, he once showed me a scar from a Rzurkin's cryuille, a crystal spike that grew on their backs like hair. The cryuille at first glance looks like a bright-pink crystal, but it was a combination of microorganisms solidified as one with spiky ends, a weapon that was javelined into Roy's gut in Galactica XLV. The hit wasn't fatal, on a short-term basis. As for a long-term, time would only tell. Terrans were always told by Rokian legends to avoid cryuille at all cost because of how fragile and viscid the microorganisms could be. To this day, there were still a bunch of tiny parts of the cryuille internally splintered in Roy's stomach, which could poison his body or develop into a xenoncologen, a cancer produced by alien tissue. One of the few scars endured by Roy's tenure as a racer. It made me wonder if there were more injuries that he was suffering from on a daily basis, like the neurological injuries Dr. Perris mentioned. Was there a reason why I always saw the ghost of my father covered in blood? Was there a reason I always heard Gradite and Tokyn's voice in my head? Dreams of me dying in my Atlas? Was I one bad day away from losing me, not my life, just me?

The importance of Midas' life didn't help my state of mind. Something I thought long and hard about during my departure from Florida. I still had Dr. Perris' business card, wondering whether or not I should make the call on the short jet ride north. I decided to hold off on it once the ice kingdom appeared on the horizon. Holoboard signs crowded the country, advertising the Gold family. A country that used to be known for its icy white glaciers now had acres of gold blanketing the snow, golden statues of all the exosuits manufactured by Luke's company, and bedazzled penguins marching around in golden flippers. Here I was, judging the presentation of the Lotus, Cronus, and Midas himself, thinking there was no way a man could exceed the threshold levels of a golden caricature. But here I was, leaning my head against the window of a landing jet, officially giving birth to a golden migraine. My saving grace was the pilot's gift to me, a pair of shades masking the beaming lasers of golden sparkles on this sunny day. The port itself wasn't as big as the colors made it out to be—a spacious country floating on a glittered iceberg. Scattered on the landing strip were drivers, each awaiting the next racer. No reporters, no security, no fans, just drivers near limousines that were surprisingly black, considering all things. I didn't overthink my choice of driver, I pretty much eeny meeny miny moe'd the pick to quickly shade myself inside a vehicle.

Trace sent me a message on Way/Point telling me to head to the Hans Egede hotel not too far away from the port. I didn't realize that I had landed in the capital of Greenland, a country that quite frankly was Goldland. The migraine fostered hatred towards everything revolving around the term "gold," the word, the element, the surname. Sharing my annoyance were several supporters of the FMJ movement, vandalizing some of the statues of Midas by spraying an "X" on the eyes and sketching the words: *Pierced by my Pierce* across the chest. Their acts reminded me of a vital fact. They were as capable of killing Midas as any other foe in this series, especially if anything were to happen to Law by the hands of Midas. God, I had to find out how to *bestow the cold*.

I settled my mind with a few drinks in the car on the way to the Hans Egede, a large white and blue twenty-floor hotel. The walls to the entrance were crimson, the mosaic floor tiles were dark-brown, and the cinnamon fragrance, reminding me of my father's, welcomed me to the sanest place on Fort Knox's plateau. The quiet of the hotel pushed my head in the right direction when I needed most to relax my soul. The hotel's Danish attendant informed me of Trace's reservation on the fifteenth floor. When I got to the room, I was greeted by the true knight's image of myself on a wall-sized TV paused on the Unican Network. To the right of the TV, in the kitchen, Trace was preparing a cocktail next to a tailored-up buzz-cut man who had his back to me.

"There's my boy!" Trace greeted, causing his friend to turn around. It was Midas in a gold-edge black blazer with a gray turtleneck to complement the slim gray denim jeans.

"Mr. Knightfall himself," Midas added, chewing on some gum.

"What took you so long?" Trace asked me with a wink. I knew what he was getting at.

"It's only been a day Trace," I told him, resting myself on the couch in front of the TV.

"Hey, a lot can happen in a day. Isn't that right Midas?"

"I'd say so, especially if Craven was with um. I don't know, my sister," Midas said, bringing me a hair's breath away from snapping Trace's goddamn neck. The past twenty-four hours had just been a coaster ride, and all I wanted to do was rest. Trace started to chuckle as I gave him an angry look. He must've invited Midas here for the drama because that was all Trace had been causing was drama.

"There's no need to sugar-coat it, I know that you two are seeing each other. I'm trying to make sure that the feelings between the both of you are real. She's my little sister, and if anything happens to her, well, it won't come to that, right?" Midas said, giving me the family talk. My emotions were tangled. A part of me wanted to say that he was going to die if he didn't shut the fuck up, but it wasn't like he was intentionally trying to be a dick. He was just genetically gifted with the damn gene. Either way, the secret was out on Way/Point, so it was time for him and I to tango.

"I'm not gonna hurt her. It's actually impossible to hurt her. She's as tough as nails and then some," I replied seeing her eyes in him. My response did bring a smile to his face and light to the bicolored pair of eyes.

"That's where you're wrong, Craven. She's not as tough as nails, she is nails. I've seen that girl pick up her loose teeth with broken fingers. Of course, my father doesn't see it, and my mother refuses to say it."

"Then there's no point of threatening me if we're both aware of her strengths."

"I'm not threatening anybody. I've just learned over the years that there's two different types of men in this universe. Ones who look at the brand new 2200 Hermes model, and the ones who stare at the model in high heels unveiling it instead," Midas inferred. He was looking for a nervous reaction but instead saw a tempered man trying to not do anything stupid.

"That's funny, because I've learned something too. Typically, there's only two types of racers. Winners and losers, but staring at you, I've learned that there's a third type, chea…"

"Champions!" Midas interjected, jumping ahead of the comment. The arrogant smile made me wonder if he actually knew what I was going to say. "I love it, Craven, till next time though."

"Already heading out?" Trace asked, glancing at the clock.

"Yeah, I just wanted to give Craven the big brother talk, but he already knows what he's gotten himself into," Midas stated, shooting one last stare at me before leaving.

"For someone who's not medically cleared, you really create a lot of fucking drama!" I told Trace.

"What? He already knew you were seeing her. We saw you both leave the party together," Trace explained. "And besides, he's alright with it, everything's okay."

"No, it's far from okay."

"How? You're dating Miss Earth. Millions of men and possibly women would kill for the position."

"If I tell you something, would you promise to keep it a secret?" I asked him, who quickly nodded. "I mean it Trace, would you swear on our friendship?"

"Yes dude, I swear and cross my heart," he replied before covering his mouth. "Is Gabriella… pregnant?"

"Nooooo!"

"Then what?"

"Gabriella's Krueger!" I finally revealed. Trace punctured his spleen as a response. It took him a moment to actually take things serious again. I hadn't seen him laugh like that since Kira's match with Zane on senZation.

"Get the fuck outta here dude. There's no fucking way Krueger's a girl and out of all the girls in the world, Miss Earth?"

"Don't try to be as ignorant as everyone else because you're not. You've heard her speak about Versa in native terms, and on top of it all, she's a Gold. She's got the money and resources to create something as innovative as Krueger," I explained, drilling the truth deeper into his head. He knew I wasn't a liar, and I wasn't creative nor clever enough to think of a story like this. I went on to confirm the controversial issues surrounding Midas and how he was a cheater who denied the responsibility for Orin's death. Knowing how impulsive Trace could be, even if it was with good intentions, I chose not to touch upon the repercussions of Midas' death. I bent the truth, making it seem like a story of Gabriella hoping to save her brother from Law and the Carnivores. I knew that Trace would buy it as a love story he couldn't let me fail. He made a strong point about Lucifer's flames being unreliable in the next race because of the colder environment, but I had personally been more worried about his blades. Trace also provided some information regarding the tumblers. They were extreme when it came to the theatrics. They liked to play with their food instead of eating it, a huge weakness that could pay dividends, but it didn't stop me from doubting Midas' survival in Greenland. There were just too many threats on Peak's track that could end one's life, if not Midas'.

"How about this, instead of trying to protect Midas, how about you and Gabriella do what we did back in the Semi Leagues? You know, the clash & crash tactic?" Trace proposed as a pretty good idea. It was a plan he and I used to pin racers into fighting one another instead of focusing on the main objective, winning. Manipulating two or more racers into fighting one another provided an advantage to the puppeteers, developing an opportunity to take a big lead or shove the skirmish off the track. It worked so well back in the Semi's, especially because of Zane, who happened to be one of the thirteen racers.

The mentioned clash & crash tactic brought a smile to my face. Before I could respond, I received a message from Gabriella regarding the location of her workshop thirty klicks due south. She had an idea too.

ACT II
CHAPTER 10

OFF THE
GRID

AURUM SCHEMES FADED AWAY THE FURTHER SOUTH I VENTURED INTO A MORE RURAL ENVIRONMENT. I had to travel in a 2180 Corolla, an ancient piece of shit without hovering functions. Don't know how the hell people drove around in these things. I'd been driving for ten minutes, and I was already annoyed from the bumpy hydraulics. For a golden country, I expected better. I would rather have been in the damaged version of Atlas Sr. The destination was a quarter-mile out on the GPS, a questionable read from the flat landscape of snowfields as far as the eye could see east, west, north, and south. There wasn't even a frost-covered road to drive on anymore. It died a klick ago. A countless number of ditches crisscrossed the area, enough to hide the bodies of an entire platoon. The eerie winter silence stuck in the air, adding to the loneliness, making me miss the blinged out penguins.

I stepped out of the car and onto the tundra. Shivering, I fully zipped my jacket for the first time in my life. I was used to the underworld of the Chicagolands, the part of the city cloaked beneath the harsh weathers that infamously slid in during the winter. Here I was, trying to figure out how to bestow the cold when it was bestowing itself into me. Even in their pockets, my hands froze. Close to a breaking point, I heard the sound of rust breaking loose from underground. I looked to see a pile of snow slowly bursting into the air to unveil a metallic pair of trapdoors opening their arms to me. In the brightness, my eyes had a hard time adjusting to the darkness inside the doorway. One concrete step, then two, three and ten more until I saw Gabriella on the stairway.

"How's the weather up there, cold?" Gabriella inquired. Her smile diminished the darkness.

"It's been more gold than cold honestly," I responded, following her down into an oval-shaped bunker that seemed more like a laboratory. Chrome textures on the walls, computers, and workshop tables ran all across the room to the two descending stairwells, sandwiching the entrance. The blue-tinted windows to the lab drew my eye to the race track that could be seen hooking around the room's perimeter one level below.

At the lab's center was her custom-made suit cased in a glass container, displaying the artifactual carbon fibered coating. Like a tourist, studying the highly acclaimed exhibit in this museum, I felt the jitters the longer I admired the room. There was just so much to take in. It was not the big things that create a masterpiece, no, it was the little things. Tiny touches like the digital pixels of the holographic skeleton layered all over the suit's body, the slim diamond veins wrapped around the stainless retractable krone claws, or the extremely dark-red spectrums of fiber on the pectars patterned into claw marks. For a moment, I felt like a kid inside their first toy store, a giddy feeling that subsided after realizing how long I'd been staring at her exosuit without saying a single word. I saw the reflection of Gabriella smiling over my shoulder in the helmet's visor.

"I thought I saw a smudge on the suit's abdominis…" I eventually said. "I was wondering, what's on the claws?"

"Whatchu mean?" she replied, caught off guard by the question.

"Come on, you were controlling reliQ's suit back in Dessnia, and I have a feeling that it has something to do with the diamond veins on the cla…"

"LIKE IT!" a man cried out from around the corner of the display, scaring the shit out of me. "Do you like it?"

"Who the hell are you?" I accidentally blurted. The scrawny man had to have been 7-feet-tall with salmon colored skin, and black eyes with white irises.

"Relax Craven, this is my Ryth companion, Nito," Gabriella affirmed. He must've been her mechanic too because he was wearing a gray snow cap to season the greased-up coverall that must've been pearly-white long ago.

"He never answered the question," Nito said really fast. It was almost impossible to decipher whatever the hell he was trying to say.

"He wants to know if you like the suit-controlling trick?" Gabriella finally translated, bringing a smile to Nito's face.

"Can put trick in suit for ya," Nito offered.

"No, no, it's an exclusive trick," Gabriella stated, gesturing the Ryth over to a computer at the end of the room before focusing back on me. Stepping over to their computer revealed a recognizable holomark behind Gabriella's suit display. It was a black man standing tall in a mesomorph-shaped Versa suit designed to an elegance that would even leave JoKer speechless. He had a black metal jacket over the outer layer with a black vest top underneath. Within the vest top, a black metal tie over a white collared dress shirt. If the metal top hat didn't give his appearance away, the chainsawed forearms leading to the double-stacked hands over the golden gripped cane planted onto the ground did, or in this case, a hologramer's grid. The man's name was J.C. Ripa, also known as Jack the Ripper.

"One of 'the surviving seven,'" I blurted once the man's identity had been deciphered.

"One of the what?" Gabriella asked. I explained to her that it was a name my father gave to himself and six others during his bout with *The Golden Evolution's* revolutionary suits. There were always stories about him and The Terran Triforce, taking on the other worlds, dethroning multiple apices in the galaxy. Those were the tales told by a bonfire. On the other hand, there were hasty accounts about racers like Adonis "The Perfect

Angel" Angelos, Catelyn "The Lone Shark" Brannigan, Fiona "The Wintry Viking" Welsh, and especially J.C. Ripa—someone Trace told me was the most vicious of the seven from his readings and confirmations from Roy. To see for myself, I perused the information.

Name: J.C. Ripa
Sobriquet: "Jack the Ripper"
Weight: 212 lbs (96.2 kg)
Height: 6'3½" (1.92 m)
Native: Whitechapel, Londinium

Appearance: A bald cleft-chinned rebellist with a drop of dried-up blood always on a bruised cheek above a scruffy beard. Though, J.C.'s nature is brutal, he doesn't shy away from elegance. This is why he paired himself with the Versa company, *Freya*, creating a sole suit called the 2220 Rapture. A double-layered mesomorph suit w/an inner layer designed as a vest top suit and an outer as a black trench coat. The loose armoured helmet only covered the upper-region of his face like the Phantom of the Opera with a black top hat modified to jam A.I. signals.

Bio: From the hard streets of Whitechapel comes a vigilante notorious for setting their city right. J.C. believes that blood must be shed to protect the substance from entering the heads of Whitechapel's youth. A man who has been coined as "Jack the Ripper" by most for his blood-ripping essence and also because the origin of his initials are unknown. Extremists have even gone as far as initialing J.C. as a Jesus Crisis who has come back for condemnation versus reconciliation.

 On October 17th, 2217, the vigilante was caught by MI6 and sent to the deadliest prison on Earth, Tartarus. An exclusive prison associated with a death race series called The Pit. Stuck in Earth's favoured capital punishment system for publicity rates, J.C. would flawlessly rip his way to an apex status within the slaughterhouse, claiming the winning prize of a pardon. Realizing his capabilities within the sport of Versa, J.C. entered Galactica XLVI the following month post-release for a chance at winning the series to aid Whitechapel's financial burdens.

Status: Deceased

There was more info regarding his highlights in The Pit and Galactica's XLVI-XLVII on several tabs to the holomark. The readings provided me with another chapter of Gabriella's precious commentary. She talked about how J.C. inspired her to sketch her exosuit. For instance, J.C.'s use of the top hat was how she uses her claw-trick. The holomark claimed that J.C. only used his top hat as a jammer, which was true and false according to Gabriella. The hat was a jammer, but it was also electrical, and J.C. used it to electrocute his victims whenever he slammed it into their helmet's, freezing them for either an incision from his cane's hidden blade or a pulverizing maneuver from his chainsawed forearms. I knew how brutal Jack the Ripper was, but also knew another piece of valuable information from Trace. It was also something Gabriella didn't know. I knew what J.C. stood for, and it wasn't Jack—a name that inspired Gabriella's Jack-o-lanterned theme—or Jesus Crisis—the name that inspired the extremists. His name was Jasper Callum, and he was definitely one of the main reasons why the Re-Versables existed. The activists believed that someone like Jasper should've been sentenced to death versus being placed in a series that would inevitably lead to Jasper's pardon. They strongly stood against the idea of a death race series designed to kill most of the prisoners with an exception of one, mainly because it pertained to Earth's connection with Galactica. The United Countries were aware that killers in our world should be condemned, but when it came to the best killer, the United Countries slapped their wrist claiming that Galactica was a death sentence of its own. This was why the best killers in the world represented Earth. No doubt, providing fuel for Re-Versables, and I couldn't say what we did as a planet was ethical, at least when it came to our judicial branch. Hell, my father kept the stories about Jasper brief and limited. He didn't want his son to get the wrong idea about Jasper, and here Gabriella stood as an inspired offspring of The Ripper himself.

I always knew that there was another side to Gabriella. Almost as if there was a devil beneath her skin, which made even more sense when she showed her angelic smile. Even Satan was an angel prior to falling far from grace. But this was something that Earth needed, a Terran powerful enough to level any battlefield, any dilemma. A Terran who committed brutality out of love, just like Jasper versus revenge like Law and co. All she cared about was saving her brother's life, and she was willing to do anything in her power to stop it. A trait I couldn't help but admire. She was someone I wanted to support and had a hunch that I was one of the few things keeping her close to grace. I was still confident about being the luckiest man in the world. I mean, I was the one man in this world who had a front row seat to happiness. She also gave both Kira and Zane a run for their money when it came to intelligence. From the idea engraved on Gabriella's exosuit to the envious hologramer in her workshop, it illuminated a hallway of ideas I should explore. Gabriella could see it on my face. I stared at Jasper's holographic image and broke into a star-studded grin.

"I honestly can't tell what you're more fond of, me or my workshop," Gabriella stated as I pulled out Jasper's holomark.

"It's just…" I paused, realizing that I was looking at her like she looked at Jasper. I was a true fan of her talents. "I've been an owner of a workshop for a couple years now, and I have never thought about adding something as small as a hologramer or something as big as a track. How did you come up with something like this?"

"I didn't. The construction of this workshop actually came from my mother," she explained, knowing I desired more details. The entire workshop was a sight for sore eyes, but I could tell there was more of a personal connection to this place. For the first time today, her smile vanished which caused her to look away at the track downstairs. "My father wanted a son who could be a Galactic Champion, and my mother wanted a daughter who could be a Galactic Belle like her, but Midas never had the natural interest towards the sport, and I hated the modeling industry. I always wanted to be like

Jack the Ripper, or even..." she paused and tilted her head towards Nito who seemed to have another holomark near the computer. One he would quickly place in Gabriella's outreached hands. After applying the holomark, an image of my father standing tall in a pristine version of his 2200 Hermes appeared.

"...The Heart of Earth," she finally continued, immersing me in the narrative. "You always knew something special was gonna happen whenever your father stepped onto the track whether it was in the Perseus, the Legacy, or the Hermes. As for Jasper, you knew the crowd would cringe from a fatality. Both of them were my role models, Crank for the skills that saved our world and Jasper for the kills that protected it. My mother, she would always try to steer me away from the violence of the races so that I could find some connection to her career, but she knew I had zero interest. That's when she came up with a compromise, something that involved me getting an off-the-grid workshop in exchange for a modeling debut. At first, I said hell no, but then she changed my mind by throwing Nito into the deal, the only mechanic from my father's company naive enough to help a little girl capture a dream."

There was always a deeper meaning to every story. Nothing was ever simplistic, and that was when it registered. Throughout her story, Gabriella wasn't looking at the track, my father's image, or even me. She was looking at nothing. Back in the hotel, she had said that there were only three things her father cared about, and she wasn't one of them. There was sorrow from neglect in her gaze, and she didn't want to admit it. She never had a good father, and must have been using mine or Jasper to fill in the void.

"You mentioned that Luke abused the things closest to him?" I questioned, now standing beside her. "Did he abuse..."

"Yes, Midy more than my mother. Surprisingly, he never really laid a finger on me. As you can see, I tend to be a little more rebellious like Jasper. Back then, I didn't realistically think that I would ever be a racer under the circumstances, so I taught Midy everything I learned here. But it backfired as his success grew, bringing out my father's arrogance within him. Midy actually believed he was the best, that he couldn't be beaten. Then the competition became better than him, and the bigger it got, the more desperate he became. I expected a minor injury to happen, but instead, an electromagnetic pulse did, and now I'm responsible for all of the crap that has happened. Orin's death is my fault. I even see his ghost every day on the streets and every night in my dreams. That's why I created the delphian racer fans named Krueger. A racer that could dethrone Midas, and it's a good thing too, because that's when Claire tracked down this place to tell me everything, which brings me to Nito's idea of control," Gabriella explained, leading us over to Nito's computer station. Trying to understand him again was still difficult, but a few nudges from Gabriella slowed down the Ryth's speech. Their plan involved us getting close to Midas so that she could use her Jasper-inspired trick with the claws that would shut her brother's exosuit down the same way she had done reliQ's. The only problem with the plan was actually getting to Midas before any of the vengeful racers. I brought up Trace's strategy. The clash & crash tactic impressed both masterminds and became the main tactic we would use to protect and possibly dethrone the champ in the cold environment. Because of the frosty factor, I made a special request back at the nest.

My mechanics quickly relayed a supply drop on the surface above Gabriella's den. The drop came with thermal cushioning to warm the body temperature, an air tank and mask for the change in altitude, and Thornland wheels that could manually produce a layer of spikes from within the tire to create traction on snowy surfaces. They could also be used as a weapon, if necessary. And, to my surprise, an Atlas Jr. comfortably treating the supply drop's base like a bed. I couldn't believe that the guys back at home sent this. They could've at least sent the bulkier Atlas Sr. It would've made me look like the Incredible Hulk in front Gabriella.

The native resources of the 2249 Atlas piqued Nito's interest. It turned out the Ryth had an ego when it came to who could supply the better exosuit. Nito claimed that Gabriella's had more advancements than any suit I could think of because of the foreign gadgets like the Rokian cloak. It could make her suit invisible, letting Gabriella suddenly appear and disappear on the tracks in the blink of an eye. A thorn in my ass cheek Nito was, and Gabriella found it hysterical. It brought out the competitor in me. I challenged her to a single lap race on the track in her workshop. I personally felt like the win at Dessnia was a fluke, and needed to know whether or not I could actually beat her, even in Atlas Jr. Before the race could start, she gave me a communication mic to place inside my helmet so that she could hear my reaction to an ass kicking I had no plans on receiving.

Being on her turf was clearly a major disadvantage, but I was always up for the challenge. She explained how the track was designed by both her mother and the *Holo* company to create an adjustable difficulty ranking to the track. The ranks ranged from "Puny"—an insulting amateur level recommended by Nito—to "Atrocious"—an incomprehensible set of obstructions mastered by Gabriella. A damned if I do, damned if I don't notion marinated in my head as I gave a perfunctory nod to the "Atrocious" level. Gabriella quickly adjusted the difficulty down for the sake of our relationship. The level was graded as "Heavy," two levels above "Norm." A backhanded compliment fitting a race I never stood a chance of winning.

I gained an ounce of confidence at the curve from the starting line outside of her workshop. I kept a side-by-side pace, leading into a sudden slope. Prepared for it, Gabriella slowed her suit down. Unprepared for it, an idiotic knight rocketed into the roof and plunged down the slope that led to a flooded surface. The aquatic element made my Atlas hydroplane. Gabriella let me catch back up in the next obstacle, a series of sharp turns. As if that wasn't demoralizing enough, the insults coming through the mic were.

We came to a long straightaway with *Holo's* identity inscribed all over. It was a tunnel that would randomly morph the holographic scenery every ten or so seconds. The first environment was volcanic, shooting geysers of lava. The next environment was windy, producing typhoons that slowed us both down to 10km/h speeds, even though the wheels to our suits said 200km/h. In this section, my strength outmatched Gabriella's, and I was able to edge closer using a workout of forward lunges and mountain climbing skills. The last environment—a jungle—threw a tree branch out of the floor and into my face. The hit disrupted the momentum I had reclaimed in this race. We entered the last obstacle of ascending turns leading back the perimeter of her workshop, ending the catastrophic performance I had endured in front of a Gold and Ryth.

"I thought you were supposed to be Mr. Knightfall?" Gabriella mocked as I finally crossed the finish line, a bit fed up with myself more than anything.

I slowly built the strength to reply, taking my helmet off for a breather. "I thought you were supposed to be Miss Earth?" I had to stay seated due to the burning sensation in my legs. Those lunges in the race must have done a number. That was the last time I would skip leg day with Trace. Gabriella could see the discomfort as she came closer, giving me a chance to return her mic.

"Keep it, we'll need it for the next race," she advised, trying to restrain the laughter.

"At least you're in a happier mood."

"It's always the little things you have to enjoy, right?" she replied, taking a seat next to my tired body still sprawled at the finish line.

"If it makes you feel any better than, you're not the only one who's haunted by a ghost. I tend to see my father whenever I'm on the track. Believe or not, he stood right in front of you during the start of last night's race."

"So, he's always around? Damn, this race must've really broke his heart," she joked, leaning her body into mine. As we sat close, Nito took the liberty to play some smooth 20th Century jazz through the speakers around the track. I looked at one of the overview windows in time to see the Ryth winking at Gabriella. Turned out, she had a Trace of her own.

Towards the end of the song, Nito raised a small box through the window, catching our attention. We ejected out of our suits to investigate. He claimed the box came from another supply drop during our race. I took a brief glimpse at the label: *Komodo Fire*

"Yama, you son of a bitch. It's a boost engineered by one of my mechanics. He claims it's the fastest and longest boost in the galaxy," I explained with Nito holding on to the gas tank and Gabriella reading its formula.

"Holy crap, the formula's wrong but on the right track," she said, beginning to change parts of the formula by grabbing a few chemicals stored underneath one of the workshop benches. She formulated a better version of Yama's product and handed it over to me, sealed up in a gas tank.

"Where did you learn how to do that?" I asked her in amazement.

"Thank Nito, he's the professor," she acknowledged. Nito gave me the most arrogant nod of approval. The only reason I could enjoy Nito's presence was because of my own experience with Trace. Nito was Trace's twin from another planet, a twin that could make the hounds envious, which was why I made Gabriella promise me that she'd keep her mechanic far far, and I mean far away from Burretta.

A telephone grid appeared on Gabriella's Dreamcatcher iCube sitting near Nito's computer. It quickly killed her smile. She took a deep breath before answering a one-sided conversation that could be summed up in her bicolored eyes as stressful. When the conversation came to a close, she looked at me and said, "Looks like my parents finally know about... us. Craven, they wanna meet you."

ACT II
CHAPTER 11

CONSTRICTION

OUR DRIVE BACK TO AN AURORA SKY OF NUUK WHERE GABRIELLA'S PARENTS LIVED WAS AWKWARD, BUNGLING, AND CHILLING. Like wizards of Greenland's Oz, they had a golden brick road leading to their neighborhood of crystikular mansions, an architectural adaptation of Crystallite's style and material. The richest currency in the galaxy was the Cryzen from Crystia. Gabriella explained that the houses on the outer rim of the neighborhood were owned by her father's workers. They surrounded the Chief Executive Officers of *Tsarina* and *Freya* closer to the nucleus in an analytical game plan of keeping his enemies close. So far, the move had kept the peace in Earth's essential heaven. A place I assumed Dick was reaching for through his gambling skills. The residents here even walked out of their houses with the same hylec gear, rich enough to cover the entire body like a corium.

Each house was grand, but Gold's manor was the grandest at the heart of the land. Like the neighborhood, nothing on their house was gold. It instead mimicked Crystallite's taste, beaming brief waves of white, green, pink, blue, and yellow from the crystal's transparent structures. The glass itself had a translucency that blurred the mansion's interior for seclusion.

I've mentioned before how Trace and I chose Pasydanya and Gigalus as our planets for the required intergalactic courses in middle school. We chose them because they were the planets that spoke to us versus choosing them based on class. That was why most kids tended to sever the arteries of their parent's bank accounts for courses about the Elysian half of Legios, the transformable thrills of Graviathen, and the unfathomable gems of Crystia. Those three planets were the richest within the galaxy, but that was it. They relied on their wealth and tended to be more self-centered than most. Something my father wasn't, which was why I think he was more than proud of me being paired with the Burretta family. It prevented me from becoming like the kids here, urinating on holomarks of Minoris planets like: Mars, Earth's solaric rival, Derry, the smallest Minoris planet of meticulous specimens, or Sylum, a tiny jaundice jungled planet filled with armless animalistic creatures only capable of racing and hunting—incapable of anything else.

Unaware of what to expect from the belly of this rich beast, Gabriella and I journeyed across the lengthy snow-covered walkway to the gate-sized entrance of her parent's manor. The obstacle proved to be too much for The Clawed Cardiac. As strong as an ancient Amazonian, she couldn't find the strength to knock this barrier down.

"In all honesty, there's no love lost from my family if you bailed," Gabriella finally said, unable to make eye contact.

"No way, I don't ever want you to feel alone, this is what I'm here for," I replied, knocking at the door for her.

"My father's not gonna like this. He'll find a way to come between us," she said as the doors opened to reveal Midas for the second time today. His sister instantly swung her fist into his jaw. The hit jarred loose his piece of gum, sticking it onto the door's hinges. "That's for telling them about Way/Point."

"Way/Point?" Midas remarked, placing pressure on his bruised jaw. "For fucksake, they already knew. It's all over the news." I was now a third wheel, stuck in an argument between the golden siblings.

Midas led us into the stunning crystallized interior of the house. The entrance hall was massive and had a pair of stairwells curving up to a balcony over the dining room straightaway. To the left was the west hall, curving rightward, containing exosuits lined up against the wall with paintings in between. To the right, was the east hall curving leftward, mirroring the exact same concept.

"Can you two stop acting like children for once, there's a guest in our house," a woman called from the balcony, quickly silencing the two. The striking lady had long brown curly hair, slightly tan skin, and similar heterochromia eyes wearing a pearlescent Pyscean dress made out of shyre, a material produced by solidifying Pyscean rain. The molecules from the clouds of Pasydanya could sometimes leave a silky cloth on their surfaces unlike the puddles of Earth's rain. The silky dress radiated a melody of colors. The first would be a creamy-white, instantly balanced with a soaring violet stream along the edges before the teal and pink colors could join the party. The colors were cut short by the dress' length, which revealed a pair of heel-flexed thighs.

"Sorry, mom," Gabriella replied, leaving me stunned. I could not believe this lady was Catherine Gold. She practically looked the same age as Gabriella.

"It's okay, my dear," Catherine said, walking down the stairs. "And you must be Craven. I can see why Gabriella likes you. There's a heart that beats on the outside of your body, I don't know how to explain it."

"Apple doesn't fall too far from the tree," I replied, referencing my family.

"No, no it doesn't. If only my apples could've done the same," Catherine issued, glancing into her daughter's eyes.

"If only," Gabriella added, annoyed.

"Your father would like to speak to you both in his study, now," Catherine commanded, ushering the siblings up the stairwells, gracelessly leaving me by myself. "Do make yourself a home," she called back to me. "It won't be long for dinner."

Being left alone in the main hall rekindled some memories of me and Trace back when I would spend the night at his house whenever he and his parents were at war.

The only difference was that I knew what the problem was this time. I'd be an idiot if I didn't know what the Golds had to discuss. The glass walls were thicker than their discretion, but that wasn't going to stop me from getting comfortable. I began to venture. I traveled down the east hall first, getting a closer look at some of the statues that were actually first-place trophies chiseled into the winner, Catherine Gold as Miss Earth, and it wouldn't be fitting if it wasn't next to the trophy of Gabriella. Her trophy made me chuckle. Gabriella was in a golden dress worn by Belle from Dessnia's most popular film. The only differences were the small onyx strips of jewels around the collar and hip, with an onyx tiara to match the presentation. The dark tones spoke more to Gabriella, but then again, she was wearing a pair of golden heels, so the princess design felt a bit cliché for my liking. I'd become used to the leather jacket and skinny pants, more fitting to Gabriella's personality. Appearances could hook the eye, but the personality, that's what hooked the heart.

Next in the line-up was a silver trophy of Catherine with an orbit of planets, labeled: *Miss Galaxy Runner-Up*. Made me wonder how Luke felt about that outcome, a Gold unable to claim a gold. Must not have been too bad if it was in the line-up. The silver trophy stood in front of a cracked open door to what seemed like a workshop covered in walnut-colored glass mosaic walls. Inside was a virtual sandbox of stripped parts to an exosuit scattered over the dark-gold trimmed tiles and stardust-black countertops. The gray cabinets matched the starlit sky seen through the crystallized ceiling. On one of the mosaic walls was a remixed version of Michelangelo's creation of Adam. A robed Midas was in the place of God touching an Adam who was turning into gold.

"Gee, I wonder whose room this is," I muttered, surprised at how Midas' workshop was the polar opposite to his sister's, and closer to my old sloppy ways. I remembered the "Sloppy Joe" remark and now knew what it felt like to be the one coming up with the jokes versus being the joke. One could say that Midas' messy room took the gold medal. Yeah, I'd leave the jokes for Burretta from then on. Realizing how short-lived my career as a comedian would've been, my eyes locked onto the white sleeveless 2245 Icarus, lying on an operating table. There'd only been one man on this planet worthy enough to race in an Icarus model, and that was Roy Fathom, leaving me a bit stunned that Midas had it in his arsenal. Especially since the exosuit's manufacturer was *Tsarina*. There must've been a sense of trust between the companies as they had even crafted a traditionally white and black Guy Fawkes mask for the helmet. Pinned under the suit's arm was a folder labeled, *The Midas Touch*. I went to reach for it but was startled by a knock at the doorway.

"I'm no genius, but I think sabotaging another's suit is illegal," Midas said seriously and then smiled. "I'm only kidding, do look around though."

"I would, except I've never been in a junkyard."

"And yet, my special folder caught your attention."

"Every junkyard's got a relic."

"Precisely," he said, coming closer to grab and open the folder. "My father named me after the iconic Greek King Midas, a figure with a mythological power of turning everything he touched into gold, an innovation I hope to bring onto the track someday."

"You can't turn everything into gold."

"On the contrary, I…"

"Dinner's ready," Catherine stated from the doorway. A part of me was a bit disappointed as I was still curious about the delusion Midas was referring to. If the stars aligned, maybe this trick he had up his sleeve would save his life. "I hope you like fish, Craven. We caught a chinook earlier this week and have had the cravings for it ever since." She led the way back to the dining room where two Golds sat in silence. One, Gabriella, the other, a man I'd waited years to meet in person. A hazel-eyed man in a black long-sleeved dress shirt and black pants with a black shiny edged belt that had his company's logo as the buckle. The reflectively bald cranium and smooth jawline showed him freshly groomed, but his aquiline nose, thick brown brows, and sharply green eyes suggested intimidation. An image his son has been trying to replicate since our first meeting. Luke slowly stood up once I was in the room, and reached out his palm.

"It's a pleasure to finally have a peaceful encounter with a McGuire," Luke said as our hands shook. For a split second, I was worried that he was going to feel my raging pulse through the handshake. "My princess sure knows how to find her charming."

"Yes, she does, and I'm racing him," Midas added.

"I didn't ask for a fool's opinion," Luke said, shutting his son down completely. The unnecessary comment made Gabriella clinch my hand. A quick glance at her twitching eyelids showed how much aggression she was truly holding back.

"What can I say, he had me at hello," she finally told her father while a group of chefs marched out of the nearby kitchen. They placed down entrées of salmon en croute with sides of asparagus and clam chowder. From all of the extraterrestrial foods I'd been ingesting lately, it was nice to have a native refreshment, ones that seemed more fitting than usual. Salmon wasn't something I typically ate, but there was something about this dish that felt so right.

"How about you Craven, did you feel the same way?" Luke asked, digging into his salmon.

"I'd be lying if I said no," I confidently replied, shooting a half-raised smile Gabriella's way, releasing some of the tension in our grip. "She caught my attention before she even knew me."

"Of course she did. She's the seed of the most beautiful lady in the galaxy. She catches everyone's attention. I'm just a little shocked that she's with you," he finally revealed. It was a damn shame, too. Here I was thinking that we were going to have a civilized Terran talk. Here I was thinking that the steam of a well-cooked salmon was going to settle properly in my stomach. Here I was thinking that a golden date wasn't going to be like Jasper's tenure at Tartarus, but oh no. All it took was a glimpse into Luke's heart to wash it all away.

"What do you mean by, me?"

"Craven, please don't," Gabriella pleaded, knowing a declaration of war was on the horizon.

"What I'm trying to say is that your legacy is fading away. I just thought that she would pick someone with a more promising future," Luke explained while continuing to calmly eat his dish. He spoke with a sense of irrelevance as if he was having a conversation with his shit. The disrespectful demeanor gave Gabriella a taste of her own tightly-gripped medicine.

"I still don't know what you mean," I responded, finally able to wipe away the fucking smugness on his face. It might have been his house in his country, but that's all he had on me. He wasn't God. He didn't rule the world. The only prospering things to his name were his company, his bank account, and possibly a few good suits here and there. I, on the other hand, was trying to save the world. I, on the other hand, was trying to avenge my father and the McGuire name. I, on the other hand, was plausibly the only person in this world that Luke Gold feared based on the devilish stare the man shot at my chair. "What's not promising about my future?"

"What you're doing right now is what's not promising. You're just like your father, ignorant and unable to know better. It inevitably led him six-feet-under to most likely burn in hell. I'm not afraid to venture deeper down this rabbit hole, Mr. McGuire, but if you still want to continue the discussion, then be my guest."

"My father was trying to defend his planet in a life-threatening sport because that's what he loved to do, and here you are, a man who's made a living off of exported merchandise to the same specimen that beat Earth. If there's a spot in hell for anyone, I suggest you take a look in the mirror since your house and cranium's full of them," I angrily defended almost causing Luke to choke on his food from the sudden chuckles.

"Foolish boy, your father was a nuisance. I tried to help him by offering my gear, but he turned it down and made a fool out of me during the process. That's why I believe in Karma. She has no deadline and ironically killed him in a suit made by yours truly," he said, getting up to take him and the rest of his food elsewhere. "Do stay on this path, Mr. McGuire, you'll end up in a grave next to his."

"Where are you going my love?" Catherine asked, attempting to get a grasp on her husband's arm.

"Upstairs to my office, I think the fool and I need to have a little talk. Craven, I'm glad we could finally meet, you've helped me realize how blind my princess is when it comes to love," he finished, leaving the table with Midas. Gabriella then exhaled, finally letting go of my hand.

"He's wrong Craven, you're not a dead man walking. You've got heart, I can see that, and I know my daughter sees it too. If you stay on this path, you'll surpass your father, and that's a legendary accomplishment of its own," Catherine said, beginning to rise up out of her chair. A tiny tear slithered down her cheek from the green mascara before she made her way into the kitchen.

"I'm sorry about everything, this is on me," Gabriella said, worried about her mother.

"It's alright, I think I've got an idea about what you've been dealing with your whole life."

"To be honest, this was him on a good day. Wanna head out?" she desperately proposed. I was ready to finally escape the household, but she first had to go check on her mother to say goodbye. She was one of the few people Gabriella genuinely cared for, and it made me feel bad. I didn't know how the family could put up with the Marado of a man I could hear violently giving an earful to his son up above. Gabriella eventually came back with a few plastic containers for leftovers, rescuing me from back-to-back crimes of uneaten food. We left, spending the rest of the day in her bunker. Seeing how ungolden The Golden Scion was made me more committed to saving his life, even if he sometimes abused it. Gabriella and I had a plan for the next race, but that was the thing. When did anything ever go as planned?

ACT II
CHAPTER 12

WINTER

PROTECTING THE GOLDS AND BESTOWING THE COLD WERE THE OBJECTIVES STUCK IN MY HEAD ON LOOP FOR THE PAST FEW DAYS. It was the only thing that mattered, and the race hadn't even started. As of that moment, it was just me traveling to the top of the Schweizerland Alps via hovercraft. The specialized vehicle adapted to the change in pressure and oxygen levels so that each racer could get to the locker located at the ice station on the top of Mont Forel, a mountain said to be over 3,000m, and I thought both the Sirius Tower and Castle of Dessnia were a tad too high. The best thing about the height was the clear view of the race track named Peak running along the mountain's side and into several tunnels leading to the worst thing—a B- rating on the Naturis scale. I learned that miserable fact from Trace who kept placing bets on where he believed Law would kill Midas on the track at the cabin by the finish line. I just hoped the medical staff was ready for the catastrophe because at least one of us was flying off of the mountain.

The unsettling thoughts increased the higher I got, closer to the King Kong ice station resting on the top of the Empire State mountain top. I pulled into the entrance bay of the multi-layered frosted station where I was able to depressurize safely. The bay had a warm welcoming staff willing to take some of the gear I brought straight to my room for legalization. The bay itself was icy-blue from the light-blue larkspur-scented candles all around the light fixtures and walls, trailing to the title of the station embedded on the ceiling—Skaði's Sanctuary—and beneath it, an imposing ice sculpture crafted out of Villa, Arythro's unmeltable cryogen. The sculpture was the Norse Goddess of Winter herself, Skaði. Her skin was as white as the snow outside with dark-brown tree branches protruding upwards out of her white hair and eyebrows. The top of her forehead transitioned to a dark-blue, matching the color of her lips and breasts. I briefly closed my eyes and respectfully prayed for her to send whatever wrath that might be stored for us all to me instead of Midas or Gabriella. I opened my eyes and made my way to the main semicircular whitewood counter. Behind it, a giant window gave me a view of the tunnel and the starting line. Above the window, a board with the list of racers and where our starting positions should be.

Know Your Lanes!

1st lane: Midas Gold (30)
2nd lane: Craven McGuire (28)
3rd lane: Krueger (28)
4th lane: Spade Amaryllis (28)
***5th lane:** Lawson "Law" Pierce/Credo "Creed" Velasquez (26)
***6th lane:** Lawson "Law" Pierce/Credo "Creed" Velasquez (26)
7th lane: Zane Maddox (24)
8th lane: Warlock Neit (24)
9th lane: Heart Amaryllis (24)
10th lane: Diamond Amaryllis (23)
11th lane: Lucretia "Lucifer" Xiagra (22)
12th lane: Club Amaryllis (22)
13th lane: Kira Brink (21)

**Tiebreaker to be decided by a coin-toss*

The list itself only hinted at the stories behind it. All of the head-to-head tiebreakers proved this wasn't just the premier bracket, it was the rivals' bracket. At least five racers would be leaving this mountain with zero points, making it that much more vital to safely eliminate Midas. We had a plan, and the bird in the seventh lane should help us fulfill it.

A green light above the main counter signaled that my new gear checked in as legal, but before I could walk away, the red-bearded Irishman entered the bay. One of the staff members guided us to the locker.

"Damn MaGuire, you seem a bit different since our last encounter," Warlock said as we were escorted through a hallway and up a set of stairs.

"I've got something to die for now," I replied.

"Something, eh? More like someone," he rephrased as we went up the stairs.

"The hell are you, my therapist?" I remarked, making him laugh. At least someone in this world enjoyed my comedic skills.

"I love tat fire, MaGuire. Can't wait to see it melt tee mountains," Warlock said before he was ushered into a room on the second floor. On the journey through the third floor, we passed an absent Krueger, a harmonically immersed Lucifer, and a gun-loading Law. I was led to the fourth floor in a room next to Zane and Kira's. The locker was silently tense, making me miss Dick's presence. Someone, I assumed, had acquired a brand-new hylec sleeve.

In my room, an Atlas III was attached to a wall similarly styled as my previous locker. Knowing the importance of today, I wasted no time adding the new gear. It was almost impossible to determine what I needed the most, the Thornwood tires, the thermal neutralizers, or the oxygen tank. It might actually be the new and improved Komodo Fire.

Either way, I was glad to have my regular exosuit back and fixed up like usual. Acclimating my Atlas to the new environment did remind me of the bruises still barking their agony on my back. Definitely not as bad as before, but still rough enough I would want to guard from any big hits. I thought about having MIKA launch a quick check-up on the minor injury but remembered the mic Gabriella lent. Maybe it was about time I figured out what she did during pre-race.

"Are you even near the station?" I asked after I planted the mic into my helmet. The moment of silence made me a bit embarrassed.

"You know me, I'm just chillin'," she finally responded.

"Where? Outside? Do you ever get cold?"

"I'm Greenlandic, out here, we embrace the cold," she said. I overheard shouting coming from the room next door. I took the helmet off to venture over and see what the commotion was all about. The dimmed room belonged to The Raven who was pacing back and forth, back and forth, not at all making contact with his Nevermore nor his robotic raven in a cage.

"I've got to do it. I can't lose. I can't lose. I can't not do it… I have to do it…no can't do it," Zane kept chatting back and forth to someone that wasn't in the room. I couldn't get a great look at his face, but it was still scarred up from our last bout at Knightfall.

"Zane, are you alright?" I calmly asked. He glanced at me over his shoulder and then gazed over at his caged raven.

"Craven, I remember you, yu-yu-yu-you're the one that did this to my face," he spoke softly, revealing the scars all over the left side of his face. The tissue was oozing a red-and-yellow substance from the peeled scabs. "Yu-yu-you and Trace, Trace, I swore he was competing!"

"Zane, are you okay? You're not quite yourself. This act is odd, even for you."

"I've been never better, I just have to do it… I can't lose… no one else will do it. Only I can. Trace, I swore he was competing," Zane began to repeat, causing me to back out of his room.

The staff in the station were now signaling for us to head to the track. I rushed back to my helmet. I quickly booted the Atlas to wake MIKA up and urgently ordered her to search the Versarchives for Zane's medical records over the past few months. The history showed a cracked frontal bone, a cracked superciliary arch, a cracked glabella, a cracked maxilla, a slightly fractured nasal bone, and a dislocated mandible, all coming from the same race, Knightfall.

"Gabriella, there's been a change of plans, we can't use Zane as our pawn. He's not mentally right and is probably the biggest threat to your brother." There was no response. I quickly realized that I would need to explain to MIKA about the mic as I entered the suit. I then noticed a tamed Zane in his adrenia-injecting Nevermore gently walking down the stairwell with the uncaged raven attached to his dell. I feared the inevitability of his actions post-siren. The next racer I saw was a smiling Kira in her Venus without a helmet on.

"Can I ask you for a favor?" I quickly proposed as I joined her down the stairwell detaching my helmet. It didn't take long for her to nod. "Can you help me protect Midas in this race?"

"Let me guess, Miss Earth told you to look after her big brother?" she mocked, almost causing me to blurt out the truth, but I instead went along with her theory. I owed her one and would someday have to explain the importance of this act.

I suddenly realized how big a baker's dozen was from the line-up of racers assembled in their lanes, ready for the frozen obstacles. The starting line of Peak apparently took place in a tunnel attached to the station behind the large disk-shape pressurized doors, temporarily closed. The confined space made me wonder how the hell Gabriella was going to get in here, but the idea quickly died after noticing her standing in the third lane all suited up.

"If we're being honest, it's times like this when I swear you're Batman," I said over the mic.

"Is this permanent or temporary?" MIKA asked, a bit annoyed. I could sense the jealousy in her tone.

"Don't worry about her, instead take a guess at where we're at." I tried to change the subject.

"You added some thermal gear, so I sense somewhere cold," she answered, browsing through the map on the bottom corner of the visor. "Mont Forel on a storm-approaching day, great."

"It was beautiful when I got here," I explained making my way to the second lane. Every racer was set, all of them in suits modified for the altitude. The racers I'd had a history with wore their normal suits. The new encounters, their suits presented a different story.

Warlock had on *Tsarina's* shamrock-green 2250 Celtic, a mesomorph exosuit carrying a silent battle cry from his bloody-red claw designs. There was a sense of familiarity from the racer's deck, but I could not say the same for the other fresh combatants like Creed, Law, and the Quartet of Amaryllis.

Creed wore *Tsarina's* white 2245 Roman with a giant black cross stitched onto the torso and back, etched droppings of black ink on the hands and feet, referencing a crucifixion. A controversially menacing, yet unique design for a suit, let alone for the abusive Roman lacking acceleration; a black cat surrounded by cheetahs.

Law, on the other hand, had a more direct presentation in *Freya's* beige and dark-brown 2235 Ares, and would win the coin-toss, claiming the fifth lane. His helmet had three detachable sections: the brown magnetic cowboy hat, the snowboarding goggles over his silver eyes, and the gray-skulled metallic bandana wrapped around his mouth connected to an oxygen tank. The adapted suit suffered a big flaw, three wheels creating room for the armed revolver within Law's right hand, and an arm coated in molten magnesium-filled bullets that could've illuminated the entire tunnel as the lone star.

The Quartet of Amaryllis children had on white 2250 Aces dedicated to their names based on presentation and also a suit I had some familiarity with since the manufacturer was *Ion.* This was their first prototype for an aerial suit, and the Amaryllis family must've been fond of it. Spade and Club had their black visors designed with their names and a king's image wrapped in black vines. Heart and Diamond adapted the same presentation, except they had red colors and a queen's image wrapped in red vines. On the back to each suit were holographic wings arching out of their backs like the scorpion-shaped legs of a Rachnidian Tarhandric. Each wing matched their schematics with the addition of a royal crown at the helm of each cranium with an onyx or ruby symbol of their card's suit displayed for all eyes. If it wasn't for *Ion's* logo on the dells of every suit, one would believe these exosuits were *Tsarina's*. The *Ion* logo was a jumbo "i" with an "O" shaped atom as the dot with an "N" implanted into the nucleus.

Each racer had their goals set on either first or Midas. I could maybe argue both for a few and neither for one. I didn't like the odds at the moment and had too much hope in a thirteenth-lane Kira, knowing that this plan was easily going to go south. *But at least it was sunny* was my final glass-half-full thought as the tunnel doors opened, revealing the snow-globe storm now occurring on the mountain top. We weren't at Gabriella's obstacle course anymore. No, this was the real deal with real life-threatening outcomes.

"I thought you said the storm was approaching?" I instantly blurted. A surprising sight that even brought Midas up on his wheels.

"Oops, I'm only artificial," MIKA responded as an alibi over the thunderous claps from Warlock, the lone racer excited for the damnation of nature.

"It doesn't change anything, we'll use the snow to our advantage," Gabriella affirmed without a stutter, composed in the frosty elements. The lights in the tunnel began to turn red, then yellow, then green. All of us sped into the drone-less storm down the slope of an opening straightaway out of Skaði's sanctuary. Through the icy starfishes sticking to my visor, I could see the slope got steeper. I could not hear much noise in the suit, only the strong exhales fogging my sights. I could barely see Midas' wheels a few meters ahead, what seemed like a mile away. The peripheral image of a racer crept up the left side, briskly passing by to claim their leading target. My attempt at preventing disaster failed, though I was unaware of the boost being wasted by The Greatest Showman.

"Catch Spade, I've got the others!" Gabriella demanded through her grunts. I heard screeching metal over the mic and hoped that she was holding her own. Meanwhile, MIKA locked a racer-sized target onto Spade while adjusting the visor's lens to the blizzard.

"You're welcome," MIKA said once Midas, Spade and the track unveiled itself. A sharp right turn into a tunnel approached, and I quickly battered the braking Spade into the outer wall, full speed. I could feel the crackling vibrations of bone through his suit, leaving a huge dent on the concrete wall. The Atlas took minor damages, something I overlooked to keep a tail on Midas.

I was surprised that Midas executed the turn easily considering his issues in the past week. Then again, this wasn't a bad race to kill poor habits. The orange tunnel widened the further we went providing hazards like pits, spikes, and arising walls at random spots detouring us toward the outer walls for avoidance. The sudden set of obstacles made it hard on Gabriella as a pair of tumblers turbo'd past me to attack Midas. Kingsley must've made an impulsive call to take down Midas, punishment for my actions against Krueger and Krakyn at Dessnia.

I had a clearer sight of the tumblers at the tunnel's end opening onto a narrow cliffside. The two attackers, Diamond and Heart, were failing to dethrone Midas as he took no time establishing his defensive stance. He braked when they tried to sandwich, he shimmied when they tried to leap onto him, and he jumped over the icy puddles they tried to guide him across. His passively aggressive actions drained the sister's energy, shifting Midas' stance to offense. He shoved Diamond into the projecting walls of the mountain. The tumbler's body flopped like a fish over the rubble and into the dells of my suit where Diamond somehow latched herself, eventually contorting her limbs around my torso for a better grip. The weight of The Greatest Contortionist decreased my speed while Heart extended a brachial blade out of her right arm aimed at Midas. The traumatic experience with Yama's boost kept me from triggering it, allowing Warlock to catch up. I saw his grin through his visor while he shoved his wheel into Diamond's face, shattering her helmet. She lost her grip on my suit. Warlock then gave a quick thumbs up before a hatchet planted its bladed-end into his dell. We both glanced back to see an airborne racer latching themselves onto Warlock's spina, using the handle of the engraved hatchet like a mountain climber for leverage. The clash slowed Warlock, and I noticed the dogfights occurring behind us all.

The skirmish involved Gabriella, Lucifer, and Law. A hate triangle at best, each inflicting pain on the other. I'd heard Gabriella's groans and roars inside my helmet from the beginning of the race. She clawed open the upper-left pectar of Law. He then unloaded an entire round of molten bullets into Lucifer's left femoralis, provoking the unphased Satanian to slice off one of Gabriella's front-wheels. An alliance quickly formed between the two reapers, aimed at Gabriella. Kira came to Gabriella's aid choosing her side wisely. Focused on their fight, I was suddenly blindsided, and shoved into the mountain's rocky wall by the piston-back racer driving along the cliffside. The hit cracked the right side of my visor. The beaked-racer passed me as more cracks branched across my visor, disrupting my view and blinding me in the snowstorm. The only thing I could see of the racer in front of me was a bird latched onto their spina now torpedoing itself into my face, completely destroying the visor.

"Close your eyes and stay straight!" MIKA demanded, protecting my eyelids from the impact of ice shards. The sharp pain then stopped as I opened my eyes to another tunnel. I could see a clear image of the adrenia-injecting Nevermore inching closer to Midas and Heart, laterally extending their brachial blade out for the kill. "Your boost is ready!"

For the first time in my life, I didn't think twice about using the Komodo Fire. The powerful boost created a boiling sensation around my legs, and I squinted through the extreme velocity of gusting winds. I had the Aegis shield assemble itself before I passed Zane to magnetically engulf the sharp brachial blade with my hæmalytes in order to snap it in half. With The Raven's blade destroyed, I gained a quick lead before triggering my brakes to ram Aegis into Zane's right-front wheel and dell. He lost traction, eventually colliding with Club. I then turned my attention back on Midas by boosting closer to take care of Heart. The lone tumbler shifted her attention to me—a distraction that suddenly caused a molten bullet to penetrate her legs. The resulting spinout sent her into the walls right before the end of the tunnel.

Instead of closing my eyes, I kept them squinted through the blizzard as the tank of boost emptied itself beside Midas. I couldn't believe it, but the chances of Midas coming out of this race alive seemed legit, and the Komodo Fire could arguably have been one of the reasons why. I felt a moment of relief as Midas and I raced side by side along the mountain's cliffside. From my journey to the ice station, I knew that there were no more tunnels, only icy hazards that could result in a fall. An idea that I would have to focus on, knowing we weren't even halfway through the race. I could see another sharp leftward turn coming up, which drained our speeds upon our approach. The Golden Scion gave me a brief cold stare before shoving his entire weight toward my body during the turn, successfully guiding me off of the track and mountain. With my eyes shut, I felt the impact of each hit from the mountain's side, impacts that would twist and crush my bones as I heard both MIKA and Gabriella screaming my name before I finally lost my grip on reality.

ACT II
CHAPTER 13

REQUIEM

I **FADED IN AND OUT AS A BLINDING SKY BLURRED MY VISION THROUGH A BROKEN VISOR.** Loose strands of blood coated the edges of the visor's remaining glass shards, slowly dripping onto my cheeks. I gently twisted my head to the left, seeing the towering rock cutting the clouds at its peak. There were chunks of metal lodged onto its side—an evidential trail of my recent journey down the mountain. Still in a severely damaged suit, the bones to my left arm protruded out cleanly, flashing the bright colors of snow-covered blood. The brutal injuries continued down to my left thigh which bent outward, signaling another fracture. My breathing patterns suggested internal injuries. From the pain, I knew my ribs were cracked. The pain made me cough a great deal of blood into the inner parts of my helmet.

"Craven…" a voice spoke softly by my side. I looked to the right and saw a warm body standing tall in an exosuit. The figure shaded the sun's light before crouching down. The beardless man with light-brown eyes had facial features similar to mine. I smiled at the unforgettable image. An image of my father, intact, unharmed. "Why are you here, kiddo?"

"Ar-Are…Yu-yu-you…r-r-r-re-real?" I stuttered through the pain. The question brought a smile to my father's face.

"No, kiddo. I'm only here to help you make your next choice," he calmly responded as if we were back in his study.

"Am I d-d-dead?" I eventually asked, my vision severely blurred before adjusting to his smile.

"That choice is up to you, something I wish I had in the end," he said. I couldn't comprehend this conversation I was having with the ghost in my head.

"W-w-w-why are yu-yu-yu-you here?" I struggled to ask, involuntarily coughing out more blood.

He was unharmed and purified, just like those nights in the library or in his office. A tear fell and froze on my cheek.

"I'm here to tell you that this ain't it, this isn't how I greet my son in the next world," he finally revealed, bringing some life back into my chest from the haymakers in my heart. "I don't wish to greet you in the next world for a long time, so wake up… wake up…"

The words began to grow louder, echoing through the winds and looping within my head. My heart grew anxious like a caged animal desperately trying to claw its way to freedom. The rush of adrenaline briefly caused me to close my eyes, only to hear my father's scorching voice morph into a female's. "...wake up, Craven… CRAVEN, WAKE UP!"

Heat from the sun's rays were magnified through the chipped visor. I opened my eyes again to the sight of my battered and broken body. There was an intact appendisc on my left arm, trying its hardest to magnetically attract itself onto the Thornwood wheel merely inches away from my left hand.

"CRAVEN, WAKE UP!" the female voice shouted once again. It was MIKA's.

"Damage report?" I asked, now trying to reach my good arm out to the Thornwood. I could've sworn there was a Gigallian resting on my left arm from the energy it took to lift it a millimeter off the snow. A millimeter then became a centimeter before finally peaking at an inch. Desperately trying to keep the shaking arm high and long enough for magnetic attraction, I began to cry out the energy left in my lungs while the Thornwood wheel rattled closer to my palmix. After finally pairing up with my appendisc, the wheel's pull jolted me onto my stomach, burying me in the casket of snow. This lone wheel was my last hope out of the graveyard my father claimed was premature.

"Oh my god, you're back. The Atlas is in a critical state, and your body is suffering from multiple fractures within the ribs, the left femur and humerus. The entire left shoulder is dislocated, but aside from that, you're fine," MIKA reported as each spike in the wheel began to point outward, creating traction on the snow. I had zero sense of direction, but I was going forward, and that was all that mattered. Even the sharp pains of my broken ribs pinching my lungs made it damn-near impossible to breath. I maintained a steady forward motion until the sand-like surface turned into asphalt. "Stay alive Craven, just stay alive."

A river of blood streamed out of my mouth and created a puddle within the helmet. From the sounds of sparks and screeching metal, I realized that this wasn't just any asphalt surface, this was the ground layer of the race track. Not only was it a straightaway, it was the final straightaway of the race. I saw a herd of people in the distance, each of them with hands masking their mouths, standing over what looked to be the finish line. I could not understand how it was possible that I could be in a position to finish this race. But that wasn't the strangest part to it all. No, the strange part was the lack of racers at the finish line. There weren't any exosuits, any fan-bases going nuts, or even a tire trail in the snow. It was almost as if I was in first place. Unable to talk from the pain, I could only observe the reactions from the people once I crossed the finish line, and when I did, nothing changed. The crowd stood as frozen as the tears to my face. The only ones who were moving were the pack of medical staff rushing to get to me.

"MIKA..." I tried to say before they removed my helmet. Blood spilled across the track. They kept beaming their flashlights into my eyes for a sign of life. Words were then exchanged by the medical team before they quickly levitated me into a hover stretcher for transportation. Images blurred again, but that didn't prevent me from searching for more racers. I took one last glance at the finish line only to see the black-and-gold mask crossing the finish line. The bicolored racer then pulled his helmet off to reveal a haunted expression just before the agonizing pain caused me to lose consciousness once again.

V
ACT III
LOVE, I HAVE WOUNDS

ACT III
CHAPTER 1

BROKENLY UNBROKEN

ONE BEEP, TWO BEEPS, THREE BEEPS. Constant and steady. The soft beeping noise was beside me. Dry mouth, chapped lips rubbing together in the cold room. I lay on a soft cushion. Another beep pitched into my ear again and again. I pried my eyes open to the white lights, an annoying sight.

"I'll be damned," a man said, leaning into my sights. Trace. "Your spirit really is unbreakable." The friendly face was comforting.

I could no longer feel the entire left side of my body. Did I dare look? I was afraid of what might've been replaced or completely taken away. The beeping sounds sped up as I glanced down to an intact body, heavily casted and nurtured by IVs, blood, and sanitatium.

"How long have I been out?" I finally built the strength to ask.

"Only a couple of days, believe or not. They weren't expecting you to wake until next week," Trace explained, taking a seat next to the bed I was in.

"And Midas?" I asked after a long pause.

"Ummm… How can I put this… Midas is dead."

"What!" The monitor's beeps raced again.

"I'm fucking witya, he's alive, chill out," Trace revealed, proud of his lie. Of course, Trace being Trace, he began to laugh and mock my reaction.

"Keep it up, and I'll make sure you don't make it to your wedding," I threatened, lowering my heart rate. If I had been given more time to heal, it would have been him in this damn bed making my injuries seem like a chipped nail compared to his.

"Jokes aside, I do have some good and bad news," he gestured as I saw the table of zarquoyse flowers, a Pyscean color-changing flower that never dies, over a get-well card from Gabriella sitting next to him. "Good news is that the Pro League's board is not deducting ten points."

"What ten points?"

"The ten you got from your last race, you know, the one where you fell off a mountain and still won. Technically, it should've been illegal, but I guess they felt bad for ya and decided, why not give the man a win," he explained, answering the dying question I had prior to blacking out. Go figure, I got the biggest win so far in my Pro League career, and I couldn't even remember half of it.

"So, what's the bad news?"

"Well, you kinda missed a race, but you still have a score of thirty-eight points. You're not too far from the top, but you have fallen behind, and you must be able to compete in the next race tomorrow or else you'll be disqualified from missing two consecutive races."

"Could be worse," I responded, knowing that there wasn't much to be mad about at the moment. Midas was alive, Gabriella had to be doing well from the look of the flowers, and I was not in the danger zone point-wise.

"Craven, I haven't even gotten to the kicker, the next race is at The Grand Summit, and you won't believe who's competing in it," Trace revealed, pulling out his iCube to place the line-up of racers involving: Kira, Krakyn, reliQ, the unclassified Bayne, and the Rokian Primax. Six racers, all competing on one of the toughest tracks on the planet, The Grand Summit, a track that took place on Mount Everest in the Himalayas. The last race track I saw my father win, again competing against the four-horned Satanian. The impeccable noir flames could've left Chomolungma as a lonesome monolith surrounded by an ashfield if not for my father's momentum-shifting skills against the four-horned brute. The basking heat combined with Sularis Snatchera's offense left Everest shaken, generating several avalanches strong enough to bury the two gladiators colliding like Gods on Olympus. My father came out victorious, respectfully raising his helmet to the Satanian, who in return did the same.

"Could be worse," I repeated a little more nervously.

"Now you're startin' to sound like Crank," said an older man standing by the doorway—an old vet who should've been resting on a beach in Pasydanya enjoying the perks of retirement. There was no doubt on how thankful I was to see Roy during a time of need.

"Did you come all the way here to see little ole me? Roy, you shouldn't have," Trace remarked over a bright smile.

"Don't worry, I didn't," Roy said to kill the smile. "I came to see Craven, who's been gardening a golden pile of shit. What the hell are you thinking, pairing yourself up with the golden smug's daughter, out of all the fish in the sea?"

"It's complicated," I reluctantly replied, seeing him stare at Gabriella's flowers.

"But it doesn't stop there. I forged a lot of heavier armor onto your Atlas trying to protect your ass from another tumble off a mountain, discovering this," he lectured, pulling out an A.I chip. "Being in possession of MIKA isn't a smart move, Craven."

"Why?" I asked, catching the chip when he tossed it.

"She's old; chips have to be replaced every decade or they wear out. When that happens, they lose control of your suit, leading to injuries worse than the ones you've already endured."

"After the big fall, she kept trying to wake me up. Never giving up on me for one second, so I'm not gonna give up on her," I said to the pair of weary looks. It may not have been the smartest choice, but it wasn't gonna stop MIKA and I from finishing this series together. In my first race, where I debuted with a sore abdomen unable to maintain a planked position, she became the wind beneath my wings, manually binding the intervertebral discs within my suit's spina to stiffen my back. It relieved pressure in my abdomen. She did that. She'd been the one who provided me with viable reports from the Versarchives. She was the one who always spared an ounce of boost when I was determined to empty it. To her, I was the closest thing to a redeemable ticket she believed she deserved. She always blamed herself for my father's death—something that wasn't her fault. So, who was I to deprive her of the much-needed mental antidote.

As a response, Trace jokingly offered me Dr. Perris' info card—a reminder of my mental state. I decided to reveal that I'd been seeing my father's ghost, haunting me everywhere I went—something I knew couldn't be normal. I saw flashbacks of my father in Roy's eyes, but I explained that my visions were of a half-dead cadaver. Roy stayed silent. Trace, on the other hand, explained how these mental responses to traumatic events were normal. He'd been aware of my mental disturbances in the past, and so had Roy. I mentioned Zane's condition during the last pre-race, which silenced Trace.

"I once knew a racer who went through the same shit," Roy began. "A mental breakdown after she lost her girlfriend in Galactica XLVII."

"Catelyn Brannigan," Trace said gently. The Lone Shark, one of "the surviving seven" I knew so little about. It was crazy how their stories had continuously popped over the past week.

"The tragedy broke Catelyn's mind, but never her spirit. Eventually able to convince herself to compete in Galactica XLVIII for closure, killing the shithead responsible," Roy said, connecting the dots for me. "But the vengeful path ended up taking her life as well. I don't need to be a shrink to know how much you hate Thorax. I only wish you'd search for a better path. Maybe then you'll find serenity."

"Thorax has nothing to do with this, with my head," I defensively stated, somehow able to say the Rokian's name without stuttering.

"Why MIKA then?" he asked. I explained that her experience with my dad translated well to mine, but he countered with an objective statement about how any A.I. chip could do the same thing. He was digging deep into the parts of my head that had not been explored since my father's wake. "I think it has everything to do with closure. I think that you are as smart as your father, if not smarter. You own a shop, and from my understanding, have been able to smuggle in shit that hasn't even hit the market. An impressive risk that I believe can be the roots to your eudaimonia, so tell me, what is your eudaimonia?"

"Being the best racer," I responded, causing my eyes to water.

"Bullshit," he shot. "Never have I ever heard you say those words. You couldn't even say it without tearing up."

"That's enough," Trace stated, coming to my aid.

Roy walked over to the table of zarquoyse flowers. He took a long look before nodding to himself, now turning back at me.

"I know why you see your father, Craven," he said. "But until you can tell me what your true endgame is, I don't think you deserve the answer."

The Prestige Angel then left the room, his words drilling into my cranium. I couldn't believe he knew. I couldn't believe he had an answer, a plan. He knew what my intentions were past Four Seasons, and they didn't involve my hatred towards Luke. This whole time, he knew the hate had been reserved for… a Rokian. A blue-eyed Rokian that would force me to break a promise I'd made to my mother. A Rokian who deprived me of a father, a Rokian who could morph his face onto every Rokian, even the one waiting for me at Everest. Thorax, the Rokian who brought out the worst in me, the worst that I'd kept locked up in the basement of my head. This was something I had to confront sooner or later, the battle against my demon. But I didn't expect the resolution to involve my mental instability. I always figured it was just PTSD, the typical disorder, but if Roy knew the real reason why I always saw my father, maybe crossing that bridge now wasn't such a bad idea.

"I've never seen the old chap so pissed," Trace finally said.

"Could be worse," I muttered, noticing the sparkling silver revolver hidden in the shadows of Gabriella's bouquet. "Why is there a gun in the room?"

"Oh yeah, I almost forgot," Trace blurted, rising out of his chair to the firearm. "You're brokenly unbroken resilience at Peak caught the love and attention from The Full Metal Jacket."

Trace tossed the nihilistic gift to me for further examination. It had a chrome nose with a special cedar grip that would adhere to any moist palm. On the center of the multi-sided grip was a gray logo of a skull wearing a cowboy hat with black letters of "FMJ" carved into the frontal lobe. Still attempting to understand the gift, I ejected it's 9-hole cylinder causing a pack of golden bullets to fly out onto my hip. It was a good thing, too, because I was getting ready to unload the damn gun at Trace for throwing an armed gun at me in the first place. Then I noticed Midas' name etched onto each bullet.

"Those crazy fuckers were at the finish line too. You should've seen the look on their faces when they saw your carcass drive across the finish line," Trace explained. I tried to remember the image, and instead could only muster up the faces of the medical staff. "They were prepared to kill Midas right there on the spot, but you stopped them. You gave them hope that the sonuvabitch could be taken down."

"I did that?" I questioned. If both Law and Midas were to qualify in the championship race, hell would scorch the Chicagolands. I ripped off all the heart rate pads stuck to my chest.

"The hell are you doing?" Trace inquired.

"Getting ready for the next race."

"Dude, if I wasn't medically cleared after losing an arm, what makes you think they'll make an exception. You should be lucky you weren't paralyzed from the fall, there isn't an herb in the galaxy that'll heal…"

"TRACE! I'm competing, now help me," I demanded. Half of my body felt like it was floating, and I could hardly stand with the cast on my left leg.

Trace used his hibrix to break the stiff coatings. The doctors had surgically installed vises in my left leg and arm, braces acting as fresh layers of bone around the femur and humerus so that it could withstand an extreme amount of tension. Vises could cause unimaginable levels of pain freshly attached. It was a good thing I was still unconscious when they were installed.

I instantly felt the weak muscles after Trace helped me onto my feet. I almost collapsed without half of my nerves which didn't help the proprioception either. Things got a bit smoother the more I walked around in the room, but it didn't feel quite right. The race didn't require running, nor would I want to at Everest, fully healthy. As long as I stay in my suit, I should have been good. Then again, I had to remember the four extraterrestrial Carnivores awaiting me.

Feeling as ready as I'd ever be, I told Trace to get a doctor to sign us outta here pronto because the trip to Nepal was a long one. While he carried out the task, I got back into my blue jay jacket, feeling the heavy pressure in my left shoulder, struggling to even raise it above my chest. Things could have definitely been worse. I mean, I fell off of a mountain and survived, ready for the next race, an impossible one at best. A lot of things felt broken, but just like Catelyn, my spirit was anything but. The only difference was that the one closest to my heart at the moment was alive. Roy advised taking a new path, so that's what I would do. I glanced down at my dad's championship ring on my hand in order to take it off, replacing the token of support with one zarquoyse now changing its color to teal. From a presentational standpoint, I would've preferred the blue colors, but beggars can't be choosers. The teal wasn't a bad color for the loving token. Something I hoped could keep me strong at Everest, a desperate measure in a desperate race, a race I must survive, no matter the cost.

ACT III
CHAPTER 2

CHOMOLUNGMA

ON THE LENGTHY FLIGHT TO NEPAL, TRACE AND I STUDIED THE FAULTS OF THE GRAND **SUMMIT.** There weren't a lot of moments on the track where a racer could fly off, thankfully, but it evened out the playing field with hazards such as: hanging icicles, eight-inch high snowfields, and of course, warnings of avalanches. Holding onto a Naturis rating of B+, the mountain tripled Mont Forel in height, standing over 9,000m high. The competitors might be tough, but Trace reminded me there were only six of us. There would be more space on the track, fewer moments of frenzy, and guaranteed points to the last racer across the finish line. Points that would keep me in the top-sixteen. Throughout the entire flight, Trace was more supportive and serious than ever, aware of how treacherous Everest was. He could only watch his severely battered brother attack the feat. It wouldn't have hurt to have had Gabriella's support, but she was busy competing in a race of her own. The zarquoyse flower was the only part of her I had, and I wasn't taking it for granted. In order to make the flower pocket-sized, I ripped off most of its stem during the flight's landing.

Trace and I wasted no time traveling to the ice station and listening to Gabriella's race on the radio. It was a bloodbath on a track at K2 between Gabriella, Law, Creed, Jackal, Lucifer, Warlock, and many others. The announcer swore multiple times that Gabriella was a Tasmanian devil swiveling its claws all over each racer—one of the many stories on the second highest mountain in the United Countries of Earth. The other stories involved sequel clashes between Warlock and Creed on top of an arsenal-heavy Jackal dropping thousands of bullet shells, butting heads with Law who brought out the spiked lasso. He wrapped it around Jackal's neck for Lucifer to dismantle with his sword. The two Carnivores then blitzed the outlaw, creating an unbelievable alliance between Law and Gabriella. An overwhelming pair proving to be too much for the Carnivores. Gabriella clawed off one of Jackal's machine guns for Law to lasso onto his suit, now using Gabriella's krone claws as a target for the bullets to ricochet into the Carnivores. Gabriella walked away claiming second with Law stealing a last-second lead for first, glazing K2 red in the bloodiest race of the series thus far. This served to increase the anticipation for what awaited the world on Everest.

Working on good time, we were able to reach the station by sunset's end. It was not nearly as big as Skaði's, mainly because this station was one of many scattered around the bottom of Everest. The staff actually had to communicate with the other stations so that my suit could be transported. I also found out the lanes to the starting line were helicopters, and that we were going to be dropped onto the track—an overlooked start to The Grand Summit that tended to wipe racers out early on. The info made me shiver after realizing my body wasn't prepared for punishment after all. Trace reminded me that it could be worse. I damn-near choked on the words.

The staff then had to separate us both once the Atlas finally arrived at the locker. *Give them hell, brother*, were Trace's final words along with a fist-bump. I thanked him for getting me to this point, now as ready as I'd ever be for grandeur. Kira was the only other racer at this station, getting ready in her Venus, wearing several layers of clothing. She looked in disbelief once she noticed the unbroken knight prepared for siege.

"No mountain high enough?" she stated, walking up for a hug. It may have been gentle, but it was still painful. An analytical move, on her part, to observe how race ready I actually was. I stifled a groan which seemed to impress her. "Try not to die on this mountain."

"I was trying to protect someone," I reluctantly replied.

"And he sure as hell repaid the favor. Why the hell are you protecting him?"

"It's complicated."

"Complicated enough your girlfriend couldn't do it herself?" she questioned, fully attracting my attention. "I know she's Krueger."

"How?"

"All eyes have been locked on Krueger since the debut. The one racer with special behind-the-scenes treatment, krone claws, a handmade suit not even on the black market, and an undisclosed profile, meaning they have to be rich, smart, and important. That limits the options of Krueger's identity. Someone who hasn't laid a finger on you during competition, narrowing the options down to your mom, your best friend, or your girlfriend. I've never seen your mother compete and Trace has too much pride to mask, leaving only one option. Based on your reaction, I take it I'm right," she explained, Sherlocking the truth. "I'm not gonna tell anyone, just know the difference between a friend and an enemy before it gets you killed."

The brief discussion came to an end as she gave a ready signal to one of the guards that would lead her to the helicopter outside. I knew that Kira and I had been friends since the start of my career, but was it that easy or was she just that smart? The limited time didn't help as I rushed to get ready. New parts for the Atlas made a noticeable difference in the suit's appearance. The dells were broader, the abdominis had been replaced with the ones from Roy's Icarus, the patallises stuck out more for increased stability, and the tiballises were much thicker. Roy was aware of my injuries and had installed additions to the exosuit that worked in my favor, even though it took away speed. That was what the remaining fluid ounces of Komodo Fire would fix. Stuck on the newly repaired helmet was a post-it note reading:

GET THE JOB DONE!
Your Guardian Angel,
Roy

It was the final dose of confidence my body needed, but I added one final touch to the Atlas—a zarquoyse stuck to the side of the helmet's interior. A reminder to set my friends apart from my enemies. MIKA was the only thing missing. I heard Roy's advice in my head, but ended up sticking with my decision by applying her to the helmet as well. I wanted to hear her voice once again.

"Hello Craven, it's good to see that you've healed," MIKA said.

"Thanks. Could you give me your status report?" I asked.

"The suit has had repairs and looks like..."

"No, I want YOUR status report," I insisted.

"I'll be alright," she replied.

"I've been told you're hanging on by a thread, should I be worried?"

"Chips are known for deteriorating after a decade and I've been around for almost two. There's no doubt my time's coming to an end."

"I'll make sure we see this series through to the end, together, I promise."

"And I believe you Craven, but what happens when the series is over?"

"We hang up our capes and ride off into the sunset, how's that sound?"

"It sounds like the way to go," MIKA replied, brightening the mood as a staff member entered our room and waited to escort me outside and onto a helicopter.

Inside the aircraft, an Initiator was signaling me to take the helmet off as the propellers began to spin. He explained the dangers I'd already studied during the ascension, advising me not to do what I did at Forel. A lot of things he addressed were not pleasant but he concluded on a positive note, stating that my thirty-eight points were still the highest among the six. That meant the race would start on my leap out of the helicopter. I'd always been in every lane except first, so this had to be a twist of fate. I'd be able to enjoy it more if I didn't have to fly onto the track. My body wasn't ready for another fall. The air pressure and oxygen levels began to change as we got closer to the other five choppers floating still above Mount Everest. The Initiator made it clear that he'd nudge me when the time was right prior to placing our helmets on. MIKA quickly adjusted the airflow to the Atlas once we arrived next to the other racers patiently waiting.

Half of the aircrafts were super-sized military grade choppers for the likes of Krakyn, reliQ, and the now impatient Rokian, Primax. Krakyn and reliQ were polar opposites. The Pyscean felt foreign to the frozen conditions. As for reliQ, he was sitting on the edge with dangling feet, playing a tune on his guitar. In our previous encounter, Krakyn and reliQ walked away with a combined total of three points. Breakout performances wouldn't be a surprise.

The aircraft carrying Primax swung back and forth from the Rokian's uncontrollable movements as he embraced the high-altitudes. He had on a raisin and nickel 1955 Daconix, a suit native to the Ragnarök with an immeasurable amount of horsepower. There were light-blue veins for the distribution of xenon gas.

Primax dismantled the visor to his helmet, whipping it at my aircraft. I dared him to toss the helmet too, knowing he'd suffer without the xenon gas. He roared the words, *I am going to hurt you.* I ignored the threat and sensed another Carnivore staring into my soul in *Freya's* black and silver 2240 Grymm covered in Hyper Velocitative Armour. The heart of the freakshow, Bayne, hid their face under a black metallic hood and a giant silver scythe attached to their back. The unknown originated from the same red moons that gave the universe Skorge, a beast incarnated for havoc, except there was no way of killing IT. Bayne would always heal from any type of impairment wreaked onto their body. IT calmly waited for me to initiate the race.

The moon shone bright in the cloudless star-scattered sky, reflecting off the snowfield sheeting of the first descendent ramp of the track. At the edges to each part of the track were nightcam lights, high in lumens, killing any need for night vision. I couldn't help but gaze at the sky, a peaceful habit my father and I did from time to time, taking away the pain, the stress, the damage, helping me comfort the nerves in the left side of my body.

The Initiator gave a nudge. I then balanced my wheels onto the landing skids of the aircraft, readying up the racers. From all of my homework on the track, I knew that this race could only be determined by speed and durability from the long curves and straightaways. The finish line was all the way at the bottom of Everest within an underground tunnel. I glanced at the teal zarquoyse flower and then saw the ghost of my father jumping out of Kira's helicopter in his Hermes, landing perfectly on the left side of the snow-covered ramp. He disappeared only to reappear in Kira's helicopter in order to do it again. I wondered if he was trying to tell me something, perhaps the left side was the sweet spot.

The specter from above propelled me off of the helicopter. I impacted the track, smoothly sailing through the snow and quickly discovering traction. For the first time in my life, there was no one in front of me at the start. I soon felt the rumble of racers unable to land the same way. The snow blew into the air as the wheels continuously plowed through the field, not once slowing down to the white height. Up ahead was an entrance to the first golden-lit tunnel introducing the next hazard—spiky icicles hanging from the tunnel's ceiling. I led the way inside, avoiding each spike, enjoying the snowless asphalt in the tunnel. I maintained the lead, going flawless against the hazard as the track got steeper. A menacing shadow appeared over my dell, provoking me to trigger the brakes. I could feel my pair of rear-wheels colliding against bone and metal, shattering them at first contact. Parts of their upper body now leaned over my right dell, revealing the face of a blue-eyed Rokian, the face I swore never to forget, the face of my dad's killer. It felt like I stared into those eyes for an eternity, a sight that changed with a single blink, now showing me the bicolored eyes of Primax in a lot of pain. His body still blanketed mine after I triggered the boost, attempting to sway him off, but his wheels created a minor problem. His legs may have been fractured inwardly, but the wheels were still attached, causing him to wrap his arms around my torso once I mule-kicked the rear-wheels from under his legs. The wheels attached to his arms then began to shred off parts of my abdominis.

"Craven, you've got to do something before his wheels penetrate your skin," MIKA informed me as we left the tunnel now driving on a rail-less track curving leftward. A blunt rocky obstruction stuck out on the mountain's wall. I used it to my advantage by leaning towards it, reaching back to grab a hold of the Rokian's platys-plate so he'd impact it face first. The rocky collision ripped Primax off of my back, causing the entire mountain to quake.

"Please tell me I didn't cause what I think I caused," I asked MIKA as the curve transitioned into a long downward straightaway on the mountain's side with a tunnel at the end of it. A shitload of snow slid closer to the tunnel's entrance from above, and would bury anyone unable to reach it in time.

"You talking about the avalanche? Oh, heavens no, Craven," MIKA sarcastically responded, signaling that my boost was ready. Before I could trigger the boost, I heard a woman scream. I twisted back to see Kira with a scythe impaling her back. Bayne was on her tail, attempting to slice open her vertebrae. "Craven, you'll be buried if you don't use your boost!" MIKA tried to talk me out of the choice she assumed I'd make.

I slowed down, ramming through Bayne's front-wheels and into their face, destroying the visor. I placed a lot of strength into my legs so that the wheels would cause abrasion to the skin. Bayne tried to retaliate by impaling me with their weapon but eventually spun out of control and into the mountain's side. Now in the clear, Kira and I both triggered our boosts to beat the avalanche. The Komodo clearly outmatched her boost as she fell behind causing me to shift in front so that she could draft. The chilling clumps of snow briefly showered our exosuits before reaching the tunnel's entrance soon closed off and buried in snow. Kira and I were basically the only two racers left. The realization made us ease off on the boost and come to a complete stop.

"You alright?" I asked Kira, partially taking my helmet off. Bayne had clearly done a number on her from the pain her face expressed and the amount of blood dripping onto the track.

"Glad to know I'm a friend and not an enemy," she stated through her helmet. A series of rumbles drew our attention to the tunnel's entrance. They must have come from one of the Carnivores.

"Damn it, Krakyn doesn't know when to quit," I muttered to myself, getting back on all four.

"The Pyscean injured himself at the landing, it's Titan," Kira said as reliQ busted through the pile of snow with one neck of his bladed guitar. He grew closer and closer to us even though we were draining the rest of our boost tanks. The giant tried to slam the bladed-end of his guitar into my suit, but Kira pushed me out of the way to take the hit, letting him slice open her thigh. She then triggered her Thornwood tires, shifting them from rubber to spikes, now shoving them into reliQ's dell before boosting away and into the lead. She was unaware that my boost tank was empty, leaving me alone with the giant. Choosing not to attack, reliQ gripped the back of my neck, twisting me in his direction. Unable to decipher his next move, I gave a headbutt, cracking the glass to my visor. The hit left the giant disoriented and defenseless to the spiked wheel Kira launched into his face, forcing him to let go.

I caught back up to Kira before the tunnel could come to an end leading us into a maze of icy-walled pathways, each leading to the same underground tunnel. Some of the pathways were longer than others, but Kira and I had to focus on surviving versus racing, so we took the same pathway. Titan accidentally got stuck in a different pathway before he could regain his focus. Kira seemed to be losing control of herself as her stomach grazed the track. I hadn't thought much of the cut on her thigh until then. It had the ivory glow of Irizan leaking out of it. I decided to grab a hold of her, unsure of what the nerve agent was doing to her, but I knew it wasn't good. The icy walls exploded as the giant rammed through the icy walls, rediscovering our location from behind. He tomahawked one of the guitars at us, missing by an inch. Now seeing the underground entrance in the near distance, I quickly kicked one of Kira's spiked wheels from underneath, sending it into the giant's head once again. That prevented him from launching another projectile. We found ourselves in the tunnel of fans shouting our names from the stands as we crossed the finish line. Kira took second place and I, first. At this point, Kira's body felt limp and lifeless, attracting the medical staff. Unsure of what could possibly cure the Irizan, I followed the staff into the nearby bunker, escaping the fans, ignoring the reporters, and surviving the mountain.

NO REST FOR THE WICKED

URGENTLY, THE MEDICAL TEAM TRANSFERRED KIRA'S BODY INTO A ROOM FOR TREATMENT. They were having problems extracting her from the exosuit, something I aided them with while still stuck in mine. Afraid of what I would see, I carefully took off her helmet, quickly noticing the pinpointed pupils of her hazel eyes and the light-green vasoconstricting veins squiggling around like nightcrawlers brought into the daylight. The veins had thorns growing every few millimeters. Kira grunted—a sign of the struggling life hanging by a spider web. In this case, I hoped the web was made out of wethro from Arach. If anyone in the galaxy could hold on, it was Kira Brink. She couldn't have come all this way to save my life just to give up hers.

"What's the substance around her leg?" a doctor inquired after Kira was fully extracted out of the Venus. The glowing ivory colored fluid had now coated her legs and displayed the veins and arteries clawing out of her corium as if they were trapped inside a frozen lake.

"Er-eri-eye-Irizan," I blurted out. Half of the medics scanned the room for an antidote while the other half started cutting off parts to her clothing to see how far the nerve agent had traveled internally. It didn't help that she had multiple layers of clothing, creating an obstacle for the medics that would cost crucial seconds. Once a proper incision was made to strip her out of the corium, we could see the glowing fluids traveling through the erratic veins around her breasts. I didn't know much more than what Gabriella told me about the Ghastallian drug, especially not the fact that it had its own life. Its own spirit. Whatever was inside her bloodstream could now be heard crying through the skin of its host. One of the physicians informed me that if the Irizan found its way to the cerebral, she'd be as good as dead. There had to be an antidote somewhere. Urgently, I pried open every unopened medical cabinet mounted on the walls. There was nothing in the first cabinet I checked, but in the second were the letters "Prali-" etched onto the side of the vial glass half-full. Pralidoxime. I quickly grabbed it with my quivering hands and hustled it to a doctor with a syringe at hand.

All hearts were racing faster than the endangered Terran in the room while the doctor filled the long-needled syringe ready for penetration. Once the syringe penetrated Kira's bare skin, the Irizan let loose a loud screech as the antidote went straight into the heart. The scream of death trailed to silence as Kira's glowing skin began to dim, and the Ghastallian substance was eradicated once and for all.

We all sighed in relief. The medical team had just saved another life and began to hug one another. The doors to the room burst open, and the worried hounds rushed in looking for their friend. Confused why his girlfriend was lying on a table half-naked, Beta shoved us all away from Kira. He temporarily froze at the sight of her pale body. Kira feebly reached up to gasp Beta's tremulous arms. Everyone who thought that she was merely a ventriloquist pulling the strings of a gullible hound should've seen how fixed their eyes were on one another. Could this be eudaimonia? Whatever it was, it deserved privacy.

I escorted the entire medical team and Meta out of the room. The head doctor thanked me on the way out, adding that the cold weather had been Kira's saving grace with regard to the Irizan.

I ejected out of the Atlas and slid my battered body down the outer wall of the medical room. Meta took a silent seat next to me as Trace appeared for an update. Expecting a hyped boy ready for the Spring week, I, instead, got a man worried for Kira's health. Guards and a few practitioners circled around our perimeter, protecting us from those who dared to disturb the peace. They guided the fans to an exit and answered all questions. As we sat there, our exosuits were prepared for transportation. Everybody had been guided out of the vicinity until it was just the three of us and a few guards patiently waiting for the couple to come out of the room. Once they were out, Beta offered his jacket to cover his love's ripped attire.

"Craven," Beta began to say, but instead gave me one of the most painful hugs ever. "Consider this hug as a thank you, but forget you saw my girlfriend naked."

"I'll try," I yelped. He then loosened his grip, setting me free for a more heartwarming hug from Kira. I could sense her gratitude and the feeling of being in debt. But she would've done the same. The five of us had come a long way since our days competing in the Semi's, and we were still growing, actually aware of where we were going next.

Trace claimed that he had a hover truck warmed up and waiting for us outside. He had a plan to defeat the frosty conditions—getting us all the hell out of Nepal. He did not anticipate the nightmare waiting for us.

A dozen or so cars sat outside, waiting for a driver. In between us and the lot was the Carnivore family, newly warmed from their long tenure in the eight below. The elderly blonde patriarch, Kingsley had on his traditional white dress pants, white vest top with blue buttons over a blue tucked tie and white alligator shoes. His gray wife, and matriarch, Gwenylin had on her snow-white dress and silver heels. I wondered if the capes around their shoulders had something to do with their comfort in the cold, standing tall in front of the only alien at the bottom of the mountain, reliQ. That's when it hit me. They weren't waiting for us. They were waiting for the rest of their family. I glanced up at the tip of Everest where a number of aircraft were flying a search & rescue mission.

"Terrible things, oh you have done terrible things, MehGuire," Kingsley stated, unveiling a sword hidden in his long winter cape. The guards quickly came to our side, now waiting for the patriarch's next move.

"We don't have time for this shit, old timer," Trace said, pulling up the sleeve on his hibrix arm. Gwenylin glared at him.

"You should respect your elders," she thundered.

"I do, and I respect them enough to call them ignorant assholes whenever they're ignorant assholes," Trace informed her.

"I admire your spirit. Clearly it has taken an arm at some point, but your ally has not been loyal to his word," Kingsley explained, raising the sword's end at me. I could only wonder what was going through the minds of Kira and the hounds through all of this.

"I'm aware, why punish him now instead of on the track? What honor comes from it now?" Trace questioned, trying to rescue me from the peculiar dilemma. His words dug into Kingsley's emotions and he reconsidered the situation. Kira saw it too, addressing what might come after the crimes that may or may not have been committed.

"Justice…is…now," Kingsley answered, stepping closer before a pair of masked-figures squeezed past the giant directly to Kingsley's side. The pair planted a knife up to Kingsley's carotid arteries. I realized they were the Quinn siblings, now willing to commit a bloodletting act. Harley stood to Kingsley's left wearing dark-blue face paint with silver swirling around the outer rim of the cheeks and eyebrows. He also had long green-and-blue hair formed into a pair of ponytails. His sister Harlene stood to the right with the same presentational configuration. Her colors, instead, were red and silver with long red hair in three ponytails.

"Justice…is…futile," a man suddenly announced from behind the family. A stick batted the ground in a slow thud before a man in purple with a cane appeared. It was Joseph Kershaw, now in a purple top hat suitable for the occasion. "You kill the boy, I hit you with a lawsuit that you won't be able to afford, and that's if we make it out alive."

"So that's it," Gwenylin cried, "We just let them leave?"

"You catch on quickly, my dear," JoKer replied to a disapproving Kingsley, sheathing his sword. "Justice is coming, it's just not here."

"Like I said, we don't have time for this shit," Trace restated, leading the way to his truck. Kira and the hounds followed, convincing the guards and reliQ to lower their weapons. For the time being, the Quinn's kept their knives planted into Kingsley's neck waiting for me to pass by. Like before, JoKer's hands were firmly gripping his cane. He gave me a wink when I walked past him. I still had no idea whose side he was on or what game he was playing. But I was grateful for the escape, making my way to the others.

Trace was determined to get us out of the Himalayas, instantly driving away once we were all in his truck. After hitting the halfway point, Beta decided to break the ice by asking what the confrontation was all about and how Trace knew exactly what to say during the debate. Sensing my best friend's stress, I decided to take a leap of faith by explaining everything to the twins and Kira, and I mean everything. I told them Gabriella was Krueger, explained the deal with the Carnivores involving Midas losing and Jackal winning, and even decided to suggest what would come after Midas' death—information that Trace didn't even know. Each of them shared the same look of disbelief. Unsure I'd explained it correctly, Kira translated part of the story. Her words confirmed the part about Midas' guaranteed death by the FMJ, if not Law, and the research her family had dug up about Luke Gold being impulsive and abusive. She quickly became the proper wing support I needed to get everybody on the same page prior to our arrival at the airport.

"This series is a lot bigger than us, so what I'm asking is for you all to win out. The more friends we have in the Semi-finals, the less likely Midas dies," I said, knowing it was easier said than done. But it didn't take long for the runner-ups of Knightfall to make a promise of doing just that, win out.

Trace then pulled out his iCube to check where we all were heading next in the series. I had forty-eight points, sending me back to the forty-plus-point premier bracket of the Amazon. Unfortunately, Kira and the hounds were headed to the islands of Samoa. They promised to keep their word before getting on their flight while Trace and I waited for ours. We stared out of the airport's window to the star-scattered sky.

"You stable?" I finally asked, aware of how different he'd been since the end of the last race.

"I don't know," he answered, watching our friends' flight sail off into the clouds. "Katia, she called me just before your race. She had something important to tell me."

"What was it?"

"She's pregnant," he revealed. As his best friend, and as his brother, I wanted to congratulate him, but the displeased look on his face told a different story. There wasn't a hint of cheer in his eyes, only sorrow. "At first, I was a bit scared of the bittersweet news, as any new father would be. I knew that it would affect the way I compete in Versa, and that's if I'll ever compete again."

"You can still compete. A child didn't stop my father."

"I know, and that's why I'm scared. I haven't mentioned how scared Katia would be if I did, but those were my first thoughts. I didn't know about the extinction section of your story," he responded. The hot seat I was in became hotter, but more importantly, it made my final words to Kira and the hounds that much more important.

"Me being in this series is the start of change," I promised, butting our foreheads together. "You've done your part by bringing me here, now let me do mine."

The hug between us grew tighter. He'd always pushed me in the right direction, even when I felt like falling, every single time since we first met. Sure, he could be a thorn in my ass cheek, but he was my brother, and I hated seeing him unable to cherish the beautiful gift that life had given him. It'd be a sick joke if life granted my brother a child only to take it away.

ACT III
CHAPTER 4

SPRING

A NEW DAY, OFFICIALLY UPON US, BRIGHTENED EVERYTHING AS THE SHINING SUN ROSE OVER OUR DESTINATION, MANAUS, BRAZIL. The fields of clouds were so close to the jet that the sunrise seemed like the cliché image of heaven. If only our lives were equivalent. So much chaos, all of it for peace, and we're only halfway done in the series. At the start, prior to my Pro League debut, I had listed the Amazon jungle as the unluckiest destination, not once questioning the mountains that would almost kill me. More injuries and missing cases plague the racers within the jungle, all unavoidable. It was the one set of tracks that depended more on luck than the skill I'd been leaning on. It was the one set of tracks that deserved a Naturis rating but lacked it due to the calm weather.

With my confidence level sinking again, Trace stumbled upon an urgent announcement from the Unican Network regarding Four Seasons. He had an idea of what it might be. Spring week tended to be the half-ass week of the competition due to the top-sixteen racers clinching their positions—something I had to keep an eye out for. The sooner I clinched, the fewer races I had to endure. Less time in the jungle.

The plane began its descension into the jungle, revealing the beautifully green city of Manaus lying below. We were foreign to the weather as midwesterners coming off a cold week, and were now restless behind doors to the port. We both inhaled deeply on our first steps onto the tropical land. The warm atmosphere didn't seem too bad, at first. The air was dry and hot. As the shock of the heat cooked our skin to a rosy pink, we hurried towards a nearby vehicle. Thankfully, the air conditioning inside the car had been on full throttle. Acclimation could be a bitch. It was short-lived, but I think I missed Everest.

"So much for defeating the cold weather," Trace said as he set a course to the nearest hotel. I was used to seeing Re-Versables, or FMJs, but neither were here. The Versa symbols all around the city were pristine. The kids on the streets had on shirts, hats, and tattoos to support their favorite racers. The male elders favored my image of an unchained knight while the youth preferred a golden scion. The women, on the other hand, showed their devotion to the most popular female competitor in the Pro League, Kira. Some of them even added the Yin and Yang Hound symbol in deference to her personal life. Some wore a neon-blue chain as a necklace to honor my life-saving act. Manaus felt… normal. The city was a true fan to the sport and kept a lot of the fluff surrounding Versa out. There weren't too many cities on our planet that could say the same thing. Greenland was tamed, but the blinged-out penguins were just so… No, on second thought, I missed those damn penguins. They were the best thing about *Goldland*.

Though Manaus wasn't as flashy, the calmness made the heat more bearable. Before we reached the northernmost hotel named Wyndham Garden, I'd decided this was a destination I would have to return to someday. The hotel was sandwiched between two minor stands of palm trees. At the entrance was a navy-blue fountain. Just like the other hotels, a valet met us at the door and provided us a direct passage to our reserved room not nearly as big as the previous one. It had a soft carpeted floor with strips of cinnamon, vanilla, chocolate, and glaze that led to the soft white recliners and couches all around the oak wood dining table. The lone Fornia King bed catered to royalty with its quadruple-tucked blankets beneath the dozen or so pillows. Trace and I argued about who got the bed because there was no way in a Satanian hell that we were both going to sleep on it. We loved each other, but we didn't love each other that much. We chose to resolve the dilemma with rock-paper-scissors. From the past match-ups against this imbecile, I'd learned that when he was in doubt, he rocked it out. I chose paper. The cynical bastard went scissors, almost as if he had planned this moment from the start, quickly flopping onto the mattress.

While he sank into the foam, I took the liberty of ordering a few meals to our room. For Trace, I ordered a medium-rare raptr cooked to his liking, while I treated my craving for a lachli salad to help heal all the wounds inflicted on my body in the past week. By the time the food arrived, an announcement from the Unican Network popped up on our iCubes. We rearranged the overstuffed chairs around the bonfire of a television grid while the network informed everyone that the premier, axial, and danger brackets had been dismantled—an action that altered the designated tracks for several racers. Delays were enforced on every race except the one I'd be competing in tomorrow. It was a major change that would postpone a much-needed reunion with Gabriella, someone who had their race relisted to Australia along with Law, leaving Midas safely here with me. It also unveiled the top racers of the series, classifying anyone below the sixteenth rank as endangered, and listed the potential clinching scenarios.

Four Seasons Rankings

1. Midas Gold (56)*
2. Lawson "Law" Pierce (50)*
3. Craven McGuire (48)*
4. Jackal "Jack" Amaryllis (46)"
5. Warlock Neit (44)*
6. Krueger (43)*
7. Credo "Creed" Velasquez (42)*
8. Zane Maddox (42)*
9. reliQ "Titan" Qalmantine (39)

10. Kira Brink (38)
11. Spade Amaryllis (36)
12. Beta Breckenidge (35)
13. Meta Breckenidge (35)
14. Lucretia "Lucifer" Xiagra (32)
15. Heart Amaryllis (32)
16. Club Amaryllis (32)

__Danger Zone__

17. Krakyn Avenya (31)
18. Diamond Amaryllis (31)
19. Bayne V'XIII (30)
20. Amir "Cobra" Al-Otaibi (30)

__*Clinching Scenarios:__

Midas Gold (next race)
☐ If finishes in 4th place or higher
☐ If Beta, Meta, Lucifer, Heart, Club, or Danger Zone finish unscored

Lawson "Law" Pierce (next race)
☐ If finishes in 1st place
☐ If Danger Zone finishes unscored

Craven McGuire (next race)
☐ If finishes in 1st place & Kira, Spade, Beta, Meta, Lucifer, Heart, Club, and/or Danger Zone finish unscored

Jackal "Jack" Amaryllis (next race)
☐ If finishes in 1st place & Spade, Beta, Meta, Lucifer, Heart, Club, and/or Danger Zone finish unscored

Warlock Neit (next race)
☐ If finishes in 1st place & Lucifer, Heart, Club, and/or Danger Zone finish unscored

Krueger (next race)
☐ If finishes in 1st place & Lucifer, Heart, Club, and/or Danger Zone finish unscored

Credo "Creed" Velasquez (next race)
☐ If finishes in 1st place & Lucifer, Heart, Club, and/or Danger Zone finish unscored

Zane Maddox (next race)
☐ If finishes in 1st place & Lucifer, Heart, Club, and/or Danger Zone finish unscored

Trace hadn't been kidding about the clinching scenarios blowing up, a logistical pile of what ifs. It should have been a simple win and we're in. Instead, it showed how many points one needed along with a little help. At least Midas' scenario was direct. It would be damn-near impossible for him not to clinch a berth, altering my objective of making sure he got there tomorrow, avoiding any type of Spring week disasters.

All eyes would be on us in the next race due to the scoring scenarios, leaving the date for Gabriella's race in the air. As for my race, it involved me, Midas, Warlock, Creed, Zane, Jackal, and Bayne, who I was sure would be much worse in the Amazonian climate. I'd have been baffled if IT went after Midas instead, flattered by the grudge IT held against me. Trace explained that the Pro League Committee worked out the match-ups to increase viewership, a notion similar to Thardus' Semi League tactic. I could see why, though. It pits Midas against Jackal I, Warlock against Creed IV, and Me against Something outta hell X.

Like always, I had to wait for the big race, but then realized how far Gabriella had fallen from the top with her forty-three points. She had only acquired one point after I fell off the mountain and six the day after, probably still startled by my injuries. This reminded me of the first-place victory stolen by Law at K2. I pulled my iCube out and opened Way/Point's grid. Still by my avatar's side was Miss Earth. Realizing I should have done this days ago, I made a call.

"Hey," she finally answered. I relaxed to the sound of her voice. "The word going around is that there's a mountain slayer on the loose."

"Well, I didn't get the luxury of bloodying up another one like you," I said.

"In my opinion, the highlights of K2 didn't do the blood justice."

"How are you?"

"Shaking off a few bullet holes from Jackal. Don't take him lightly, Craven. I'm sure he's gotta bullet specifically made for ya," she advised, knowing him better than I ever would. "And how are you?"

"I'm alive," I said. I told her that I'd get her brother through to the following week with help from our new allies. She didn't take kindly to the news that I'd leaked her identity. It took a moment, but she agreed to trust me and the plan I had in motion. Five-out-of-sixteen changed our odds dramatically. The news did boost her confidence. She actually seemed a bit impatient for her next race against Law and whoever else. She was in a position to clinch and was set on doing so with the help of a diabolical plan her and Nito devised for a drone-heavy race like Sydney. "Remind me to stay on your good side," I responded.

The both of us eventually agreed to use the remainder of our day for rest & recovery. She advised a hot bath to re-stimulate the regeneratives still on my body. It was great advice, but I almost fell asleep to the pleasure of lachli and medicine. The one thing that kept me awake was the constriction of the vise in my leg. It needed more time to adapt, unlike the one in my arm. I found myself truly appreciating the innovations of Rokian technology. The Ragnarök was the first alien species to give Terrans a chance, but I couldn't even look at them without growling. I was judging millions by the act of one I saw at Everest. I tried to take a new path, a better path, but my eyes wouldn't let me forget. I saw Thorax's face every time I closed them now, replacing the words I'd always heard Tokyn preach at the start of each race. When my hands began to shake, I thought of Zane. The bigger question now was who will snap first in this series.

Fortunately, I slept well. It was a weird morning where I felt energized. I typically hated the mornings, but I woke up with a positive outlook towards the jungle, skipping a highly recommended breakfast, claiming the Wyndham's pão de queijo cheese breads were out of the galaxy's realm of ancient savories. It may have been impulsive, but I had a good feeling about the race as I made my way down to the bay of the Rio Negro River behind the hotel. A seaplane and its pilot awaited me, ready for the private expedition deeper into the jungle.

We flew for half an hour over the misty tropical features. Beneath the trees, I could see several tracks, both short and long, asphalt and dirt, inhabited and uninhabited. I couldn't tell which track was for the Semi, Pro, or Galactic League. I wondered why they would intimidate the racers with a galactic track if we were just going to be sent to a Pro League course. The plane then circled around a black semi-octagon roof to an ancient barn-shaped building that had a straightaway to a race track running longitudinally through it. We descended into the bay of the building near a repugnant river. Walking out of the plane and up the bay's wooden stairwell gave me a better look at the building's brown-bricked walls with foggy glass windows looking into a set of stables. The lightshow within suggested that this place wasn't just a barn, it was a station, heavily guarded, sheltering the track's starting line.

There was an emphasis on the station's privacy. No fans nor reporters were there to persuade the other racers like Zane, Midas, Creed, and Warlock to arrive early. The lightshow came from Warlock's stable. He was running pre-race experiments with his krone knuckles, sparring against an exosuited "dummy." Less proactive was the defending champ, Midas, enjoying a nap next to his Cronus. Creed, with a bible at hand, stood preaching his sermons to Zane who seem to find holy words more soothing than Midas' slumber.

A lone racer stood tall on the track at the north end. They were already suited up in their hooded Grymm, staring at the jungle stretching as far as our eyes could see. The racer then slowly crept towards me, causing some of the guards to arm their assault rifles. A black hole was the only thing I could see through the hood's darkness—a soulless being far from home. There were stars in the darkness, arranging themselves into a smile. I gave Bayne a slow nod as we both took another look at the track's endless straightaway. I realized what type of race this was—a circuit. The big catch was the number of laps. Some circuit races could be a marathon consisting of twenty-five laps. The simpler ones, a traditional tres.

Wisely, I left Bayne to itself and went over to The Unchained Knight's stable, now sub-labeled "The Mountain Slayer." I couldn't help but chuckle at the fresh sobriquet, mainly because I thought Gabriella was joking about the scuttle on me.

I concentrated on the Atlas, too far from Nepal, still conditioned for a tundra on Arythro. Unsure of how much time I had, I detached as much weight from the suit as I possibly could, including the additions given to me by Roy. The boost tank was empty. The Committee provided a generic Pro League tank, but it wasn't the same. My body was addicted to the Komodo, and I felt dopesick without it. I could be called superstitious, but I'd been 2-0 whenever I'd competed with it—a stat I wished to increase today. I spotted the zarquoyse still lodged inside the helmet. The flower radiated a yellow light, a color that made me question if it referred to anything.

"So, you're the man my big brother wants dead," a deep garbled voice stated from the stable's entrance. Standing there, leaning on the jamb was a tall muscular man in a sweaty gray tank top, camouflage pants, and black combat boots. The smoke from his cigar fused with the unpleasant onion odor blowing towards me. When the smoke cleared from his cigar, I saw a man with a black-trimmed beard, hazel eyes, and long blonde hair wrapped into a ponytail. A Carnivore. Why was it always a Carnivore? "I don't believe we've met. I'm sure you already know me as Jackal, but my friends call me Jack."

"You here to threaten me?" I said, giving my exosuit more attention than he wanted.

"Did I not just say my friends call me Jack?" he questioned with his arms raised, providing a more potent stench that watered my eyes.

"Are we though?" I countered.

"We can be, if you play your cards right," he answered, walking closer to my suit. "Ahhh, the mountain slayed Atlas that got back up to slay the grandest mountain of them all. This bad boy just reeks a hypertrophic heart."

"That's not the only thing that reeks," I muttered to myself while he took another inhale of his cigar. He blew the mist into the Atlas' visor.

"Has she kissed it, yet?" he asked.

"Who?"

"Gabby," he replied, now hooking my full attention while he flicked his cigar into the wall. "She kissed mine."

"No, she hasn't kissed my helmet." I responded, as he leaned onto the suit, his frowning face close to mine.

"It's alright, she doesn't kiss everything, but do tell me something, friend. How does she taste down below?" Jackal knew exactly what he was doing—saying this shit to me instead of Midas. I had no choice but to take the verbal hits this man was throwing. "Oh, do you not know? I thought you two would've done something by now. She just couldn't wait to claw her hands into my hair, down my back. Spoilers, it tastes like raspberries."

"You better hope the jungle eats you alive," I blurted. We both rose to a standing position. He clearly had the upper hand in height, but I wasn't afraid. In fact, it was his heart I could feel pumping out plasma to the arteries. He may have been pissed, but he was silent, and all ears. "Because if it doesn't, I will."

"Is that a threat, friend?"

"No, it's a promise," I said, determined to enforce my words today.

"ALL RACERS MUST REPORT TO THE TRACK! MIDAS IN LANE ONE... CRAVEN IN LANE TWO... JACKAL IN LANE THREE..." an Initiator announced, breaking the standoff between us.

"The McGuire fire is what Earth once said about your father. Let's see if it still stands," Jackal finally stated. I expected worse from the inevitable threat before he left to get suited up. I did the same, meeting him and the others already on the track. He had on *Tsarina's* aerobic crimson and gold 2230 Corallinus with black strips touching the red, all coated for war. A golden 0-gauge plasma shotgun was on the right with a 10-barrel rotary machine gun on the left. *A bullet with my name on it*, eh, more like an infantry. The shells, grenades, and combat knives extending around the exosuit's torso were numerous on the man heading to the third lane. Behind him, in lanes four through seven, were Warlock, Creed, Zane, and Bayne, all in that order, competing in their regular suits. The only differences came from Zane's purple Nevermore with black designs of a raven spreading its wings across his back and arms like the blue jay on my jacket. The fresh color scheme also adorned his patented plague mask with a purple face and black beak. A new presentation from a man and a robotic raven that seemed a bit more stable than on our last encounter, but one could only guesstimate the status of a man within an adrenia-injecting suit. Hell, I wondered if the dosages had acted as a catalyst for his mental deterioration.

Once I was in my lane, set and ready, the Initiator of the race revealed the magic number of laps as dos. A number I felt comfortable with on an unfamiliar track, evening the odds for all of the racers. The wheels then shifted down each limb while MIKA initiated the operations of the exosuit, though there was static in her voice.

"Is everything alright?" I asked her a little worried.

"Mos... Mostly... We... get through it," she responded fading in and out. It was the first time since our partnership that I worried about her age. I could only pray that the problem didn't cost me time and preparation. What started as a positive day deteriorated quickly before the siren could finally scream us all into the jungle.

ACT III
CHAPTER 5

IN THE HEART
OF THE JUNGLE

THE ZOOM OUT OF THE STATION INTO THE JUNGLE STARTED FREE, SHIFTING TO CLAUSTROPHOBIC AS THE TREES GOT TIGHTER DOWN THE FIRST STRAIGHTAWAY. So far, there hadn't been any malfunctions inflicted on the Atlas by MIKA's mishap, easing my stress levels. All of us were forced by the tightening track to assemble into a line, drafting behind one another as the track became extremely narrow. The asphalt surface then transitioned into the tree branches, pushing the magnetic attraction of every appendisc to their limits. The bumps bounced some of us into the air, smacking us into some of the vines along the way into the first big right turn. Midas was the leader, attempting to slow down but, instead, glided across a muddy surface. All of our wheels turned brown before we each could slam into a tree, unintentionally overshooting the turn. To maintain his lead, Midas brushed the fault off, boosting out of this position, and into the next straightaway. I did the same, staying right on his tail, cherishing the mud-less ground.

This portion of the race gave us all opportunities to pass or punish one another in the spaces between the denser portions of the rainforest. Midas had no reason to go all out in this race, smoothly avoiding all of the mossy elements trying to jam our wheels. I followed his lead, and his slower pace, until I heard metal cranking out a storm of bullets from behind. I transformed my right arm into Aegis, protecting Midas from Jackal's fury. Not only did the auto-fed bullets destroy the hæmalytes, they leveled a great portion of the rainforest before we were guided into a cave with multiple pathways. My agenda was to follow Midas, but that changed with the detonation of a grenade heaved into the cave, sparking a flash that temporarily blinded me. I couldn't tell where anything was and eventually got shoved into a descending pathway by multiple racers.

Continuously pin-balling against the rocky walls, my vision returned to see a scythe hovering over my head, dropping down into my left dell. The sharp blade didn't drill too far, but that didn't stop me from triggering the breaks. Two dark racers passed by, their identities revealed by the skyline holes in the beautiful sapphire cavern. The two in my sights were Zane and Bayne. They wasted no time getting even, an objective that turned in my favor as the two maniacs began to fight each other down the slippery slope that dropped us out of the cave, back onto an asphalt track. I wisely allowed the two in front of me to handle their beef, while I noticed the flooded portions of the track up ahead. There was a river to the right of us. We raced down one side of the riverbank, and on another track, paralleled with ours across the way, were Creed, Warlock, Midas, and Jackal.

As expected, the viewers got the clashes they were looking for—a sequel to the Irishman versus the Argentinian, and the debut of the iron against the Gold. Luckily, Jackal was trying to throw knives instead of bullets at Midas, while Warlock and Creed focused on throwing one another into the river. It was only a matter of time before their chaos got out of hand. I searched for a way over to their side of the river. I eventually spotted a ramp up ahead that would leap us across. The only things in my way were a raven and a reaper.

The clash between the two escalated. Zane produced a brachial blade to disarm Bayne's scythe, and took advantage of the light armor by destroying the sections of Bayne's right brachialis. Zane then rose up, shifting both front-wheels to his elbows in order to get a good grip around Bayne's arms. He used his brachial blade to amputate one of them. I couldn't prevent a sadistic smile as I dodged the loose arm flying back at me, mind-boggled by the fact that I was actually rooting for The Raven. The brutality continued as Zane drilled his wheel-attached elbow into the right side of Bayne's gut followed by the blade, slashing the entire gut wide open so that the small and large intestines would drag the track's surface. I sped up over the trail of blood so I could dive onto Zane's back, gripping his pistons while destroying his robotic raven from the impact of my wheels. He extended his bladed arm backwards, attempting to shove his wheels into my chest, but that was a big mistake. Zane reaching back gave me the upper-hand, and I broke said arm. The bones shattered while I pinned my right-front wheel into the side of Zane's beak, demolishing his helmet and penetrating his flesh. Blood shot onto my visor. The Raven was practically two-faced when I broke his blade off, using it to slice all the wheels from his Nevermore.

I had to quickly leap off of his body before the final wheel was dislodged, sending the beakless raven into the river after he lost control. My eyes then locked onto Bayne regenerating another arm. Puzzled by how I could defeat the reaper, their loose intestines suddenly tangled the Grymm's rear-wheels. The mishap opened an opportunity for me to shove Bayne off the track. I was somehow able to survive and smash the two threats. The path to the ramp was free. In one giant leap, I rejoined the others across the river.

The landing placed me at the back of the pack. I felt a little better about Midas' survival, especially since Jackal was triggering his brakes to seek vengeance for what I had done to his ally. Regaining speed to stay in front, the one-man army prevented me from passing, dropping grenades that were flammable, electrical, corrosive, and explosive— pretty much everything that wasn't flashy. I avoided all of them as we slowed down for a hard-right turn into another tree-scattered straightaway.

Still focused on punishing me with grenades, Jackal accidentally grazed one of the trees which spun him out across the branchy surface. Instead of going around him, I triggered my boost to T-bone him, sending a message to all of the Carnivores watching. Sounds of metal scraping across the branchy surface filled the air as Jackal pulled out a combat knife, impaling it into my dell. I was forced to push him off to avoid another incision. The black strips of his suit were now demolished from my attack, the crimson and gold smudged into one another.

The long straightaway soon led us back to the station and across the starting line for the second lap. Midas still had the lead. The fights between Warlock and Creed gave way to the realization of how important first place was to their clinching scenarios. We aligned ourselves for the narrow section one last time. The tightened path became more dangerous as flammable grenades flew into the vines from behind. It helped having Creed directly in front of me. He used his hatchets to slice the flame-coated vines in half. But the racer on my ass churned their gun for another wave of bullets now impacting the Atlas' spina. The narrow track prevented me from using Aegis, leaving me vulnerable to a bullet that eventually perforated my boost tank.

"Detach the tank," I commanded when MIKA didn't respond to the whistling screams of the tank. I couldn't detach it manually, still stuck on the narrow track, now fearing for my life. "MIKA, DETACH THE FUCKING TANK!"

The cylinder capsule then detached itself prior to exploding, ending the barrage of bullets. MIKA stayed silent while we executed the muddy right turn. I saw the evidence of our first lap on the trunks of bruised trees. The tree stand, this time around, was decided by a game of speed instead of strength to avoid the leveled trees resting on the ground. With Jackal out of the picture, the race revolved around skill. Midas slowed down, basically handing the race to Warlock, Creed, and I as we entered the cavern dividing into five pathways. Warlock and Creed confidently chose the far-right pathway. I followed, trying to avoid separation through the sapphire cave. I was at a disadvantage without a boost tank, now relying on my drafts with Creed. Warlock maintained his lead out of the cave. He was a surprisingly fast brute, and Creed knew it, now whipping his final hatchet into the rear-wheels of Warlock as an act of desperation. The hatchet destroyed the wheels as Creed boosted closer to reclaim his weapon. Both racers now had a good lead on me.

Searching for another miracle in the same location, I realized we were on the right side of the river. A racer driving on the other side of the bank launched himself off of the ramp, spraying his gun at the two leading racers. The bullets from an airborne Jackal punctured every front-wheel attached to Warlock and Creed's suits, slowing them down for me to pass before the sharpshooter could land. First place was up for grabs between him and I as we entered the last turn. Drained and battered, the two of us took turns shoving each other into one of the trees on the last straightaway. Jackal then reloaded and aimed his plasma gun at me. I desperately defended myself with Aegis until his clip was empty, quickly shoving the plasma-coated shield into his face. This blinded him for a last-second shove into a nearby tree, gifting me with first place for the last 100m.

A bad feeling crept into my heart as the yellow zarquoyse inside my helmet turned red before I noticed the hooded reaper, scythe in the hand of a fully regenerated arm, standing on the finish line. Armed guards surrounded IT, aiming at Bayne's suit. Everyone except for Bayne jumped out of the way as I approached. I tried to leap over IT. Bayne swung their scythe, only able to tag the rear-wheels as I flew over the finish line. The hit stripped away my momentum, resulting in a crash onto the asphalt, where I waited to endure the hell that would come next.

ACT III
CHAPTER 6

VENOMOUS

IN A KNEELING POSITION, MY BODY TREMBLED FROM FATIGUE. I hoped the situation with Bayne wouldn't escalate. The armed guards had their rifles aimed at the reaper's head, ordering Bayne to drop the scythe or else. Unafraid of the threats, Bayne took off their helmet, unveiling the gray bandaged face with holes exposing the black scleras with red irises. Rushing across the finish line, Jackal begged for his celestial friend to calm down.

"This ain't the right time, stand down," Jackal pleaded, causing the reaper to ease up while Midas crossed the line, followed by Creed and Warlock.

"What the hell is this freak's problem?" Midas viciously inquired, forcing Jackal to restrain the reaper's attempted charge at The Golden Scion. IT finally let go of the scythe's handle.

"Look upon your work, McGuire," Jackal said. "You've brought hell onto everyone here." He took his helmet off, throwing it at my feet. The guards aimed their guns at both Carnivores. "Being engaged to the golden whore won't save you anymore."

"The hell you call my sister?" Midas questioned, slamming his helmet into the ground, rattling the Scythe resting near it.

"A fucking whore!" Jackal shouted, raising his shotgun at Midas. The guards threatened Jackal and suggested that he rethink his next move. Suddenly, the reaper laughed aloud, a deep malicious sound that caught everyone's attention.

"I dare ya to pull the trigger, kill the champion you sore losing piece of shit!" Midas antagonized, showing more of his father's rage by kicking the nearby helmet at Jackal's patallis.

"Don't encourage him," I desperately implored.

"Why not?"

"Because he'll do it, and you have no idea how important your life is right now," I responded. Out of anger, he brought up the engagement, telling me that his father would either have a bounty on my head or die before allowing his Gold to sacredly bond with a McGuire.

"We'll be more than happy to claim that bounty," Jackal stated, causing Bayne to kick the handle of their weapon up for a grip, decapitating the nearest guard.

The blade of the scythe sharply blurred through the air, slicing off arms and legs. The surviving guards emptied their rifles at Bayne while the wounded stared and screamed as their organs dropped to the gore-stained floor. Jackal, in turn, unloaded a sudden assault at the guards focused on the bloodletting reaper. Before the last guard could be killed, Midas sped away in his suit while Creed and Warlock teamed up to deal with Bayne. While I watched the bloodbath, Jackal aimed his steaming shotgun at my shell-shocked body. He pulled the trigger, but the chamber was empty. I ran out of the station as Jackal dove at the nearest rifle on the ground and sent a hail of bullets my way.

Still untouched but able to evade Jackal, I continued to run towards the uncharted territories of the Amazon. Our suits slowed us both, but he was armed with a dead man's rifle. The pellets continuously ruptured the trunks on either side of me. If only the Atlas' helmet was on my head instead of the station's floor.

Jackal eventually stopped firing, so I used the nearest tree as shelter. There had been nothing but big trees in this forest, but in my time of crisis, the tree trunks seemed very skinny. I saw thicker trees at the bottom of the steep hill—a possible pathway to freedom. Trying to leave my suit as a decoy, I scrambled out of the Atlas, but before I could pry off any parts, a tiny green capsule landed on my feet. It lacked a pin, armed and ready to blow. I escaped the worst of the blast, still tossed down the hill from the shockwave.

I scrambled to my knees and saw the image of the creek turned red. The blood on my brow from a flesh wound caught the attention of a hissing predator now rising out of the water. A large green-headed predator with a never-ending brown dotted neck stretched out of the pond and licked its hungry mouth. My eyes locked with the anaconda's as it slithered closer. Inches separated our faces as it slowly opened its mouth wider than my head. Sounds of someone crashing down the hill caused the snake to retreat into a nearby tree.

"Eat me alive, you said," Jackal reminded me. He stepped in front of me and pressed the nozzle of his rifle into my gushing forehead. "You couldn't even eat Miss Earth."

"Wait!" I yelled, watching the grin grow on his face.

"What's your last word, friend? I'll relay it to her," Jackal stated, oblivious to the reptile hanging off of a branch over his head.

"The jungle beat me to ya," I said just before the snake leapt onto Jackal's exosuit without warning. The anaconda's mouth gripped his dell before plowing Jackal into the ground. I desperately crawled out of harm's way, watching Jackal try to overpower the anaconda's strength with an upward squat. The snake easily wrapped its body around Jackal's torso and then matched the power of Jackal's contracting muscles, constricting the life out of the sharpshooter's hands. The game of strength continued as Jackal somehow pulled his arms out of the snake's grip, and with the rifle at hand, searched for the reptile's head.

"Help," The Blackjack exhaled with protruding eyes, his skin turning red. Jackal was going to die unless I did something. I got up to grab the rifle. Initially, I was going to point-blank the snake but, instead, held back to watch Jackal's suffering. He didn't deserve my help. The veins in his eyes began to rupture and his skin turned blue. Before his eyes could finally roll into the back of his head, a click followed by a boom of fire and blood masked my face, blowing me back into the water.

My body sank to the bottom of the deep pond. On the surface, I could see flames, followed by the guts from both bodies. I still had the strength to move, but chose not to as the Atlas' spina sank into the muddy depths of the pond. My face, bare to the water, felt the air bubbles kissing my cheek. What should've been painful became pleasurable. Like the combination of lachli and regeneratives from the night before, my body felt energized, not even afraid of drowning. I waited for the flames up above to disappear. I ejected out of the Atlas and tried to drag both it and my body out of the pond. The weight of the exosuit reminded me how Terran I really was. There was no way I could get the Atlas out, but there was no way I was going to leave her here. I'd spent years trying to conceptualize the charmer, and months trying to perfect her. Here, at the bottom of the pond when she needed me most, I couldn't even save her.

I finally realized how long I'd been below the surface. My Atlas was gone. I planted my hand onto the pectar for one last goodbye. To some, it may have been just an exosuit, but it was my friend, a friend I had to leave behind. The neon-blue glows from the chains shone onto the shoal as I ascended back to the fiery surface. Burning leaves sprinkled into the air as I rested my body by the creek. I glanced around to find the explosion's origin, and saw the reality of death. The first death I'd actually witnessed since my father's. Except this time, the blood was on my hands. Nothing good was going to come out of this, only damnation.

Then I remembered the stream of blood that had been flowing down my head. It was healed. I was not convinced of the illusion, so I crawled back over to the pond. In its mirrored reflection, I saw a pristine face without a bruise, without a burn, without a scar. Was it something in the water? Was it my own body? What the hell was I? But I knew I wasn't going to find any answers here. I needed to get away, to leave the crime scene. Jackal Amaryllis was dead.

Unaware of where I was going, I shoved my way through a tangle of leaves before ending up back at the track's riverbank. I heard footsteps from the direction I had come, and suddenly the reaper appeared swinging their scythe at my arms. The blade impaled my right bicep, drilling through the bone marrow, somehow missing the artery. In pain, I quickly broke the scythe's handle with my other arm and elbowed it into Bayne's stomach, slicing it open once again. The reaper retaliated by pulling the blade out of my arm and tossing it into the river while their organs piled onto the ground. IT then tackled me into the asphalt. The reaper wrapped its own intestines around my neck in an attempt to suffocate me. Just like Jackal, I felt my life slipping away as the reaper pulled their intestines tighter.

"Say hello to your father," Bayne whispered before a hatchet sliced through their cranium, loosening the grip IT had on me. Creed snatched the hatchet out of Bayne's head and decapitated IT. Suddenly, Warlock punted Bayne's head into the river before they could reassemble back together. Struggling to reclaim air, I was unable to shove Bayne's corpse off, leaving me vulnerable to whatever the two remaining racers had in store for me. I was officially out of lives. A smiling Warlock crouched down and displayed the gushing wounds he'd received from the alien's wrath.

"Should we help him, or leave him?" Warlock proposed to Creed, an unexpected ally.

"Do I have a say in the matter?" I gasped.

"Why? Tee locker's a slaughterhouse because of you," Warlock responded, spitting out blood with each word.

"Not to mention the parts of the forest you and Jackal disintegrated," Creed added.

"This was the Carnivores' doing, not mine."

"Well, we'd ask 'em, except teir bodies are…" Warlock replied, chuckling at the reaper's remains. "Fuck it, I vote yes. Pandora's gonna pin tis shit on us anyways. Maybe MaGuire can be our alibi. Whaddya say Casper?" Glancing at Creed, the two came to another agreement, convincing Warlock to toss the reaper's corpse into the river while Creed helped me onto my feet. I placed pressure around my right bicep as the three of us stared at the body floating down the river. Did Vanta's Thirteenth have one more trick within their skin? Once the corpse was out of our sight, we heard choppers overhead. They quickly landed near us, and several new guards locked their guns on us. Just as Warlock predicted, we were in a shithole, but I oddly felt calm about being in it together. There was a chance that they were now my allies—allies that deserved to know the truth beyond the jungle about Midas, about Gabriella, about everything.

ACT III
CHAPTER 7

THE HONOR AMONGST

IT FELT LIKE HOURS IF NOT DAYS, STUCK AT THE TRAGIC SCENE. SEVENTEEN DEAD. I should know the exact number since they told us seventeen times on seventeen occasions. Warlock and Creed were in the same situation, facing another interrogation within their stables. Zane, somehow discovered at the riverbank, was being evaluated for any type of mental anomalies. And Midas, well, from the policía's intel, Midas was last seen on a plane ride back to Goldland. I'm sorry, Greenland.

The Amazonian Military's Captain made another attempt to dig more information out of me once my right arm was finally patched up. Apparently, Jackal and I had drifted off to a blind spot during the chase, and my story of an anaconda blowing up The Blackjack didn't fly. I would have had them check the recordings of my visor, but that was impossible. I couldn't have been caught more red-handed if I had tried. At least Warlock was having a blast. I'd been hearing nothing but laughter from his stable followed by a frustrated soldier close to throwing in his white towel. Leave it to The Devil's Shamrock to prevail in a psychological game of checkers. I could assume Creed was in the same position. Nothing but Spanish and Portuguese dialects came out of their stable.

The circumstances changed once the jungle's evening inhabitants began to howl. The nocturnal animals drew gunfire from some of the soldiers outside. Though the Captain was keen on getting to the truth, choppers arrived to ruin his night. Members from the Pro League Committee, formally dressed in their black suits with the Versa logo, began issuing orders from Pandora to set us free. They also retrieved some of the exosuits for the next race. There would be a next race. For all of us. The main problem was, I no longer had an exosuit. I was forced to provide the Committee with the nest's address for a replacement. Thank the Galactic Gods that it was the Atlas and not my helmet. MIKA was the only thing that couldn't be replaced on the suit.

After the Committee's work was finished within the station, the three of us were officially sent back to a Manaus hospital along with Zane on a separate chopper. When Warlock claimed that Pandora was gonna be on our asses, the last thing I expected was a rescue mission. I envisioned wrath over mercy. Pandora, of course, didn't save us in person, postponing our inevitable encounter. I didn't know how I would react. The closest I had ever come to meeting the woman was at my father's funeral. She was supposed to show up out of respect to his career, but instead got caught up in an intergalactic meeting. A part of me was bitter from her absence, but she'd redeemed herself today.

In the helicopter, our iCubes blew up with messages. My mom, Trace, Gabriella, Kira, and the hounds all had sent messages of gratitude that quickly became troubled at the sudden turn of events. What they saw was much worse than what I endured. Being in the dark was a scary thing, especially when it involved the life of someone close. I wasted no time responding. My mother, of course, came before everyone else. The conversation between her and I was more compassionate than worrisome. If it hadn't been for the unfortunate conclusion, she might have claimed that my race in the Amazon made her list of Top 10 Races. I didn't know there was a damn list to begin with, but then again, she and I had only started to really connect. After my father's death, she grew very sad and silent. Staying out of trouble was the best I could do, though having Trace around made that very challenging. But it also made him closer to me than my own mother. She didn't come around until after my Semi League debut, which, in turn, made me keep my distance for her sake. I wanted to make her happy again, for my father, for myself, and ultimately for her. Our Versa talk was as comforting as the feeling that came over me while I was underwater. Something I wanted to run by her, but instead, I chose not to for the sake of the moment. There was something different about me. I didn't know if there was a connection to my father's ghost. Whatever the revelation was, it would come, but for now, a great chat with mom wasn't the worst thing.

The jade-colored city of Manaus appeared on the horizon as the chat with my mother came to a close. The chopper dropped us off by the bay of the Wyndham Garden where Mr. Burretta awaited me and my two new friends. "I'll be damned" escaped his mouth when he noticed the new set of battle scars we all wore. Warlock called our wounds the bright *tickles of life*, an analogy that brought on a drink offer. Without hesitation, Warlock wrapped his muscular arm around Trace's shoulder so he could lead the way to the bar near the pool deck. Trace designated himself bartender by hopping over the counter for requests.

"So, which one of you fuckup's gonna tell me what happened after the cams went dark?" Trace asked, pouring us all a glass of whiskey.

"Depends, whatcha see?" Warlock responded, requesting rum instead.

Trace explained that the first decapitation was shown prior to the cameras shifting back to the Unican Network. Gradite then took control of the story, relaying updates that were a bit fuzzy at times. The network delayed announcing the deaths of Bayne and Jackal Amaryllis. Pandora would be holding a press conference. We then confirmed to Trace what he had wished to be false.

"All we know is that there will be another race," I said, putting a smile back on Trace's face. "And that we'll be in it together."

"Well, I'll be damned," he said, raising his glass for the cheer. "To honor among fuckups."

"To honor among warriors," Warlock ferociously joined.

"To honor among saviors," Creed added.

"And to honor among friends," I said as our glasses collided. Trace eventually pulled out his iCube, leaving on the Unican Network for updates as we all joked around. Before long, the network switched to an African American woman walking up to a podium in a room filled with reporters and flashing cameras. The woman looked to be in her mid-60s, wearing a teal suit matched with the laurel wreath resting on her long black-and-gray hair. It was the Shepherd. The sight of Pandora Winfrey silenced us all.

"Today has been a memorable one," she said, "and it is not for good reason. As I'm sure you have heard, we lost the lives of nineteen men and women during the Amazonian Massacre, and it breaks my heart. Four Seasons is supposed to be a skillful series where we determine our planet's best, not worst, and it is because of days like this that the armored 'V' becomes an armored question mark.

"Earlier today, I spoke with the families of the deceased. Through the many tears on both sides, I concluded each meeting by taking full responsibility for the bloodsport's past, present and future. I told them exactly what I tell Re-Versables everyday. Versa is a bloodsport for a reason, and every racer signs an agreement, aware of the emphasis upon blood. They all are aware of the risks and take full responsibility for the unfortunate outcomes. Today is another day for mourning, and tomorrow will be another day of rejoicing, because the series will continue just like the sport," Pandora said.

There was a mixed reaction from the reporters—some of them yelling protests.

"Why?" one activist called out. "We've made our money from the sport, so there's no reason for continuation. It makes us more unethical than our history of disease and war combined!"

"You're right, we have made our money, but you have to remember what the UCE is to the galaxy. A Majoris planet. We are a member of an alliance that must be sustained. Is the sport perfect? No. Am I a fan of the sport? Yes, when performed appropriately. Why, because we've built power and respect. Unlike Derry and Sylum, our planet isn't being raided, raped, and ruined by Maradoes. Because of that fact, I can live with the deaths of a few over the many," Pandora explained, silencing the crowd. "The deaths of the nineteen are unfortunate, but the show must go on. That's why I'm also here to announce the playoff berths of Midas Gold, Lawson Pierce, and Craven McGuire due to the expulsion of Bayne and Jackal. Analysts will set up another series of clinching scenarios around the same time of tomorrow's race."

Trace suddenly muted the television grid with all eyes on me. It was official, I was one of the top-sixteen. Warlock begged for more rounds of whiskey. Joyful. Optimistic. Relieved. These were the only emotions at the bar. Both Midas and I had moved on. A pair of enemies eradicated, along with a pair of allies initiated. Warlock rambled on to Trace about his friend Darragh. It helped the two hit it off while they exchanged war stories. Warlock brought up the bare-knuckle lifestyle he and his friend shared which inspired Trace to bring up his mixed martial arts background. I could only laugh at the sight of the two fighters jabbing at one another. Trace got me a girlfriend, I got him a boyfriend. Looked like his cupid skills were rubbing off on me too.

"So, what's the eudaimonia?" Trace proposed to the group, pouring another round.

"Dunno, retirement's sounding pretty good," Creed answered.

"Say it ain't so Casper, we were beginning to have some fun," Warlock replied, jabbing the Argentinian's shoulder. He then ran through some of their barbaric highlights of krone knuckles destroying Creed's visor at K2. Creed defended his stance with a highlight of his own—a hatchet hammered into Warlock's left ass cheek at Neotokyo. The chuckling brute even showed us the second crack perpendicular to the original. A masterchef of comedy, Trace favored us with his infamous story of rupturing Zane's testicle with a tire shot. Creed let out a high-pitched laugh that sent our heads into the bar's countertop.

"I didn't think it was possible to make the pastor laugh," Trace stated.

"Like I said, dunno. I've always wanted to compete in Galactica, but that's not looking like an option," Creed finally said.

"Lockdowns can be a bitch," Trace added. "What about you Lucky Charms?"

"My eudaimonia?" Warlock questioned. "Shai Gora." The brute slammed his bottle of splashing rum onto the countertop—a response strong enough to make both Trace and Creed spit take. "What are ya, jealous?"

"Who the hell is Shai?" I asked.

"She's one of the Gora sisters—the craziest of the three," Trace explained.

"She loves blood, and dreams of becoming a Galactic champ one day. I tried to catch her attention by beating the shit out of Hauschka," Warlock explained, reminiscing back to the previous Four Seasons.

"The racer card said it was out of rage."

"Oh, it was outta love," the winking Warlock reassured us.

"Sounds like a match made in a Satanian hell," I stated.

"You're too kind, MaGuire. How bout you?" Warlock finally tossed at me.

"I guess, riding off into the sunset with the girl," I replied to the booing group. "Come on guys."

"What about Thorax? There's gotta be something there," Warlock said. Even a bit buzzed, Trace kept his mouth shut on the topic. I think he was actually surprised I didn't snap at the sound of the Rokian's name. Our discussion with Roy may have been the reason why he brought up the eudaimonia discussion in the first place.

"A wise man told me to search for a different path, and the sunset sounds like a difference," I explained, grinning at Trace's approving nod. The Prestige Angel wasn't the only one who needed an answer to that question.

"Most wise guys aren't tat wise," Warlock eventually responded.

"Even Roy Fathom?" Trace questioned, sparking a bigger discussion among the three.

My body now emptied its energy tank. I truly wanted to know how their discussion was going to conclude, especially after someone mentioned The Terran Triforce. I wanted to support the trio's case, but my body urged me to find a mattress instead, so I journeyed up to my room. It had been a rollercoaster of a day; I would take it over most if I knew it would end the same way—with me lying in a bed without the pressure of the world on my shoulders.

Different than the previous night, the dream I had wasn't a black blur turned into reality. It didn't even involve snow. The foretelling hinted from that dream made me focus on the images of a golden dreamcatcher dripping blood. The crimson puddle reflected an unmasked Gabriella kneeled in her suit, gasping for air, grasping out a prayer. Blood flowed down her cheeks, down her lips, dripping to the gash on her hip. She mouthed the words *I'm sorry* before a flash suddenly destroyed her gruesome image.

"CRAVEN!" a voice shouted. I opened my eyes to the rising sun. Trace moved back and forth in the room, packing our bags. "We might have a problem."

"Wh-what is it?" I struggled to say, hoping to reclaim the haunting images of Gabriella. I didn't know what they meant, and before I could close my eyes again, I noticed the paused image of Krueger on the bedroom's TV screen.

"Gabriella was originally in a race with Law against others, but now she's by herself against others."

"Who are the others?"

"The eight remaining Carnivores!"

ACT III

CHAPTER 8

DETERRING
DETOURS

"SHE'S NOT ANSWERING!" I YELLED AT TRACE.** We were on a Peregrine, the fastest jet on Earth, and yet the travel felt agonizingly slow. I was a hair-string away from a panic attack. Trace and I were the only ones making the life-saving trip. Creed and Warlock stayed back at Manaus for their next race, a Summer-clinching race if they obtained the right amount of points. I wished that they had achieved those points yesterday as I could use some of Warlock's positivity combined with Creed's laughter. Another story about Darragh would've been the entrée with a blinged out penguin as the dessert. I needed something to take my mind off the dream about Gabriella. I refused to believe that I could see the future. The snowfall dream had to be merely a coincidence. I knew that there was going to be snow on the mountain that day. I was not Claire Voyant. That was her ability, not mine. *Craven, I swear to every damn god in the galaxy that you can't see the future, so get ahold of yourself.* Gabriella was going to be alright. It was just like her brother said back at the Hans Egede She was not as tough as nails, she practically was nails. I'd been trying to save Midas' life this entire series, so it was only fair that his words would save my sanity. "She'll be alright, she'll be alright."

"Of course, she'll be," Trace said, rushing to a seat across from me. "We're gonna be there for her, Sydney's only an hour away," he informed me. Tonight's race was the lone event, *Krueger vs The Carnivore Family* as the Unican Network's headline read. But it didn't have to be. She didn't have to race. Live to fight another day, right? If only that were the case. Knowing her mindset, there wasn't an excuse on the planet that would keep her away from the life-threatening challenge. Gradite and company measured the forfeiting route as a coward's move, something that could taint Krueger's career going forward, no matter what. "It's the smart move."

"Not to her," I refuted, watching the sorrowful sun shoot rays into the ocean. I refused to look away.

Trace shut my television grid off, distracting me. He wanted to talk about him and

Katia towards the beginning of their relationship. They were in trouble one night outside of a bar. Clearly outmatched in the fight against a gang, he only had one thing on his mind—Katia's safety. He fought with everything he had until she got away. He then was overwhelmed by the assault until a gunshot forced the gang to retreat out of fear. It turned out that the savior who fired the gun was Katia. So, focused on being the protector, he didn't realize that she had the capabilities of protecting herself. They both finally understood each other's strengths. It was in that moment when they realized they couldn't live without each other.

"Things working out the way you want them to, that's a fucking fairytale," he told me, grasping my shoulder. "The detours you take are reality, and reality makes you who you are, not the fairytale. Sooner or later, reality turns into the fairytale you've been praying for your entire life," he said as the Peregrine cut in front of a storm and back into the light. "No matter what happens, just remember we're on a detour, brother."

The Peregrine soared over a bay and into Sydney's airport. Trace then led the way to the rentals but stalled after struggling to find a goddamn truck. It was always a truck with him, never a sedan, a motorcycle, nor a sports hover. The man craved his trucks and wasted at least 15 minutes hunting one—time that could haunt us later in the congested flyway of hover vans. Though the slow pace brought out the worst of our hover rage, it let us appreciate the capital of the FMJ movement that was Sydney, Australia. Like Greenland, the environment was saturated with its iconic presentation. Holoboard signs displayed images of the FMJ's infamous skull in a cowboy hat, but with silver irises this time around. The FMJ crowd celebrated on the streets beneath. Near the bottle seals on every corner of Sydney were platoons of Re-Versables, brave and ready to collide with their antithesis. We missed the fireworks, though, somehow able to fly past the riot just before it engaged. The world here was turning into a battlefield, showing us the animosity that has been around since the beginning of this series. If Law's prayers were answered for a race with The Golden Scion, we were doomed. It didn't matter if both Gabriella and I were competing. If Midas escaped that race alive, or worse, victorious, the FMJs would stop at nothing.

"What has the world come to?" I questioned as the traffic loosened up. Trace stayed silent, drifting into an exit leading us closer to the night's main event. It would take place on a track called Curtain's Call, built around the landscape of Sydney's Opera House, the starting line at the house's boardwalk. Once we were a few miles out from the steel caterpillar-shaped building, a convergence of drones flew into the sky, illuminating the colors of each racer competing. The colors were then overshadowed by the brighter bursts of fireworks. A storm was brewing, but we could beat it on our race to the track. Not as easy as reaching the house from the airport due to the herds of non-FMJ fans crunched together at the track's checkpoint all the way back at the Royal Botanical Garden—a roofless environment that quickly became sheltered below a massive swarm of drones with metal shields on their backs. Lightning from the storm tested the drones' durability. At first, the crowd was startled by the storm's offense, but then became amazed by the drones' shielding, turning a fierce storm into an art show. Trace and I used the show to our advantage, floating past the crowd like ghosts. We made our way to the Opera House's doors where security gave us a pass inside the east building for exclusive reservations instead of the west building where the regulars entered. The exclusive building had pathways that lead to celestial restaurants, VIP booths, and even an auditorium for an Evolutionary Reality. This was where one became transcendentally attached to the drone they'd rented for a robust connection to the races. Some racers in the Pro League donate their helmets for an intimate recording of their races that others could look back on through an ER experience. That's what my dad did at times to study his mistakes and was honestly something I'd forgotten all about. I was thankful for the virtual reminder. Hopefully the people attached to experience weren't here to witness a golden funeral.

Aside from those pathways, the rest of the building was restricted. I was confident Gabriella was inside. We snuck through the vacant areas in search of a goldmine. Taking a number of Trace's detours, we ended up in the northern foyer and spotted the boardwalk's starting line through a mile-wide window beneath the striped glass of an angled ceiling. Beyond the window, a drone flashed an orange spotlight onto the violet carpets of the foyer. Tables, bars and sunken couches were scattered about the large room. It was anything but comfortable when we noticed most of the Carnivores. In their royal attire, Kingsley and Gwenylin tended to the Aces of their four children. On one sunken couch, the hammerhead shark with a missing end sat beneath a rain cloud of his own. Lucifer, in his Hades, crouched behind the couch and conversed with the Pyscean. Without his helmet, Lucifer noticed us right away. For some strange reason, he didn't say a word, giving Trace and I a second to assess the situation. Another pair of eyes locked onto us.

"Looks like the stars can align," Spade stated, quickly marching up to us with his brother, Club.

"And here I am thinking that Karma's lost her way," Kingsley added, pulling out his sword. The rest of the family followed by pointing their weapons at us. Trace and I glanced at one another, each hoping the other had another spare life before Spade and Club could yank us away from the exit and into the foyer's window. They had their brachial blades out, waiting for their parent's signal. Diamond and Heart stood near their mother with their weapons raised, staring at Kingsley who now covered the exit. There just wasn't a way out of this situation, no detours of any kind, and yet Trace kept laughing and mocking the family.

"Hell's so funny? Joka ain't here to saveya!" Krakyn shouted, poking his bladed arm at my friend's cheek.

"Because you're all so fuckin stupid. The Satanian's the only smart one here," Trace responded, prompting the family and I to focus on an unarmed Lucifer.

"Loosh?"

"Raise your sword," Kingsley commanded, but the Satanian refused. "Remember your family, boy."

"I do," he answered, "but I also remember my race, my religion. That's why I refuse to kill a Terran in cold blood."

"If Bayne could do it, so can you," Kingsley replied, getting more frustrated by the second.

"I'm not Cresciennic, I'm a Zatanian. I serve Zata, therefore I hunt the strong for honor," Lucifer explained. The Satanian's culture may have been responsible for his mother's death, and his departure from home, but it was still his by heart, and he wasn't afraid to show it.

"Your kind also kills the weak like they did your mother," Gwenylin insisted. In response, Lucifer pulled his katanas out, raising one of the sharp ends to her throat. Kingsley defended her by extending his at the Satanian. Lucifer then gave The King a cold stare as they both knew the sword was no match for the Satanian's obsidian shell. Gwenylin let out a squeal before Lucifer lowered his weapons in order to grab the horse-skulled helmet before exiting the foyer and, possibly, his allegiance with the family. The Carnivores had nothing but cruel words for the Satanian.

Kingsley's sadness turned to madness. "First, you kill my brother… then my prize… and now my son," he said, choking on each word. "What else will you take?" he questioned raising the sword back at us.

"H'boutya life?" a voiced suggested. A cowboy hat overshadowed Kingsley's crown as a gunman stepped off to the side and cocked his revolver. He had caramel skin and a short nappy beard that hadn't been trimmed in weeks. Piercing through the hat's shadow were silver eyes aimed at the revolver firmly planted into Kingsley's hip. Of all the people who could save us, the Aboriginal outlaw ironically coined as Law never entered my imagination. It was the first time since Greenland that we'd encountered one another. He wore a mask then and, if'd I remember correctly, his racing bio distinctly stated that he always had a mask on. "Ya willin tu give thet up, mate?"

"Picked a helluva time to ruin my night, Law," Spade said, pulling his brachial blade away from my neck.

The outlaw shrugged. He wore a dark-brown vest with a line of buttons running down the outer edges. Underneath the vest was a black compression shirt that had one long sleeve down the left arm and a short sleeve down the right which was shielded by a small dark-brown poncho covering his shoulder. He wore skinny black jeans with holsters strapped to the thigh for a revolver and the left oblique for a combat knife with adhesive wethro gripping. Capping the outfit were the gray cowboy boots with a bronze base and spurs.

"S'like a neva-endin love story between us, ay?" Law added, causing The Greatest Showman to smirk. His two sisters stood at their mother's side, shaken like a pair of baby ducklings lost in an ocean.

"What do you want?" Gwenylin begged.

"Foya tu leave, else we'll need an ambo," Law proposed, constantly tapping his finger into the revolver's neck.

"You don't have the guts," Spade challenged, triggering Law's revolver. The small explosion produced a bloody hole through Kingsley's hip. Pellets of Kingsley's blood splattered onto the pectars of his daughters' exosuit before he could collapse. Law then walked up to Trace and I, blowing the steam from his gun while the Carnivores screamed in horror, rushing to Kingsley's aid.

"Toya," Law confirmed as the family placed pressure on the wound. Krakyn then picked Kingsley up to carry him out of the foyer, followed by the rest of the family. A vengeful Spade hesitated, provoking Law to shoot near their feet as a warning, scaring them away for good.

"Detours," Trace muttered, now bringing me back into reality. "I'd thank you Law, but I don't know why?"

"Savin Craven, not you," Law said, finally holstering his gun. Briefly revealing the burns of a tattooed right arm before cloaking the weapon within the poncho. The tattoos were tribal and had the head of a sleeping dingo on the bicep with the word *Altjirerama* beneath it. The rest of the markings sleeved the arm. The markings and a brief glimpse at the FMJ buckle on his gray belt reminded me of how slim this man's friends list was. I questioned his motives for helping me in the first place. Him and I hadn't even laid a Versa-finger on each other, and yet he was here for me? "You helped meh cleench ay spot fo' next week. If it wasin fo' you mate, I be as good as dead in tis race."

"Seriously, I think you'd fare well against the family, especially after..." Trace began, now gesturing toward his hibrix on the carpet drenched in Amaryllis remains.

"I'm good at fendin mehself against Terrans, and mehbay a Payshen, but not against a Satonian. May magma rounds can't affect a Satonian, it'd only backfiya," Law explained, glancing at the track. "RIP Kruga, ay?"

"Yeah, RIP," I softly agreed, noticing the bands of golden bullets around his left bicep, forearm and wrist, "How did you find us?"

"Came here tu see the end of Kruga, then I saw ya straddlin around the house, and thought I should thank ya. Now I'm here claimin tis lounge for mehself," he explained, taking a seat on a couch, continuously coin-flipping one of his golden bullets. I thanked him, considering us even, and then followed up on a hunch that he had knowledge of the house. I asked him about the most private parts of the building. He mentioned an Utzon room one floor below, typically an event room that could be rented for specified venues. "It's as private as a space-drifting porta potty," he said, questioning why we were interested. I almost blurted out the truth, mistaking him as a friend. But that was the thing. He was one of the biggest threats, and I was responsible for giving him a free ride to the Summer week. To save myself from anymore speculation, I told him that Lucifer chose not to harm us, and that he was probably looking for a private room, considering he was a fan of the Opera. The alibi was clever enough to help us escape the foyer.

When we entered the room marked as Utzon, we instantly saw the bay east of the room's mile-wide window. The room had been redesigned into a locker with dirty workshop tables all around, each covered in scrap parts for an exosuit. If this room didn't shout Gabriella, I didn't know what would. There wasn't a racer or a body in sight. There was nowhere to hide in the spacious room. Lying on the ground, we saw a broken iCube with a symbol of a dreamcatcher on its shell—something I remembered Gabriella had on hers.

"Craven?" she said, her suit suddenly appearing out of thin air. It scared the shit out of Trace who took a moment to process everything.

"How did she...?" he exclaimed.

"Rokian technology," I answered, understanding how confusing this may have been.

"How did you find me?" She placed her helmet on a table.

"I took a lot of detours," I said as Trace chuckled. He knew what I was here for and ended up giving us the room. "I had to come here to see you, I tried calling."

"Yeah, sorry about that, I had a rough conversation with my father. Midy told him about the fake engagement. I don't know how he found out. Did you say something?"

"No, it was Jackal."

"At least you're alright," she finally stated, walking up to hug me.

"Will you be?" I questioned, subtly gesturing to tonight's race. She backed away.

"No... I'm not hearing this from you. This was my plan, so I'm going to see it through to the end," she angrily defended.

"You're going to die, and I'm not just gonna stand by and let it happen."

"Sydney is not my graveyard, Craven," she replied, getting a grip on her helmet. "You've been calm under pressure throughout this entire series. What's changed?"

"My feelings," I revealed, striking a nerve within her. I couldn't tell if it was a positive or negative thing from her expression. "I…"

"I love you too," Gabriella said, beating me to the finish line. I suddenly saw the path Roy had advised me to search for. The peace, the serenity, the bright future that could kill my demons if I let it. For the first time, my heart opened itself to another. Gabriella came up to me, resting her warm soft hands on my face for a kiss.

"This is the reason why I'm not dying today. It's the same reason why you didn't at Greenland, Everest or Brazil. We've got each other to lose," she explained, turning on the activation phase of her helmet. "I love you because you appreciate me as Gabriella, not as a Gold or as Miss Earth. When I'm around you, I feel free and unmasked. So, I'm going to ask you one more time, for the last time. Do you trust me?"

"I trust you," I answered. It may have been a few weeks late, but it was something she needed to know—an answer that seemed more meaningful than our declared love. It was all she needed to hear before putting on her reflective helmet. She left me alone in the room to stare out at the intense lighting strikes from the storm. The waves outside burst against the shoreline, contrasting stark white against the dark sky.

Trace re-entered the room. "Why did you let her leave?"

I couldn't respond. Australia, along with the rest of the world, was in store for one hell of a battle. It just so happened that Law had given us a front row seat. Tonight would be the second time in my life where I had no choice but to sit back and watch the person I loved compete in a culminating race, except this time, I hoped I wouldn't be on the wrong end of tragedy.

HELL'S BELLE

"DO YOU TRUST ME?" I ASKED CRAVEN, ONCE AGAIN. He had never given me an answer back at the amphitheatre. Now, his light-brown eyes were steady and frozen. They weren't scared. They were promising, they were real, and I could tell prior to his answer that they believed in me tonight.

"I trust you," he had answered. Better to hear those words late than never. They enamoured my aching heart for what I had reserved for the Amaryllis family. There were just so many things that were falling apart today. First, the news that Law had clinched a spot for next week. Then, my loving father decided to telephone, calling me a succubus slut. There were just too many damn diversions, but that was all about to change. I felt confident about it. There was no way I was going to die while my father was watching. I wouldn't give him the satisfaction. There was no way I was going to die in front of Craven. He'd already witnessed the death of one racer close to him—one that haunted him to this day. I would not become another ghost for him as Orin Pierce was mine.

The death of Lawson's brother was always on my hands. I let Midy have the pedestal, the schemes, and the electromagnetic pulse to save him from my father's punishment. Luke had been willing to amputate parts of Midy's body for Rokian supplements. I saw the appointments for *Transcendence* on the countertop, and thought *over my dead body*. This was why I created the monster Midy had become, why I gave birth to the boogeyman that haunted him in his dreams. I didn't care if he hated me in the end, as long as he lived to do so. That was the price I was willing to pay, and I planned on taking it out on the family that should have made my life ten-fold easier.

Linking an alliance with the Amaryllis had been my biggest mistake. The goal was to dethrone Midy. It wasn't supposed to be a death threat on his life or on an entire planet. But everything happened for a reason. While I'd made things worse, Craven has been the one changing everything for the good. There was no way I could've built the strength to kill Jackal, not after all the things I'd placed him through. He felt for me, and I couldn't return the gesture. All he wanted was a pretty assistant for his carnival act, he only loved Miss Earth unlike Craven who seemed to be more interested in the real me. With full knowledge, Craven had stepped up to help Midy and I—something no one else had done for me, let alone my family. As a wise woman recently said, I'd take the lives of a few over the many. That was how we maintained stability.

"He's going to live, he's going to live," I repeated in my head all the way to the backyard of the Opera House. Beneath the flaming-orange cloud of drones sat the tools of my staged masterpiece: a bleacher of fans as the audience, a hovertron set of drones as the camera, a family of enemies as the actors, and myself as the up and coming director. Above it all, within the clouds, was a vibrant vortex gifted to me by Mother Nature.

"How's the weather, Nito?" I asked, modifying the Hi-Fi system in my helmet to a slower playback speed for his accelerated speech.

"As close to an Arythro evening as I'll ever get," he replied through the speaker transmitting from homebase. "By the way, I'd like to be called Smitty Johnson for the night." The ridiculous name couldn't have been more appropriate for the crime we were willing to commit tonight. We had to utilize the drones to our advantage with Smitty Johnson acting as the technologist hacking into some of them. Having eyes in the sky was not just a luxury but a necessity.

"I'm sending you feeds of Smitty," Nito informed me. Livestreams of a dozen drones appeared on each corner of my visor providing visuals from the sky. I could now be seen by all of the drones. The crowd went silent.

"Kruuuuueeeeeger… Kruuuuuuueeeeeger!" they all began to sing over the thunderous lightning impacting the cloud of drones. Now attracted by the Anthem of Hell, the hateful eight had their spotlights on me. I glanced over my shoulder to stare their parents in the eyes but, instead, saw both Craven and Trace through the windows of their reserved lounge. Trying not to show my confusion, I gazed back at the Amaryllis and noticed the stains of blood scarred on Heart and Diamond's pectars.

"Nito, who's blood is that?" I asked, hoping he could use his hemovision through the drone's eye. Nito's race of Ryths could identify blood to an owner—a vampire-like skill, hearing the voices and seeing the memories of one's life from the simple sight of blood.

"It's from Kingsley himself. Law shot him…and now seems to be allying himself with Cravy-boy," Nito revealed, decoding a major story from the minor evidence. Craven befriended Orin's little brother? The revelation made me glance back at the lounge. There he stood next to Craven as the lone FMJ in my audience. Most likely, he was here to witness my death out of respect for our bouts over the past couple of weeks. A silver-eyed avenger was fully unmasked for once. The only thing the outlaw kept hidden was his burnt arm, sustained from the molten-magnesium bullets to his exosuit and suffered on purpose to symbolically align the tattooed arm with his brother's scorching fate. Orin "The Serene Dingo" Pierce was someone who Craven would've loved just as much as I did. Someone who came from a humbled aboriginal tribe, sharing Crank's penchant for showcasing skills over violence. Falling not too far from the tree was Lawson, usually cheering his big brother in the stands. There was even a time when Lawson and I were in the same booth, arguing about how our brothers were the better racer. He had my brother's poor turning skills to use against me in those debates. I countered with his brother's pacifist approach to racing. Lawson taught me his native term *altjirerama* that day. It was carved onto every exosuit in Orin's garage and meant, *to see God*. It was why Orin never had any intention of taking a life in the sport of Versa. A bright philosophy that Lawson could get behind before… before I ruined the Pierce family's life. Lawson, he admired the dreamcatcher I always wore, something that wasn't a part of his culture, and yet he understood the meaning and why I should always wear it. He even nicknamed me "dreamer" from the relic. He lost the smile he wore that day in the booth. Maybe one day, he would wear it again.

"Nito, do you think it's still possible to befriend Lawson?" I eventually asked now locking eyes with the avenger.

"If he can't kill your brother, he'll probably settle for you instead, so no," Nito replied, helping me realize how far gone Lawson might actually be. The fact that the avenger stood next to Craven, a mirrored image of Lawson's past-self, proved how one bad day was all it takes to fall far from grace.

"I can't kill another Pierce," I softly stated, still haunted by the image in my head of Orin's face melting.

"Then let's keep you masked as Hell's Belle," Nito said, rekindling the flames booked for the Carnivores.

The chants of my name grew louder the closer I got to my lane at the end of the curved starting line. Prior to entering the reserved first lane, I gave each Carnivore the daring opportunity to look Krueger in the eyes. The first candidate was the Rokian Primax who lacked proper parts for his body. Most of it was the usual purple rust, but his legs resembled strong spaghetti whenever they stood tall—an action he attempted after noticing the lantern stare I lobbied to him. I could probably take on the former Rokian-General considering the injuries sustained from Craven, but that wouldn't have been fair. I had better plans for him. Like *An Amaryllis Exosphere*, he was going to be the star to my bloody show.

Next in line was the hammerhead himself, already spitting pellets of saliva onto my visor. He wore my father's Glaucus, the earliest of many exosuits manufactured by my father's company. Short a hammer-end courtesy of Craven, the Pyscean was at home, embracing the stormy tears of Mother Nature that would give them a native advantage over us even though he was in the second to last lane. He was definitely the wild card who could potentially spoil the show. I just had to hope he was more boneheaded today than usual.

Then there were the souls worried about Kingsley's health, three of the four tumblers in lanes five through seven. The Greatest Acrobatic, Club, made eye-contact—rage beginning to build for our big bout. I was hoping the rage triggered by Law and Craven would make him as dumb as he was young. Only seventeen. As for his sisters, they kept their eyes forward, pretending I didn't exist. Diamond, The Greatest Contortionist, would be an idiot if she tried any of her body-twisting moves against

Krueger, and she knew it. She may have been fifteen and an intelligent Amaryllis, but she lacked experience. She could easily top her older sister, Heart, The Greatest Aerialist who had to be the most mismatched one of all the Carnivores here. I believed that Curtain's Call only had two ramps and was underwater for half of the race. She was as foreign as an aerialist could be and would strongly suffer tonight. The same could not be said about their eldest, Spade. The Greatest Showman called the shots between them, and he was impatiently awaiting Krueger in the third lane. As tempting as it was to jump straight to him, an unkindled Satanian stood in between us in the fourth. I honestly didn't know what was saddest about Lucifer, the fact that he couldn't breathe fire or that he was using flamethrowers as a supplement. I might receive a kiss from his Goddess Zata by the end of this sorrowful tale, but I preferred to think of the rain washing him down the waterspout.

"Hey, there's something you should know about Loosh," Nito informed me as the Satanian's horse-skulled helmet locked eyes with mine. "He rebelled against Kingsley after being told to kill Cravy-boy. Not sure this gives him a pardon, but I thought you should know."

"You saw that through the bloodstain?"

"Gabby, I saw who Kingsley lost his virginity too, and it wasn't a Terran," Nito answered, clarifying how robust his hemovision was.

"Will I regret sparing him?"

"It depends, how many lives are you willing to take tonight?" Nito asked while Lucifer kept his eyes on me. The Satanian had never given me a reason to take his life, and sparing Craven only made him more of a paragon.

"I'll spare him, but the same can't be said for this asshole," I said, finally walking up to the anxious Spade now pressing his visor against mine. One of us was prepared to die. I honestly found it funny that Spade believed he stood a chance against me in *Ion's* failed project of an exosuit. *Only a Matter of Time*, they said. *Keep Dreaming*, I countered. An Initiator had to quickly tear us apart as the crowd booed. To avoid any more confrontations, the Initiator took the liberty of guiding me past the giant Gigallian lacing his guitar with Irizan in the second lane.

The Anthem of Hell played once again as the countdown began on the hovertron. Lightning struck harder than before. Everyone's lives were about to change from the show I was prepared to give them. They'd continue to worship me as the hero, and that was the point. They would have a future with me in it and a choice of how to perceive their heroine named Krueger. I was not a nightmare, only a savior, which was why I took one last glance at Craven. I wanted to remember what he saw, what I truly was and what I was not—the man next to him.

"Our drones are ready for combustion on the final straightaway," Nito informed me as the Carnivores and I got down on all fours. "Let's get you there in one piece."

The horn's roar matched the crowd as I drained a bit of boost to keep the margins fair from the others for now. All of the drones flashing red and black followed us along the edges of the track as we left the sky of tears. We entered a sharp right turn leading to a long left turn curving inward towards the ocean's head. I knew I could keep a lead on the first turn, but the waterfall now pouring onto the second was going to create the first major clash of the night.

I slowed down to impact the water at a reasonable pace and saw a giant overshoot the turn, hydroplaning close to the track's edge, nearly falling off and into the drones. Titan had to drill one of his guitars into the track like an ice axe for the save, while Spade copied my strategy against the rain. He leapt onto my latis to disrupt the control I had. He then attempted to impale my spina with his brachial blade. For his pleasure, I presented an x-ray of my suit that revealed a fractured vertebra. This prevented a second strike. I then triggered the gastrolocks to brake and whiplash his head over my dell, reaching my clawed hand over the same shoulder to impact Spade's eye. The bloody puncture trembled my claws long and hard as the eldest tumbler screamed. I wanted him to suffer for much longer, but Krakyn drifted into first place and made me think otherwise.

Seeing the drones change their identity, I dropped my bloody claws back onto the track to match the Pyscean's speed heading up a ramp. Spade's body impacted the water with a loud splash as Krakyn and I took the big leap off the ramp and into the opening of an underwater tunnel. It reminded me of Mr. Knightfall's championship race.

"How big is the lead?" I asked Nito, landing in the tunnel with the Pyscean.

".985 seconds," he answered, which was as good of a lead as a racer could get, except I was sharing it with the hammerhead now ramming the side of his head into my right dell. I responded by impaling his platys-plates with my clawed-right hand. With the left-angled motion of his head, he pinned my right hand into the ground while pushing me away in order to fully stretch out my right arm. I knew what he was trying to accomplish, now noticing the Satanian boosting closer to us for an amputation. Krakyn always raced far from the ground, leaving enough room for a body to hide beneath, possibly my saving grace. My tyres deflated back into their holster. With my clawed hands free, I impaled them into Krakyn's pectar and abdominis, beating Lucifer's fatal blow. Everyone heard the screeching strike from Lucifer's katana once I was underneath Krakyn. The Satanian shot his flames at me. My position may not have been the best, but it was good enough.

"Gotta make a move, Gabby," Nito said. "Primax is catching up, and the tunnel is about to split into four pathways." The urgency forced my tyres to inflate again as I peeled my claws away from Krakyn's chest to slide out from underneath. The ramming force of my rear-tyres impacting Krakyn's catapulted his into the air, leaving me on my back, vulnerable for the incoming Carnivores. Parts of the scraped-off metal pierced a crack into my spina's rocketing boost tank, which ironically kept me near Krakyn's dangling feet before my front-tyre could inflate me out of the peculiar position.

To avoid the collisions, I twisted my body back into a planked position and drove up the tunnel's wall all the way to the ceiling. I knew that I was the only one with adhesive tyres, so I used that to my advantage as the multiple pathways approached. In the lead was Lucifer who decided to take the center-left path. As for second place, Krakyn oriented himself towards the center-right path leaving two paths vacant. The remaining Carnivores began to slow down to trace the pathway I was going to take. As a counter attack, I used my clawed-right hand to slice off my igniting boost tank and dropped it like a nuke from the ceiling between the tumblers and Primax, sending the Rokian and I far-right, and the three remaining tumblers far-left.

Fortunately for Primax, the pathway we took had several dips that were essentially hills for me on the ceiling. This granted him a good lead. The path then led us into a series of ascending loops, providing me with an opportunity to fall onto Primax from above. Impatient for the moment, I blindly pushed myself off of the ceiling, only to be impaled in the hip by a sharp object piercing through my corium layer. A bladed-end of a guitar had lodged itself into my left hip, and I had to quickly pull it off from the Irizan saturating my wound. The giant edged closer, forcing me to drive back up the wall with the blood-dripping wound.

"Shake it off. Most of his Irizan drained away from the rain," Nito informed me, but that didn't stop the giant from using his remaining guitar as a weapon. All Titan had to do was stand up in order to get a proper swing at my injury—an offense that prevented me from catching the Rokian, now approaching another section of splitting pathways. The track divided into two instead of four this time, causing the giant to leap into the air for a tackle, finally bringing me back to the surface below. The fall slightly injured my left shoulder, but it wasn't bad enough to keep me off the Rokian's tail. The desperate tackle actually disrupted Titan more than it did me. I could only imagine what a leaping semi-truck felt like from a hard fall.

After surviving the Gigallian's onslaught, I followed Primax into the same path, using his draft as a way to help me catch up. The Rokian knew how much closer I was getting and decided to take a blind swing with his right brachial blade. Avoiding the amateur move was too easy, giving me a third chance at driving up to the tunnel's ceiling. I aligned our suits once again, successfully able to fall onto his, impaling all four of my claws, deflating my tyres once again. For safety, I glanced behind, hoping Titan was nowhere in sight. Instead, I saw a giant dwarfed in the distance. Titan might have been mute, but he was no idiot. He knew exactly what I was trying to do to his Rokian ally since I did the same thing to him at Dessnia.

"The pathways don't merge for another klick. Make it count," Nito said as I began to manually hack through Primax's programming system. This was my secret weapon—artificial veins granting me access to all of Primax's Daconix through my visor. This form of Iris-scrolling placed an arrow mouse travelling wherever I looked within the visor, and clicked on what I wanted with a blink. The idea was ironically inspired by the Rokian body which was half-artificial and half-organic—something right now that was more overwhelming than expected. Whenever I hacked into a racer's suit, I typically only got the codings of the suit, but with Primax, I got the codings of his organs, too. If I wanted to, I probably could have shut down his artificial heart, which would corrupt the organic one. There was so much I could have done to him in so little time, giving me an idea of what I could alter in his brain. "400m," I could hear Nito announcing in the background while I gave Primax a temporary virus that made him believe we were competing in a Wreath-based series with all of the Carnivores as his primary targets.

The walls of the tunnels turned transparent as we all approached the grand merge. The first racer coming out of it was Krakyn, who I assumed had the lead. Behind him, Lucifer, followed by the three remaining tumblers: Diamond, Heart, and Club. Titan's guitar hammered a continuous thud in the background as he desperately tried to warn his family of the hell approaching them from behind. The first to notice was Club who didn't hesitate to attack, most likely riled from the crappy day his family was having. Taking matters into his own hands, he bladed both arms and took a screaming leap directly at me. Obstructing the attack was a giant blade from Primax, which entered Club's gut, tearing the tumbler's body in half. Chunks of Club's stomach flew into my face while the intestines wrapped around Primax's neck.

The sound of disemboweled organs caught Heart's teary eye. Titan tried to attract Diamond's attention with his guitar. They could only see the aftermath of their brother's death, causing them both to mount a challenge. I had one of Primax's tyres transition to my arm as Heart took a leap, only to be caught by Primax's hand. To prevent Diamond from saving her sister, I underhand-pitched the new tyre at her head, which drew her beneath Primax's rear-tyres. From Heart, I heard crushing metal and cracking bones, while Diamond screamed at the shattering glass. The agony abruptly came to an end, triggering a spine-tingling scream from Titan which deafened us all. We all glanced back at the grieving giant. Parts of my visor began to crack, deactivating the virus I had on Primax. I couldn't believe how powerful the Gigallian's scream had been, still ringing in my ears. Trying to get ahead of the full destruction of my visor, I scrolled through my codings to shut down Primax's suit, preventing any retaliation while I leapt off to catch Krakyn and Lucifer.

The tunnel turned into a ramp, launching us back onto the streets of Sydney. The landing onto the straightaway labeled High St. burst the top-right corner of the visor, to reveal my blue iris and brow. The cracked hole restored some of my hearing as the navy-blue drones spotlighted on my face, searching for more skin.

"Nito, am I exposed?" I asked, realizing the straightaway was inside a neighborhood. Blockades separated us from the houses full of cheering families.

"No, but you'll have to defend the left side of your visor," Nito responded as the blockades turned us sharply right down Clark Rd. "Your blue eye won't reveal anything, but your red eye will."

"I hate playing defense," I muttered, driving down the curved road. It eventually turned left down a short straightaway that made us turn left again. This placed us underneath an elevated motorway. The crammed straightaway gave the giant behind me an opportunity to catch up, causing Lucifer to aim and blow his flamethrower. The attack forced me to use my right-front tyre as a shield so I could kick my left-rear tyre at Titan's head, slowing the giant. The flames then crisped my shielding tyre into aluminium, causing me to adapt a motorcycle position as the road surface led us out onto a bridge over the bay, directly back to the Opera House. On the bridge, Krakyn and Lucifer teamed up to send one final attack my way while Titan inched closer from behind. Defense was never my strength, causing me to stand on my rear-tyre while launching my front-tyre at Lucifer's gas tank. I leapt onto Krakyn's spina. A backwards headbutt from the hammerhead fully destroyed my visor.

"Hold on, Gabby," I could hear Nito screaming before a tyre launched at the back of my head destroyed my helmet for the first time in my Versa career. My long curly hair covered some of my face while several drones soared down onto the track, kamikazing into Lucifer and Titan. Nito's life-saving offense gave Krakyn and I some privacy for first place as I jammed my claws into his front-tyre just before the finish. My body catapulted over the line first. My own claws grazed my forehead as I tumbled, finally halting on my patallises. I heard the crowd at the boardwalk gasp. Streams of blood dripped down my face as I stared at the ground, remembering the gashing wound in my left hip. My drenched hair hung over the sides of my face, still hiding my identity, but the emblem of my dreamcatcher swung down to my pectar. Claire may not have been here, but I heard her words as I looked up. Each fan in the crowd stared at me as if I was a ghost. Krakyn kneeled next to Lucifer and Titan.

"Kruuuuueeeeeger… Kruuuuuuueeeeeeger!" A brave voice slowly chanted, followed by the rest of the crowd increasing in volume. Like Zane's adrenia, their support helped mollify the cuts on my head and hip, helping me forget about the quantity of red on the ground. I kept turning until I had a direct view of the disappointed expression on Craven's face. This unmasking was, in Claire's words, important. I was no longer Miss Earth, I was Krueger, and my true colours were now exposed for the world to see. I eventually mouthed the words, "I'm sorry," at Craven. I loved him and he loved me, but I also loved my brother. I was willing to take an avenger's bullet to save them both.

ACT III
CHAPTER 10

WHAT
COMES AFTER

❝I **'M SORRY," WERE THE WORDS I READ ON GABRIELLA'S BLOODY LIPS, LEAVING ME DOWNHEARTED, FRIGHTENED, TROUBLED.** Most of all, I was immobilized by the unstable Law who stood beside me, finally stopping the flip of his bullet. The cold metal of Trace's hibrix touched my shoulder, gently pulling me in his direction. He wanted us to safely escape the booth while Law was distracted by the sight of Krueger.

"Dreama," Law gently spoke, stopping Trace and I with the clicking sound of a gun aimed at us. "Where do ya think ya goin?"

"This is why we can't have good things Crave…" Trace started to say before Law took a warning shot at the door behind us.

"Look, we're on your side," I said, trying to reach a peaceful resolution.

"Are ya? Havin relations wit Kruga sounds like an enemy tu may."

"Yes, her and I are together, and yes, I did know about her alias. But we all have the same agenda, stopping Midas once and for all," I explained.

Law loosened his grip on the revolver's trigger. "I don't wanna stop him from winnin, I wanna keep him from livin," Law rephrased, slowly stepping closer and closer. "In vain, may brotha died wit the golden boy walkin away free from true justice. Them rich cunts thought ol' Law would waltz away wit a green donation, but green was neva the magic cala. It was red." The muzzle of his revolver now pressed my forehead. Beyond the gun were the silver eyes. He knew I wasn't his enemy, he just didn't give a shit. He was merely a triggerman, ready to off me like he did Kingsley.

"You want justice for your brother, I get that, I really do," Trace said, "So does Craven, his father…" He tried to reach the silver lining inside Law's head. "He loved his father like you loved your brother. He also loves Gabriella the same way she loves him. And that is the same Gabriella who just dismantled an entire fucking family out of spite like it was child's play. So, if you're prepared to pull a trigger on the man she loves… God forbid what comes after." It was an unorthodox way of negotiating for our lives, the gunslinger smiled and lowered his gun.

"We're not enemies," I restated.

"Nah, but we ain't friends, eitha," Law replied, holstering his weapon to take another look at Gabriella now limping back into the Opera House.

"Okay, we're not friends, but we are Terran, and killing Midas will…"

"Killing Midas will hurt Gabriella, and that's something Craven will try his best to prevent," Trace interrupted, shaking his head behind Law's back.

"You're dancin wit the devils, McGuire. The Golds don't need ya protection. They deserve reckoning, and Kruga is no exception. She's still a Gold, and they always leave a trail of blood soona o'lata." The hovertron had its cameras on the deceased Carnivores bathed in their own remains. Law then turned around to unveil his burnt arm. "So, take a long look at may, see that I'm what comes afta."

Through all the blood and hate Law had embraced, he still was trying to be a decent Terran. Could she really hurt me like her family had hurt him, or was this merely a song sung from sorrow? Law tipped his hat and then pulled out another golden bullet to flip in the air while exiting the lounge.

"Why did you stop me?" I eventually asked Trace.

"Because you don't want a man blinded by blood as an ally," Trace answered.

"That's a significant decision you just made for our planet."

"And I don't plan on regretting it. Both you and Gabriella, I mean Krueger, can take care of Law. And speaking of Krueger, don't you think you should check on her?" Trace advised, reminding me of her condition and skillfully changing the subject. Midas was nowhere near safe, and the one guy who was most likely his killer could've been our friend.

"Trace… brother… I hope this doesn't come back to bite us."

"It won't. Now go," he insisted, pushing me out of the booth.

He was right about Gabriella's condition. The amount of blood coated on her body was worrisome even though it wasn't fatal. She always seemed to walk away victorious from the most gruesome of races. She'd dominated a Wreath-based series with most of the kills and turned a white mountain in the Middle East red. Now, in Sydney, she had tested the temper of our Shepherd, Pandora. I wondered if Gabriella was still qualified to compete in this series.

At her room, and with her identity exposed, she left her door opened and unsecured, finally giving up on discretion. Inside the Utzon, now utilized as a clinic, Gabriella attempted to strip out of her black corium. I quickly moved to her aid.

"It's a good thing I wore black, eh?" Gabriella joked from all of the blood sopping the corium. Her face was bleeding badly, and the deep gash on her lower left hip revealed a lot of skin. "It looks a lot worse than it actually is."

"Well, it doesn't necessarily look like a day at the spa," I replied, trying to search for some alcohol wipes or towels. She directed me to the medical box on the bench closest to the window. It had syringes of morphine sulfate, sanitatium bandages, a spray can of alcohol, wipes, and pralidoxime, the antidote for Irizan.

"I've been through worse," she claimed, once we were next to each other by the center bench. She needed me to unzip her out of the corium, revealing the massive scars from past races. One large one on her right side expanded and contracted with each breath. Parts of her black underwear sheltered a scar diagonally stretching out of the left side of her butt cheek. An archipelago of rock-size marks ran down the right side of her ribs, dropping down to the large incision on her hip. Protruding out of her left thigh were thorn-like veins which we would treat with the vial of pralidoxime. The image of a naked and flawless Miss Earth may have been a thing of the past, but that didn't stop her from smiling at the wounds. It was almost as if she was begging for more to tattoo her body. "During the Bermuda series, I mistimed a landing that dislocated my shoulder and fractured a rib into my lungs."

"How the hell did you survive that?" I asked, infusing the syringe with the antidote before the organic nerve agent could scream for mercy. A vein in her left thigh dilated with the injection, quickly killing a Ghastallian substance.

"Whaddya think I did, I drove my butt to the emergency room as soon as I won the race," she answered, making us both laugh.

"Of course you won that race," I told her while grabbing the wipes.

The best thing about the cut on her face was how fresh it was. I'd learned from my dad how hard it was to clean dry wounds. He consistently preached how we were filled with paint instead of blood. *Warriors* create their art on the battlefield, my father once said. If only he had known how stressful life could get when that warrior was someone you loved. Was a warrior even the right title for Gabriella? She was beautiful when she smiled, even through all of the blood, but she was Hades-like when she didn't. She was a freak of nature, and now the whole world knew how dominant she could be as a racer.

"I don't win all of the time. I lost a couple races when you were still comatose," she replied after her face was clean. She then grabbed the syringe in order to fill it with morphine before injecting it into the veins of her right arm.

"Those don't count, you were just a little lost then," I stated, now shaking up the spray can of alcohol. I gave her time to breathe deeply before spraying the hip's incision. The morphine must've kicked in at the right time because her reaction wasn't as expressive as most. Once the alcohol saturated the wound, I firmly placed the santatitium bandage over it.

"And now I'm found," she said.

"Why does it seem like I'm too late? I mean, weren't we trying to avoid the unmasking"

"Craven, I don't plan on dying for a long time. You, Midy, and my mother are all I've got, and I'll fight through hell to keep you all safe," she promised, leaning in for a kiss followed by a long hug. Spring week had been one race too long for both her and I, but it still felt like a championship week to a certain degree. There were so many possibilities, good and bad, none of them as unpredictable as the one her and I were living in. Who could have foreseen the number of deaths that would take place in back-to-back races? Sure, we had Claire, but even she didn't predict a massacre. Were we on a questionable path? Could this chaotic path even produce a peaceful outcome, or was it leading to a much darker story?

I had to rethink the harsh reality and envision a more beautiful outcome. One where Trace and Katia got married in front of their newborn child, where Luke Gold finally had a date with Karma, and where Gabriella and I could sit on a beach in silence enjoying the life we'd busted our asses to create. I shared my thoughts with Gabriella. She, of course, cherished the thought of her father's fate.

"I didn't realize Trace was having a kid," she said, with the same look on her face I'd had when I found out. "Being a racer… that's all I've wanted to be. I didn't care about modeling, fame, or money. I just wanted to be on a track doing the things I saw my idols performing, not once thinking about the life I could possibly have outside of it," she explained.

It gave me insight into her feelings. We had gotten so caught up in the present situation, we forgot about the future we could change for those incapable of witnessing it just yet. Something I found related to my father's motives.

"Do you remember the race my father had here in Australia?" I asked, taking a seat next to her. "Well, in that race, he had a near-death experience. It wasn't anything new, but it was good enough to make him drive far away from the track to a beach. No one knew why he did it, but it was a good thing that he did because on that beach, he ran into a lifeguard who would eventually become my mother. I say this because I think he was just like you, thinking about racing on a daily basis. Always finding new ways to make his life better on the track, not once thinking about the possible life he could've had outside of it."

"Where was the beach?" she suddenly asked.

"Up north in Newcastle."

"Then let's head up there and enjoy that life," she proposed. I was uncertain if it was her or the morphine talking. She then got up to clean and pack everything in the room. I joined her, now understanding how locked on the idea she really was. Newcastle changed my father's life and prepared him for what came after. Maybe it would do the same for us.

ACT IV
EARTH, WIND, & FIRE

ACT IV
CHAPTER 1

FROM ASHES
TO NEW

MY CHEEK PRESSED AGAINST A COLD FLOOR INSIDE A NEON-BLUE ROOM. Disoriented, I looked around and found a holder on the wall for an exosuit. This must have been a locker of some sort, but where was my suit? It wasn't on the cracked walls or on the blue-and-gray checkered floor with a hard-water stench of a damp basement. No, it was still on my body, destroyed in several sections. The vastus around my left leg spiked outward like bloody bayonets. The sight shocked me, as did the crushed helmet next to the broken leg. Crushed like crumpled paper over shards of glass. What the hell had happened? What had I missed? Why was I here? I couldn't remember anything. Blood suddenly poured out of my mouth. I tried to escape the gore by crawling to the wall. Unable to identify all of the injuries, I leaned against the wall and read the writing above the locker's doorway. *AD INFINITUM* it said over the armored wings of Versa. The words seemed familiar but lacked an associated link to my archive of memories. Below the symbol and unfamiliar scripture, The Raven patiently waited in the doorway. Inside the Nevermore, his brachial blades were directed towards me, both covered in red. Was he the source of my injuries, or was he merely the executioner? As I attempted to speak, more blood streamed down my chin. I was dying, numb, broken, helpless. The only thing I could do was bleed, breathe, and stare. Zane's face had been ripped apart in several areas, and yet, through all of the pain, he somehow managed a smile. I closed my eyes to his violent intentions, shutting them to darkness, and opening them to radiance. Blinded by the sun's rays, I heard pelicans, winds rustling the trees, and the dance of waves from the ocean.

"Another nightmare," I softly affirmed, coming back to reality. I embraced the soft cotton fur, the smiling sun over the rich blue body of water. A complete turnabout from the unforgiving weather the previous night. Gabriella and I had been thankful to arrive at this hotel. She had been determined to reach Newcastle. This view of the ocean was why I believed the United Countries was one of the most gorgeous planets in the alliance, if not the galaxy. A subjective opinion considering that I'd never been to any other planet.

"What?" Gabriella suddenly asked, stepping out the bathroom, rinsed clean of last night's blood. With curls now drenched in water, she took on the persona of Miss Earth once again. Outlines from her Way/Point black bikini peeked from underneath the white tank top and lace coat. She wore very short shorts, revealing some of the bruises on her leg from the series. "Did you say another nightmare?"

"Um… yeah, it's just something I've been having lately," I revealed, bringing her to the edge of the bed. "It's nothing though, I hadn't had one since we were in Dessnia."

"What are they about?"

"Sometimes, I see myself dying, and other times it's someone else," I replied. "It's just a dream though."

"How do you get hurt in these dreams?"

"Well, the first time around, I was covered in snow and blood with broken legs and ribs. My father was watching. This time around, I'm stuck in a locker losing a lot of blood with Zane watching instead," I explained trying not to relive the moment.

"So, you had a dream about getting injured in a snowy environment, and not even a couple days later, it actually happened. Doesn't that seem a little too coincidental?"

"It was just a dream."

"You told me that you sometimes see your father's ghost. Did you see him at the bottom of the cliff?" she questioned. I nodded. "So, you had a dream about falling off the mountain with the same injuries, seeing the same ghost at the same moment before it actually happened. Again, that doesn't seem strange to you?"

"I mean… maybe, but it doesn't prove anything," I stated. "In Brazil, I had another dream where you were dying. You're not dead. If I can dream about the future, I suck at it."

"Yeah, only being half accurate is pretty much crap," she replied, making us both laugh. She then pulled me out of the bed, guiding me into the dining room to the smell of cinnamon and bacon. The kitchen was a crime scene of egg remains, battered bread, and greasy pans. On the dining room table, she had laid out bacon strips, cinnamon toast, and scrambled eggs. The TV screen was paused on the Unican Network show, Vice Versa. Gabriella searched for the remote, ready to resume the show and eat.

"First, we had The Son of Earth, then we had The Heart of Earth, now we have Miss Earth," Layla Rose announced, ready to open a discussion while the camera zoomed out, revealing a shaken Lenny Jackson and an anxious Gradite Monroe. "What do you two make of last night's events?"

"Lenny, in my time, I've seen beauty, and I've seen beasts, but never have I ever seen both combine in the sport of Versa. You and everyone else can call her Miss Earth, but I refuse to do so. Until the day I die, I will forever admire Gabriella Gold as Krueger. Let's get that straight," Gradite said, almost leaping out of the screen. "I wholeheartedly believe that Krueger is going to change not only this sport, but the United Countries of Earth."

"You're telling me, Krueger, Miss Earth, Gabriella, whateva the hell she wants to be called, is betta than her brotha, Midas, her lova, Craven, and her arch rival, Law?"

Lenny questioned, pulling out highlights of his referenced racers. The highlights showed Law at K2, Midas at Greenland, and me at Brazil.

"Yes, and I'm ready to take it a step further. I think…" Gradite paused, waiting for the full attention of Lenny and Layla. "I think Krueger can win us a Galactica championship!" The bold statement quickly made Gabriella cough up the eggs she tried to swallow. Everyone on Earth knew how electrifying Gradite could be, but never to this extent. He seemed prepared to tattoo Krueger's name and image onto his very bones. Some said he had done the same thing for my father.

"It's funny that you bring up Galactica after this race, because I wanna lead us into the next big question. Should Gabriella be expelled from Four Seasons?" Layla asked of the gentlemen and audience, referencing the polls conducted at the bottom of the screen. The polls gave an option of "Yes or No" causing me to tomahawk my knife at the "No" as the percent for "Yes" surpassed the 50% threshold.

"Absolutely not," Gradite answered before Lenny could interject with the clips of Primax slaughtering the three tumblers. The sight mirrored the showcase at Dessnia with the exception of Gabriella on the Rokian's back. "We can't conclusively prove that she was controlling Primax. There are rumors that her and Jackal were a thing in the past. If that's true, who's to say her and Primax weren't allies, hmm?"

"Grad, there have only been two bloody races in this series, and she has been the catalyst for both. Where does the committee draw the line for her? What makes her different from the Gora sisters of Egypt?"

"The difference is that she can win a race without killing, Lenny," he said, leaning over the table.

"I hope you're right Grad, because as of right now, Gabriella is only a monster in the eyes of the Re-Versables," Lenny concluded with the camera transitioning to the rallies happening in the streets of both Old and New York. There were activists painting "666" on some of the Miss Earth posters scattered around the city. I was amazed that the activists were willing to treat her like a Xenner. Gabriella looked startled. She hadn't eaten a single thing on her plate since Gradite's bold statement. I turned the TV off. The dead sometimes haunted me because of the races, so I could only imagine what was haunting her.

"They cheered for Krueger's image at Dessnia, now they crucify it? Am I really a monster?" she softy asked. "If it wasn't for me, Earth wouldn't need saving. If it wasn't for me, Titan wouldn't have screamed. If it wasn't me, Orin, Jackal, Bayne, Diamond, Heart, and Club would still be alive."

"If it wasn't for you, I'd still be half a man wondering whether or not he should or shouldn't pray for the chance to race Thorax. If it wasn't for you, I wouldn't have been admired by the FMJs after Greenland, changing the course of history," I explained, getting out of my seat to hug her. She might have been the toughest racer on Earth, but she was still Terran, and Terrans felt the pressure of hate. "How are you a monster if you're the best thing that has ever happened to me?"

That seemed to bring her back to the light as she had done for me back at the carnival. I never thought I'd have an opportunity to repay her. Bittersweet as it was, it was still good to know that I wasn't the only one who could lose their grip on reality. And it was even better to know that we could bring each other back whenever we got lost, but we shouldn't have been struggling in Newcastle. The point of coming here was to take a timeout away from the sport and be a normal couple, not to be what others thought we were. I wanted her to remember that, and once she did, we finished breakfast to finally discover what the city had in store for us.

Outside of our hotel, NOAH'S On The Beach, was an immaculate environment of Pyscean architecture with pearlescent roads, arch-shell rooftops, and peach stem trees spiraling up with pink leaves. The only native things about Newcastle were the brick bases of the buildings, the light posts which seemed misplaced due to their gray colors, and the people, or at least some of them. A great portion of the pedestrians were Pyscean. Alien races like the glimmering iridescent-purple and teal female Syames, the sunny iridescent-orange male Goldlyns, and the neon-blue and red Tetras. Earth typically acted as a retirement or vacation destination for the Pysceans, especially for the Tetras who were one of the working classes on Pasydanya. Apart from the upper-class were the Goldlyns and the Syames. The Goldlyns acted as the athletes of Pasydanya, competing in both swimming and Versa races. The Syames acted as the beauty, always participating in fashion competitions. I'd only read about these competitions at home, never seeing them in person. Similar to Krakyn, each of them had their questionable Terranoid body form. As expected, the Goldlyns were more wet from a recent swim, the Syames were fashionable to catch the eye, and Tetras were resting on the benches. This was a small part of Pasydanya's cultural diversity, something I had never been around, and yet it felt like heaven. What should've been a culture shock felt more like a sense of belonging. I'd never felt homesick until now. There was something about Newcastle's Pyscean architecture that enhanced the aromatic smell of the ocean. The odor of seaweed was absent. Restless, restless was the word that best described my attitude. I chose to ignore the restlessness and followed Gabriella to the beach.

She claimed a spot away from the ocean's edge. Around us were parties of people playing beach ball. A couple of families watched their kids construct sandcastles, and a few Goldlyns sprinted into the ocean force for a race. On a normal day, we would probably have joined one of the active groups, but this wasn't a normal day. The soreness in my body reached a peak. Over the past couple of busy days, I had no time to consider that my body lacked rest, but today, I felt like I was stuck in a body cast. My legs could barely bend, forcing me to fall onto the beach towel. I wanted to lie there forever, but the sun turned the beach into a skillet. I sat my ass up on the towel and looked at the countless number of bruises on Gabriella's skin, each slowly revealed as she stripped to her bathing suit. Visible was the scar now present on her left hip, along with a slashing scar on the lower back. She wore the scars proudly. My body wasn't any better. I mean, it did fall off of a mountain. Physically, we racers endured a lot of shit without complaining, but as my father had stated in the past, mentally, it could take a toll unlike anything else. This morning proved that claim. There was only so much we could go through, but being with Gabriella was the proper antidote.

Lying under the warm sun, her and I began to talk about the good memories of our families, leading to why she called her brother "Midy." She explained how her and Midas didn't have a lot of friends growing up. They were each other's best friend, a lot of secrets shared between them. One secret was how much hate Midas had towards his father. Luke wanted his son to not only be a Versa racer, but a king that could turn whatever he touched into gold. The notion never pleased her brother, so she nicknamed him Midy. At first, he hated the name as much as Midas, if not more, but then she told him its origin. It came from an old book about an ancient land ruled by a tyrant who always claimed the land's wealth, leaving his people poor and his militia rich. The corrupted system persisted until the circumstances killed the male protagonist's family, giving him the abilities of super strength and invulnerability. The extraordinary powers helped the main character overthrow the tyrant and their militia to become the land's new ruling class, spreading wealth across the community for a happy ending. The main character's name was Mite, but most often referred to as "Mighty." Gabriella altered it to "Midy"—a name her brother could get behind with an appropriate backstory. It allowed him to avoid Luke's wrath by keeping the roots in the name Midas.

Her dreamcatcher provided a follow-up story, something I'd been interested in since I first laid eyes on her Way/Point avatar. The token came from Midas, or Midy as a thank-you gesture for her Versa teachings. He knew how unhappy she was about going into the modeling industry and wanted to give her a symbol of hope. Though he didn't understand the dreamcatcher's meaning, to Gabriella, it was the thought that counted. The symbol came from the ancient Ojibwe tribe with the word *dreamcatcher* translating to *spider* in their language. I would never tell Trace that. Eight legs are six too many for his liking, especially when it came to the Rachnidians. I could only dream about Trace taking on a Rachnidian in a race someday, but that was just a small tangent. The important thing was how alike Gabriella and I really were. The spider theme was something Gabriella chose to incorporate on her adhesive wheels while keeping the dreamcatcher emblem on her necklace. Like my father's championship ring, she always felt safer with the dreamcatcher around her neck and would continue to wear it through dire times.

I envied the sibling love represented in the pair of stories. Sure, Trace was my brother, but he was not blood. He and I didn't come from the same beginnings. Whenever issues erupted in the Burretta household, Trace was pretty much missing-in-action. I explained that to Gabriella after she asked about my family background. The relationship between my father and I was good, but it wasn't durable, which damaged the one between my mother and I. Gabriella could see how my father's death affected me. It may have been depressing, but it was getting better. The bridge between my mother and I had been sturdier, so things were coming around. I tried to sell that idea to my love, but failed miserably, considering I didn't make eye-contact with her once through the depressing stories. I stared into the ocean, remembering my unusual experience under the water in the Amazon. I chose not to run it by my mom.

Roy had planted the seed last week that I was different, which made me restless about what that revelation could mean. Because of my bout with Jackal, I ran an odd idea by Gabriella. I wanted to see my grandparents' grave. They were buried in Salt Ash, Australia. It had to mean something that we were so close. Gabriella didn't hesitate. She quickly planned our voyage to Salt Ash.

We plugged the city's destination into my iCube on the way to the car, discovering that it was less than an hour away in a rural section of Australia where the ocean and sand were replaced with acres of hills and grasslands. It was a much different vibe from the beach side we had acclimated ourselves to. The area was ancient, less terraformed. It felt like a picture from an 18th Century history book—grounded, not hovered. Roads were freshly paved. Tractors, yes tractors scattered the landscape, and farm animals roamed through the fields. Gabriella and I embraced the scene on the search for my grandparents' graveyard in a town that had three separated from each by a few klicks.

The first one we traveled to was small and easy to venture through. The second was vast, unorganized, and was filled with names like Wade, Wayne, Laurie, and Laila. No Ward or Lauren. There was one named Luke.

By the time we reached the final necropolis called An Angelic Channel, the sun was going down. Unlike most cemeteries, it was an island surrounded by rivers and required a bridge to enter. It was an unorthodox cemetery. Just as at Newcastle, I felt a tingling in my head, almost as if a spirit was calling to me. It seemed to be directing me. We then found two graves, side by side, with my grandparents' names engraved on the tombstones. My grandfather's, Ward Freud, was a more traditional tombstone—a stony block with his name, date of birth, date of passing, and what he was best known for. Proud father, loving husband. My grandmother's, on the other hand, revealed much more than expected. For starters, her name wasn't spelled like "Lauren." It was, instead, spelled "Luryn," engraved on a teal-colored marble with black zarquoyse flowers that turned blue upon us as we watched.

"Craven, are you sure that you're a hundred percent... Terran?" Gabriella questioned, crouching down to grab a flower. I couldn't answer, even though I had a hunch. I remembered the dinner we were having with Gabriella's family, the taste of the salmon. I should have made the call back at the jungle, but I didn't want to believe it. I didn't want to admit that I might be a Xenner. The thought of it brought me down to one knee, now realizing why my mother kept her distance, why she didn't want to reveal our bloodline. It would've ruined our lives and more importantly the McGuire name.

"Not anymore. I never asked my mother, so she never told," I replied, bewildered. For the first time, I was thankful that someone like Thorax existed in my life. Without him, people would desperately have tried to investigate my background. Being a part of a Xenobred family tree would be scandalous. Terrans viewed Xenobreds the same way Whites used to look at Blacks prior to the Evolutionary Era—worse than how the activists treated Gabriella earlier. In the past, there had been cases around the planet of Xenners being crucified on an upside down cross. Merciful compared to the punishments carried out on other planets. I could only imagine how much worse my life would become if the world knew about this. I felt sick.

"You asked me earlier if you were a monster," I said, looking with pleading eyes at Gabriella. "Am I?"

"Hell no," she replied without hesitation. "You're just a little more unique." She pulled one of the zarquoyse flowers off of the marbled tombstone and explained why Pysceans favored the ever-changing blossom. The flower would bond with Pyscean blood, translating emotions into color: green if one was happy, orange if one was mad, white for a newborn, and black if one was dead. Pysceans would place the flower near a loved one's grave, hoping it would change into any color except black. As proof, Gabriella gently laid the flower on my shoulder, causing the bloom to turn purple. She gave me a tight hug hoping to turn the flower green. "You held on to my secrets, so I'll hold on to yours."

Cushioning the hard fall, Gabriella's softness in my arms turned the rest of the flowers green. Suddenly, my iCube rumbled. A message marked as urgent appeared on the device's screen.

**Congratulations,
Craven McGuire, you are one of the top-sixteen racers and have been invited to Pandora's Palace for a mandatory conference**

ACT IV
CHAPTER 2

SUMMER

I **WAS BACK IN THE NEON-BLUE LOCKER, STANDING, NOT DYING.** The room was still cold. Instead of a raven, I stood at the doorway and stared at a bench with a dozen cards lying side by side. I was aware within the vision that the accuracy was a coin-flip. I would stay skeptical even as I weighed my choices. I could step into the locker and look at the cards, or I could convince myself to wake out of this nightmare. Torn, I stood wearing the blue jay jacket with cold hands pushed into the pockets. In my right pocket was a pile of change rattling around. I pulled out one piece that had the words *wake up* on one end and *explore dumbass* on the other. I laughed and flipped the coin. It fell to the side saying, *explore* already.

Unlike before, the locker had a series of tree branches with vines streaming across the holey walls. Like the *AD INFINITUM* scriptures, I wasn't sure what they meant or if they meant anything at all. That important message was reserved for the twelve unique cards. The first four cards were a four of a kind of fours. The first was burnt, the second, soaked, and the third, crumpled. The fourth was unharmed but would randomly fly off the bench only to return back to its sedentary position. The next three cards were the ace of hearts, clubs, and diamonds, all ripped into pieces with an ace of spades underneath a grenade. Next in line was a bloodstained Jack, a sobbing Queen, and a bandaged King. Finishing the line-up was a Joker with the words *Are you a believer, now?* next to an arrow aimed at the card's edge. I reached down to turn the card over. It read *Meet me at the garden?* The branches and vines began to cover the locker's wall before the grenade flashed, illuminating the room with a blinding light that suddenly tossed me back into reality. I woke to the beauty of the woman sitting across from me, her bicolored eyes locked on me.

"Another nightmare?" she asked.

"Possibly," I replied, gazing out of the jet's window to an ocean.

"What was it about this time?" she asked. I explained the dozen cards I saw, now correlating them with recent events. The fours explained the elements, the aces explained the tumblers, and the named cards were self-explanatory. The only part of the dream I left out were the words on the Joker, seemingly as irrelevant as the room's jungled theme. "These dreams could mean something."

"Possibly," I said. "Keeping Midas alive is all we need to worry about. Not my dreams."

"Overlooking your dreams is absurd, though. It's not like you're all Terran."

"Wo-wo-whoa," I quickly interjected.

"Craven, it's only you, me and the pilots. I would never say something like that in public," she proclaimed, laying back in her seat. "Or would I," she joked, now reading a book she'd been invested in since we left Newcastle. It was a book about the Pyscean culture. A laymanized version compared to the more sophisticated ones in my father's library. Given the circumstances, I should have read those books instead of looking at the cool pictures. I even took a course about the Pyscean culture in high school. I guess I should have thanked my ex, Chastity, for taking my mind off of the lectures. Gabriella continued to state fun facts, like how the female Pysceans have two gills on their neck instead of three like their male counterparts. She then took several quick glances at my neck prior to reading aloud more facts about the Pyscean monarchy on Pasydanya. Currently, they had a Kyng named Maryne, a Qyn named, Shya, and a Prynce named, Treska. Gabriella enjoyed emphasizing Maryne as a real king compared to Kingsley in the golden bio. The best fact in the book came at the end which gave us a great deal of information on how Pysceans grieve. We knew about the rituals surrounding the zarquoyse flowers, but I didn't know that Pysceans could see the dead spirits of loved ones—misconceived as remarkable when it was actually haunting. The spirits clung to the last appearance the living had with the loved ones. In most cases, this image could be graphic and hard to process, like that of my father. Out of all the extraterrestrial abilities to inherit, this would not have been the one I chose.

Learning about the Pyscean culture was interesting, but it wasn't enough to keep us occupied on the long journey to Pandora's Palace located at UCE's capital Honolulu, Hawaii. To pass the time, I pulled out my iCube and kept us updated on the other qualifying racers. The Unican Network showed highlights from races Gabriella chose to ignore. Apparently, the remaining Carnivores, Krakyn, reliQ, and Lucifer, rebounded from their horrid performances in Sydney with a flawless Top-3 finish on a track in Perth, Australia. The sweep helped them each clinch a spot for the final week. It was worrisome, but it was quickly followed by the highlights of races taking place on the Islands of Samoa where our allies, Warlock, Creed, Kira, and the hounds clinched spots in a bloodless race that, notably, didn't acquire as many ratings as the massacres in Sydney and Brazil. With all the final spots taken, Vice Versa provided a list on their intro.

Four Seasons
Championship Contenders

Midas Gold (17.7%)

Craven McGuire (15.9%)

Gabriella "Krueger" Gold (11.9%)

Lawson "Law" Pierce (10.3%)

Lucretia "Lucifer" Xiagra (9.4%)

reliQ "Titan" Qalmantine (8.1%)

Krakyn Avenya (6.6%)

Warlock Neit (5.3%)

Credo "Creed" Velasquez (4.6%)

Kira Brink (3.1%)

Meta Breckenridge (2.2%)

Beta Breckenridge (2.2%)

Zane Maddox (1.4%)

Ferra D'Angelo (0.7%)

Amir "Cobra" Al-Otaiba (0.4%)

Hotaru Fukumaru (0.2%)

(X) = Probability of Winning Championship

Those were the names, half of them friendly, a quarter of them hostile, and a few of them unknown. Whether it was due to Gabriella and I changing the course of history or it being set in stone already, these were the final pieces of the puzzle. We just needed to make sure the final image was a bearable one.

As time flew, we could see a massive wall hovering over the ocean in the distance—an obstruction labeled as Athena's Grace. It acted as Hawaii's guardian angel. The wall was filled with soldiers ready for anything. Beyond the wall sat an archipelago of islands with beaches as beautiful as Newcastle with a fusion of ancient Roman and Samoan architectures. Along the edges of each island were cabanas, tiki torches, and palm trees. In the islands' interiors, Pantheon-size structures with columns all around. The biggest and most important building was Pandora's Palace. A light-almond building with eleven columns in the front symbolizing our involvement with the Hendecalliance. Wrapped around the columns were vines with ribbons that matched the primary colors to every Majoris planet.

The palace has been regarded as one of the most imposing landmarks on the planet. One reason was the circular skylight over the palace's garden in the main hall. Another came from the shrine behind the palace where a statue of every Terran Shepherd could be seen standing tall. The pond in front of the palace was gorgeous, but we weren't here to admire Earth's most prestigious landmark. We were here for a completely different reason, and that reason became clear after we got off of the jet. The Global Enforced Officers escorted us all the way to the palace. We felt like prisoners in the awkward silence. Gabriella gave one of the officers a death stare, again reminding me to never get on her bad side.

Considering it was my first time at the palace, I welcomed the sight of the more ballistically armored GEOs. It was flattering more than intimidating. An arsenal like this was generally flexed towards the most dangerous people in the galaxy. The palace housed fewer soldiers. The roof stretched ten-stories high with paintings that told stories of their own. Some about love and others about war—a war that could occur depending on how the top-sixteen racers were split for the Summer week. A fountain lay at the center of the garden beneath the skylight with a view of the small stage with a podium at the end of the main hall. Near the fountain, the hounds flipped coins into the water, hoping for a safe championship week. Meta started flicking the coins into the fountain, creating a pattern across the water. Kira, next to her love, didn't know how to properly master the technique causing Beta to come to her aid. The hound grew close to her from behind, grasping her arm, motioning the right way for the proper flick of the wrist. The romantic sight attracted a group of photographers, ruining the romantic moment. I noticed the other racers in here with us. Attracting a faction of GEOs was Law in the far corner of the room, staying away from Midas who couldn't wait to see us.

"What the fuck is your problem?" Midas asked, walking up to his sister. "Do you have any idea how neck deep up shit creek we are?"

"How are you in trouble?" she asked, confused.

"I'm the older brother who should be keeping you on a damn leash!" he said, sounding more like his father. Gabriella yanked him closer by his golden tie.

"Say something else, I dare ya," she challenged. "You have no idea how much I've done for you out of love. I built this golden pedestal for you, and can knock you off it whenever I please, so I'm advising you to leave it behind. It might just save your life."

"It's not my life that needs saving," he stated, snatching her arm off of his tie. "Dad's been on my ass since your headline and has given me the green light to Orin your ass."

"Orin me? Are you even listening to yourself? You're turning into the man you swore never to be."

"There's a lot of things I never wanted to be, but who's fault is that? Who taught me everything I know about this sport? Who gave me the EMP? Who's really responsible for Orin's death? Who's responsible for the outlaw barking bullets at my ass?" Midas questioned, backing his sister into a mental corner. Like a Gigallian clashing with an ant, Gabriella was outmatched and, for the first time, tears glistened at the edge of her eye. He continued to pummel her before I finally intervened, unable to bear anymore. He gave me a devilish stare that he and his sister genetically shared. "There's no happy ending to this love story."

"For your sake, you better pray for one," I calmly stated, moving inches away from his face. Several photographer's cameras flashed for the money shot. We pulled away from each other when we noticed the crowd of bewildered racers watching. Among them was a lonesome Law enjoying the show. We pushed Midas away, resolving the tension suffocating Gabriella. She kept her composure, but that didn't stop me from giving her a reassuring kiss on the forehead. The hounds and Kira came over to us, and I introduced them to Gabriella. I remembered the story she told me on Newcastle's beach. I wanted to prove that we went there for us, for a new beginning. Allies came with those beginnings. It was also great to see the two smartest women I knew actually talk Versa with one another. Kira was interested in the x-ray component of her suit. Meta, well…he was asking for a signature on a picture he had of her in the black bikini as Miss Earth. That sparked an argument between the two hounds as Beta attempted to jump to my girlfriend's aid, claiming that she was Krueger, not Miss Earth. That was true, but a fire brewed between the two, creating a new sibling clash within the palace. *The Breckenridge Bout*, the headlines usually read, and as of right now, it was the follow-up to *The Golden Grudge*.

Saving us from any more arguments, Pandora called for everyone's attention. All lenses turned to her for the conference. She stood in front of the podium. Behind her stood a muscular light-skinned man with a short beard, buzz-cut face, and a linear scar running diagonally across his face from the left side of the forehead to the right groove of his jaw. Beside him, a platoon of Lynches armored in *Freya's* gray 2240 Wraiths with a peace symbol on their pectars made of a dried sacramento-green substance. Adding to their presentations were black hooding helmets with sacramento-eyed visors and pointed tops. The Lynch specimens came from the planet Legios and were only used in extreme circumstances to administer peace and, by the looks of the spiky black-armored waist capes on their Terranoid exosuits, they would be doing more than that. In person, they looked like Terrans in an armored costume. But were they?

"Hello and thank you for coming on such short notice. I apologize to the racers who qualified last night. I'm aware of the rest you need, so I'll try and make this brief," she opened, going into detail about the overview of this series as a virtual screen above the fountain projected footage of the previous races. She mentioned the highs involving Midas' dominance of the series opener, my comeback performance on Everest, and the Carnivore sweep this past week leading to the lows regarding the events at K2, Brazil, and Sydney. Blood covered the footage, cueing the light-skinned man to step forward for introductions. His name—Commander Cage. His goal—to lead his extraterrestrial task force provided by the Shepherd of Legios, Kane, to oversee the peace in our remaining races. He also had the power to extradite anyone responsible for another homicide directly to Legios for justice.

"The measures I've taken to prevent more deaths may be drastic, but are necessary," Pandora explained while her and Cage eyed Gabriella. "The activists are only getting stronger as a result of the deaths in the Pro League, and I refuse to let them flourish. Killings are not appreciated in the series anymore. I repeat, killings are not allowed."

"WE WANT BLOOD!" the hammerhead screamed to the pounding strike of reliQ's guitar.

"AYMEN!" Law added to anger the Shepherd.

"If you wish a fate worse than death, be my guest," Pandora countered, leering at each of the bloodthirsty individuals. Our Shepherd certainly was intimidating as she stared down and silenced every Carnivore. "Now that we understand one another, I guess it is time for you to learn where you will be competing." Following her announcement were the line-ups for the championship week of Four Seasons, separating the qualified racers into the four expected quadrants reading.

WATER
"Battaglia D'acqua"
Venice, Italy

- Lawson "Law" Pierce
- Meta Breckenridge
- Amir "Cobra" Al-Otaibi
- Hotaru Fukumaru

FIRE
"Scorched Earth"
Blackstone, America

- Midas Gold
- Gabriella "Krueger" Gold
- Krakyn Avenya
- Ferra D'Angelo

EARTH
"Knievel"
Grand Canyon, America

- Warlock Neit
- Credo "Creed" Velasquez
- reliQ "Titan" Qalmantine
- Lucretia "Lucifer" Xiagra

WIND
"Ad Infinitum"
Solitude, America

- Craven McGuire
- Kira Brink
- Beta Breckenridge
- Zane Maddox

There it was, set in stone, a line-up that would've given Thardus Leone a mindgasm of ratings, of expectations, of headliners. In the Earth Quadrant, my favorite band of war-ready allies against The Anthem of Hell. The crazy thing was that I had just come up with that nickname on the spot. I didn't know what Gabriella called reliQ and Lucifer, but I was using The Anthem of Hell. It had a nice ring to it. I would have to run it by Gabriella someday if this week worked out for copyrights. Aside from my impressive nickname, I had faith in Warlock and Creed. The Grand Canyon track was called Knievel for a reason. It required a racer to land an extreme leap across the canyon, something I highly doubted the Gigallian could pull off, leaving the Satanian as Warlock and Creed's biggest obstacle. Law's race, on the other hand, seemed to have no obstacles: two nobodies, and a lonesome hound. The Pro League Committee couldn't have given the bloodthirsty avenger a better path to the Finals. That left Gabriella's match up with her brother as the most vital. If anyone was going to stop Midas, it was her. She said it herself, she was his creator, therefore his destroyer. She no longer appeared vulnerable to the emotion. Midas seemed troubled as he made his way out of the palace. The green light from his father seemed more like a ruse than a promise.

"Sonuvabitch!" Meta shouted, appalled, realizing his brother was absent for this week. "The ol' divide and conquer scheme, they weren't ready for us bro."

"You two had a good run," Kira added.

Even Beta had to step away to his brother's side.

"Good run?" he then questioned.

"Are we really doing this?" she responded.

"They ain't ready for us," Beta restated, side-hugging his twin. Distracted by the debate, I barely noticed Law rushing over to the entrance. He had a golden revolver cloaked within his poncho and his silver eyes aimed at The Golden Scion, still not yet out of the palace. Aware of his intent, the GEOs stood by to let the aboriginal decide his fate. I intercepted the outlaw, quickly grasping his burnt arm before he could pull it into the light for a killshot.

"The fuck ya doin, mate?" he growled.

"Rethink it," I insisted. Midas approached the staircase, narrowing Law's opportunity.

"What if that was Thorax, huh? Wouldya make the same choice then?" he questioned, attempting to trigger the rage within me. The statement caught Gabriella's attention. Law took off his hat and stared directly at me. "Ya look may in the eyes and tell may ya makin the same choice."

"Fine, you're not wrong, but the timing is. Did you not hear anything Pandora said. You'll be given a fate worse than death."

"I'm already dead, mate. The series, the movement, there's no turnin back. I'm one man wit a billion bullets," he concluded, snatching his arm out of my grip. He made his way to the same staircase as Midas, but chose to keep the gun covered and headed in a different direction.

Gabriella reached my side. I killed any worrisome thoughts she had with an assuring smile. I then took a glance at the line-up in my quadrant. Solitude, the metal city inside a dome protecting it from the infinite number of tornadoes generated by a supervolcano in the past. Since the eruption, tornadoes had constantly roamed the southern areas of North America, an area nicknamed Fujita's Province. Ad Infinitum was the perfect name for a windy environment. It wasn't capitalized as in my dream's scripture, but the fact that I was not the only bird soaring the asphalt meant something. Joining Kira, Beta, and I was The Raven himself. Gabriella remembered his importance to my dream as she watched him headed for an exit. Gabriella taking on Zane for a race, that was something I wished I could dream about. That thought was short-lived as the pack of Lynches suddenly circled the two of us. In their Wraiths, they maintained silence, their visors hiding what could be hollow interiors. The commander himself entered the circle, stretching a grin across his scarred face.

"Halt!" Cage ordered. The Lynches puffed up their chests and locked their hands together behind their bodies. They raised their chins and visors toward their commander. Gabriella was unimpressed by the show of power. She matched their cold stares with one of her own as the remaining Carnivores walked past, briefly glancing at our situation while heading to an exit. "Mr. McGuire, the Shepherd awaits your grace at the garden."

"We're already at one," Gabriella asserted.

Cage grinned. "Not this one," he declared. "The one out back."

"Then lead the way," she demanded, attempting to leave the circle only to be stopped by the Lynches.

"Not you, sweetheart," Cage added, glancing at me. "She only wants to see McGuire."

"Like hell she does," Gabriella challenged. I gave her a reassuring smile and told her to wait with our friends at the fountain. I gave her another kiss before Cage could lead the way to the garden out back.

As seen on the flight here, the garden was massive and designed to resemble a city. There were towering bushes mixed with red oak bridges over a few small ponds. At the center of the garden was the Shrine of Shepherds. Earth had had ten Shepherds, but the most notable three had been: Bishop Graves, Adam Wreath, and Mathis Newman.

Bishop Graves' statue stood tall and strong like the Lynches did in the circle. He was decoratively suited in Earth's green and blue, his infamously chapped lips always pressed together. Like Cage, he had a scar running down the right side of his face partially covered with an eye patch. Bishop may have been the first Shepherd from 2055 to 2075, but he was relentless. He taught us never to declare a war veteran as Shepherd. Bishop's major emphasis was Earth's defense against the dangers of the galaxy, He constructed an alliance with the Wardens of Legios, an alliance Pandora was currently using to her advantage. But Bishop didn't care much about the internal affairs of the United Countries which created a few civil wars during his stay at the palace.

Adam Wreath, on the other hand, utilized his internal connections, creating many links with the people of Earth. His statue wasn't as tall nor as strong as Bishop's, mainly because Adam was a paraplegic from the injuries sustained in his final race within the sport of Versa. Some called him The Cardinal, others, The 1,2,3 Punch. He was the first Terran to get a kill in Galactica, the second to be elected as Shepherd—2075-2095, and the third to be inducted into Unica's Land of Fame. Decorated in different ways, he taught us to never declare a Versa racer as Shepherd. Mainly because he placed too much emphasis on the sport, pioneering the Wreath-based series around the planet to determine our best killers. Even so, he and his fellow Terrans were horribly outmatched during Earth's first Galactica appearance.

Mathis Newman didn't come into the picture until 2135 as the fifth Shepherd, teaching us to never vote for an entrepreneur from Wall Street. Mathis provided the right funds within the Hendecalliance on top of paying off every debt Earth had with Crystia's currency exchange. The problem didn't occur until 2155, the year Mathis grew stubborn as Shepherd. Unfortunately, he attempted to alter the Absolution Act before the summer solstice elections. Mathis spent most of his term growing lustful of the power, attempting to buy another 20-year-term—an act that would lead to his point-blank assassination by a Terran named Connor Mccoy. Mathis was the first and only Shepherd to be assassinated. The history books told us that Connor was sent to Legios to carry out an eternity-long sentence, whatever that meant. Mathis didn't die in vain, though. No, he was the reason why Luke Gold would never be a Shepherd, no matter how rich he was.

Still writing her own history lesson was Pandora Winfrey, acting as the tenth Shepherd and the first female to hold the palace. As Terrans, we hadn't decided whether or not a female should be added to the list of never-agains, but I thought she had been a fair leader to this point. Her philanthropic background had a certain appeal to the Minoris planets, she acknowledged the alliance's common ground, Versa hadn't gone unnoticed, and her emphasis on Earth's defense with the creation of Athena's Grace had made her the best of all worlds. Like her statue within the shrine, she awaited a knight, smiling when she first saw me. I crossed the circular stone floor shining with the colors of sunset as Cage left us alone.

"I believe this is the first time we've met," she confirmed, her purple lipstick glittering in the low sun. "Being a fan of a McGuire has been something I've become accustomed to over the years, but if we're being honest, misery loves your company, and I am not a fan of misery."

"Trust me, I ain't a fan either," I stated.

"Great. Now let's fix it. Let's take care of said misery," she proposed.

"How?"

"The Golds," she answered. Meta said it best, *divide and conquer.* Separate me from the heart and convince me to drive a stake through it. "As the Shepherd, it's my job to be a target for others to throw their problems at whenever shit hits the fan. As the Shepherd, it's also my job to uncover what slithers behind these problems. The recurring pattern has been the golden snake. The Golds are the issue and can be given a one-way ticket straight to Legios with the proper evidence."

"I'm with you to an extent, but you're saying this problem as plural," I replied. She took a deep breath, sensing the direction of this conversation. "Midas, Catherine, Gabriella, they are not the problem."

"The Full Metal Jackets, Midas' problem. The Re-Versables, Krueger's problem," she said. "But that's the thing, Krueger has recently been identified as Gabriella."

"Have you ever been in love?" I quickly asked.

"This isn't about love, Craven."

"It is because I've loved and lost my father. I'm in love again, and I can't lose again." I wasn't trying to make Pandora my enemy, and if I were in anyone else's shoes, I honestly wouldn't have thought twice about her offer. But that was the misconception about the Golds. The problem was the head of the snake, not the body.

"One life, Craven. She is just one life. Midas is just one life. Taking care of the Golds can save millions, or are you blind to the riots that happened on the streets of Sydney. Have you forgotten about the alleged bounty Luke was prepared to place on your head, a bounty that caused two racers to kill nineteen innocents," Pandora reminded in a rage.

"I haven't forgotten," I quickly responded. "I love her, and she loves Midas. They stay out of this deal. As for Luke, there's no love lost."

"You're in no position to make demands," Pandora stated.

"Then this conversation is done." I stared at the stone floors in disappointment. I could have had a powerful friend. As soon as she realized I wasn't folding, she made her way to an exit before briefly stopping to apologize about her absence at my father's funeral, making the claim that everyone else made about him and I looking alike. Then she left me in peace.

I thought about following her back to the palace, and then remembered the message on the Joker in my dream. It mentioned meeting someone in the garden, and I highly doubted that someone was Pandora. A sylonzer suddenly bubbled around me, and both Harley and Harlene Quinn, with knives at hand, cartwheeled out of the bushes. I had no weapon or friend to defend myself with, no moves in my arsenal as the Quinns entered the bubble, pointing their blades not at me, but at the statue of Shepherds to my back. There was no way I was going to turn my back to them, which caused them both to drop their blades, initiating peace.

"They're not gonna harm ya," a man announced from behind. He had a familiar accent which made me finally turn around to the smiling sight of JoKer in his conventionally purple vest top with hands pressed onto the grip of a cane. "So, tell me Craven, how have your dreams been lately?"

ACT IV
CHAPTER 3

IN FOOLS
WE TRUST

THIS HAD TO BE A JOKE FROM A JOKESTER. THERE WASN'T A SPECIMEN IN THE GALAXY, I THOUGHT, WHO CAN ENTER OR CONTROL ANOTHER'S DREAM. The idea was stranger and scarier than my Xenner roots. The silence within the sylonzer didn't help, either, but merely enhanced the awkwardness. The impatient JoKer steadily limped his way towards me.

"No words? No questions?" he asked, gesturing the Quinns away with a wink.

"How?" I finally replied.

"It's funny that you ask how," he began, limping around the sylonzer's inner perimeter. "I've waited weeks to tell you my story and couldn't. Not until today, because today is the day where you're more open to the impossible."

"I'm here, aren't I?"

"You are, but today's the day you realize we're one in the same," he stated while dropping his cane. With a series of convulsive cracks in his spine, his posture became more hunched as he dropped to his knees. "One hundred percent Terran becomes the dream, the false truth."

"You're a Xenner too?" I questioned, rushing to his aid. Parts of his teeth began to fall onto the stones, causing his cheeks to deflate. Joseph's horrifying true identity. An identity that would've sent me in another direction the week before. I realized that his third eye allowed him to choose this day specifically. More potent than Claire Voyant's gift, this man could tell time, he could see events that hadn't happened yet. And somehow, he could extend his presence into another's subconscious. Like a parent watching their kid solve a jigsaw puzzle, JoKer allowed me some time to puzzle out most of the questions. He then pulled his left sleeve back to reveal a weird wristband with five buttons schematically designed into an "X" with the largest purple button at the center. He pressed down on the button, which caused his spine to convulse again. The device within the vest restored his posture to normal. I picked up the cane and handed to him, only for it to be pushed away. JoKer then got to his feet and reached into his pocket for a pair of dentures. Once again, he was the JoKer I'd grown accustomed to seeing.

"How about that for a magic trick," he announced.

"How did you...?" I questioned, shocked by his metamorphosis.

"A magician never reveals their secrets," he replied, retrieving the cane from my hands. "For you, I'll make an exception. It's a vise handcrafted by Primax. It's the reason why I acquired the Rokian. Without him, I'm as crippled as Shepherd Wreath."

"Where is he now?" I asked, remembering the killings at Sydney. Most believed that it was carried out by the Rokian, not Gabriella.

"He's been banished from Earth. It's the reason why I'm here. I had to negotiate the Rokian's future, repayment for him keeping my background a secret," he explained, going into details about how the Rokian was now on a much more crucial path that may be a problem for our planet in the future.

"If you're a Xenobred who can see the future and enter someone else's dreams, then what's your mix?" I inquired, mentally scanning through all of the books in my father's library. The curiosity stopped JoKer in his place, and he flashed a smile.

"Story for a different day, yeah?" he said. "Last time I checked, a raven was a bigger problem."

"Is he my executioner?" I asked, gulping at the notion.

"At the moment, yes, but that doesn't mean it can't change. That choice is up to you," he explained.

"How do you know for sure?" I questioned.

"The dreams aren't good enough?"

"I'm still not sold. Make me a believer," I tossed back at him for a laugh.

"You're a tough nut, you know," he remarked, pointing his finger at me.

"Well, you should know."

"You're right, I know a lot of things about Craven Joseph McGuire. I know that he owns a workshop called *The Blueprint*, no, *The Blue Jay's Nest*," he revealed, continuing to pace circles around me. "You picked the name because it was merely a blueprint without a creator."

"I-I-I've never told anyone that," I stuttered.

"Just like you haven't told Gabriella your amazing nickname for Loosh and Titan," he added, sinking my heart further into my stomach. "The Anthem of Hell, right? You were thinking about running it by Gabriella, yeah? I wouldn't. She's recently coined the nickname for Krueger's chant."

"Timeout!" I demanded, stopping Kershaw. I turned around to see the startled expression on his face. "You're revealing these things without explaining how you can do them."

"You're right, I got carried away," he softly spoke. "Your iris, to almost everyone in the galaxy, it is merely a color, but to my breed, it's a gateway. The second we lock irises, it is my job to remember the coding it gives me. The minute I access it, well, we become one and the same. I live your life, while you're still frozen in yours. Like the coasters at Limitless, I sit back and enjoy the show... until I reach the cliff."

"So, you know my next move before I make it?" I questioned.

"Yes, with the exception of today. We're on a new path, you see," he answered, relieving some of the tension.

"And the cliff?"

"The cliff is death, Craven," he revealed, renewing the tension. "Death is something I refer to as a cliff because I cannot witness one's death. It'll take my life, too, or at least that's what the research suggests."

"So, you can sense my death, but you can't witness it?"

"Correct, but that doesn't mean we can't change it. Whenever I enter another's iris, I am merely a spectator. I am not the director, which is why I've taken the liberty of opening up to you," he explained. I finally understood the importance of this meeting. He was trying to prevent my imminent death—one I could never foresee; hidden by the hot streak I'd been on as of late in the races.

"Does this meeting save my life?" I finally asked.

"Well, this week is the cliff. And it's all about you walking out alive at Solitude, do you understand?" he asked as the Quinns began to return to the sylonzer. JoKer frowned. "Looks like our time is running out." The Quinns then reclaimed the sylonzer, allowing me once again to hear the sounds of birds chirping in the ponds, of winds pushing through the bushes, of people laughing on the palace's streets. JoKer's cane began to tap each stone as he made his way to an exit.

"Wait!" I cried. "What about Gabriella's race? Isn't it more important than mine?"

"Possibly."

"Is there a cliff at Blackstone?"

"Yes, but if I told you who, wouldn't it affect yours?" he queried, now leaving the shrine with the Quinns. His last words left me shaken. Death was making reservations for Blackstone Park, a race where both Golds would be present. Before I could think it through, Gabriella walked to my side.

"Is everything alright? I saw both Cage and the Shepherd come back without you," she said, a bit winded. Part of me wanted to discuss Blackstone, but JoKer said it himself. Things could change for the better, or even the worse. I didn't have a coin this time around, so the decision was a game-time one.

"Pandora, she…she had a lot to say about my father," I began, improvising a lie. "It just made me realize how much I miss him."

"He may not have been my father, but I miss him, too," she said, comforting me with a strong hug. I wanted it to last forever. Hell, I wanted us to be back at Newcastle. I didn't want this to be the last time I could touch her silky hair or smell the raspberry fragrance. JoKer left me with a lot of questions, but only one answer. I now knew what it was like to be in his shoes. I was now a spectator to the Gold's future at Blackstone Park—an appropriate setting to torch our hearts.

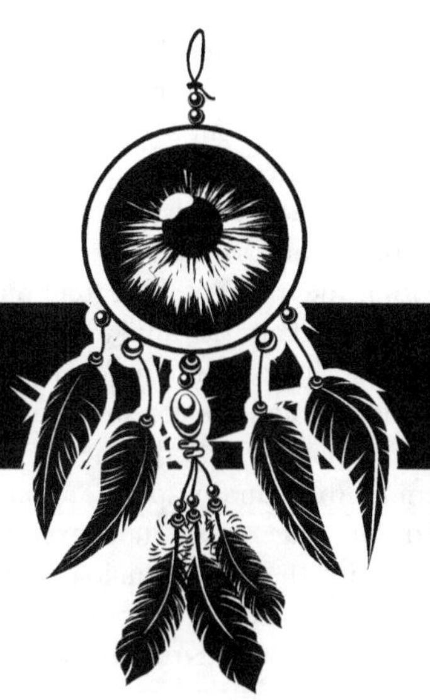

THE MERCY
TO MY...

BLACKSTONE PARK, THE FINAL DESTINATION FIT FOR THE GOLDEN SCION, THE END OF THEIR GOLDEN LINE. It only seemed fitting that it'd be him squared up against his creator, his destroyer, while giving him an opportunity to fight for his future in a sure-to-be great race. The golden bloodline had never been a weak one, with evidence to prove it, but it was the false strength that had corrupted us—the same attribute that had morphed my loving brother into our spiteful father. I never wanted him to turn into the monster he swore never to be and, at the same time, I'd created a monstrous image of my own, destroying Earth's belle of the decade. I was still unsure of how costly the move had become, especially because of how shaken Craven seemed back at the Shrine of Shepherds. His meeting with Pandora seemed to leave him more threatened than reassured. There was something that he wasn't telling me, a feeling similar to the one I gave him prior to Claire's revelation. If there was something he had to hide, he obviously was doing it out of love, which was why I was choosing to trust this path instead of pressing for the truth.

The path was an eerie one, a lonely one. The flight to Blackstone turned darker the minute the jet flew over America's soil. Like the pollution in the oceans our Pyscean cultures had fought so hard to cleanse over the years, the clouds over the lava fields overshadowed the Satanian colours. Yellowstone was what we used to call this land. The eruptions of the early 21st Century changed everything. What was once called Los Angeles, Phoenix, Salt Lake City, Denver, and Boise was now a land of ash, obsidian, and magma. The only surviving metropolis had been Volador Vegas, but that was only because it grew wings, flying high above the hell that should've encapsulated it. That was all it took, right? Just a pair of wings. By no means was I a God-fearing woman, but I prayed to whoever was listening that another pair of wings were gracefully stitched onto Lawson's back. He hadn't deserved the life my family gave him. He was currently flexing the flames of hell throughout his race in Venice. Battaglia D'acqua was the track's name, translated from the Italian to *The Battle of Water*, and ironically, this race was anything but. Law was vaporizing the rivers with bullets, annihilating the high hopes of his competitors. A Meta without a Beta, the thought of their disadvantage may have been more depressing than my autographed picture in his locker. The upside was that he currently held first place. As for securing the lead, Law was treating the half-less hound like the leftover crumbs on his silver platter, constantly toying with the mutt until he had him within the grasp of his rarely unspiked lasso, or in this case, leash. Law strangled Meta's carotid arteries until the twin was unconscious, leaving the door open for a flawless victory. Icing on the untouched cake was Law's disfiguration of *Ion's* coverboy, Hotaru, and Arabia's prince, Amir. Law didn't even break a sweat, let alone a smile as he stood victorious. He stayed stone silent, staring each of his followers in the eyes, signalling them to fire rounds into the cotton clouds. The bullets flew into the sky until Lawson eyed the image on the hovertron promoting the next race, my race. He and his followers turned their aim to unload at Midas' image.

I shut off the tellies, wishing I had Craven, or even my iCube right now. Like Meta, I was alone and back to my original ways, Krueger's ways. I shouldn't have been scared because I was in love, I should have been driven by the new future Krueger and I were willing to create. With an avenging Law hopscotching his way to Oz, all eyes and spotlights were on Blackstone Park, and Krueger and I were now more than ready. My attitude changed along with the altitude, finally landing at the northern entrance of the Scorched Earth track in Montana—not nearly as packed as the other airports, nor as big. Similar to Salt Ash, there was nothing but grassland, but it was more grey than green with a single charcoal road leading to more desolation in each direction. But I wasn't here for desolation. I was here for destruction, therefore my path led south into the volcanic heart of the park.

I rented an ancient Jeep—possibly the only automobile capable of getting me to the starting line. There were no hover components capable of surviving the extreme temperatures. They even had Jeeps specified with each racer's colours, my colours, black and red lying in its sedentary position, waiting for The Clawed Cardiac. Was that even my nickname anymore? I continued to question it as I entered the Jeep. The answer was emblazoned on my locker's doorway. The thought of using an actual locker rattled my mind. It would be the first time, and there was no turning back considering the Committee had acquired my exosuit back at Sydney. But that was the problem. It was the only suit I'd ever made, and it was as foreign to this environment as Nito. There was no way either of them would survive the molten conditions now throwing up curtains of magma in the distance. Mount Vulcan was the name of the undead volcano, always oozing its pyromancy. To Law and I, it was Orin's necropolis—a man I feared I would see within the belly of the beast. I hadn't seen him since K2 and could only plead for forgiveness when we met again. Today had to be the day where his story arc came full circle, where he could finally rest in peace, saving both him and his brother's tainted spirit.

As expected, the temperatures rose the closer I got to Mount Vulcan, making me thankful for the windowless Jeep in my possession. The humid winds brushed through my hair, drying it out. I had no choice but to remove my jacket, setting it in the passenger seat. I questioned my choice of black skinny jeans. At least I had on a Dri-Fit tank top, sports bra, and underwear. It made the dense air more bearable, but I would have to strip out of them when I entered my suit or else I would be baked alive. It also meant that I would have to protect my pectars or else Krueger's image would become more erotic than exotic. Maybe Craven would forgive me for the exposure if it came to that.

Bishop's Arch, a historical landmark, could be seen in the distance as the road ascended into a bridge over the black-and-orange ocean of lava fields scattered below. The arch itself was a notable one as it was Scorched Earth's starting line, standing tall between a pair of two-story buildings acting as our lockers. Outside, the Lynches stood as security with a few drones broadcasting the live footage. Past the arch on the horizon was a teary Mount Vulcan, flashing streams of lava down its cheeks, somehow missing the track's entrance into the cavern. Parked outside of the left locker were Jeeps painted in the colours of Midy and Ferra, a young 16-year-old from Italy who had no idea what was in store for her today. She would've had more success back at home against Law. If she got in Krueger's way, I would not show mercy to the young. Spade Amaryllis could vouch for me. If he were here, he would probably be at Krakyn's side, pleading for restitution.

The hammerhead himself actually shared the same building with me, I noticed as I read the sign on the large navy-blue Gigallian-sized dune buggy parked outside of the right building. The Lynches were kind enough to lead the way inside, guiding me to a locker room larger than the Utzon's with more workbenches than lava lakes here at Blackstone. Surprised to have the luxury, I quickly rushed to my suit stuck on a wall at the far side and sandwiched by a pair of windows displaying the furnace of bubbling lava fields. Lucifer would've killed for this view. I was sure Krakyn was killing himself over it in his locker one floor above mine. I was almost positive that the water veins in his suit were evaporating, a major disadvantage Krueger would definitely manipulate. But I was not Krueger, not yet at least. I had more than enough time to get into character for our next big act, a culminating one. Initiating my transformation, I tossed the suit onto a workbench just as I spotted the beautiful woman standing at the locker's doorway.

"Hey, Gabby," the woman softly spoke, stepping into the locker with a very large briefcase rolling beside her. Of all the people in the world, my mother was the last I expected to see. She might as well have been a disco ball from the amount of jewelry she wore. Her shyre tank top matched the slim white pants and shyre heels.

"What are you doing here?" I asked, running over to her side.

"Could you...?" she gently asked, aiming her eyes at the briefcase and then over at the closest workbench. On the side of the heavy casing were the latches connected to a hand-recognition padding serving as the key. "I'm here to make things right again."

"Make things right?" I questioned, connecting the padding's size to my mother's hand. "You're here to make another deal, aren't ya?"

"Wow, you never cease to amaze me. You are definitely much smarter than your father," she complimented. "Nito told me that you're in need for a much better suit capable of sparring with a volcano. His words, not mine."

"Clearly," I chuckled.

"The main problem is that he can't survive in Blackstone…"

"And you can, so what's the catch?"

"Krueger's death," she revealed, pulling me over to the windows. She didn't understand that there was no way I could kill Krueger, not after all we'd been through, after all we'd accomplished. "I want my children to love each other again."

"I've never stopped loving Midy," I stated, quickly glancing back at her.

"Then why the separation? Why do you two seem so far away?" she asked before her jade mascara crept down her cheek.

"Orin," I answered. She nodded, proving that she already knew the answer. This meeting was merely confirmation. She knew how pissed I was that day two years ago. I never thought that Midy's actions would take the life of another and only had myself to blame. That was why I had to fix it.

"One race, a race that kills the demon within your brother, and a race that kills the demon within yourself," she proposed, slowly walking up to grab my hands. "I could care less about what happens to your father and I, but as for you and Midas, I can't imagine, no, I refuse to imagine a future where you're not by each other's side."

"I can't either," I admitted, attempting to hold back my own set of tears.

"Then let me hear you say it, let me hear you promise. After today, Krueger stays dead," she finally insisted with a tight grip around my hands. Her eyes caught mine, now able to see through all of the rubbish. If I lied right now, she would know. My palms began to sweat. I was trapped, and there was no other way I was going to beat Midy unless I had the acclimated suit in her casing.

"I promise… that Krueger dies… after this week," I hesitantly answered, forcing her to retreat back to the suit. "Wait!"

"One race Gabby!" she declared, grasping onto the casing's handle.

"But if I win today, I'll be required to compete at the Finals, or else the runner-up to today's race will substitute, which could be Midy," I explained.

She loosened her grip.

"Why does it matter?"

"Because it's the only way we save him," I replied. She didn't need to know the whole truth, but at least she knew my plan. "I swear on my life, that I won't compete in another Versa-sponsored race after this series."

"Good, because if you're going to go out…" she started to say, planting her hand into the padding to open the treasure chest, shining its gold rays into the air. "…then you're going to go out like a Gold."

I walked over to the casing, now seeing *Freya's* golden 2250 Demeter, a cooling hypoventilated suit specifically catered to a female, ultimately capable of surviving the harsh volcanic furies to the south. Golden spirits traced across the heavily-coated pectars, the pointy dells, and the smooth scapulars with velvet craters as the tyre holsters. At the moment, the holsters were empty, but I was sure Nito had done that on purpose so I could use my original pair of tyres still attached to the other suit. Continuing the colour scheme were the dark-gold spina, the only armour around the torso as the Demeter lacked abdominises and a large latis where a boost tank labeled as Komodo 2.0 sat. *Thank you Craven.* The only parts of the Demeter that were heavily armoured were the lower extremities where the suit lacked fortitude along the arms, only able to provide dark-gold gauntlets, which had Krueger's exclusive claws. They could only be used if my tyres were detached from the velvet appendisc fixed to the gauntlet's palm, a risky maneuver I was sure I'd have to resort to.

"Nito really outdid himself," I stated, stripping out of my clothes.

"It wasn't Nito, it was me," my mother revealed, smiling. A revelation. "Your father isn't the only genius in the Gold household."

"Of course not," I declared, hesitantly pulling off my tank top. Back in Sydney, I feared doing it in front of Craven for the exact reason I feared doing it now—the markings left on my body from the races. It may have been something that Craven appreciated, but I could clearly sense the opposite reaction brewing within my mother after my pants were off.

"Jesus Christ, Gabby," my mother blurted with hands masking her mouth. I wasn't sure what was more ghastly, the scars of broken ribs from last year, or the laceration on my left hip from last week. Maybe it was the claw marks on my right bosom from the first test run with krone claws.

"I'm sorry," I quietly whispered to myself, but it was loud enough for my mother to hear. She stiffened as she pulled out the lower sections of the Demeter.

"There's no need for apologies, this is what you always wanted, the price you always wanted to bear, bare," she stated, helping me into the Demeter's pants. The frosty inner coating made my butt cheeks clinch. "What's wrong?"

"It's… it's cold," I answered, breathing in and out for the next wave of chills.

"You're supposed to be Greenlandic," she remarked, handing me the upper set of armour more compressed than the Dri-Fit sports bra I had on prior. It was times like this when I hated having breasts. They always pressed inward like a bear hug around the heart. At first, I was incapable of breathing correctly, but the Demeter automatically adjusted it's armour, becoming a little more expansive and bearable for my figure. Once my mother could see how cosy I was, she attached the spine from the scapular all the way down to the hip threxis. I could feel the long metal strip attaching itself to the lumbar sections of my skin, causing my actual spine to gently crack from the chiropractic adjustment. With most of the suit now on, I took the custom tyres from my original, connecting them to the holsters, but realizing there were no magnetic pathways that could transfer down to my hands. The only way they could become attached to my gauntlets was if I manually planted my hands into the back of my neck, initiating magnetic attraction. The unfamiliar maneuver was one I had to practice while my mother pulled out the last piece to the Demeter, the specialized helmet designed as a gas mask with a dark-tinted visor transparent enough to reveal my multi-coloured eyes.

"Is there a reason why the visors are this transparent?" I asked.

"Yes," my mother quickly replied, pulling out a small capsule from her pocket, extracting a pair of contacts from inside. "To make you Miss Earth. I thought it was in your best interest to cover the red eye with a blue one. Now I think it's in your best interest to cover the blue eye with a red one." I quickly claimed the surprising gift, almost poking my eye out while covering my blue iris. I rushed over to the mirror once the new lens was on, now seeing the red-eyed racer looking back at me. My mother walked to my side and stared at the bruises on my stomach. She grabbed some makeup supplies from the casing, disguising the scars so the other racers might ignore them.

"How do I look?" I asked her.

"Like the most beautiful badass to ever live," she answered, gently lying a kiss on my cheek before I could place the gas mask on. The red eyes lasered through the visor. Attempting to ignore the sinister appearance in the mirror, I skimmed through some of the controls to the suit within the mask, unveiling the new attribute to my claws. They were now bluetooth.

"Midy doesn't know what's coming," I muttered to myself, embracing the new identity of the nightmare named Krueger.

The Initiator entered my locker, letting us know that the race was about to begin. Outside, the Lynches boarded a chopper to act as the eyes in the sky this time around. Not all of them were in the aircraft, though. A trio stayed on the track in their exosuits waiting for a signal from the Initiator—a signal that would bring them on all fours, now driving south into the volcano. Flying in that direction, the helicopter took the majority of noise with it until the starting line was more silent than a snowfall night. There were no crowds, no bleachers, no anthems, just a black-stoned arch with a pair of racers beneath it.

In the violet and orange 2250 Tigress was the 16-year-old, Ferra D'Angelo, a talented girl who I was sure wished she were two years older due to the Pro League rules constricting her body. *Tsarina's* Tigress may have been similar to the Demeter armour-wise, but that didn't mean she was as bare. Because of her young age, she was required to have a corium layer beneath her suit in case of a wardrobe malfunction. She was a female minor, and the Pro League would not tolerate any nudity to avoid the ancient 18th Century laws. It was honestly hysterical. A minor getting burnt to death, sure, we can show that to the world. A minor exposing an inch of skin, God have mercy on whoever saw that. At least Ferra was having fun with the rule as the torso section of the corium had violet-and-orange tiger stripes to complement the tiger-head-helmet with smoke vision goggles. The Initiator eventually guided her to the far-left lane.

Next to her in the sleeveless white 2245 Icarus was Midy. The Icarus was the EMP suit I knew he'd bring back to Blackstone. Hinting at the crime he was ready to commit were the black-and-gold lightning strikes multiplying out of the boost tank on his spina, the location of the EMP. If I could get close to him in the race, I could easily destroy it, or I could wait for him to use it so I can see the look on his face when he realized that the Demeter wasn't operated automatically like his. Never in my life had I competed in an automatic, and I never would. Midy's expression would be more priceless than his reaction to Craven surviving Mont Forel, but at the moment, his Guy Fawkes-masked helmet graced me with its vulgar smile. If this was anywhere else, I would have matched his smugness by contracting the lantern's grin of my other suit. As I thought about it, I'd never have an opportunity to do so after this week. I had promised mom, and I plan on keeping it until the day I died if it meant that both her and Midy could be safe and happy. I didn't know how Craven would take it, but it was for the best, I told myself. Everything happened for a reason, right?

Fate not only granted me an opportunity to dethrone my older brother, it granted me the lane directly next to his. In the Semi-finals, points were tossed into the fire, and the lanes themselves lacked any advantage being symmetrically aligned. I wasn't too sure how accepting Midy would be to my presence, but our respectable silence spoke volumes. We chose to stare at the volcano screaming its inferno into the black sky, underscoring the name of this park. The eruptions rumbled the track, throwing us off balance and bringing us down to our suits' patellis. Crashing into the largest Jeep on the track behind us was the hammerhead. Indisputably the unluckiest one here, he released some of his pent-up rage by flipping his Jeep into the air and onto the lava fields. When emotions were high, logic was low, and Krakyn proved it by destroying his only ticket home. He was now stuck in hell, wearing the worst suit a Pyscean could wear in the hottest place on Earth. Even my mother knew better since another model of Krakyn's exosuit lay in the halls of our home. Stepping out of the locker, she could only gasp and chuckle at the Pyscean's poor choice.

The Initiator had to usher her back to one of the Jeeps while pulling Krakyn into the far-right lane next to me. His mouth produced steam instead of saliva, signifying the limited amount of time the Pyscean truly had. His suit trembled from his anxiety, but like any Pro-racer, it all changed once he was on all fours. Sloth-steady Krakyn was shooting the volcano's shining reflection off his visor and onto mine. Our eyes locked for one last time before the Initiator could make his way in front of us for the Fire Quadrant announcement. He readdressed Pandora's words about the Lynches' motives here at Blackstone and forewarned us about any intentional killings. *A fate worse than death* became the recurring statement of the week. He then concluded the spiel by explaining how the starting signal would come from a bright-green firework launched into the sky by one of the Lynches in front of the volcano's entrance. We all nodded as I snatched the tyres from my holsters, planting them firmly into the road surface. Another series of rumbles alerted a more prepared set of racers now eyeing the explosion of lava bursting into the black sky. The magma's potent colours winging across the sky turned green, instinctively pushing my tyres past everyone else for the early lead out of Bishop's Arch.

The crisp feel of first was quickly tainted from a hard hit into my right-rear tyre. My brother's swinging arm made me spin out. My eyes then shifted to the hammerhead boosting out of the archway and into the exposed side of my gut with the blunted-end of his cranium. A near-fatal hit, great enough to raise my body and pound it hard into the ground to crack the lower portions of my rib cage.

An anatomical MRI of my body presented itself onto my visor, revealing a contusion in the ileum of my intestinal tract. Entering late to the party, my nerves sent razor blades into my colon, pushing a stream of blood up my esophagus. Attempting to beat the bloody stream, I detached my left-front tyre and retracted the claws to snatch my mask off, now puking out the buckets of plasma. The hot air turned the red puddles into steam clouding my vision. I could still see the other racers' trail of fumes becoming smaller by the second causing another wave of blood to pour out of my mouth.

"GET UP GABBY!!!" I could hear my mother screaming in the background, creating the first real smile of the day… of the race… of my shining hour.

"Who's Gabby?" I questioned, spitting out one last pint of blood before placing my helmet back on. The name of my former self only brought out more rage. Miss Earth was no more. I was someone else, and it was going to take more than a cheap shot, more than a false promise, to kill Krueger.

ACT IV
CHAPTER 5

WRATH

TO REVIVE MY POTENTIAL IN THIS RACE, I TRIGGERED THE KOMODO, RAISING MY FRONT PAIR OF TYRES INTO THE AIR LIKE A STALLION IN THE KENTUCKY DERBY. I regained my balance by slamming them back onto the ground, demanding more speed from the Demeter. The bright lava veins of lakes at Blackstone became blurry lines in my peripheral as the volcano in front of me grew in size. Unlike most tracks, this race was designed to be a distant one with Mount Vulcan being several klicks away. The only parts of Scorched Earth that were similar to Earth's traditional tracks were the inner sections of the volcano. A close-quartered section I was more than ready for after practicing in Dessnia's cavern. Another obstacle to my comeback in this race was the volcano's stream of lava now slithering its way down onto the cavern's entrance. The time was officially ticking, proving the reliability in the Komodo's durability. I finally saw the racer in third place—Krakyn. The angel of Karma hovered over his spina, creating a few long curves that disrupted his balance while enforcing mine. A couple of body-lengths in front of him was an ongoing dogfight between Ferra and Midas. Lava poured onto the surface of the cavern's entrance which still seemed so far away. Ferra and Midas were fighting for the lead while the clock was ticking before a waterfall of lava could close the entrance.

Aware of my shadow, the Pyscean quickly became a barricade, trying to take up as much of the track as he could. With arms and legs spread out, I saw an opening that revealed the hammerhead's genitals. I took a page out of Burretta's book by whipping my left-front tyre into Krakyn's crotch for the cup check. The hamstrings quickly closed the thigh gap, unintentionally gripping the tyre I tossed, now acting as an anchor, altering the Pyscean's speed. Unable to see how much closer I was getting, Krakyn kept his eyes on the streams of lava creeping down Mount Vulcan. I didn't waste any time with the distracted Pyscean, impaling his gastrolocks with my claws, quickly detaching my other front-wheel tyre to climb up further onto Krakyn's spina.

Now on the Pyscean's back, I saw Ferra and Midas entering the volcano. They were successfully able to beat the waterfall of lava. As for us, we were still a good 400m out.

The intensifying hot liquid made Krakyn brake for dear life, but I countered his life-saving maneuver by hacking his suit in order to trigger the boost. He shouted *What are you doin?* as the lava door quickly closed in. To save myself from the magma, I crawled down the side of his torso until I was sheltered beneath. Once he realized what I was doing, he dropped his weight onto the track to use my body as a brake. The sparks from my screeching spina almost yanked me off his suit before I could hack it again, overriding his scapulars and dells to push us upward. He was officially my umbrella from the lava merely meters away, but there was still a puddle I had to avoid which made me thankful of Krakyn's race of hammerheads. He was my saving grace, I just had to use him correctly. I impaled my clawed-right hand through his jawline in order to pull his head onto the track's surface by arching my back inward. In the nick of time, his hammerhead ploughed through the thick puddles of lava, giving us a golden entry into the heart of the volcano.

The lighting within Mount Vulcan dimmed the further we travelled inside, illuminating the bright-orange liquid oozing from Krakyn's eyeballs. The disfigurement could be seen as the insoluble claws sliced out of his face like butter, causing my body to slide out from underneath Krakyn's melting corpse. His body rammed against the wall and shook the cave before the momentum of my body could come to a complete stop. I noticed two light sources keeping the darkness at bay. The north source was the waterfall of lava at the entrance. The south source came from the remains of Krakyn. The salvageable parts of the Pyscean's body were his legs, but that changed once I got back up to my feet. Even with a gas mask on, I could smell the burnt scales of salmon left on a skillet. If Krakyn was lucky, the cause of death would've been my claws. If not… um… I was sure Karma wasn't that cruel. The stains of blue blood still coated the claws of my left hand so I hoped he didn't suffer for too long.

With one racer down, I began to jog further into the cavern, prepared to overcome anything else within Mount Vulcan. The two sources of light quickly died down the further south I travelled through the volcano where the smoke became more prevalent. The foggy atmosphere triggered the smoke vision in my visor, providing thermal images within the cavern now as green as moss. My vision was then disrupted on the first turn when the visor rebooted. Midas must've finally triggered his electrifying trick. I didn't know whether I should be surprised or disappointed in Midas. Him resorting to the EMP meant that Ferra put on more than just a great fight, she actually scared him. That also meant that he had a straight shot to the finish line.

"What a pity," I muttered to myself, travelling further within the cavern. There were a multitude of corkscrew loops within the volcano that I had to navigate by spider-crawling with the claws, but I had the time to pull it off. There was no action, adrenaline, or close calls. It was just me, time trialling with my tyreless self until I came to a sharp right turn on the leveled track where a body lay, hyperventilating. It was the young talent Ferra, suffocating from the tiger-striped corium around her torso. Her tyres were scattered around her body—something I gladly took as my own as I prepared to exit the volcano.

"Aren't ya forgettin somethin?" a random voice inquired near Ferra's body. The tone was masculine and had an Australian slang. I knew who it was and should've kept driving, but the race was over, and Gabriella's demons weren't going to haunt me. I should do her a favor by killing this ghost once and for all.

"Shouldn't you be dead," I replied through my mask, now on my feet. The ghost of the silver-eyed Orin stood next to Ferra's body. He had on the same caramel corium that matched his clean-shaven skin and long black dreadlocks.

"Ya might have a new look, but ya still Gabriella," Orin stated to test my anger. I made sure that each claw on my hand was expanded before stomping closer. "Ya gonna kill may twice?"

"I'm sure I'll find a way."

"There is a way, Kruega," he said. He then glanced down at Ferra, her breaths so faint. "Save the girl, and I'll fade away."

"You've got a deal if it means shutting your ugly accent up," I answered, severing Ferra's exposed corium to aid her breathing. I then slung her over my dell and carried her out of the volcano.

"Try not tu git her killed," Orin demanded.

"Ferra will be fine," I replied.

"I wasn't talkin about Ferra," he said. I turned around to an empty sight. The ghost of Orin may have been gone, but I couldn't be sure that he was dead. Either way, the silence was priceless, and this tough nut on my dells was the answer. Her body kept sliding off too. Like holding a toddler, my hands had to continuously grip her body which made me contemplate killing her on several occasions. After passing the last turn on the track, I saw the exit to the cavern through the thermal vision. The thought of dropping this girl's weight off my dells inspired me to speed up until the muscles in my legs strained themselves. My legs eventually gave out, but not before she and I were out of the cavern on the southern side of the volcano. A lava-less side, I should add. I gasped for air. To make the recovery process easier, I pulled my helmet off, tossing it at Ferra out of spite. For a 16-year-old, she was heavy, but at least she was safe and suddenly surrounded by a pair of Lynches checking to see if she was alright.

"I'm alright too," I sarcastically shot at them, quickly taming my anger after seeing the racer lying on their back without a helmet several meters ahead. The racer was pretending to be exhausted in his Icarus, quickly pausing his act as the last man alive at the sound of my voice. He eventually tilted his head my way, opening his multi-coloured eyes to the red spiraling in mine. Just like a Mexican-standoff, we knew what each other's next move would be. The question was, who would attempt it first? Echoing his helmet, a smile crept onto my face before I could snatch Ferra's tyres out of my holsters. I leapt onto the track which granted me the lead to a race that should've been over a long time ago. It didn't take long for Midas to catch back up, emptying his boost tank to make an attempt at an attack. He attempted several swings with his front-tyres and missed, causing me to mule-kick his nose with my right-rear tyre. The hit should've broken it, but my legs were still weak and exhausted. He grabbed a hold of my right leg, Midas began to abrade the armour off with his tyres, causing me to push my body into the air for a clockwise corkscrew flip, roundhouse kicking him with my left-rear tyre, freeing the right from his grasp. The tyre's impact to his cranium came close to jarring him off of the track while I crash-landed onto my spina. But like any Pro-racer, we adjusted back onto the groove of the road's surface, ready for round two.

With great control of first place, I followed the track as it dipped into more caverns before rising out of them a second later and onto a small ramp that leapt us into another dip down another cavern. This section repeated itself several times, shifting the leaps more westward at the start and more eastward towards the end until we came to the last straightaway with the finish line a kilometer out. As my eyes locked on our final destination, a tyre impacted the back of my head like a bullet, ricocheting my face off of the road's surface. The hit blurred my vision, but I could still sense the racer passing me to the side, instinctively forcing me to leapfrog onto their back before they were out of jumping range. I planted each claw into Midas' spina, but there was one major problem that I didn't realize until I felt the hot breeze shooting through my curly hair. I didn't have a helmet on, which meant I couldn't hack Midas' exosuit. The armour to Midas' Icarus came alive, magnetically attaching the scapulars and sacrums to my arms while shifting their vastus and femoralis to my legs. It took me a good second to realize his suit was turning inside out and latching itself onto mine, ejecting Midas' vulnerable body onto the track. Growing a mind of its own, the Icarus triggered every gastrolock, braking my body to a complete stop one meter away from the finish line. Here with me were a pack of drones, aiming their feeds at the official line for an undisputed winner. Out of desperation, I extended my clawed hand, but lacked sufficient length to claim first place. Still confused at how Midas pulled this trick off, I glanced back at The Golden Scion limping his way closer. Around his stomach and thighs, sections of his corium had been ripped open by the ejection. A risky move that should've been idiotic, but from the control band around his left wrist, it proved to be dividend. Sprinkling salt on my wounds, he crouched down next to my body, stretching out his control band synched to the Icarus coating the Demeter.

"I thought of the idea myself and forgot to run it past ya during one of your lectures," he began to say, dramatically pausing for the drone's spotlight. "Call it… The Midas Touch." With that statement, Midas sealed the race with one giant step across the finish line. I had played right into his hands and only had myself to blame. I would have made the same mistake even with my helmet on because this was his counter-attack, specified to my hacking maneuvers. For the first time in my short life, I was outplayed. Maybe Gabriella should have played this game, because her lover, Craven McGuire, was now our last hope for the planet's survival.

ACT IV
CHAPTER 6

A TALE OF
FOUR BIRDS

BEING WITH BETA AND KIRA PRESENTLY PRODUCED MORE POSITIVE VIBES THAN NEGATIVE, **EVEN THOUGH THE PLANE RIDE TO DALLAS WAS SILENT.** The bright side was that JoKer's cliff referred to Krakyn even though Gabriella's life seemed pretty dim in the beginning. In the end, her brother came out on top with a cheesy one-liner to capstone his victory. *Call it, The Midas Touch*, were his words for the cameras, for the fans, for Gabriella. The words weren't just cheesy, they were familiar. I recognized them from a folder at his house. If I was not mistaken, he was going to explain the concept. If only I had listened or peeked at his trump card, maybe it would have been Gabriella providing the final statement instead of her brother. Either way, Midas was moving on to the Finals along with another racer who was one step closer to closure. Midas and Law, maybe this was what the racing gods wanted, if there was such a thing. This was the predicament we had to deal with, the truth we tried to avoid, but at least I could use the term, "we." The lovebirds next to me were friends I wouldn't trade for the world. They were definitely a pair of racers I was thankful to be competing against tonight. The same couldn't be said about The Raven standing strong as one of the obstacles in our way. The Unican Network claimed he was already at Solitude. As for us, we were still in a small subway heading to the dome city.

As an inhabitant of the Chicagolands, I could admit to the world that it's nickname, The Windy City, was severely overrated and misconceived. Solitude was the real windy city as it could only be entered from underground. The dome to the metal city stayed closed until races were in progress, hiding the city from the immortal twisters battering against the perimeter—arguably the biggest challenge to a track that none of us were familiar with. The lovebirds had only heard stories about the city and how it was primarily used for a Wreath-based series with the exception of today. As for me, I had only seen pictures of the dome city, fascinated by its unique construction. The dome's peak reached up to 1000' with a latitudinal ring every 100' for retraction. This fully opened the dome until there was nothing left but a sturdy 100-foot wall to keep the racers within. Never in my wildest nightmares did I imagine competing here, but again, at least it was against Kira and Beta.

"Soooo…" Beta began, getting our attention. "With Gabriella eliminated…"

"Beta!" Kira interrupted, mistaking my blank expression for an angered one.

"What, too soon?" he questioned, receiving a punch from Miss Brink while the subway began to rumble. The staff attendant at the Dallas station had forewarned us about the quakes. It meant that we were entering Fujita's Province with Solitude only a dozen klicks out.

"With Gabriella eliminated, one of us has to win… at all costs," I stated. The hound sighed, aware of the stakes. I was sure that he was going to play a heavy hand tonight. He might not have had his brother, but he had the next best thing, his lover, who now had her arms around his waist from behind.

"That someone is you," Kira declared.

"Yeah, Kira and I discussed it while you were sleeping on the plane ride here," Beta said. "Without Meta, I can't excel."

"And I almost died at Everest," Kira reminded me, causing Beta to tightly grip her hands.

"What we're trying to say is that it's all you, Mr. Knightfall," Beta said, stripping away the tension I usually stored for big races. "But after you're done saving Midas and the world, you owe me a championship."

"Me too," Kira added, laying a kiss on Beta's cheek.

"After today, I'll send you lovebirds to a beach on Pasydanya, how does that sound?"

"Sounds like a deal," Beta quickly replied while the lights to the subway tunnel became brighter. The A.I. conductor announced our arrival at Solitude as we came to a complete stop at an underground station. The doors to the train opened to unveil the luxuriously gray hallway with chrome gardens along the walls. At the center of the hallway, a statue of Shepherd Wreath sat on a large stone with a scripture on it reading:

> *My fellow Terrans,*
> *I give you a future engraved in stone,*
> *Forged by Gigallians in krone.*
> *All mistakes must be atoned,*
> *Or spirits will be broken to the bone.*
> *To coat every racer's heart with chrome,*
> *I've capped your battleground with a dome.*
> *Like our barbaric bloodlines from Rome,*
> *Solitude tests the might that'll bring you home.*

The deceased Shepherd pioneered the Wreath-based series for the Terran race so we could make our mark in Galactica. Again, a move I should have been thankful for as it became the stepping stone for my father's success. But this wasn't a Wreath-based series, which made us question the setting while noticing the pillars past the statue with names of the fallen embedded on them. There had to have been over a thousand fallen souls, driving the bad omen deeper into our thoughts. Beta softened the grim tone by stating that he'd rather be here than at Chernobyl, a radiated city that hosted the Windy Quadrant two years ago. The reports claimed that all four racers walked away contracting some form of cancer like most do at Chernobyl's track. The hound's positive attitude was one more reason why Kira fell in love with him. Hell, it damn-near made me fall for him. He was a lot less annoying without Meta and had a spirit that couldn't help but bring a smile. The only man in the world who ever embodied the same spirit was my father.

With hands gracefully locked onto Kira's, Beta led us to the large stairwell at the end of the station's hall, ascending to the empty streets of Solitude. The first thing we could see was the gray sky of the dome's interior. On the surface were metal buildings designed in the 20th Century. Like Calumet, things were more grounded, except Solitude had a dome that deprived it of the sun rays. It made the three of us feel lost in time with eyes on the asphalt street stretching north to a three-way intersection. Kira then caused us to turn around and eye the entrance to a large arena labeled Wreath Arena at the city's center. The street's sidewalks were painted with arrows next to the word, "Locker." We entered the arena, marveling at how spacious the interior was. The entrance had us at the top of the bleachers that circled the entire building. At the center was a submerged court with a rectangular marble stone. Lying against the four sides of the stone were statues of Beta, Kira, Zane, and I, with mine pointed at us in a reconstructed version of the late Atlas III. We didn't understand the purpose of each statue until we glanced at the hollow openings on each statue's chest.

"It's a goddamn suicide race," I announced to the lovebirds. There were traditional races, circuit races, rally races, and even relay races in the sport of Versa, but the worst category of them all was unarguably the suicide races, which explained why the city of Solitude was large and empty. In Wreath's words, *a battlefield*. In suicide races, the Satanian's structure for a race, there was a homebase with a racer's statue and a heart/beacon for said statue randomly scattered around the homebase's vicinity. The catch to a suicide race was that it was based on luck. If a racer discovered their beacon on the first try, they immediately had an advantage because all they had to do was suicide back to homebase in order to end the race. The luck changed, however, when two racers acquired each other's beacon, creating a brutal dilemma which was why these races were specifically used for a Wreath-based series like Galactica. I honestly thought the Pro League Committee needed to be drug-tested for even considering the Satanian's concept of a race in a Merce-based series.

"I see y'all finally arrived," a muscular man said, coming out of the nearest tunnel to the bleachers. He was suited in a black and white camouflage outfit with an assault rifle strapped to his back. The diagonal scar on his light-skinned face revealed it was Commander Cage, but the black and white striped chest armor also informed us that Cage was the Initiator.

"The last time I checked, you were a soldier, not an official," I remarked, leading us down a flight of stairs to the court. Lynches suited in Wraiths suddenly appeared from the other tunnels to join us courtside.

"I'm here to make sure that every life is preserved," he stated. "Being the son of Crank McGuire, I take it you're familiar with the concept of a suicide race."

"Yeah, considering my father never won one," I responded.

"All streaks eventually come to an end," Beta commented, raising Cage's scarred brow.

"Graceful words for a competitor," Cage declared.

"We're friends and friends stick together," Kira added, producing an unconvincing smile at the commander's face.

"Loving words from the loving birds up against a raven, and… a blue jay?" Cage raised his arm laterally to signal over to the one Lynch who differed from the rest. Their Wraith was chrome instead of gray and had war badges pinned onto their dells and abdominises. They handed a folder to Cage for examination. It had disclosed information about my workshop. "*The Blue Jay's Nest* is what you called it. Why a blue jay?"

"Why the interest?" I countered, causing him to toss the folder back at the chrome Lynch.

"No interests, I just wanted to know why I'm conducting a tale of four birds," he revealed, trademarking Solitude's race. "I wanna know why this tale piqued my interest. Why does it feel like this is the tale to keep an eye on?"

"I don't know. Maybe you've been reading Wreath's preamble too many times," Kira remarked. Cage chuckled before he could signal one of his Lynches over to guide the two lovebirds to their lockers leaving me at the arena's stone with the chrome Lynch still by our side. Cage stared at the Lynch for a minute before glancing back at me.

"Why do you think this Lynch is as decorative as it is?" Cage then asked. I stayed silent. "He's the most driven one, with a spirit stronger than any metal on Gigalus. They were brave enough to save our planet from a tyrannic Shepherd, but at the cost of enduring the Wardens' wrath. Do they still teach your generation about Shepherd Newman's assassin?"

"There's no way this is Connor Mccoy. He'd be over a century old," I responded. Cage then explained the rituals performed on the darker side of Legios where the Wardens were more tortuous than solicitous. In Cage's paraphrased words, the Warden had the resources to kill and revive any kind of specimen. Their tortuous resurrecting rituals brought the specimen back emptier than before. The Wardens did it to destroy the specimen's soul until they were permanently reformed for a better purpose, or in Connor's case, as a Lynch. It explained why the ones currently on Earth seemed more Terranold than most. Cage explained this process to reveal his true motives as the Initiator in this race. He believed that he would be escorting one of the four birds directly to Legios for the reformation process, leering at me before a blonde-haired woman with black mascara could come out of one of the tunnels.

"Cage, you have to disqualify Zane," the woman demanded, coming into the light in her high-heeled business casual attire. It was Dr. Azzrelia Perris. "He's not here anymore."

"He left the arena?" Cage questioned.

"No, he left his head," she answered, pulling Cage towards the arena's entrance.

"I've lived among mentally ill soldiers, I'm sure he'll be fine," Cage said, finally leaving the arena.

"Craven, can you help me?" Perris eventually asked out of desperation. She seemed pretty invested in The Raven's health, but I was anything but interested. Perris went into further detail. Since Knightfall, Zane had been exhibiting schizophrenic tendencies and had been a vital patient of Perris' studies over the past few months. She truly believed he was not only a danger to himself, but to everyone else here. The next choice I made could plausibly decide a lot of lives, including my own. JoKer told me that it was my choice to change the future, to change Zane's. With Gabriella eliminated, it was up to me to change Midas', too. In the past, Zane had been my best friend's enemy. Perhaps this was another sign for change, convincing me to aid Dr. Perris. She quickly escorted me into the dark tunnel and into Zane's locker.

The walls were black, and the fluorescent lights were ultraviolet. Pinned into the corner were large purple clothes over box-shaped objects that began to rattle, slightly exposing their secret. Sitting calmly on a bench, suited up in his Nevermore was The Raven, nodding his head to the jingles of ringing metal. His helmet was off and firmly stationed near the hip.

"Zane?" Perris hesitantly said, putting an end to the jingles. Zane lifted his head up to the hollow holster on the wall. "I brought a friend."

"A f-f-f-friend?" he questioned, gently looking over his left dell with the abraded side of his face still unable to heal correctly from all of the Versa hits tormenting it. "C-C-Craven, I remember you."

"I hope so. We've been racing each other for a few years now," I responded, slowly walking closer to him while Perris stayed at the doorway. "Do you remember our last race?"

"T-t-t-the jungle. You won that race," he replied once I was seated at the edge of the bench.

"You took a nasty hit in that race."

"Yeah, and at Greenland…and at Knightfall…" he paused like a robot attempting to scan through an archive of memories. "Y-y-you won both races."

"I did, but enough about me. What's going on with you?" I asked. His hands clawed his face to hide the purple eyes scrunching together from the contracting cheeks.

"I-I-I made a deal with the devil," he slowly answered, each word struggling to squeeze through his hands.

"The devil? Are you talking about Lucifer," I questioned, also proposing The Devil's Shamrock as a plausible candidate.

"N-n-no. Trace, I swore he was competing. T-t-the devil gave me a present… just for Trace… over there," he explained, repeating several words with an arm pointed towards the covered objects at each corner. "It's just for Trace… just for Beta… just for Kira… just for you…"

"What are…?" I tried to ask until his cold purple eyes froze my soul. I didn't have JoKer's abilities, but I could see the violence projected into The Raven's irises. It instantly brought me to my feet and out of his locker. Perris attempted to stop me, but I would rather live on a hot Satanian moon than to have stayed in the room with who I knew to be my future killer. I hurried to my locker located in another tunnel. I had to convince myself that death was not in my near future, a plan that lacked internal persuasion when I smelled the hard-watered stench of my locker. My eyes fell on the AD INFINITUM writings hovering the Versa logo and then onto the blue-and-gray checkered floor. This was it, the neon-blue locker reserved for my death. The thought of actually being here sent chills down my spine. Then I saw the lone object differing from any dream I had about this place. Within the wall's holster, the elder, the ol' reliable, my most notable creation. The 2248 Atlas Sr. She may have been bulky, but she was hope, my guardian angel. Still attached to her arm, the first BrachiShield I ever tested. It did lack oxidized hæmelytes, but it was a shield nonetheless. A protector sent from home with a note on the pectars reading: *Try not to drown suit again.* I had to smile at Vector's broken English. I had another spare life, one that would make Trace envious.

"Solitude is not my cliff," I confidently stated, realizing my confrontation with Zane had been the right choice. I now had knowledge about his "gift" and had to warn Kira and Beta. If we were prepared for the trick, we could avert the trick. I leapt into Atlas Sr. with a tight grip on the last remaining piece of Atlas III, the helmet with MIKA still attached. Once I was geared up, I ran back to the court with eyes on the lovebirds at the top step of the bleachers. The Atlas Sr. was heavy and required all of my strength as I hurried up the stairs to catch Kira and Beta. I finally met them outside on the street circling the arena where they were standing next to Cage. Around them, a baker's dozen of Lynches in their Wraiths, the guardians of Solitude, ventured away from our location.

"There's number three, where's four?" Cage questioned.

"We can get away with three," I answered, walking up to the lovebirds. "Zane's a danger to us all."

"How bad is he?" Kira asked.

"He's rambling about a deal with an unnamed devil and supposedly has brought a gift for us and Trace," I explained.

"Trace ain't here, though," Beta pointed out.

"He's been rambling about Trace in every locker to this point," Kira said as Beta sat down on the curb. "If this 'gift' is partially intended for Trace…"

"…then it can't be good," I finished as Dr. Perris ran out of the arena and up to Cage.

"Please disqualify Zane Maddox," she pleaded to Cage who seemed annoyed by the request.

"Thirteen Lynches, I have thirteen Lynches!" Cage stated. "If one Terran can take down thirteen Lynches, I'll give you the official right to backhand me with a krone-knuckled hand." After a moment of silence, the purple Nevermore stepped out of the arena. "Mr. Zano, you insano, or are you goodo?"

"Reado," Zane shouted through his beaked-helmet. He gave a thumbs up before his wheels transitioned to the appendages while the pistons injected more doses of adrenia.

"He sounds sane to me," Cage announced while gesturing Perris off to the sidewalk. He then advised us to enter the Versarchives for the city's layout and the locations of each beacon. I quickly tried to carry out the task, only hearing static from MIKA's audio.

"MIKA, are you there?" I asked.

The static came to an end. "Yes," she stated very clearly.

"To catch you up to speed, I need you to access the logs and pull up the mapping to Ad Infinitum," I commanded, simultaneously eyeing a display of Solitude on my visor. It began with Wreath Arena, then the street circled around it with straightaways directing north, northeast, east, southeast, south, southwest, west, northwest, and finally north which was where we were. The north and south straightaways led to three-way intersections. Past those, a small maze of turns stopped at the major landmarks to the city. At the northernmost section of the dome, a graveyard, and at the southernmost, a schoolyard which were where two of the beacons were located. The other two beacons were at the junkyard to the far east and the boneyard past the sewerage infrastructure below an interchange to the far west. Solitude was big, and easily meant for galactic-size race, but that was something we could use to our advantage. As Cage had said, this was a tale of four birds, and we had a lot of space to soar. I pulled my helmet off in order to say one more thing to the lovebirds.

"We've got this," I promised.

We each had outlines of the official map within our visors. Cage brought his arm up to initiate a set position. Once we were on all fours, Beta pointed to the westward section of the dome, claiming that we could escape the dangers at the interchange, but that's when the dome began to retract, opening to the swirling coal-black sky. The screams of Mother Nature blew into the center of the city until the dome was fully open, unveiling the completely formed tornadoes to the far west. Like the fingers of God, the large gray vortexes whipped across the Earth.

"On second thought, east sounds better," Beta rephrased, his voice cracking. The large pack of tornadoes seemed to have a mind of their own. Half began to veer northward, the others southward. Either way, our plan was to stay far away, praying to Mother Nature herself that my beacon was at the junkyard.

When Cage's arm fell, the three of us instantly rushed towards our intended destination. The Raven stood at the starting line like his statue within the arena. Wary, we kept our eyes on him while driving east. It was not like Zane to hand over a win. Suddenly, a flock of robotic ravens blasted through the arena doors, flying high into the sky to form a small tornado of their own—his "gift" to us. Zane was accustomed to only having one robotic, but a swarm? I knew there was no way in a Satanian hell that he had created that many on his own. His mind may have been lost, but he wasn't a liar. He most certainly had made a deal with someone behind the scenes. Were they actually a devil?

The ravens eventually dispersed in every direction, forcing us to trigger our boosts to the junkyard. We had a distant head start from the few headed our way, but the flock brought us to the fields of crushed vehicles stacked into small buildings. With us in the junkyard was Connor and a fellow Lynch, overseeing the area in crouched positions at the top of the tallest stack. Unafraid of their presence or the situation, Kira led the way deeper into the junkyard until we were at the dome's eastern wall. A smaller wall of stacked vehicles stood in front of it with a small glowing ball at the peak. Kira quickly declared herself the climber, naming Beta and I as lookouts. The big attraction in the distance was the lone tornado at the arena. I was sure Cage and Perris were inside, but I questioned their comfort levels. The thought of Cage in danger even worried the pair of Lynches as they hadn't taken their eyes off of the arena. Ignoring their immediate surroundings, a pair of ravens forcefully impacted their dells from the side, tossing both Connor and his fellow Lynch off of their tower.

"You don't think they're dead, right?" Beta asked after our helmets were off.

"Technically, they're already dead," I replied as soon as Kira dropped down with the glowing basketball. The illuminated color matched Kira's Venus, and written on the base was her sobriquet, The Cerebral Assassin. This was a beacon, but more importantly, it was hers. The thought of having the key out of this race made her contemplate the next move.

"Zane's gift did just take out two Lynches. Maybe you should be the one who wins," I proposed, knowing she'd make a strong case for Earth's survival at the Finals. She had the capabilities to win the big races, especially for a female. Fans and several racers often overlooked the gender because of their anatomical disadvantages, but I could proudly speak for Gabriella, calling those disadvantages bullshit. Kira supported me in the beginning and even witnessed my victory in Knightfall. Both her and *Brink Industries* had seen me create big moments. I wanted her and her family to have one, also. Beta seemed startled by the gesture.

"I'd be honored to defend Earth's survival in the Finals, but I'm not a savior, you are," she stated, gently tapping her beacon's groove at me. "You saved my life multiple times at Everest, so this is me repaying the favor."

"But…" I tried to say before she heaved the beacon far away from us. I could only imagine what the viewers of this race were thinking. What the hell was the flamboyant Gradite going to say? But Kira was set to Beta's plan, and wasn't going to stop until we found my beacon. I hugged her before turning to face a new problem. A tornado might have been better than the pair of menaces staring at us. It was the Lynches, but attached to their dells, with sharp talons dug into the armor, were the ravens. Brachial blades extended out of their arms, which tossed our helmets back on for the great escape.

"MIKA, I need you to pull up live footage from the beginning of the race," I ordered while the Lynches chased us out of the junkyard. Kira and Beta led the way to the south side of the dome. We kept our eyes on the tornadoes racing us to the schoolyard from the west. A small box-sized screen then appeared on the lower corner of my visor, exposing the flock of ravens dispersing out of the arena. In sync with a hunch I had, MIKA paused the screen and zoomed in on their talons. Running down the sharp claws were diamond veins similar to the ones on Gabriella's krone claws. "Shit!"

"Is Gabriella friends with Zane?" MIKA questioned as we approached the school, bracing ourselves for entry into the landmark. To protect the lovebirds' exosuits, I turbo'd into the lead to ram the bulky Atlas through the brick wall and into a large classroom. The impact tossed the desks like bowling pins. I was able to stop at the farthest wall, but Kira and Beta impacted my suit, bursting us all through the wall and into a hallway of lockers.

"No," I remembered to answer while the dust and debris settled onto our suits. "But someone has learned how to mimic her trick, and I don't think it was Zane."

Kira and Beta were resting on each other's stomachs for the landing. The lovebirds quickly noticed that the lockers around them on the ground lined up into a heart. We laughed and then readied our search for the next beacon. Windows in the hallway revealed the library at the center of the school. A glowing ball attached to a clawed hand rested on the librarian's cherry oak desk. The beacon glowed purple, and once we got closer, we saw "The Raven" carved onto the base.

Suddenly, a Lynch burst through the library's window and attempted to leap towards the beacon. Beta snatched it before the Lynch could claim it, while Kira tossed her spiked Thornwood wheel at the robotic raven on the Lynch's dell. The hit destroyed the raven but quickly attracted Connor, who rammed through the wall near me for a fatal blow. To avoid the hit, I triggered my BrachiShield, now prepared for Connor's swinging blade, ricocheting it backwards. This forced me to sweep-kick Connor's unbalanced legs, bringing him onto the ground. He tried to blindly swing his bladed arm, but I countered by grasping the arm in order to fracture it inward so that the blade would slice off the head to his robotic raven. I then pulled the raven's talons out of the dell. Quickly, I noticed a unique image on the raven's back—a naked man growing crystallized wings, golden wings.

"Does that answer your question?" I asked MIKA, showing *The Golden Evolution's* logo to both Kira and Beta.

"A devil indeed," she responded.

"It's a clever trick, but at least we know where Zane's beacon is at," I inferred.

"You're right, and the puppeteered Lynches will stop at nothing to retrieve it..." Beta began to say as the school rumbled, signaling the tornado nearby. Beta grabbed the beacon. "We can use his plan against him."

"What are you going to do, toss it into the tornado?" I asked. It was what I would have done.

"No, the Lynches will probably attack us if I do that. I'm thinking of acting as the distraction, giving you two a straight shot to the other beacons," he proposed, leaving Kira uneasy about the plan. She declared it dumb and suicidal, but that didn't stop the hound from heading to the school's exit. We saw a pack of Lynches driving our way from the north. Kira gripped Beta's arm. With his chrome hand, Connor held Beta's dell while aiming his arms back toward the junkyard to avoid the tornado coming from the west. Just in time, the other Lynch still loyal to Connor came to Beta's aid. "I don't plan on dying today, not with these two as my guardians."

"Again, I owe you a trip to Pasydanya after this," I told him, convincing Kira to loosen her grip so that her lover could create the diversion east with Zane's beacon in hand. Connor and his fellow Lynch protected Beta's six by following before the rest of the traitorous Lynches from the north could divert east, providing Kira and I a direct pathway out of the schoolyard. With tornadoes all over the boneyard still, we ventured past the arena and straight to the graveyard. It was the fourth one in the past week I'd been to, except this time, The Raven sat against a large leafless yew near the dome's northern wall. In his hand was a neon-blue beacon. Of course that would be the beacon Zane would find first. Kira and I had a two-on-one advantage against The Raven who had no Lynches, but he did have a trio of robotic ravens circling around the graveyard. It made our next move a crucial one. Adding to the list of problems was the swirling cloud just beyond the north wall, attempting to configure a tornado. It deprived us of valuable time, so I did the dumbest thing I probably could've done. I walked directly into The Raven's view. To make matters worse, I took my helmet off.

"You still here Zane?" I asked once we were merely meters away from one another. The Raven stayed in his Nevermore, seated, while Kira kept her distance and eyed the trio of birds circling the graveyard. Zane eventually nodded. I followed up by asking about his alliance with Luke Gold. He nodded again. He detached his helmet by the beak, tossing it at my feet. His face was battered and lacked pigmentation compared to the vacation tan he usually had.

"H-h-h-he told me that you did this to m-m-me," he explained, pointing at his face. "Y-y-y-you and Trace."

"We did," I answered, gently stepping closer so that I could possibly snatch the beacon from his grasp. The robotic ravens landed on the top branches of the yew behind Zane. Their caws stopped me in my tracks when I saw each opened mouth with a blade for a tongue.

"Trace, I-I-I-I swore he was competing," Zane repeated as the tornado from the north became more developed. "T-t-tell me where he is an-an-and I'll give you the beacon. It's t-t-the only reason why I agreed to the g-g-gold one's plan. H-h-he promised me Trace."

"I…" I began to say, quickly stalling as soon as the spiked wheel impacted Zane's pectar, pinning him into the yew with a loud trembling roar that caused his ravens to soar at me. I braced myself for the flock's wrath, raising my BrachiShield—a prototyped that never stood a chance against the blades that would now impale themselves down to the bone marrow. My entire right arm oozed blood, but Zane was still pinned and vulnerable. I snatched my beacon and rushed back to Kira's side. With one of her remaining wheels, she instantly destroyed the three ravens stuck into my arm. The hit didn't destroy the shield, but it did leave the blades buried in my bone while I led the way out with my beacon tightly pressed into my chest with the left arm. My right arm might have been injured, but I had no choice but to use it as the front-wheel, constantly grimacing through the pain. In a worse position was Kira with only two wheels left and with the tornado from the north now fully developed. We watched Zane escape to the east out of the graveyard just before the tornado could enter it. The northern tornado seemed to only have two targets. The funnel acted as a gravitational force of air, slowing Kira and I on the last straightaway back to the arena. The wind became unbearable once we were only 100m away from the arena, the stairway down to the underground subway to our left. With the tornado's pull matching our speed, we were brought to a complete stop and had no choice but to try and pull ourselves towards the stairway. Kira had healthy arms, so crawling was a bit easier for her even though she was still several meters behind, much closer to the tornado. But my arms were injured, forcing me to use the sharp edges of my shield as a hatchet into the ground, pulling myself forward, gripping the beacon in my left hand.

I heard another loud caw as a raven soared towards us from the arena. Its blade was already stretched out of its mouth. I used my beacon to deflect the blow, veering the raven past my body. Glass shattered behind me, and I glanced over at Kira. A series of cracks rivered across her visor, and the raven's blade lodged into her left eye, stopping my heart. Blood seeped through the cracks in her visor before her body went limp and flew backwards into the tornado's grasp.

With tears blurring my vision, I had no choice but to continue crawling. Once I got to the stairs, I used the tornado's grip as gravity for my legs so that I could walk up the stairs even though I was actually going downward. I didn't escape the twister's grip until I was halfway down to the subway's hall. The change in pressure launched both my body and the beacon down to the hallway's floor. To make sure that my beacon was safe, I tossed it further into the hall while the tornado passed by. More furies from Mother Nature screamed outside, shaking the underground hall until a loud quaking thud cued the silence. The only thing I could hear then were the heavy breaths fogging up my visor.

"Craven," MIKA gently spoke, hearing the pounding in my chest while the tears flowed down my cheek. "Are you okay?"

"It's… my fault," I slowly replied to MIKA's static. I took off the helmet to fully embrace the quiet. I could think of only one thing. I had to prevent another death from going down in vain. The beacon had to be my focus now.

I made my way back up to the surface. The gray sky of the dome seemed bright compared to how dark the actual clouds were beyond it. Beneath it, a battlefield of dirt and debris, the markings of the tornado that chased us… that chased me. There wasn't a trace of Kira's body in sight. Azzrelia and Cage stood at the arena's entrance doors. I walked over, leaving a path of blood dripping from my right arm—evidence against Cage's poor promise of safety. I reminded him that Azzrelia owed him a backhand.

I made my way down the bleachers, slow and steady, until I finally reached my statue. I wasted little time shoving my beacon into its heart. The force collapsed my body to the floor, planting my back at the statue's feet to finally end the race. Now came the aftermath. The position of my battered body and the path of blood mimicked the ones in my dreams, except I was in the arena's court instead of my locker. Waiting at the arena's doorway wasn't a raven, but a hound—a heartless hound. Oblivious.

"I could use that trip to Pasydanya right about now. Man, you should've seen how I used the sewerage to escape the Lynches," Beta explained, coming down the bleachers. He only saw the success of his plan but didn't realize the price we'd paid. "Where's Kira? Is she in the locker?"

"Beta…" I softly spoke while he made his way to the tunnel. I repeated his name. "She…"

"Where is she?" he asked again, now seeing the tears in my eyes. I couldn't muster any more words and, instead, just shook my head. It brought the hound down onto his knees in misery while I fell onto the puddle of mine. Claire once said that changing history came at a cost. Our choices saved a blue jay by killing a lovebird.

POSTHUMOUS

THEY SAY THE AVERAGE AMOUNT OF TIME FOR MOURNING IS INCONCLUSIVE. As evidence, I could say that a few days wasn't the answer. Hell, I was still stuck in the denial stage of grief. Kira couldn't be dead, she couldn't be. Her body hadn't even been recovered. They had no choice but to hold the funeral without one—a funeral I wanted to attend; except I wasn't welcomed. The hounds had placed my avatar in their dogpound on Way/Point. Joining them on the hateful train was the rest of *Brink Industries*, and who could blame them. I was the reason why Kira was no more. Yet, I still refused to believe that she was dead. If I accepted it, she would take her place next to my father's ghost. That was why I hadn't left my office at the nest since returning home. Out of respect, Trace, Katia and the gang left me be. Even days since my return, my eyes had not unglued themselves from the footage of Kira's death. The raven was going to hit me, so I had to defend myself, but I continued to analyze the footage, wondering whether or not I could've swung my arm upward, or even downward. I questioned why I swung to the left. I should've been aware of the trajectories. I should've known it was going to hit her. I should've been the savior she labeled me as, not the heartbreaker responsible for the misery. I didn't know if Beta would ever smile again, this was why I had to find a reason, a piece of evidence that suggested Kira could have survived.

I must've replayed the footage on my iCube for the millionth time before another grid suddenly popped up, showcasing the trial underway at Pandora's Palace. The Shepherd and Pro League Committee were attempting to declare the proper sentence for Zane Maddox. He had apparently been pinned as the culprit for the shitpile within the dome. By The Raven's side was, of course, Dr. Azzrelia Perris, trying to reason with the jury. She made the case that Zane should never have been given the green light to compete, using documentation as evidence. The big issue was Pandora's word with Shepherd Kane regarding punishment for the next kill within the series. Pandora must've been a hair string away from allowing the extradition before the true devil showed up at the palace. Luke Gold. He was smug, and loaded with journals on his so-called "Project Raven." The writings suggested the plausible malfunctionings of the robotic ravens. A suitable claim followed by a blank check firmly planted in front of both Pandora and the Committee. He was prepared to buy a pardon for his associate in case his evidence was insufficient. The action sparked an argument between Luke and our Shepherd. She reminded him that his family was the "accidental" cause of every death in Four Seasons over the past few years. The derogatory statements then forced Luke to end the debate by reminding everyone of his historic markings on the alliance and how it was because of him that the United Countries of Earth lacked Maradoes. He quickly reminded them of Pandora's own words about accepting a few deaths over a million—a concluding statement strong enough to leave the court silent. Luke walked out of the palace with The Raven in hand.

Four Seasons, the United Countries of Earth, I had almost forgotten about both since my tenure at the office. A messy office for that matter. It resurrected the nickname of "Sloppy Joe" to Trace's liking. The court case reminded me that it was Friday, a day out from the big race at The Twilight of Hera. Both Law and Midas had already qualified on Monday's doubleheader, and I didn't end the windy mess until Tuesday. Who was the fourth? The question quickly answered itself the second I changed the channel to the Unican Network. I had hoped for the grizzly smile of The Devil's Shamrock. Hell, I would even have accepted the walrus-wrinkled grin of Creed, but neither were to be seen. It was, instead, a Satanian—the Carnivore's last hope for redemption, if they'd still accept him as a Carnivore. I had a lot of respect for Lucifer, but with both Krakyn and Bayne dead, I knew I could call him anything but a friend. Earth's future was endangered, and Kira made sure that I would be the one who saved it. But the cost of saving the planet would just have to be next week's problem.

"So, this is the big workshop you always mentioned," a raspy voice called from the doorway. I looked up to see the bicolor-eyed belle gracing me with an angelic smile. Gabriella. It was the first time I'd seen her since Hawaii.

"It was originally my father's idea, I merely continued the dream," I explained while she came closer to the desk. The grid of Kira's footage was still on replay. I swiped it away, but not before Gabriella could see it. The guilt crept back into my mind; I closed my eyes to push it away.

"Are you alright?" Gabriella asked in a soft tone. "I know that she was close." I opened my eyes to see Gabriella seated at the edge of the desk.

"Claire… she told me that the cost of saving a life is to give a life. I didn't think it'd be Kira's," I replied.

"I know this is soon, but the cost wasn't for nothing," she stated, inferring Midas' life. She didn't know about my meeting with JoKer. I almost blurted out the truth about his Xenner background, about his foresight, about me being the actual life saved in the process of leaving Midas' up in the air. I chose to keep it all a secret, not because I didn't trust her, but to relieve her of the stress that had been placed on her shoulders over the past few weeks.

We talked about every court case that happened this week. I'd forgotten that she had one of her own for the events at Blackstone. Pandora and the Committee attempted to pin Krakyn's death on her before Ferra could appear as Gabriella's saving grace. The odd part about our talk was how convinced Gabriella was that she'd blacked out in that race. She didn't remember anything after the big blow by the hammerhead. The only thing she did remember was the infirmary after the race. Her mother explained the race and condition her body was in.

"I promised my mother at Blackstone that I'd retire Krueger" she said. It had been a hard decision, but Gabriella explained that she had no choice. She didn't really know what to do with her life currently. Knowing what Luke was up to with Zane, I decided to offer Gabriella a once-in-a-lifetime deal, co-ownership of *The Blue Jay's Nest*. The offer almost sent her off of the desk. At first, she didn't know how to take it, but I explained myself by stating how much she loved the sport and how being retired from the track didn't necessarily mean the end. I truly wanted her to be a part of the sport, somehow. My company could use her knowledge. Then I explained how we, together, might deliver a fatal blow to her father's company, especially after he'd stolen her hacking schematic.

Above all else, I wanted Gabriella to be happy. She had the most convincing smile I've ever seen once she shook my hand in agreement. She then pulled me up for a tight hug.

"Is this a bad time?" a woman standing in the doorway asked. The words pulled Gabriella off of my body. She turned to see my mother for the first time.

"Mom," I said, rather immaturely. "How did you find this place?"

"Trace gave me directions," she answered. "He was worried about your health and thought I could treat it, so here I am."

"Trace, the same Trace who had his arm cut off by a lunatic?" I replied, referring to her statement a few months back. It brought out a smile I hadn't been accustomed to seeing from her.

"Don't push it, kiddo," she responded, now glancing at Gabriella. "I don't believe we've met, I'm..."

"Lacey McGuire," Gabriella blurted, beating my mom to the punch. "Sorry, I was a big fan of Crank McGuire."

"At least we have one thing in common," my mother noted. "I'm assuming there's another."

"Yeah," I quickly stated, properly introducing the two to one another. Gabriella's surname did leave a bittersweet taste in my mother's mouth, but it also produced a twinkle in her eyes. To think, a Gold in a relationship with a McGuire. She saw promise for a chance at peace. It helped build a natural chemistry with Gabriella. My mother was interested in Gabriella's background, easily linking her face to Miss Earth. It was a discussion that would have lasted for hours if not for my interjection. I reminded her that she was here for her son.

"You're right. I brought you a gift."

My reaction to the announcement didn't please me at first, but that was because the last person who announced a gift damn-near killed me with it. Luckily, the feeling unwrapped itself once I saw the cast of friends in front of the closed chamber doors to the forge downstairs. The only people I expected to see at the forge were Trace and my mechanics, Yama and Vector. I didn't expect to see Roy and his wife Kriss. No one told me that there was a reunion at *The Blue Jay's Nest*, and I was the owner, I mean, co-owner. I tried to introduce everyone to Gabriella before she could explain to me that she'd already met them.

"The plan was to leave you be while we constructed an exosuit that embodied Craven McGuire," Roy explained while he and his wife hugged my mom. "The idea came from Trace until Lacey thought of a better one."

"Yo momma one-upped me, bro," Trace said.

"Trace, we all get our intelligence from our mothers," Gabriella added.

"I like this girl," my mother said.

"I still thought of the plan first, and it was because we all knew that you were down to the very last Atlas," Trace continued to explain while Vector and Yama began to slowly open the forge's chamber doors.

"Did you create an Atlas IV?" I questioned.

"No, we made something even better," he answered as a cloud of mist suddenly escaped the forge. Neon-blue wings glowed through the fog on what looked to be the dells and arms before the fog could unveil the wings on the legs. Once the sight became transparent, a beast incarnated was revealed. It was a Hermes, and parts of it were from Trace's Knightfall suit. I recognized the Hyper Velocitative Armour on the dells, pectars, and abdominises with sturdier attachments to the appendages. It even had the Atlas' exclusive trademark of a BrachiShield around the right arm, except it was made out of krone this time. A defense system my right arm wished it had earlier this week from the trio of lacerations still upon the skin. Everyone in the room stayed silent, allowing me to examine the Hermes further. The suit presented its defense with my shield, but it also presented offense with the sword now diagonally strapped to the suit's latis. The sword was krone and had a bright-white grip with a miniature chrome-colored knight's helmet on the pommel, and a metal emblem of Atlas holding onto a chrome Earth in the center of the sword's guard. There were two black crosses on the edges. This was the sword I had won at Knightfall, adding to the Hermes' McGuire storyline, but it didn't stop there. The scapulars, sacrum, and spina were familiar. Too familiar. They were from my father's original 2200 Hermes, an exosuit I last saw in my mother's garage. I peeked over the suit's dell to see her teary face.

"You… you brought his suit?" I asked her for a quick nod.

"We tried using my suit at first," Trace explained, "but Roy advised us to scrap the thin armor for a better supplement in several sections to the suit, hence your mother's bright idea."

"I told you that the suit was yours," my mother reminded me, throwing a one-liner of her own back at me to even the score.

"Law, Lucifer, my brother, they won't know what hit them tomorrow," Gabriella said to the approving crowd, an approving family of people I could always rely on in my darkest hour. They had no intention of being anywhere else but by my side, which flashed a memory of me as a kid still in my father's office, restating his monologue about accepting the success. He said that one must take it and place it in front of them, away from their body so that it never touched the skin. He showed me the group of loved ones standing by the holographic version of himself just like my friends and family. For the first time in my life, I could sense how proud of me he really was, wherever he was. It provided me with a new eudaimonia, a new reason to fight. And my love, she couldn't have worded it better. Law, Lucifer, Midas, they wouldn't know what was coming for them tomorrow at The Twilight of Hera. A finale I determined would not end with another tragic statement.

THIS AIN'T IT

IT WAS CRAZY HOW TIME COULD PASS, AND YET THE PRESENT COULD STAY THE SAME. It was almost as if I'd repeated history. Hours away from another big race, and so far, I'd done the exact same thing I did a few months back at Knightfall. I spent all night working on the suit without any sleep. Check. A bunch of people were critiquing the shield's purpose. Check. Zero continued his gambling streak on Nexus Ave. Check. And Yama promoted his boost. Check. Speaking of Yama, he was now learning the way of Gabriella's force. The previous night, she had found out that he was the mastermind behind the Komodo Fire boost, giving him a bittersweet response to the formula. She called him a Versa Darwin versus a Versa Einstein, instructing him so they could reconfigure better formulas. He didn't take her seriously at first, but once he found about her inventions and co-ownership to the nest, he quickly became the student. Things might have started off rocky, but the two had really become in sync with one another. They had perfected the Komodo's formula to an even better state of power and durability. It turned out; Yama had forgotten to carry the one in his formula the whole time—is the reason the boost was always too overwhelming for an exosuit. The realization helped him unveil even more projects for the two to perfect, bringing *The Blue Jay's Nest* to a competitive scale against the other big chains on Earth.

I don't even know if Versa Einstein was the right nickname for Gabriella because the amount of projects she had in mind stretched out to a century-long timeframe. Maybe a Versa da Vinci was the better answer. She had only been a part of this company for less than a day and she had already suggested commodities that would take me a couple years to produce. The nest would be in good hands, its wings linked to a goddess. One only needed to ask Zero, my prodigal son. He went head over heels in love with Gabriella from the first whiff of her raspberry perfume. To float his boat, she sent a few winks his way, but that was before he made the foolish attempt at challenging her to a race in his Zeus. Yeah, one could easily predict how that would turn out. In Trace's words, *the poor bastard had a zero chance of winning.* Live and learn. No pain, no gain. Short-term sorrow for long-term serenity. Those were the lessons of the day for my student, and he knew it. He just wanted a taste of what the Pro Leagues felt like. He was only a couple years away from being ready. Right and wrong, his talents weren't far from a professional level, but Gabriella wasn't a professional. She was just a giant who had been forced into retirement. At heart, she was a Versa racer, so that was exactly what I wanted her to be at Calumet. I even allowed her to test run the Hermes around town to see what it felt like to finally be in one. From the nest's balcony, I could tell how much she enjoyed it from the endless number of laps she took around the workshop. I honestly couldn't tell what she loved more—the suit, the nest, the retro lights, or me. It would have to be a question for another day when my mother joined me on the balcony. Two McGuires on the balcony of *The Blue Jay's Nest*. Who would've thunk it.

"I might be a new bird here, but the nest does feel like home," she explained, knowing who the originator was. I would have questioned why she married the man in the first place if she didn't.

"It should've been his home, you know," I replied as Gabriella returned to the nest's parking lot.

"He dreamt of the idea, but not to this level. He never could've imagined his son being at a place surrounded by love, by friends, by residents…"

"By family," I interjected, side-hugging her. "I do see my father, you know."

"I see him too," she replied softly. "It's why I didn't want you to get involved with the bloodsport. I never wanted to see you next to him."

"When were you going to tell me that we're different?"

"For your safety, never. I didn't want your future to be ruined by my parent's past."

"My grandparents, what were they like?"

"They were kind," she answered, choking a bit mid-sentence. I sensed a stake being driven into her heart. Out of respect, I pulled back, but she suddenly chose to continue, reminiscing back to the day she met my father. She remembered being attracted to him, but also felt uncomfortable due to how isolated her and her parents had been her whole life. She never had the ability to get close to anyone outside of her nuclear family. It created a challenge for my father, but he had never been one to side-step a challenge. He kept searching for a way into my mother's heart—a journey no man had ever attempted to take in her life. She finally agreed to a date. And then a dozen. It wasn't until they were hopelessly in love that she revealed her background to him. Rather than running, my father kneeled to propose. Love, it was a light, unafraid of beaming through the darkest caverns. It was the same love she could see between Gabriella and I, especially after the smile Gabriella gave me once she was out of the Hermes. "The McGuires sure know how to choose wisely."

"I don't know who'd I be without her, and I don't wanna know who I'd turn into without you," I stated, holding my mother tightly.

"I'm sorry for being so distant."

"Any habit can be fixed," I concluded before Roy and Kriss could announce their departure to the floating stadium. I signaled everyone else to do the same in order to beat the flyway traffic. Gabriella elected to escort my mother to the stadium. She also extended the invite to Zero. Both of his cheeks blushed.

Trace had one more attachment for the Hermes before it could be ready for transportation. He had the secret ingredient sealed away in one of the workshop benches near the forge, a secret that instantly caught me off guard. It was a mechanical holster that he could quickly attach to the Hermes' hip threxis. He then pulled out the same golden revolver gifted to me by the FMJ back at the Greenland hospital.

"Wait, hold on!" I objected, halting my brother from holstering the gun. "I appreciate the gesture, but I don't even know how to shoot the damn thing."

"You won't, the bullets are here," he explained, pointing at the Hermes' pronator in the left forearm. Within the armor were small chambers linked to a small foramen along the suit's wrist. In the chambers were bullets with Law's name on them. Trace placed both the bullets and gun back onto the suit. "The bullets are for you. As for the gun, that's for Law. Call it a refund."

"Why attack first, when you can attack last," I reminded Trace, now aware of the revolver's jammed status. If Law, no, when Law dislodged the weapon from my hands, he wasn't gonna know what hit him. It was good to know that Trace understood my philosophy, proving why he was my best friend, my brother. I sounded like a broken record, but him and I had come a long way. I didn't know what our future had reserved for us, but I knew that whatever it was, he and I were in it together. Unless it had spiders. His arachnophobia would easily make a lone wolf out of me. "If you didn't know me, and I told you about Midas' death, what would you think of it."

"If I didn't know you?" Trace questioned. "Well, I'd antagonize you first."

"You already do that," I replied.

"True, a small part of me would've believed you, though. That might not mean much but the small part would've played along," he answered.

"Really?"

"Yeah, I'd take it as a hunch that Midas had to be dethroned this time around. The odds of a racer winning this series is 100-1, the odds of a racer winning four straight titles are 1000000-1. I'd reckon those odds are equivalent to the world ending so…"

"How the hell did you come up with that?" I questioned, baffled by his statistical side. "You sucked at math class. I even failed a test cheating off your dumbass."

"Katia claims that my IQ has risen since her and I met."

"It'd be a damn shame for the world to end right when you got smarter," I joked, causing us both to glance at the Hermes and then back at each other.

"This ain't it," he stated, reaching his hibrix out for a handshake. I quickly slapped it away to hug him instead.

"This ain't it," I reassured, before he could move the Hermes into a container and out to a company truck. Once the suit was ready for transportation, he left the nest while I ventured back into the shop.

Katia was changing every channel of every TV to the Unican Network, linking their connections to every iCube so that the residents of Calumet could come to the shop to watch the big race. She, unfortunately, had to stay behind to watch the shop, but once I found out that Zero and my mother were still outside by Gabriella's car, I ordered Katia to take the day off instead. I didn't want the workshop to stress her for the rest of the day, considering that her belly was becoming more expansive through her first trimester of pregnancy.

I searched the entire shop for Gabriella and discovered her in my office. She had a few files of future projects that she wanted to finalize at my desk which reminded me about the bag of goodies I could use pressed against it. I quickly grabbed it and decided to bring out one more thing from the safe.

"Have I ever told you that I've got a dreamcatcher of my own, sort of?" I asked once she was done. I slid on my father's championship ring for protection.

"I'd get used to wearing a championship ring if I were you because you're about to win another, right?" she inquired.

"Many would hope, but we shouldn't get ahead of the game," I replied while she rose up for one more hug. Her hands, gripping the stitching of my jacket's logo.

"Everything's going to work out, right?" she asked.

"I wouldn't be standing here otherwise," I answered, thinking about what I told Trace. She needed to hear the words because trust had been something we'd had since our earliest connection blurred every line. "This ain't it."

ACT IV
CHAPTER 9

FULL CIRCLE

ANOTHER CHAMPIONSHIP RACE, ANOTHER LONG DRIVE BY MYSELF. AT LEAST I WAS NOT LATE THIS TIME AROUND. I made sure to reset the company truck's clock, too. Daylight savings could get eaten by a black hole for all I cared. The nerves were the same, but the mood had changed. I'd take this mollified mood over the one I had a couple days ago, or last week, or last month. I mean, this had to be the first time I'd ventured to a big race with an out-of-this-world support system. My mom, my god, I couldn't believe that my mother would be returning to the VIP booth before her son. That sounded crazy. I hadn't been back to the booth in a dozen years. I was sure my mother was having a great talk with Gabriella. Then there was the pregnant Katia, and the fourth-wheeling Zero. He didn't know what was on the line tonight. He didn't know that he was one of the biggest reasons why I'd fallen off a mountain to kill another, why I'd survived a jungle's onslaught only to trade my fate with another, breaking hearts in the process. It had been for a future. Not just with Gabriella, but for Zero to write his story on. He was going to be something special one day, and I wanted to be there to see it. I may have brought a bag of goodies, but his spirit was the only drug I needed for the big race, my biggest race.

Taking a page from Sydney's harsh weather, the dark clouds spread their wrath across the Chicagolands out west. Forecasts on the truck claimed that it would reach The Twilight of Hera just in time for the race. At least the weather was the only thing that came from Sydney because the streets were as positive as Manaus, with crowds of fans honoring the final four competing. Yeah, even Lucifer. His fan-base apparently liked to carry small blow torches. They also tended to wear cheap Halloween costumes of black body suits with plastic bones glued to them. The Satanian's culture was a gruesome one, but the people didn't care. They were having fun, and so were Law's fans, fans who clearly weren't a part of the FMJ movement. True FMJ members tended to carry guns filled with lead, not water. But when the fans were peaceful, the Re-Versables were invisible. I couldn't complain. It made New Lake Shore Drive seem like a space cruise across an asteroid-free solar system.

The street was still sponsored by *The Golden Evolution*. Midas was competing tonight, which meant his father would be spectating. For years, I'd been waiting for the right moment to gut punch Luke, and though Midas' life or death could alter our planet's existence, defeating him would… I wondered what expression Mr. Gold would bestow on me if I defeated his son. The golden picture made me eye my father's championship ring.

"Dad, I hope you're still watching, because that reaction will be one for the ages," I said, gripping the steering wheel harder while pushing the pedal further to the floor. Restless, I passed The Kodiak's Kolosseum feeling the win there was anticlimactic. I reminisced, briefly, about the arena that gave birth to a knight, that gifted me with a sword, that perfected a shield. I could use some of that success for the bigger spectacle I was heading towards. I saw the swarm of drones in the distance clouding the stadium with golden colors. The flaming torches along the stadium's ridges became more defined the closer I got. I slowed to admire the floating stadium's exterior of Parthenon columns all around the limestone structure. The Twilight of Hera had a pair of large statues of the Greek Goddess enclosing the flyway's main entrance into the stadium. The torches were even Hera's symbol of an "X" with an upside down cross staked through and beneath the origin.

Home sweet home, I would have said if my father had been alive. *Oh death*, would have been my words even a week earlier. But now, no words were needed. Silence, for once, became my friend as I flew towards an entrance specified for Versa racers. It took me down a pathway of light-blue lights leading to the stadium's bottom entrance. The lower pathway also gave me a good sight of Lake Michinis and the strong thrashing waves. *Craven, don't fall off*, I suddenly thought. I'd survived a lot in the last month, but there might be no coming back from those waves. The important thing was not to find out.

A rich sonuvabitch named Dick, waited for me at the racer's entrance. He used the flashing grids of his iCube to guide me into the parking lot. "Uno mas mi premio gordo," he said once I was parked and out of the truck. As expected, he had on two hylec sleeves, complementing them with a hylec necklace holding onto a blue jay emblem. The flattering display damn-near received a hug from me.

"I'm sorry but I didn't take Spanish," I replied, grabbing the Hermes' casing out of the truck.

"It means, one more, my loving jackpot, or at least I think it means that. I just found a translation online and thought I'd say it," he explained, escorting the suit and I to the elevators. Again, I wanted to address his gambling problems.

"How much?" I asked once the elevator doors closed.

"Take a guess," he proposed. He had won a hundred thousand at Knightfall, and matched it at Dessnia.

"$100,000?"

"You betta add a triplet of zeros," he said. The gargantuan leap almost buckled my knees before the doors could open.

"Are you in-fucking-sane?" I questioned as we walked down the ramp of a corridor.

"I am. I keep betting on your ass, expecting things to change, and they never do," he answered. "Look at the odds."

"Not the odds. You're the second Terran to tell me about the damn odds," I complained, reaching the end of the corridor. A pair of frosted glass doors suddenly opened up to a large roundhouse room of lockers. The massive room was originally intended for a heavy population, but instead could only hold four with each locker on the spherical corners of the ground floor. The vast amount of space had to be intentional, perhaps to prevent any physical confrontations prior to the finale.

"Hear me out, McGuire," he began to say, guiding me to the locker illuminated with neon-blue glows. "Every single time I've placed a bet on your name, you've won."

"You know…" I stopped after entering the spacious locker and glanced back at him. I momentarily held onto the silence so I could hear the trembling crowds outside. I smiled and gently patted Dick on the shoulder. "You're right, thanks."

"No problema, that's why I'm the gambler and you're the racer," he said, briefly explaining how he'd give me a heads up prior to my entrance because, apparently, all four racers were to be given a "proper" entrance prior to the siren. He also handed me a square patch with an adhesive groove on its back. On the displayed side was a gray tornado. "You came out of the Windy Quadrant victorious. Every racer is required to represent their quadrant with the elemental patching. It'll go onto the left pectar of your suit."

"Thanks, again," I muttered knowing how bittersweet the so-called victory really was. The patch acted more so like a token of sorrow than gratitude. But negative thoughts would only resort to negative outcomes, and that was not an option. The final four stories were here, and there were no words in the world that would prevent their journeys from reaching a providential climax. Midas craved gold while Law sought red. An unknown spectrum blinded the Satanian while a fairytale rainbowed mine. That was how this race should end, right? An easy victory that destroyed the storms, eased the waves, and froze the setting sun. But knowing what had happened helped me see what could still happen. Death, the old friend followed. Lately, we've wandered off for a cup of coffee. I'd been trying to seduce him, but he never gave in, never stopped to save a life. I opened the case of my immortal exosuit, hoping for redemption. The neon-blue wings glowed within the room, contrasting the black. A war between the black and blue highlighted the Hermes' unfortunate history. Just thinking of the memory rattled both the suit and I. Then again, that could've been the stampeding fans outside.

"When I first saw a highlight of you," someone behind me said, "I couldn't believe the style. And then they told me your name, and I couldn't believe the story." His voice sounded familiar, and for a second, I thought it came from my head. I turned to the doorway. There was always someone at my doorway. But this man wasn't Terran. He was Pyscean, a Goldlyn to be specific. His silky iridescent-orange skin gleamed with sparkles that highlighted his sharp white teeth. The yellow irises produced their own set of stars that seemed to contrast the trio of black gills stretching down the sides of his neck, almost covered by the shoulder length, wavy blue hair. He wore an ocean-blue tuxedo with yellow buttons and handkerchief, a look only surpassed by JoKer and

Jasper. But I'd make a case for the Goldlyn named Tokyn Hampshyre. "It's a pleasure to finally meet the offspring of a legend."

"Likewise," I said, blushing his cheeks teal. Unlike the last Pyscean I'd battled, Tokyn wasn't sweating bullets, or slobbering his speech, or… attempting to kill me. My short history with Pysceans hasn't been all too great, but I was sure Tokyn was here to change that. A small part of me wondered if he could actually sense the Pyscean within me. "What brings you back?"

"Uhh, your umm, what do you call it, oh yes, you're Pro League Commission," he answered struggling with the language.

"You mean Committee," I corrected.

"Damn," he blurted. "No offense, but your language sucks. There are a lot of roles, no, rules," he said, stepping closer to admire the Atlas still lodged into the wall. He halted by the neon spirit of the rumbling beast within the case. "A Full Circle."

"I hope not. I expect to keep my head," I stated. There was a pause in our conversation that eventually brought laughter from both sides.

"I'd hope so as well," he replied, taking a long look at the Hermes' wings. "I'm sorry for not cheering for him in the end. I didn't think the tale would…"

"I didn't think so either," I added.

Tokyn walked back over to the doorway, noticing the guards coming towards my locker.

"I don't know what the next chapter looks like for you, Craven McGuire, so stay alive to tell it," he finished before leaving. Dick and company then entered to escort me safely to the track. I quickly took off my jacket and sneakers, hoping and praying to every god watching that the blue jay on my jacket had imparted its saving grace onto the Hermes. The process to enter the suit was still as quick as the Atlas', but it did feel bizarre. This was the first time I had not one but two weapons equipped. Two weapons and one receipt for Law, now being holstered. The only thing missing was an A.I. chip. I pulled MIKA from Atlas Sr. for one more activation protocol that brought a smile from Dick.

"There's no way in hell we're losing," he said, guiding me out of the locker and into another corridor. It led to one more set of frosted glass doors that opened to an octagon platform with a neon-blue sky of drones above it all. Dick instructed me to stay still at the platform's center before it suddenly began to rise closer to the light, slowly unveiling the bleachers of fans enclosing the track.

"Craven… Craven… Craven…" They all began to chant while a few drones designed as blue jays flew past. Their mouths kept moving, but the sound began to mute inside my head. I heard the "Seven Nation" chants, forcing me to hide my ghastly face within my helmet.

"MIKA, you there?" I asked. I could tell that she was still operating the suit from the schematic adjustments displayed on my visor. She maintained her silence while the Initiator walked towards me, guiding me to the lane on the far-left side of the track, symmetrically aligned with rest. "MIKA, are you there?"

"Y-y-yes…I…ere…I'm here," she answered, fading in and out while the octagon platform descended for the second racer.

"It's not looking good, is it?" I inquired, now eyeing all of the excited fans, eventually discovering the booths at the peak of the bleachers. The first had the sensational Gradite Monroe, finally accompanied by his partner Tokyn. In the booth next to theirs, Catherine and Luke Gold, along with several business owners most likely from their neighborhood in Greenland. Several booths past theirs, my friends and family. The closest one to the window, with hands grasped together in prayer, was my mother. In the final booth was JoKer and Claire Voyant who I hadn't seen since Dessnia. We were all here to see how this story would end. Even Pandora had a booth with Cage who was busy overseeing the Lynches in the bleachers. They must've been on the lookout for armed FMJs.

MIKA spoke up. "No, it's not, but at least I'm at home and I see it's had some renovations," she replied, skimming through some of the armor and weapons. "A sword? A revolver? What happened to the defense, or is this another McGuire?"

"Do you remember that thing with Midas? Well, it ain't over, but it ends here," I explained while the majority of fans began to cover their faces with bandanas, welcoming the silver-eyed outlaw rising onto the track. Law's presence was so sorrowful that even the heavens cried a downpour of rain for his lost spirit. The rain impacted the asphalt as the cloud of beige drones flew to the end of the straightaway. A line-up of Hera statues stood beyond the bleachers, configuring an arch from their outreached arms.

"Then what?" MIKA questioned once Law was ushered into the lane next to mine. He had on his trademark 2235 Ares with the same right arm coated in molten magnesium-filled bullets. The brown cowboy hat still magnetically attached to his gray-goggled face, above their gray-skulled bandana. Close to me, on his left side, the wethro gripped combat knife strapped to the oblique, and the spiky lasso, rolled up on his hip. He still only had a trio of wheels for the trigger arm, but in a race of four where traffic is loose, the tactic became a deadly one. The survivors in Italy, responsible for the aquatic patch on his left pectar, could attest to that. With Law this close, I could've tried to persuade him to take a different path. One more merciful and forgiving. One that didn't result in a one-way ticket to Legios. But his choice had been made. Waiting for our eyes to lock, he holstered his gun and tipped the hat in my direction, gently patting my dell to reveal his cruel choice.

"Craven, then what?" It was MIKA.

"Then what?" I briefly questioned, disappointed in Law's wrathful choice, knowing this race would end in blood for the pouring rain to wash away. "We ride off into the sunset as promised."

"That sounds beautiful, except it's raining," MIKA explained while another racer rose from the entrance to embrace the fire-lit sky.

"We can make one," I replied. Rising out of hell was the Satanian in his 666 Hades with double-edged katanas in its sheath along the sides of the turbo tank acting as the pyrolytic heart of the horse-skulled Lucifer. Honoring the rocky patch, the Satanian kept a stone-calm attitude, unintimidated by the stares of his competitors. "MIKA, how many races have we been through?"

"126," she quickly answered.

"How many have we won?"

"99."

"I want you to hold on for 100," I commanded.

She laughed. "That's very prideful of you. Do you remember what happened the last time you were this confident?" she asked as the platform began to rise one last time.

"I believe Trace stole the lead I had, right?" I replied while the sky turned gold.

"He did. Pride comes before the fall."

"That's the thing, I'm not the prideful one here," I said.

"Who is?" she questioned, now seeing the man in a brand new 2251 Cronus. The suit was primarily black with gold as the secondary. The lightning strikes, gold, the rims, gold, the visor, gold, the volcanic patch on the left pectar, gold, and capstoning the aurum museum were the golden facial hairs of his Guy Fawkes mask. Once the platform was leveled, it didn't take long for The Golden Scion to rejuvenate his fan-base by showboating his swinging fists through the rain. Each haymaker increased the amplitude of cheers. Where there was joy, there was rage growing in the FMJ. The head of the snake, Law, surprisingly kept his composure during The Golden Scion's taunts. Jesus, if only Gabriella had dethroned this guy a couple days ago. She was currently shaking her head.

"Wow, I see what you mean," MIKA said. "So why are we trying to save him? He pushed us off of a cliff, he promoted a bounty, and now he's making Trace's taunts seem modest."

"Gabriella, she believes that there's more to her brother, a version less like this one," I answered.

"Do you believe her?"

"Yeah, I do."

"Then let's save him," MIKA finished, transferring all of my wheels to their positions. As ready as I would ever be, I took one more glance at Midas, discovering a page taken out of Trace's book. Hyper Velocitative Armour, it was all over the Cronus' dark epidermis, thinner than any other model on the market. The armor was so thin, the gold-tipped processes to his spina protruded out like horns.

"He just had to make this day a lot tougher," I muttered before the Initiator gestured over to the Shepherd's booth. She stood close to the window with a microphone at hand, announcing all of our journey's one by one for the crowd to admire. No story was lengthier or acknowledged more than any other out of respect. Adding to her words were visuals displayed on the hovertron directly above us, all leading to her final request for a clean race for the world to witness. The Initiator signaled a twenty-second countdown on the hovertron. Clicking revolvers, blowing torches, and clanging metals echoed through the now-silent crowd. This was it, the last chapter with the world at stake. The disaster could be averted with one more win.

"No more tragedies, Craven," MIKA stated once all of us were in our starting positions, giving each other one last look at the ten-second mark.

"No more," I replied before the siren could awake the world for the conclusion of Four Seasons.

ACT IV

CHAPTER 10

THE NEW VS
THE LEGENDARY

OH, THE SKIES, ONCE UPON A TIME THEY WERE NEON-BLUE. THE LIBERATION OF GOLD TOOK OVER FOR A BRIEF SECOND PRIOR TO BEING TOPPLED BY THE FLAMES FOR LUCIFER TO ENJOY. Lacking interest in the glory of first place, Law reached back to his spiky lasso. I used my BrachiShield to knock his arm away, quickly receiving a patellis directly into my visor. The hit cracked the visor's corner and almost jarred me off of the track for an early tumble into the thrashing waves below. It had only been one straightaway, and I'd already given my fan-base a heart attack. Lucky for them, and me, the Hermes had a God-hemorrhaging speed that brought me back to the third-place outlaw. He had his lasso fully stretched and wrapped around Midas' left brachial. The constriction, combined with the rainy surface, wobbled Midas' balance, risking his position in second place. I came to the rescue, using my sword to sever the lasso in two for a lead over Law. The act restored Midas' balance, but half of the lasso was still stuck to his brachial, leaving the rest to sway in the wind. I became a target for Law once the track dipped down, submerging us all into the underwater tunnel below the stadium. Attempting to maintain the first-place lead, Lucifer used his flamethrower to rocket away from The Golden Scion who was gnawing up the aerodynamics. Both were going so fast that neither gained an advantage. As for Law and I, the war between us had officially begun.

Law had his gun ready for fury, shooting the latis of my suit. I used my shield to catch one bullet, but the molten heat from it persuaded me to swerve from side to side instead. I could feel the hot magnesium squeezing through my skin before finally solidifying. I'd have to think twice about accepting another bullet from the Aboriginal if I was going to survive this race. It was much harder to hit a moving target according to the theory. Bull-fucking-shit I would argue. I sponged more hot shells moving around instead of staying still in this tunnel. Each bullet spread its magnesium radius into my latis upon impact, eventually destroying my scapulars completely once the tunnel leveled itself onto a short straight away leading to a honeycomb hive of pathways. From the trials in the past, I remembered counting fifteen pathways. Half were filled with brutal electrical dangers. Holding onto the lead, Lucifer used his flamethrower to propel himself up to the highest opening, while Midas accepted the leftmost path by driving up the side of the tunnel's wall. The Golden Scion's choice was wise, a path I always chose in the past. But Law chose a path for us by catching up to shove us both into the one I'd always tried to avoid—the lower-right.

Fearless the outlaw was, boosting past to take a reigning lead until he pulled out his combat knife. He triggered his brakes, running me into his knifed hand, impaling my acromion so deep it snapped the shaft of my right collarbone like a toothpick. I tried to defend myself with the raised shield, but the speed of the Hermes made it impossible to counter. Law followed up with a sharp elbow to my visor, enhancing the crack already present. To further his onslaught, he shot my right wheels, front and rear, which melted the rubber off. The lack of traction spun me out into the electrical puddles up ahead. Law avoided the danger, leaving me alone in the tunnel to suffer.

"Trigger the boost!" I ordered MIKA while my muscles contracted from the tasing puddle. MIKA detached the damaged wheels as the Komodo pushed me out of the water. The axle adaptation reformed my suit into a motorcycle. It had been awhile since I'd relied on that handicapped maneuver. Sensing the number of new bruises, I determined that the defensive game plan had to die. My friends had given me the sword to promote a new mindset. It was about time I used it properly. Now on the offense, I kept the lone front-wheel attached to my shielded arm, leaving the other attached with the krone-edged sword.

The boost fused with Hermes' native speed made my two wheels seem like a dozen compared to Law's triplets. Sensing my imminent return, Law kept his focus on the tunnel's merge up ahead, blindly shooting a few bullets back at me. I altered my speed to avoid the heat wave. Zooming past the merge's opening from a different pathway was a lonesome Midas—the perfect target for Law. With his eyes locked on The Golden Scion, I aligned myself on Law's tail to sync our speeds for a draft. Anxious to finally avenge Orin, Law struggled to reload his gun, unintentionally dropping a few bullets for me to dodge during the process. So focused on blood, his wrath blinded him to the sword I was prepared to stick him with, but that was before the both of us were caught off guard by the flames coming from the tunnel's ceiling. Directly above Midas, Lucifer was using a cue from Gabriella, driving upside down. Lucifer dropped onto Midas, impaling his dell with one of the katanas. The Satanian landed the second lead of the day. Midas attempted to pull the sword out, but Law shot the bone-ended handle off. The echo of osseous matter bursting into shards drew Lucifer's violent gaze to the thick gases ejecting from Law's muzzle. That bone-ended handle was one of the last remnants Lucifer had of his mother, and the avenging Law was too ignorant to realize it.

The Satanian chose to hold onto the rage while he led us up to a ramp out of the tunnel, back onto the floating asphalt surface of the track within the stadium. The track then transitioned into a chain of corkscrew loops giving the aerodynamic advantage to Midas who slowly reclaimed a lead. But the Satanian's focus was now aimed at the reloading third-place avenger on the leveled straightaway. Lucifer shifted his front set of wheels back into their holsters to double-hand grip his lone katana. His rear-wheels began to brake so that Law would drive into the swinging blade for a decapitation. To prevent the fatality, I drove my sword into Law's hip, quickly pulling myself forward and ahead of his dells to cover his head with my shield. A firework of sparks ricocheted off of the shield causing Lucifer to wobble and lose his grip on second place. Out of respect for the life-saving act, Law chose not to aim his gun at me and, instead, emptied the remaining ounces of boost left in his tank. I tried my hardest to hang on, but the combat knife lodged into my collar bone diminished the strength I had in the right side. I slid down Law's body once Midas was in sight, entering a wide left turn. Unfortunately for Law, his boost came to an end once I was near his gastrolocks, allowing me to reclaim a grip on the krone-edged sword still fixed in his threxis.

Using the sword to pull my body back onto Law's, I sunk it further into his legs, now anchoring the point through his bone and into the asphalt. The sword sliced the track and decreased Law's speed on the next wide right turn. The sight of Midas fading away convinced him to aim his gun back at me, but before he could align the gun's nose to my visor, Lucifer turbo'd past to cleanly amputate Law's bullet-coated arm. The silver-eyed avenger roared at the trail of blood until the remaining magnesium-filled shells could cauterize the wound. Lucifer, on the other hand, maintained his momentum and caught back up to Midas. The Satanian's blade was still at hand and ready for more punishment. In a Hyper Velocitative Armoured suit, there was no way Midas would stand a chance.

"Trigger the boost!" I commanded, pulling my sword out of Law while grounding my right-armed wheel down to supplement Law's. The maneuver might not have been as crafty as Gabriella's trademark, but it was just as efficient. It gave Law's suit a quartet of wheels. Combined with my boost, he allowed the act mainly because we were catching up to the others. But Midas was swift. The downpour of rain was the only target Lucifer was slicing. It looked as if Midas was actually toying with the Satanian heavily relying on his sword.

"Do you wanna see some good news?" MIKA inquired, showing me an analyzation of Lucifer's Hades within the cracked visor. His flamethrower's gas tank was apparently empty.

"Fully unkindled," I stated as Law and I edged closer. Now as desperate as his fallen hammerhead friend, Lucifer leapt into the air to drive the katana through Midas' spina, but The Golden Scion swayed out of the way to show why he was the three-time champion. The bladed-end of Lucifer's katana instantly drilled into the track as a result of the miss. Out of desperation, Lucifer grasped the dangling lasso still wrapped around Midas' left brachial, slowly tugging his body onto Midas' spina.

Entering the upcoming series of turns, Midas' speed gave Lucifer a challenge, but for some odd reason, it seemed like Lucifer was in control of the situation. He had each wheel detach themselves into debris for Law and I to avoid. Unaware of the Satanian's plan, Law and I watched Lucifer rip his helmet off, stripping both it and his flamethrower away during the process. My visor may have been cracked and covered with rain, but I could see the amber veins spreading throughout the Satanian's body until his neck illuminated itself, revealing the skeleton within his obsidian skin. Before any of us could comprehend what was happening, a large pyromantic cloud soared out of Lucifer's mouth and onto Midas' helmet.

"Impossible," MIKA blurted while Law relayed his left-armed wheel into my left appendisc, quickly unholstering the revolver on my hip. With a fully extended arm, he aimed and pulled the trigger at the Satanian, only to see his own hand explode. The avenger gave out a loud shriek before I unloaded the real bullets within my pronator at the flaming Satanian. Midas rattled Lucifer off of his back and onto the track. Using the wheel-less racer to my advantage, I directed Law's body towards Lucifer's to successfully crash both threats into one another. The impact launched my body forward while the two slid off the track and into Lake Michinis. Coming to my rescue was MIKA's initiative of axle-adapting the pair of wheels left on my suit into a motorcycle in mid-air for a safe landing. A part of me grieved the lost sword still impaled in Law's body, but I focused on the fact that it was just Midas and I left in this race.

The rain stopped. We were down to the clash that had been predicted by The Golden Scion in the beginning. No more rain, no more threats, and no more distractions. Just a man's fate in the palm of my hands in this homestretch bout for the championship. Mano a mano. The Four Seasons Champion vs The Knightfall Champion. The Cronus vs The Hermes. The New Legacy vs The Legendary Legacy. What more could I have asked for? Midas' Hyper Velocitative Armoured suit had its qualities, but on two wheels, the Hermes' still maintained its clutch-bone ritual by gnawing up the gap between us until both suits could fuse for a draft. Cutting through the gray clouds and gold drones were the actual sun rays from the heavens. The natural light sparked a rainbow on the wet surfaces of the track. Whether the weather had been arranged by Mother Nature, God or Hera herself, Midas and I were grateful.

Now entering multiple sets of vertical loops, the race relied on skill, something Midas managed well, capturing an advantage by controlling his lead into a sharp left turn. In the past, Midas' turns had been laughable, but for the finale, he had perfected them. The poor soul here was actually me as I almost hydroplaned off of the track to join Law and Lucifer. The Twilight of Hera then gifted the Hermes with a straightaway heading toward the east end of the floating stadium. From memory, I knew this was the second to last straightaway leading to a dip curving left into the infamous final ramp of the track. With the clouds still gold, I had to make a big move by emptying the remaining fumes of the Komodo. Midas countered by shifting in front of my suit, swerving to whatever side I attempted to use in order to claim first. Midas held onto his lead, surviving the Komodo's final breath.

"If you can't pass him, go through him," MIKA instructed, convincing me to try and swipe his set of rear-wheels with my shield. The action made Midas attempt to shove his right-rear wheel into my face, but I responded by grabbing his leg, fracturing it inward on the spot. The Golden Scion tried to retaliate by swinging his right-front wheel at my dell, but inconceivably missed. The failure shook his nerves, so I took advantage of the fear by grabbing onto his spina with my left hand in order to drill my right-handed wheel into his gut while unicycling my balance on the rear-wheel. I abraded his gut until blood could coat the wheel. Now in a commanding position, I raised the wheel up to contemplate a fatal blow. Through the golden visor of his black helmet, I saw his multi-colored eyes grimace. To spare him any more pain, I dropped my bloody wheel back onto the track to officially pass Midas for what might be the last time. I had a great lead, but that didn't stop The Golden Scion from committing one last act of defiance by whipping one of his wheels at my rear one. The hit did connect, but the gap between us only increased while Midas lost a great deal of speed without the wheels. With a gripping control of first, I followed the track down into the leftward curve. During the turn, MIKA displayed the magnetic attraction of my rear-wheel. It was severely damaged. "Craven, I'd advise you to rethink the leap."

"It'll hold on!" I shouted, seeing the large ramp mimic a stairway to heaven in the rays of sunlight pushing past the track's edges.

"Don't take the leap!" MIKA cried, automatically using the gastrolocks to brake near the top of the ramp. Unable to stop the momentum, my body slid to the top of the ramp causing MIKA to detach the rear-wheel so that I could balance myself onto my feet at the ramp's peak where the sun rays were blinding. I turned just before Midas could trigger his turbo. He torpedoed himself into my gut, tackling me off of the ramp for the batter-ramming leap. With his left dell penetrating my abdominis, the momentum from the nasty hit twisted our bodies until Midas was beneath mine. He was dangerously positioned, unprepared for the harsh landing. I attempted to push his body aside, but by the time my arms could fully extend, the Hermes had finally used his Cronus as the cushion for our fall. The frontal lobe of my helmet bounced off of the pavement, but I was more concerned for the deafening crack that came from The Golden Scion's lifeless suit.

**ACT IV
CHAPTER 11**

BETTER
KNIGHTS

"W-W-W-WHAT'S HIS STATUS?" I MUTTERED, GENTLY LIFTING MYSELF UP TO MY KNEES OVER THE LIFELESS BODY. There was a puddle of blood enclosing Midas' Cronus. Adding to the scare were the buzzing noises coming from MIKA's audio that eventually became ear-splitting. I pried my helmet off for a better look at The Golden Scion's condition. Through the sun's piercing rays I could see the Cronus' sparkling black-and-gold design. My hands trembled as I slowly planted them on the sides of Midas' helmet. For the sake of my hypertrophic heart, I paused for a few deep breaths before finally lifting his helmet off. The first thing I noticed were his heterochromia eyes slowly shifting in and out of his skull until they, thankfully, settled on my face. "You're alive," I said.

"Craven... I...I...I can't," he struggled to say while my eyes adapted to the lighting, eventually settling on the hovertron's screen. It displayed an x-ray of Midas' body. The large processes of the Cronus' spina had caved into the actual processes of Midas' spine. "I... I...can't feel my legs."

I attempted to reply, unable to find the right response. I was struggling for the right words when it finally hit me. This was it; this was the fate that Claire had foreseen. Paralysis was the bestowed cold that could save a Gold.

"What... what do I do? I can't feel them," Midas cried, unable to move anything below the waist. I gently stood up to watch the crippled scion attempt to backwards crawl in his seated position. Even then, Midas maintained his focus on the championship, desperately increasing the speed.

For the sake of our existence, and remembering Claire's words, I grasped Law's wethro knife to painfully pull it out of my acromion. A small geyser of blood oozed out before I stabbed it through Midas' right leg, using the knife's blade as an anchor to the asphalt. For assurance, I gripped the broken katana stuck in Midas' dell to try and pull it out, too. Law's destruction of the blade's handle made this process a lot harder than it needed to be. I eventually succeeded and quickly impaled it through Midas' left leg for the second anchor, a better one for that matter.

"Why… why are you doing this to me?"

"You wouldn't believe me if I told you," I answered, standing next to his anchored body.

"Please take the blades out, I…I can't live like this," Midas begged, failing to get a good grip on the blades himself. I'd be lying if I said I didn't feel sorry for the guy. He gripped my legs so that I wouldn't walk away to seal the race.

"The important thing is that you're alive, the price could've been much worse."

"You don't get it, Craven. I can't live like this, not with him as my father," he explained, tears dripping off of his chin. "I know Gabriella's told you stories, she's shared the misery. He's the reason for her killer instincts. He's the reason for my unwanted dedication to this sport, and he's the same reason why your father is dead. My father's wrath and envy. I don't know what it's going to do to a crippled son."

"I'm sorry, I have to."

"No, you don't, you don't have to end this race, not just yet," he pleaded, eyeing the blades in his legs while a few drones descended from the skies for an intimate look at our situation. "Please, take the knife out and kill me. I'm giving you permission to do so, please! If you love my sister, then you love me too, so please kill me! My fate is worse than death, Craven!"

"I can't, I won't," I stated for the drones to hear. I then snatched my legs away from Midas' hands to reclaim my helmet and officially seal the race with a journey to the finish line.

Midas screamed in the background as a barrage of practitioners sprinted from the finish line to the suicidal scion's aid. As for the crowd, they were stunned, silent, only able to stare at the lone survivor crossing the finish line to officially end this turmoil of a series. Neon-blue spotlights and fireworks converged in the clouds while I gazed upon the masked FMJs in the bleachers. Entering this race, they were undoubtedly the scariest factor. If they wanted to, they could leap out of the stands, past the Lynches, to grant Midas his one last request. I braced myself for the upcoming offense, only to see one brave FMJ pull their bandana down to commence a crescendo of claps. One, then a dozen. And a dozen then became a multitude. An unimaginable outcome. I thought for sure that this race would result in the death sentence for Midas and I. Hell, I was the reason their messiah was floating in the lake below. Thankful for their forgiving nature, I dropped my body onto the track's platform. I wanted to avoid the anxious reporters, but I was more afraid to look Midas' sister in the eyes, especially because their father was giving me the same death stare I gave Thorax on that tragic day years ago. The Twilight of Hera—never had it provided a complimentary victory. It was responsible for The Heart of Earth's death and The Golden Scion's paralysis. I would argue to the United Countries of Earth that the track be renamed Hera's Bittersweet Symphony. The bitterness was more than obvious. But the sweetness, the victory, faded with the sinking octagon platform.

Privacy, that's all I wished for. The platform brought me back to the roundhouse locker. A very gracious and satisfied Dick made an attempt at congratulating me, smartly thinking twice about it from the lack of joy on my face. It made the walk to my locker an easy one. All I wanted to do was rest and talk to one person—the unsung hero of Four Seasons' finale, MIKA. Pressing my back against my locker's neon-blue walls, I wanted her to know that we did it. I sank down onto the ground while placing my helmet on, but all I could hear were the same buzzing noises from earlier.

"MIKA, are you there?" I asked before the irritating noise ended. The silence and lack of any display may have answered the question. I pulled the helmet off to obtain her chip. Whenever the chip's light was green, it was fully charged, whenever it was yellow or red, it was running low on battery. Every racer knew this, so what was the protocol for no light at all? I knew the answer, I just didn't want to accept it. Whether I liked it or not, MIKA was decommissioned, and the last move she ever made, more than likely, prevented another McGuire from a tragic ending. I haven't even thanked her for it, and the last time I checked, there was no afterlife for Artificial Intelligence. For the second time, for the second straight race, I'd lost someone close to me. But before I could even grieve, the purple-suited man with a cane stood tall at the same doorway reserved for another's presence.

"How does it feel to be alive?" JoKer asked as one of the few souls here at the stadium allowed to invade my privacy.

"You see, now I'm skeptical of your abilities. Shouldn't you know the answer?" I replied, making him chuckle.

"Actually, I thought I'd sit back and enjoy the show. I trusted your ability to win and you did."

"My mother showed up today," I revealed while JoKer took a seat on the locker's bench.

"Did she now?"

"She did, and if I'm not mistaken, she was in the same booth as before, except she was sharing it with my friends this time around. You know, Trace, Katia, Zero, Gabriella…" I explained, feeling some of the rage arise for those absent. "There could've been more people in that booth, you know. Perhaps Meta. Or Beta. Or Kira."

"I see, so that's what we're doing," JoKer replied in a disappointed tone, now standing back up. "You're blaming me for her death."

"You could've warned me."

"I could have, and then you would have died," he revealed.

"So that thing about you not being able to see my new fate, what was that, bullshit?"

"That's one way of putting it," he stated.

"Why?"

"Why? I don't know, maybe it's because my mirage put you in the right position for the right outcome, and that's the salvation of your planet's future."

"Our planet JoKer. You mean *our planet*," I rephrased for him, as he falsely smiled back at me.

"Yes Craven, our planet," he finished before his irises could turn bright-white. It forced him to walk back to the locker's doorway. "I probably should've prepared myself for this conversation. You have every reason to be mad, but know this Craven. No matter what happens next, I'm always on your side."

"What's going to happen next?" I questioned.

"A revolution," he answered, now exiting the locker. Like before, our conversation left me with more questions than answers, and I was in no position to pursue him for clarification. My job was to save Midas, and to save Earth. I'd done that, so why did it feel like my job wasn't over. Claire Voyant's words popped into my head—history always found a way to balance itself out, hence a life for a life. So, what happened when a planet was saved? What monstrous revolution had Earth's survival given birth to?

ACT V
REGENERATION

ACT V

CHAPTER 1

R X

"**HOW'S LIFE? IT'S BEEN GOOD. DON'T KNOCK ME FOR KEEPING TRACK, BUT IT'S BEEN ALMOST A DOZEN MONTHS SINCE I LAST SAW HIM.** My father that is. Out of mind, out of sight, right?" I answered, readjusting myself on the gray chaise lounge until I was comfortable. I stared at the antique nickel ceiling tiles. Then again, I was supposed to close my eyes during these sessions.

"What about Kira? When was the last time you've seen her?" Dr. Azzrelia Perris asked, filling out an evaluation form.

"Last week, and like always, she was in her Venus staring at me with the raven's beak still stuck in the visor," I replied, gripping my cold sweaty hands together.

"What triggered her this time?"

"We had a bachelor party for the man of the month, Trace Burretta. For the sake of his soon-to-be wife, Katia, and newborn daughter, Mika, we kept the party fairly modest, for the most part. The groomsmen all had tasks. For instance, I was in charge of the location, so I chose the Sirius Tower's Skydeck. Warlock, he had priorities over the food and drinks, heh. I guess you can paint a picture of what he brought."

"Let me guess, Guinness had to be the beverage," she stated, taking her focus off of the computer to brainstorm through a palate of entrées, "But I'm not sure on what the food could've been."

"Raptr," I said. "Warlock, he's entered our small circle, therefore he knows his shit, and you can't be in Trace's circle without knowing his favorite meat in the galaxy, you know."

"What about Darragh?" Perris added.

"I was getting to him, he provided the entertainment. The main problem is that he's more Irish than Warlock, so his taste in entertainment was geared more to the redheaded variations. He brought a lot of red-haired women. It should've been alright, but my head… it couldn't enjoy the stripteases. Their red hair, it turned pink, and their light-green veins turned ivory. And then it spiked itself with Irizan. I mean, I saved myself from the public humiliation by retreating to the rooftop for fresh air. And that's when I saw her coming across the imaginary finish line to claim third place."

"I take it Trace kicked Darragh's ass for that?"

"No. I mean the two do fight a lot, but never for a cruel reason, you know. Their fumes have been tamed since Gabriella added a gym to the nest. For Trace's satisfaction, the renovation came with an octagon ring. Both he and Darragh like to push each other in multi-round sparring matches. It's really a sight to see. You should come by sometime, but I wouldn't come on a Sunday. Gabriella…well…she added an Ab Lab consisting of Murder-Ab-Mondays every Sunday," I explained, gently rubbing the demolished set of abs underneath my suit.

"How have you and Gabriella been?"

"We've been…busy. *The Blue Jay's Nest* is one of the top dealerships on the planet because of her. We're even expanding the workshop to New York and Sydney, so that should be fun. A set of training league tracks are going to be attached to the workshop in New York. It just requires a lot out of us, you know. I mean, today, it'll be the first time we'll be able to enjoy each other's company in a while. I highly doubt that our busy schedules have jeopardized the relationship, it's just that…and I can't believe I'm saying this but… I wish that things were back to how they were last summer at Four Seasons. Yeah, we were more stressed than a high-blood pressure senior in the Playboy Mansion, but back then, we had time for each other. I don't know, I'm most likely overthinking like usual. Does she talk about me during your sessions with her?" I questioned, wondering about how Gabriella and the other "her" felt about me. Perris wasn't going to admit it, but she was starting to feel a bit uncomfortable about the subject.

"Let me ask you this…" she began, shutting down the computer to signify the scarce amount of time left in our session. "Is it Gabriella's perspective you're worried about or Krueger's? Is that why you're worried about the distance between you two? Is it the fear of not knowing who you might be talking to sometimes?"

"I fear losing the woman I love, and I know the difference between the two. Sometimes. Krueger wears the red contacts and Gabriella doesn't. I don't know, she just hasn't raced since Blackstone, and I'm worried that she'll lose herself one day. Ask Lawson Pierce, all it takes is one bad day," I explained to get a grip on the fear we both knew I was trying to avoid. I just wished I had embraced it earlier, now realizing there was no time left on the clock above her doorway. The therapy session was officially over, bringing both Dr. Perris and I to our feet. My tenure in the chaise lounge wrinkled my dark blue suit—a special suit for a special day.

"I know that I shouldn't reveal another's session, but hear me when I say that she loves you," Perris assured me, alleviating my mood. "What's the special occasion if you don't mind me asking?"

"It's May 21st," I answered, now ready for the drive to The Windy Lakeside of the Chicagolands, "Which means that I've got a wedding to attend, and it's about time I enjoy the greatest day of my brother's life!"

ACT V
CHAPTER 2

UNTIL
DEATH

"KATIA DURAN, DO YOU TAKE TRACE BURRETTA TO BE YOUR HUSBAND?" THE PASTOR SAID, BRINGING TEARS TO THE EYES OF KATIA AND HER THREE BRIDESMAID SISTERS. Katia, of course, stuck to the tradition of a bright sparkling white dress draped to the floor. Her sisters Katey, Kelsey, and Kasey, on the other hand, wore neon-blue to complement the company where Katia had made a name for herself. Trace and I had resisted, but she insisted on creating a legacy. Sure, she was not a racer, but she was marrying one, and he had a reputation to live up to, therefore, she insisted on building one for herself. It was the reason why the walkway up to the ceremonial stage was a blue jay spreading its wings. The Duran sisters stood behind Katia on the right wing, while me, Warlock, and Darragh stood behind Trace on the left wing in that order. At the head of the bird, a breathtaking view of the orange Lake Michinis from inside the atrium garden of columbine flowers with blue outer petals and white inner petals. Trace and I had always heard how alluring The Windy Lakeside was, but never to this degree. Trace had been shifting his eyes back and forth from the sunset to Katia. "Do you promise to love, honor, cherish, and protect him, forsaking all others, and holding unto him forevermore?"

"I do," Katia finally confirmed. The answer brought Trace's hibrix towards me for a smooth and stealthy fist-bump. Shaking their heads at the discreet action, my mother and Gabriella sat next to each other in the front row of the bride's side of the room. If I were a gambling man, I'd bet *The Blue Jay Nest's* stock that they shared the same make-up artist for the occasion. For starters, their hairstyles consisted of long curls with neon-blue tips. Yeah, I said it, neon-blue tips. It had taken a doctorate's degree in the art of persuasion for my dad to convince my mother to change her hair color, so I wondered what it took for my girlfriend to land the same deal. Then again, it helped to have a Miss Earth title on the resume. Gabriella wore her blue contacts to match the colors of the landscape. Enhancing the sapphire spectrum, she wore a sparkling neon-blue sequined dress. The sleeves were long, the back was bare, and a canyon cut was designed to reveal the thighs. This was the first time I saw her in a dress. Blame it on the wedding's spirit, but I damn-near brought myself down to a knee the minute I saw her. It felt like my first time seeing her again.

"And Trace Burretta, do you take Katia Duran to be your wife? Do you promise to never embarrass her at the end of any race, increase the amount of friends while decreasing the amount of enemies, to not lose another limb, and to survive until retirement?" the pastor said, dropping Trace's jawline. He quickly glanced back to us for an alibi he should've known he wouldn't get. Warlock and Darragh whistled away while I shrugged my shoulders.

"He ain't wrong," I muttered, snickering at Trace's expression.

"I do, on one condition?" Trace countered, looking back at his love's slightly tilted head. "I'm allowed three more enemies."

"One," she quickly answered.

"Two," Trace replied even quicker.

"One," Katia slowly responded, successfully able to master Gabriella's cold stare.

"I do," Trace wisely answered, bringing his clenched fist back for an encore of fist-bumps.

"And now by the power vested in me, I hereby declare you as husband and wife. You may now kiss the bride," the pastor finished, waiting for Trace to seal the deal, officially making his wife Katia Burretta. The rise in applause granted the newlyweds the right to walk back down the runway. The only one here who wasn't clapping was the newborn, Mika Burretta in the arms of her grandmother. Until now, she had been sound asleep. The thunderous claps opened her eyes, and the beauty that was her mother, caught the attention. With her short arms firmly extended, Katia accepted Mika's request. In the arms of an angel, Mika now was on the runway, followed by groomsmen and bridesmaids, ushering everyone into the ballroom.

The Windy Lakeside's dance floor easily eclipsed the golden one at the Lotus from the year before. This large circular ballroom had a clouded sky designed on the ceiling with blue jays soaring next to angels. Columbines covered the walls beyond the guest tables arranged to encapsulate the mirrored dance floor reflecting the heaven's artwork. At the furthest end of the ballroom was the biggest table reserved for the newlyweds and the groomsmen, bridesmaids, and front rows of the ceremony. At first, Gabriella's seat was at the end of the exclusive table, but we bargained our seats until we were eventually next to each other in between Warlock and my mother.

"I'm not one for ceremonies, but this ain't half bad," Warlock stated while the staff brought out entrées and desserts. The most notable sweet was the monolith-size Grace of Gluttony catering to the wedding's theme with toy-size figurines of Trace and Katia. "Tell me something mountain slayer, can you slay tat cake?"

"Are you kidding? I can perform the gluttonous miracle in ten minutes," I answered.

"You'll be pinching a tent for ten hours if you engulf that entire cake," Gabriella warned, raising Warlock's eyebrows for the challenge.

"Make that ten days," my mother added, raising Gabriella's eyebrows in disbelief.

"You weren't born yet, but your father did it at our wedding. Take a guess at how awkward that visit to the hospital was?"

"Thanks, Mom, that's…that's really informative," I calmly responded, trying my hardest not to gag. Gabriella sipped some of the wine while Warlock pondered the thought.

"I'd be up for tee challenge," he eventually said.

"How about we change the subject," I demanded, gesturing at Gabriella. I brought up the big gift her and I had prepared for the newlyweds. With the first rounds of food ingested, I thought it was time to offer it, but they got up to venture to the dance floor. For the wedding, I couldn't believe that Trace kept his hibrix unclothed. We all thought he'd at least make an exception for the big day, but then again, *it builds character*, and in his defense, Mrs. Burretta seemed happier than ever. Her head rested on Trace's collar bone, and she glanced at her daughter whenever the rotation brought her eyes over to our table. Mika Burretta had been relayed down the table into my mother's arms, giving us a great look at the little bird destined for success. She inherited her mother's gray eyes, which made Gabriella joke about Mika possibly inheriting her father's wit. If the Galactic Gods were civil, they'd grant genetic superiority on the Duran side of the family tree.

"I guarantee you that she's going to grow up to be an ass-kicker," Warlock remarked—a bit barbaric, and yet we all found it charming. I honestly thought that was why I love the red-bearded bastard. When it was time for everybody to join the newlyweds on the dance floor, he nudged me closer to Gabriella. I wasn't the best dancer, but Warlock's signal was the appropriate one. She gladly accepted the proposal. Now joining the crowd of couples slow dancing around each other, Gabriella and I rotated next to the newlyweds. Katia may have still had her head on Trace's collar bone, but that didn't prevent him from requesting one more fist-bump. I was more than happy to grant it. If it hadn't been for him, I would not have been holding onto the one person I never wanted to let go of. Gabriella was everything. But as I held her close, I thought about the one hiding beneath the skin, the one I didn't know much about. Krueger favored the color red and had an untamable hatred towards anyone or anything that harmed what she loved, and what she loved was Versa. I could only imagine what the alternate persona was doing to Gabriella. She'd agreed to the aid and guidance of Dr. Azzrelia Perris, but the big question was Krueger's perception of me. Did she love me like Gabriella, or did she hate me like Midas? Shit, Midas. That was a name I tried not to think about since…well…since then. It was something Gabriella had chosen for us to never discuss. I was sure the subject conflicted her. I mean, Midas was alive, but it didn't necessarily mean he was living. On a monthly basis, the Unican Network tallied his suicide attempts. It didn't help that he denied Dr. Perris' care. If the reports were correct, he hadn't left the Gold's manor in months. I was curious if that was what Gabriella was currently thinking about, or was she thinking about me? I needed to stop overthinking. I was always the one who pinpointed every little detail prior to a race, which was good, but what good was the trait when the race was over? Should I let the details haunt me for not hunting them?

Saving me from the debate within my head, Trace called me to the big table for the inevitable speech of the day.

"As a racer, I've witnessed a lot of countdowns," Trace began, "So believe me when I say that the days leading up to this wedding comprised the longest countdown of my whole life." The words snatched his wife's attention away from their daughter. "I've adapted to the fast paces required from Versa, but for once, it feels good to slow down and enjoy the little things like the undying smile no makeup in the world can perfect on my wife's face. Big things are great and all, but just ask my brother over there next to Miss Earth, it ain't the big things that craft a masterpiece, it's the little things, and I want you all to remember. Each and every one of you here is an important piece of our lives, so cherish it, capture it, and embrace it because a wise man once told me that you can never know when it'll be your last. I hereby raise my glass to every one of you, demanding you all live out your lives like I am, until death."

"Until death," Gabriella followed up on the groom's words. She then glanced at me. Again, if I were a gambling man, I'd bet a portion of the workshop's share on the green light status of our future together. *Thank you, Dr. Perris.*

We'd reached the time for gift giving, eventually bringing Gabriella and I to the newlyweds outside on the flame-tinted beach where the waves were brisk. The breeze was bliss. It was also the only spot at The Windy Lakeside worthy of the gift we were prepared to give. The verbal gift was for Katia. As for Trace's physical gift, I had to activate a beacon for an incoming supply drop.

"As you know, we're expanding the company to multiple locations," Gabriella explained as the leading statement. "And when it comes to identifying the right manager for the right workshop, both of us synced on you, which is why we're offering the executive position at New York to you."

"New York?" Trace queried, baffled by the offer given to his wife who needed the fresh air for a breather.

"I don't know what to say?" Katia eventually answered.

"You can say yes, we're even prepared to offer up Nito as one of the lead mechanics," I added, solving the unemployment problem the Ryth ran into after Gabriella's unveiled identity a year ago.

"He's got a plethora of blueprints exclusive to the shop, he just needs an appropriate administrator. Someone who's as ambitious as they are promising," Gabriella carried on before the supply drop finally arrived. It came with a pair of casings for a pair of exosuits.

"I'll take the deal, thank you," Katia said, hugging Gabriella while Trace and I journeyed over to the casings. The groom knew exactly which one was his by the bow sewed onto the container ready to be opened, and once it was, the man himself needed a moment to assess the situation.

"Last year, you sacrificed your most prized possession without question so that I could walk out of Four Seasons successfully. Gabriella and I, we haven't forgotten, so we decided last year to begin our production towards the latest member of the Hermes family," I explained. Trace pulled the gift out of the container, now seeing the exact same design he had on the Hermes both he and his father had created so long ago. The only difference to this model was the gray armored wing over the krone right brachial, specified to his hibrix. "I give you the 2252 Hermes!"

"It has the same white skin, the same golden wings…"

"And no Hyper Velocitative Armour!"

"None!" he said, immediately noticing the suit's right arm. "Krone, really?"

"Well, we figured that lightning can't strike the same place twice, but then again with your luck…"

"It'll find a way, thank you," he said, hugging me. "Too bad you're without an exosuit or else I'd smoke you in this bad boy."

"An exosuit, you say?" I questioned, kicking open the casing next to his bow-topped container, unveiling the 2251 Hermes. The exact same one that crowned me as the current Four Seasons Champion. "Ask and you shall receive."

"This motherfucker right here," he muttered, stripping off his blazer for Katia to hold so that he could enter his gifted suit for the ultimate challenge of the day. "What's the finish line?"

"I think the nest sounds suitable," Gabriella proposed even though the workshop was a couple hours away.

"The nest? Oh, we are so getting arrested," Trace said.

"What do you mean, we?" I asked, entering my Hermes, now illuminating its blue wings. "I plan on smoking your ass."

"Don't you know that it's against the bro code to smoke your bro on their wedding day?" Trace questioned.

"I've got enough money to bail him out," Gabriella answered while we both grabbed our helmets.

"Oh, this is cute, you two are too fucking cute. Let's get this win over with so I can enjoy my honeymoon." Trace blew a kiss his wife's way before sliding into his helmet. I gave Gabriella a wink, designating her as the Initiator for our brotherly bout. It may not have been smart to begin this race on the sandy surface, but I wasn't going to be the one to offer an excuse. This race had no point of return, and we both knew it. Officially lined up directly next to one another on all fours, we waited for Gabriella to raise her arm high above her head. After a long pause, she finally dropped it down to begin the next chapter of our legendary story.

www.ingramcontent.com/pod-product-compliance
Lightning Source LLC
Chambersburg PA
CBHW060624100726
47907CB00006B/1755